MUCH ADO ABOUT HIGHLANDERS

May McGoldrick

S SMP Swerve

AN IMPRINT OF ST. MARTIN'S PRESS

MUCH ADO ABOUT HIGHLANDERS. Copyright © 2016 by Nikoo and James McGoldrick. All rights reserved. For information, address St. Martin's Press, 175 Fifth Avenue, New York, NY 10010.

www.stmartins.com

Cover photographs: ribbon © Love_Life/Getty Images; heather bouquet © Diana Taliun/Shutterstock

ISBN 978-1-250-10656-8 (e-book)
ISBN 978-1-250-15481-1 (trade paperback)

First E-book Edition: May 2016

To Linda Brown
Our cherished friend . . . and writer extraordinaire from the
Land Down Under

Prologue

The ship was nearly gone. All that was left clung to the sharp rocks of the reef. The timbers glistened in the sun like the ribs of a carcass picked clean.

Cairns stared at the low waves breaking on the stony shore. Around him masts, lines, and sails lay tangled up with casks and boxes and cargo.

And bodies. So many bodies.

He focused on the remains of the vessel that had broken apart in an instant. On a clear day in a steady breeze.

Perhaps his friends had not drowned. Perhaps they died when the ship came apart like dry kindling. The vessel had splintered into four segments with a sound so terrible that his ears still roared at the memory.

Wet and cold and exhausted, Cairns pulled out the leather pouch that hung around his neck. From it, he removed the broken piece of tablet. His fingers traced the ancient markings. So small you could hold it in the palm of your hand, but it held a special gift. Together, the four pieces of the tablet held a terrible power. No one had warned them how terrible. There was no way for them to know.

The stone grew warm in his hand. The power of it raced up his arm like sunlight breaking through a cloud. It drove sharply into his chest, and then came the second sight. His gaze swept across the littered shore. All along the beach, the spirits were rising from the dead. He didn't want them to tell him how they died. He didn't want to hear their confessions. He slipped the stone back into the pouch.

Cairns steeled himself for the task ahead. Moving along the inlet, he trudged from one body to the next.

None of them belonged to his three friends. He turned his face to the sea.

Perhaps they were still alive. Or perhaps they were dead at the bottom of the ocean. It didn't matter. Long ago, they had sworn an oath. If they survived the journey, they would each safeguard one piece of the tablet. If they lived, they would travel to the farthest corners of Scotland.

Cairns knew what he had to do. Turning toward the mountains to the south, he began his journey.

Chapter 1

There was a star danced, and under that was I
born.

WESTERN COAST OF SCOTLAND
FIFTY YEARS LATER

The old saying danced in Kenna MacKay's head. *When a man comes to a birthing, someone will die.*

And yet, Kenna thought, if the man were a physician, right now that was a risk she'd gladly take.

She was in deep waters, and she knew it. She was no midwife. Her prayers were frequently ignored by the saints. And she had no interest in witchcraft. Regardless, she had to convince either God or Nature to lend a hand and turn this bairn around.

"Let's get her to lie down with her feet pointing at the roof and her head down here."

The young villager looked uneasily from the woman in

labor to the contraption of wood and straw Kenna had assembled on the floor and followed orders.

"M'lady, have you ever done this type of birthing before?"

Kenna looked down into the frightened face of the mother. Three young children were waiting with the husband outside.

"Aye, I've helped with birthing."

A fire pit in the center of the large room spewed too much smoke and heat. Kenna wiped the sweat from her brow and focused on what needed to be done. It was a struggle, but the two managed to move the pregnant woman into position.

"Our bairn wasn't to arrive till next month. The midwife promised me she'd be back from visiting her sister. I had no trouble with the others." A contraction cut the words short. The mother's cries were followed by the wailing of children.

Kenna hoped her cousin Emily would be able to keep the family out of the cottage. Delivering a baby wasn't part of the plan for their day when the two of them left Craignock Castle early this morning. But arriving here and hearing the laboring woman's cries, Kenna had vaulted from her horse and come inside the cottage to help. That was hours ago.

"I've heard the midwife say women die when the bairn

is turned this way."

Without thinking, Kenna reached up and pressed the pouch hanging under her dress against her chest. Her mother's lucky healing stone felt warm against her heart.

"The midwife is wrong. She hasn't had my schooling. I've been trained by the nuns of Glosters Priory on Loch Eil." A bit of exaggeration was excusable considering the pregnant woman's distress. Setting bones, stitching wounds, and tending to the sick at the priory's spital house were the extent of Kenna's training, but many women passed through the priory. They talked. They shared stories. Some had a great deal of experience in birthing, whether it was with their own bairns or with helping others. She recalled one long, involved story a woman told of turning a breech baby by raising the mother's hips above her head. Kenna prayed that wasn't a tall tale.

She touched the woman's stomach, feeling, pressing gently, speaking softly, encouraging mother and child to do right by each other. If she'd only paid closer attention, Kenna thought, to what the woman had said.

She searched back through her memory. The contraption only helped so much. She had to convince the bairn to turn around. Kenna focused on the stretched skin of the mother's belly. Her hands warmed. Wherever she touched, she felt the bairn move beneath her fingers. She massaged and coaxed the unborn child, whispered soothing words.

The next contraction left the mother sobbing and clutching for Kenna's hand. "If I die here, my babies——"

"You will not die," Kenna told her. "Now help me. Help your bairn. Let's show this wee one the light of day."

Kenna prayed that she was doing the right thing. She hoped that her confidence in herself was not misplaced. Many considered her gifted as a healer, as her mother had been. But eight years ago, Sine MacKay died giving birth to Kenna's twin brothers. Gifts had their limits. Childbirth had the potential of being deadly in the best of circumstances.

Her fingers kneaded the woman's stretched belly until they ached. Kenna made one last silent plea. Small ripples moved beneath the skin. What looked like a head pushed at her hand, making its position known before shifting in the mother's womb.

Kenna held her breath as the woman cried out with another contraction.

"By the Virgin, I see the head," the young villager shouted.

Moments later, the babe was born.

By the time the stiff skin that served as a door lifted and her cousin came in, the mother was back on the straw pallet and Kenna was handing the bairn to her.

The neighbor was busily gathering up soiled rags, but she stopped, eager to share the news.

"It was a miracle, m'lady. Lady Kenna showed the bairn which way to go, and the wee thing minded her. Saw it with my own eyes, I did. Turned right around at her ladyship's bidding and came out the way the Lord intended. A miracle."

Emily touched her on the arm and crossed the room.

The farmer's wife kissed Kenna's hand. "May the Virgin bless and protect you, m'lady. May you see your children's children."

Kenna took a coin out of her waistband and tucked it into the mother's hand. A swell of emotion rose in her like an ocean wave, deep and powerful. Her voice shook as she spoke. "You must stay off your feet, do you hear me? Your labor was hard. You and your bairn both need time to recover."

At Emily's dismayed glance, Kenna looked down. Her sleeves were rolled up to the elbows. Her riding dress was soiled with blood and sweat and who knows what else. Locks of hair hung loose, having escaped the once tight braid. She led her cousin out into the fresh air.

Greeting them, the husband wiped the sweat off his face and moved a toddler from one hip to the other. Two other children, not much older, clutched at the man's legs and gawked up at Kenna.

"Did she give me a son?" he asked.

Kenna's hands clenched into fists. "So you heard the bairn's cry. Do you not care to ask if your wife lives or not?"

"Does she live? Please tell me, m'lady. Does my wife live?"

"Do you want her to live?"

"Aye, o' course. Her wee ones need her. I need her."

"She could have died in there." Kenna looked at the fields beyond the hut before turning to him. "She lives today, and she lives tomorrow. And she'll live to see the harvest, if you make certain she rests now. Her work must wait, do you understand? You owe her that."

The man nodded. "Aye, m'lady."

As the neighbor came out carrying the basins and rags, the farmer and the children pushed past her and went in.

Kenna breathed in deeply. Two lives saved. Relief pushed through her as she gazed up at the bright blue sky for some time before looking back at her cousin. "Not exactly the leisurely ride we intended. Eh, coz?"

"What a blessing we were near!"

"Where are the men your father sent out to escort us?"

"While you were inside, I thought we would be here for a while. So I put them to work. Two are cutting up the fallen tree we saw down at the edge of the orchard. One was sent to the village to fetch the crofter's sister."

"What about the one you sent back to the castle?"

"Now I'm thinking he should be back in time for the christening." Emily smiled. "I'm amazed you were able to manage it."

"There were moments when I had my doubts."

"But you've done this before?"

"Not alone. Only helped."

"Is there much call for the midwife's skill in a community of nuns?"

"With the English raiding to the south, more wounded have been showing up at our gates. Many are crofters. Like this one." She glanced at the door. "They've been fighting to keep their villages from being pillaged and burned, but they can't battle an entire army. So we see a lot of poor folk coming north. They've nowhere else to go. And amongst them, there are a few women heavy with child. And others who are experienced as midwives."

Emily's gaze swept over the southern hills. "The English are coming closer all the time."

Kenna had witnessed too much suffering in recent months. She pushed aside the cloud of gloom.

"I need to wash." She looked down at her dress. "Ruined, I think."

"What does it matter? Come with me."

Beyond the hut and down the hill, a stream weaved

through a grove of trees, offering protection from any prying eyes.

"You never told the crofter if he had a son or daughter."

"He had a son. But that news should be shared by his wife, not me."

Kenna crouched at the water's edge, and her cousin perched on a nearby rock.

"Helping with that birth. Watching a new life come into the world. Doesn't it make you want to hold one of your own someday?"

Kenna stopped rubbing the hem of her skirt under the stream's clear water. She met Emily's gaze. The two of them had been more like sisters than cousins growing up. But they lost something when Kenna moved to Glosters Priory six months ago. "I try to not think of it."

"Doesn't the thought of having a bairn change your opinion of marriage at all?"

"Nay. Marriage is a sentence. A life sentence."

"Not all marriages."

Kenna recalled a time not too long ago when the two of them spoke dreamily of the men who would walk into their lives and steal their hearts.

"You no longer believe in love?" Emily asked.

"Love? Cupid *kills* some of us with those bloody arrows."

"You don't mean it." Emily shook her head in disbelief.

"Every woman dreams of hearing a man profess his love."

"I'd sooner hear a dog bark at a crow than a man swear he loves me."

Emily laughed. "Kenna MacKay, you never used to be so stubborn with your opinions."

"I'm not stubborn," Kenna replied. "But it's a topic I have no taste for."

"You do recall that I'm getting married in a fortnight."

"Why do you think I accepted your invitation and left the priory to be here? My plan is to steal you away, far from the clutches of your father and this ridiculous arranged marriage to Sir Quentin Chamberpot."

"Chamber*lain*," Emily corrected, sliding off the rock and joining Kenna at the water's edge. "And all arranged marriages need not be ghastly. Granted, he's a Lowlander and a widower, but Sir Quentin Chamberlain is quite distinguished."

"Distinguished by the possibility that he still has two or three teeth left in his head?" Kenna scooped up water and splashed it on her face.

"Come now, cousin." Emily smiled. "He's not that old."

"You don't know that. They haven't even allowed you to meet him, have they?"

Kenna shook out what was left of her braid and ran her fingers through it.

"There was no time for us to meet. The arrangements

were made when the Privy Council met at Stirling in the spring. But we have exchanged letters."

"So he can read, too? What a catch!"

Her cousin laughed. Kenna removed her shoes and socks and put her feet in the water. Large splotches marked her sleeves, as well as the bodice and skirt.

"And I suppose they told you he has the muscles of Hercules and the handsome good looks of Adonis."

"Let's see. Sir Quentin is not too tall, not too fat, and altogether not unpleasant in his looks."

"Please stop. I may swoon with envy."

"You are the devil, cousin," Emily said. "He has no heir. He's a ranking member of the Dunbar clan. He can provide me with a comfortable life. I imagine I'll have a peaceful life once I've given him a son."

"A peaceful life? You'll have no peace, living in the Borders. Not as long as the English king keeps insisting that our infant Queen Mary wed his own son." She stood up, lifted her skirts, and took another step into the river.

"Careful. The current is strong. It'll drag you down the river."

Kenna's head came around. "Heed your own words, Emily," she said gently. "Don't be caught in this torrent they're pushing you into. Don't marry him. Come with me. You don't need him or this marriage."

"You know that I cannot. I'll never be as free as you.

You and I are different."

Emily stood up and shook her skirts. They were as clean and tidy as when they'd left Craignock Castle.

"You have the Highlands bred into your very bones. You have the independence of your MacKay heritage in your blood. My father and his father before him have been politicians, not warriors. And I'm an only child. I need to honor his wishes."

"And what is it that your father is gaining from this union? Has he traded you away for a caravan of gold and jewels from this buggering Lowlander?"

"I've been told that Sir Quentin has agreed to send a company of Dunbar warriors to help protect our lands. Those English troops have been seen not two days' ride to the south."

"An even trade to get protection for the clan. That's nonsense. Your father should still ask for a caravan of gold."

Emily paused. "He is giving me away with a sizeable dowry."

Kenna made her way out of the water. "What is he offering?"

"A ship." Emily nodded slowly. "My dowry includes a ship."

She looked warily at her cousin. "Where did your father get a ship?"

"I don't know. But they have it hidden in a firth some-where along the coast, I'm told."

As Kenna bent down to retrieve her shoes, a move-ment by the line of trees drew her attention. But she had no time to shout a warning as a hood dropped over her head and a large hand clamped over her mouth.

~

A worktable was no protection. A fortress was no pro-tection. A legion of armed warriors could provide no protection.

The abbot cowered in his seat, happy to be forgotten while the two Macpherson brothers argued across the room. But at every lull in the discussion, he was certain that they must be able to hear the fearful pounding in his chest.

If his heart stopped, at least he wouldn't have to play his part in the Highlanders' insane plan. Who was to say how the MacDougall laird would react to his involve-ment in this, forced though he was? He might very well just burn the abbey to the ground.

The abbot looked at the tapestry of Saint Andrew on the wall and said a quick prayer for delivery, however it might come.

The elder brother, Alexander, strode to a north-facing

window and stared out. The man was tall and broad and powerful. The abbot had once seen the African lion they kept in the menagerie at Stirling Castle, and Alexander Macpherson moved with the same lithe grace as that king of beasts. And he was equally terrifying. As gruffly courteous as he had been so far, he had the steely eyes of a man who would take what he wanted. And God help any man who stood in his way.

"Where is he?"

The younger one, James, was a hand's breadth taller and nearly as muscular. With his dark red hair and piercing gray eyes, the royal Stewart blood that ran in both brothers' veins was more pronounced in him. But there was an aura of command in each man that forced lesser mortals to attend them closely.

"They're coming. Give them time."

"I should have done this myself."

"Diarmad lost the bloody ship," James replied, joining his brother at the window. "It's only right that he should be the one to snatch the MacDougall chit."

These sons of the great laird Alec Macpherson clearly feared nothing, but the old priest could not pretend to be cut from the same cloth. His abbey, perched on a rocky cliff, was not half a day's ride south of the MacDougall's castle, and the thick curtain walls no longer provided the defense that they once did. In this modern age of cannon and gunpowder, the abbey felt more like a ripe plum on a tree, inviting pillage by any passing marauder.

"You have to admit it's a good plan," James pressed. "Diarmad grabs the lass, and we ransom her back for the ship. Easy. Effective. And the good abbot here has graciously consented to act as our intermediary. Is that not so, Abbot?"

Not trusting his voice, the old man nodded. These Highlanders were going to get him killed, pure and simple.

"I still say we should have sailed in with a fleet of our ships, stormed Craignock Castle, and throttled Graeme MacDougall until he told us where he's hidden our vessel."

"You just hate to be left out of the action. Don't you?" James asked.

The abbot looked from one brother to the other.

They'd been waiting here all day, and they were likely to be here all night if the Macpherson captain and his men didn't get a chance to spirit away the laird's daughter. The abbot broke into a cold sweat at the very thought of it. Abducting Emily MacDougall from Craignock Castle itself. Saints preserve us!

Alexander glared at his brother. "You're damn right I don't like sitting out here on my arse. That tongue-flapping MacDougall took our ship, by 'sblood! I want it back."

"And we're getting it back."

"That's not the point. Our ships rule the western seas. When have we ever lost one? Never! That's when!"

The abbot gazed blindly at the chart of abbey lands on his table. Since the days of the Bruce himself, the Macpherson clan had been the terror of the western seas from the Orkneys to Penzance. There was a wild story that their father, along with his friend Colin Campbell, had in one day raided an English arsenal in Carlisle, sailed into Belfast harbor where they forced the lord mayor to feed them dinner, and then made the crossing back to Glasgow in time for supper with the archbishop.

But Alexander had a point. When word had gotten around that their ship had been taken, the Macpherson honor had taken a blow. And clearly, this bruising Highland warrior intended to reclaim both the ship and his clan's fierce reputation.

James wasn't giving up. "You know that while the English are hammering away at the Borders, the regent has forbidden the clans from fighting amongst ourselves. We can't draw blood going after the ship. Isn't that right, Abbot?"

The abbot cleared his throat. "That's true, m'lord. But please don't get me any deeper into this than I am already. If the MacDougall thinks I'm aiding you willingly, my head will be gracing a pike on the wall at Craignock before the tide turns."

"Well," Alexander snorted, turning his hard blue eyes on the abbot. "That would be the first time the old bugger has done anything remotely decisive in the past twenty years, a fact that makes the taking of our ship even more bothersome."

As the older brother turned his back again, the abbot sagged in his chair. His old bones were weary, and the stress of this was not making him any younger. He shouldn't be doing this. He should be reviewing the reports of the abbey farms, tallying the latest count of sheep and goats, planning his annual hunting trip to Falkland.

This was not going to turn out well. The MacDougall lass was supposed to be married in less than a fortnight. He himself was to perform the ceremony. The groom was due to arrive any time now. If the plan worked, and clan war was somehow avoided, there would still be hell to pay. And the abbot had a terrifying idea who would be paying it.

Shouts from the courtyard drew the attention of the three men, and the abbot dragged himself from his chair and followed the others down to the abbey's Great Hall.

Moments later, the door burst open and the Macpherson captain entered. Draped over his shoulder, a woman in bare feet was squirming and kicking, in spite of the ropes that bound her. The hood and gag did little to stop the violent sounds streaming from her mouth.

Behind him, another warrior entered, leading a far more docile prisoner.

"*Two* women?" Alexander asked. "Why are there two?"

Diarmad dumped his writhing burden unceremoniously on the stone floor and looked at the two brothers. "This one is no woman. It's a she-devil."

"I can see that."

"They were together. We didn't know which one was the MacDougall lass."

James walked toward the two prizes. "Well, it looks like our bargaining position has improved a wee bit. Let's just see what we have here."

When he pulled the hood off the calmer of the two, blond hair tumbled down onto shapely shoulders and doe-like eyes blinked at him.

"Well," Alexander grumbled. "At least you got Emily."

"Aye," James said in an odd tone. "And she's grown into a bonnie lass, I should say."

"What of this one, m'lord?" Diarmad jerked his head at the other woman, who for the first time ceased to fight.

Alexander crouched beside her and untied the gag. It struck the abbot that the Highlander treated her with more gentleness than he might have expected.

"Careful," Diarmad warned. "She'll bite you as soon as look at you. I've got claw marks up and down my arms from her."

Standing up, Alexander pulled off the hood. Long, chestnut-colored hair spilled out in waves.

"Bloody hell," he murmured.

Violet-blue eyes stared at him with disbelief that quickly gave way to cold fury.

"You puny, white-livered pigeon egg!" she rasped.

Alexander glanced at James and then looked hard at Diarmad. "I'll tell you what to do with her."

"Now, Alexander—" his brother began.

"You can carry my wife to the top of this tower and throw her into the sea."

Chapter 2

Sigh no more, ladies, sigh no more,
Men were deceivers ever—
One foot in sea and one on shore,
To one thing constant never.

Kenna's sins obviously outweighed any good deed she'd ever performed in this lifetime. She'd clearly bypassed purgatory and dropped straight into hell.

This was her worst nightmare come to life. She never imagined her path would ever again cross with Alexander Macpherson's.

At least, not looking like such a mess.

In her dreams she was clothed in golden armor and holding a fiery sword, and Alexander was the one in tatters, groveling in the dirt.

"Throw me into the sea? I'll cut off any man's hand before he lays a finger on me. Especially yours, blackguard."

Alexander crouched before her. His deep blue eyes

were as striking as she remembered. The long lashes and chiseled face served to remind her why women made fools of themselves in his presence. His dark blond hair was longer. Tied in the back, it reached below his shoulders. The square set of his jaw was covered with a scruff of beard.

There was a rakishness, an insolence about him that he'd contained the handful of times they'd met before. He wasn't even trying now. He gave her a slow, thoroughly insulting inspection, starting with the wild mass of curls falling loose around her face, and ending about an eon later at her bare feet. She could not help but notice that his gaze passed quickly over the state of her dress but lingered far too long on her mouth and her breasts.

Kenna couldn't control her blush. He made her feel as though she were sitting there without a stitch of clothing on.

"And how are you going to cut anything, wife? With that dagger of a tongue in your head?"

Kenna tried to kick him. With the agility of a cat, he evaded the attack. She had a dirk tucked into her belt, but it was impossible to reach it with the ropes confining her. She scrambled to her feet.

"Free my hands, coward, if you are any kind of man. Which I doubt."

"What were you *thinking*, bringing this harridan

here?" Alexander barked at his men. "You saw her at my wedding. You knew what she bloody looked like."

"We grabbed her from behind, m'lord. And we had no idea she'd be there."

"Now you know. Take her back."

Kenna turned a fierce glare on the ones who'd kidnapped them. The men were giving them both a wide berth. "You heard him. Take us back."

"Will you be silent, woman!" Alexander commanded. "No one is talking to you."

She didn't miss her aim this time, and her foot made contact with his boot. Excruciating pain streaked upward through her leg. She leaned against a stone pillar, waiting for the agony to abate. He seemed unaffected by the blow. She glanced at her cousin. Emily was still tied. She tried to move to Kenna, but James Macpherson held her back.

"Send her with the abbot," the older brother continued. "Tell the bloody MacDougall it's a sign of our good faith in the negotiation."

"Negotiation?" Kenna asked him. "Still trying to find yourself a husband, Alexander?"

"Keep her tied. And put the gag and the hood back on her. I wouldn't want to tempt anyone with drowning her before they get to Craignock Castle."

"I asked a question, you rank, half-witted pignut."

The blue gaze swung around to her.

"One would think that the disposition and character of someone living with nuns for six months might have improved just a wee bit. That some of their holiness might have rubbed off on you."

"You dare talk to me about character?"

"That a woman living with all those religious people might have become a better person. But not you. Only Kenna MacKay could end up sounding more ill-mannered than before. And why am I not surprised?"

"Because you're an idiot," she retorted, straightening up. "The only thing I needed to improve on was learning how to lower myself to converse with you, a churlish chicken stealer so conceited that he calls himself my husband."

"So you acknowledge that you have a husband. That's new."

"I did have one for a few short hours."

"You still have a husband," he said angrily, towering over her.

She glared up at him. "Nay, our marriage has been annulled."

"Nay, it has *not*. We're waiting for the ecclesiastic tribunal to meet. And since I'm the one who requested the annulment, I should know when the decision will be handed down."

"That's just a technicality. I've made my home at the priory."

"You mean you've escaped to that bloody priory."

"It was not an escape."

"Call it what you will," he interrupted. "You escaped in the night like a thief. You broke your marriage vow and disappeared, without a care for anyone you left behind."

The cutting anger in his eyes made Kenna shiver. He was a head taller than her, dangerous. But she'd never feared him. She wasn't going to start now. She stood her ground, refusing to back off.

"So you wish to speak of marriage vows? You went to a wench's bed on our wedding night. Break marriage vows? You shattered them."

"That was a misunderstanding. A prank arranged by my brother Colin."

"I don't care to hear this," she fumed. "I don't care how you got there or how long before you realized where you were. And don't say you were drunk. You didn't give a damn whose bed you crawled into, just as you didn't care a straw who you were marrying."

"Contracts were signed."

"Between you and my father."

"I don't recall anyone dragging you in chains to the kirk."

"That's enough, you two," James Macpherson ordered,

stepping between them. He glared from one to the other.

Kenna felt scorched by the heat of Alexander's gaze over his brother's shoulder, and she did her best to return the look. He opened his mouth to say more and then snapped it shut.

"This is not the time or place for you two to revisit your rosy past," James said sternly.

Kenna bit back unspoken words of anger, words pent up in her for the past six months. Turning her back on them, she looked past the line of trestle tables at the large carved stone cross set into the wall.

"Unfasten these ropes," she hissed under her breath.

Footsteps approached. A knife cut the cords. She didn't know if it was Alexander or James. The ropes dropped to the floor by her bare feet. She rubbed her arms, looked down at the stained dress, ripped in places from the fight she'd put up when they were taken. The Macphersons' reckless disregard for danger today surpassed even their own reputation. They were pirates and privateers, but Kenna knew they would not hurt a woman. Emily would be safe until arrangements were made for her freedom. But she needed to get out of here.

Negotiation. Captives. Extravagant dowries. The conversation she'd had with Emily earlier in the day filled the gaps in what she'd heard moments ago. Kenna realized why they were taken. The MacDougall laird had been dim-witted enough to think he could take a Macpherson ship and make it part of his daughter's dowry. But there was no logic in that whatsoever. Kenna wondered if Graeme MacDougall had consulted with her father about this. At least until the annulment was granted, her marriage to Alexander made the MacKay and Macpherson clans allies, and this made the MacDougalls distant kin, too.

Facing the others again, she found James cutting the ropes off of Emily's arms. Alexander loomed over the abbot, listening to whatever he was whispering, but his gaze remained fixed on her.

"Send me back with the abbot," she told him. "I'm ready to go."

Whatever composure Emily had been maintaining disappeared. "Nay! Please. You cannot leave me here." She rushed to Kenna's side. "Please, you have to stay with me."

Kenna hugged her cousin, troubled to find her shaking like a leaf.

"Abbot," James said. "We need a place to keep the two women until we make a decision."

Kenna shot a glance at Alexander, who was scowling at his brother. The abbot gestured to a novitiate hovering in the shadows by the door.

"You, lad, show them up to the tower chamber above mine."

"Diarmad, go with them," James ordered. "Make certain the two ladies are safely and securely settled while we finalize our arrangements here. And Abbot, can you send a nun up with a cloak and a dress and shoes that might fit Lady Kenna?"

A born politician and peacemaker, James Macpherson had reportedly played an active role in finalizing the arrangements for her marriage to Alexander.

"You will not cause trouble while you're here," Alexander warned, his sharp words directed only at her.

A dozen retorts burned on her tongue, but she chose silence and ushered Emily after the young monk. Diarmad followed at a watchful distance.

Kenna was relieved to go. She couldn't stand Alexander's scrutiny any longer. He undid her, and not just in firing up her temper. He was her husband. She'd not forgotten that. Not for an instant. When it came to Alexander Macpherson, she always felt like a young lass caught up in her first flush of infatuation.

Prior to their wedding, she had wasted too much time worrying about what kind of wife she'd be. She lacked the skills of the legion of wenches that he'd infamously wooed and bedded. And she had none of the refined ways of the court lasses who'd been chasing him for years. After her mother's death, she'd been raised by MacKay men. She knew how to hunt and ride a horse and use a lance and dirk and short sword, but she never cared about acquiring the courtly manners of young noblewomen.

She was not a suitable match for Alexander Macpherson. She'd tried to convince her father to break the contract. But his hurtful words, still fresh in her mind, only affirmed what she already knew.

You are so flawed in your manners. So lacking in even the basic knowledge of what you need to be the wife of the next Macpherson laird. And yet fortune has somehow smiled on our clan in him agreeing to overlook your faults and take you as his wife. Now, you will do your duty for a change and cease your complaining.

And as she'd departed his chambers, he'd called out after her. *You muddle this chance, lassie, and you no longer have a home in Castle Varrich. You will no longer be welcome in Clan MacKay.*

So Kenna made her decision before she took the marriage vow.

She would run since she no longer had a father. She would run since she no longer had a clan. She refused to be a pawn in Magnus MacKay's game. So she ran.

Emily clung to her arm and cried softly all the way up the tower stairs.

The chamber was small. The sparse furnishings included a small cot and some blankets, a three-legged stool, and a table. Kenna waited until she heard the latch drop into position on the other side of the door before checking the two windows. Three flights up, one overlooked the courtyard. The other faced the sea.

"I cannot stay here. I have to get away from him."

"Please, you cannot leave me here alone with them," Emily pleaded. "We cannot let them separate us."

"But I can go back with the abbot and arrange for your freedom by tomorrow."

"That's unthinkable, Kenna. My reputation will be destroyed if I'm left alone in their clutches."

"Listen, I would never admit this to that knave in the Great Hall, but the Macphersons are not villainous ruffians. They're as respectable a clan as you'll find in the Highlands, and they're doing this only to reclaim what was taken from them."

"Are you defending them? They kidnapped us!"

"I am not. But I cannot be blind to the fact that their ship was stolen, either. Did you know a *Macpherson* ship was part of your dowry?"

"How could I? I wasn't included in the marriage discussions. No one told me where the ship came from, exactly. Everything I know has come to me as rumor."

"So typical of our fathers!"

"But we must stay together. You certainly see that," Emily urged. "James and Alexander may not be villains, but they're no saints, either. We both know it. Everyone else knows it, too. When the whispering begins, my reputation will be destroyed."

Kenna looked about the room. She didn't want to think that it was her husband that Emily was talking about, but she knew it was the truth.

"Sir Quentin would turn his back on me without a second thought if he were to find out I was left alone with these Highlanders. My family needs this marriage to come about, Kenna. You *must* wait with me."

Kenna took the dirk from her belt and walked to the window.

"What are you doing?"

"I have a different plan."

~

His brother was talking, but Alexander wasn't listening.

He still wanted her.

Since the debacle of a wedding last winter, every time he thought about Kenna, his insides got so riled up that he didn't know what to do. Seeing her today didn't help at all.

The union had seemed perfect. The match extended the influence of the powerful Macpherson clan, adding control of the shipping lanes of the North Minch, and the MacKays gained protection from attacks by neighboring clans while the twin sons of Magnus MacKay grew up and came of age.

So what if it was an arranged marriage? he thought. He was doing his duty as the eldest son and the next Macpherson laird, and she had a responsibility to her clan. And there had been sparks between them from the very first meeting. He'd felt it, and he was certain she did, too.

And it wasn't only her striking eyes and sensual mouth and flawless skin that had captured his attention. Alexander had known many beauties in his twenty-seven years. But she had an intensity that was impossible to hide. Passion that showed through, regardless of the formality of those meetings. There were rumors of her fearlessness and her temper. Each time they met before the wedding, she had been escorted by MacKay women, guided as to what to say, where to go, how to behave. But it was impossible to hide the untamed spirit that shone in those magical violet-blue eyes.

Only once had he kissed her, on the kirk steps after their wedding. But the surge of awareness that rushed through him, sending his heartbeat skittering, had told him everything he needed to know. Or so he thought.

And then came the bloody prank. Thanks to his youngest brother, Colin, he'd ended up in bed with the mistress of a French ambassador. To this day he was certain that nothing had happened between them. Fairly certain.

He was sprawled half-naked next to the woman sound asleep when the MacKay servants barged in. The news quickly spread. Alexander was embarrassed. Colin had confessed. Apologies had followed. The MacKays knew it was a prank. Everyone knew it was a prank. Everyone except Kenna.

That was because she was already gone.

A thousand conflicting thoughts still burned in Alexander's brain. He had been ready to go after her, find her, and bring her back. But then he'd pieced together the truth about her departure. Kenna had run off *before* the embarrassing prank. He learned that she had planned her escape even before their wedding.

"Have you heard one word I've said?"

Alexander turned around sharply. Everyone else had left the Great Hall. "The abbot and Diarmad will take Kenna and our terms to Craignock Castle. We get our ship back at Oban tomorrow."

"I knew you weren't listening. Kenna stays here."

"She goes."

"This is no time to be pigheaded. Even though the MacDougall started this, we should be sensitive to Emily's position."

"We'll bring along a couple of nuns with us to attest that her virtue is intact."

"We don't need any nuns. Kenna is blood kin to the

MacDougalls. Her word that Emily was kept safe will outweigh a convent full of nuns."

For months, Alexander struggled with the insanity of being married to a runaway bride. At first, he'd hoped he could forget about her, but he'd been wrong. When he found out where she was, he was driven nearly mad over what he should do. Part of him wanted to ride to Glosters Priory and drag her back to Benmore Castle, and part of him wanted to burn the priory down with her in it.

"She goes. The plan was always to kidnap the Mac-Dougall chit. That's all."

"Her name is Emily," James retorted. "And plans change. Now that we have Kenna, we need to keep them together."

Kenna. Alexander couldn't rub out the image of her standing here barefoot, her hair wild and her clothes in disarray. She inflamed him in every conceivable way. But in those moments, the idea of her long, creamy limbs tangled with his in a bed set his heart hammering, sending fiery desire to parts of him that should remain neutral. It was no use. He wanted her, and she was his wife.

His wife. All he could think of now was that she was his. That she *should* be his. Frustration welled up inside of him. He wouldn't take her against her will. He would not crush the spirit in her, but allowing her to stay in the abbey—stay in the abbey with him—was not an option. She was like a falcon, untamable. She would have to come to him of her own accord. That was the only way, even if it killed him. But she hated him. The contradictions tore at him.

"This is a mistake, brother," he growled. "You know better than anyone where things stand between us."

"That was six months ago. This is now."

"Nothing has changed. She doesn't want to be near me. Near any of us," Alexander fumed. "You know what happened when I sent her that bloody letter explaining things. I laid it all out for her. Told her my feelings for her, by 'sblood! And what was her response?"

His brother said nothing.

"She burned it in front of the messenger and sent back the ashes, saying she never wanted to hear the Macpherson name again."

"Perhaps her feelings have changed."

"Did it look like that to you today?"

"Well, I accept the possibility that you and Kenna might kill each other over the next day or two. But that is a chance I'm willing to take. I don't care to start a clan war because we damaged the reputation of a virtuous woman."

"They took our bloody ship."

"True enough," James replied. "And we're getting it back, using negotiation."

"By the devil, James, why do you always have to be

such a politician?"

"Because we need to use our brains in this business as much as brawn. Reason is what's called for here."

Alexander's attention was drawn to the base of the stairs, where a nun was moving into the shadows and hurrying to the door of the Great Hall.

"Then you'd best direct your reason that way, little brother, for there goes Emily." He pointed. "And while you do that, I'll just take my brawn up to the tower room and make sure that my troublemaking wife hasn't murdered an old nun."

~

Roxburghshire, Scotland

The twilight air hung heavy with the scent of battle and blood. Corpses dotted the graying landscape. In the center of it all, the castle rose up beside the river like a brooding beast. The high gate yawned wide at the horrors around it. And in the stronghold's belly, the rank, dark dungeons bulged with dozens of the ill-fated.

Sir Ralph Evers moved across the bloody ground. Wounded Scots cried out for mercy, praying for a quick death, a sword thrust to the heart.

Before fighting his way into these Scottish Borders, he had been governor of Berwick-upon-Tweed, commander in the

North, warden of the East March, high sheriff of Durham. But none of these titles held a straw against what lay ahead.

In the name of King Henry, he was the Scourge of the Borders from sea to sea. Every town and farm was his to take. Every tower house and manor was his to destroy. Every Scot he came across was his to bleed. And bleed they did, for he had no time for prisoners. Unless they had a king's ransom to pay.

More than wealth, more than titles, more than the gratitude of his king, he believed in power . . . and fear. They were the only "real" things in the world. In his world.

And he saw it in the eyes of every groveling peasant and laird that knelt begging before him.

Horsemen appeared by the river. Donald Maxwell, with his sharp hawk's eyes, spotted him and led his band of renegade Lowland cutthroats up the hill to where Evers waited. An old man, his white hair matted and bloody, stumbled along behind them at the end of a long tether.

"Sir Ralph," he said, dismounting and reeling in the old man like a stray dog. "I've got a prize for you."

Evers nodded but said nothing.

"This one is called Cairns, and they say in the village that the old bastard possesses great knowledge of the dark arts. He even knows the secrets of the dead."

Evers stared at the man with little interest. These ignorant Scots. Every village they plundered had a witch or wizard.

Fools. Frightened villagers spewing nonsense to preserve their lives for an hour longer. Even the entertainment of it was growing stale.

"Well, old man," he demanded. "Is there any truth in what they say?"

Cairns said nothing, but his restless eyes scanned the field of dead bodies around him.

Maxwell struck him across the face, driving him to the ground. "You will speak when his lordship addresses you."

The old man, on his knees, stared at the blood running from his mouth to the black earth. He glanced up only once at Evers, but said nothing. Still, his wizened face, closed and guarded, bespoke secrets.

Sir Ralph's eyes narrowed. He knew nothing of sorcery or magic. But he knew about strength and control and power. These things Cairns had . . . for the moment.

"Take him to Redcap Sly," he told Maxwell. His master of torture. An artist of the first order.

Whatever Cairns had or knew, it would all be Evers's before the dismal Scottish sun rose again.

Chapter 3

If I had my mouth, I would bite;
if I had my liberty, I would do my liking:
in the meantime, let me be what I am,
and seek not to alter me.

"Forgive me, Sister. Normally, I would never raise a hand against any member of the church, but the desperate nature of our situation here demands drastic action."

The gray-haired woman, stripped of her habit, veil, and wimple, sat bound and gagged and entirely unhappy in a corner. Her furious glare told Kenna that there was no forgiveness in that old heart at the moment, no matter what the reason.

"Where are you, cousin?" Kenna peered down at the courtyard. She'd given her word that she would not climb down the tower wall until she saw Emily clear of the building and running for the gates.

Every blanket and rag in the chamber had been cut

into strips and tied into one length of rope. They had even broken up the cot and used the woven pieces of cord that supported the straw tick. The clothing the nun brought up for her had been cut and added to the lengths she'd be using to escape the tower.

Ignoring the woman's fierce looks, Kenna tested the strength of the knots.

"Finally." She smiled, seeing her cousin in the court-yard. Emily paused for a moment to look up at the tower before hurrying toward the gates.

"I'm eternally grateful for the clothes and the shoes, Sister. I'll make arrangements to have them replaced."

The nun shook her head vehemently. Kenna moved to the window facing the sea and opened the shutter. The sun was dropping quickly toward the horizon, and the cool breeze whistled through.

"Don't worry about me. Even as a young lass, I was climbing greater heights than this." Usually using good rope, she added silently, but that wasn't going to stop her now.

Always given free rein as a child, Kenna had enjoyed every rugged adventure she could find. After her mother's death, she had been essentially cut loose to run wild. Her father had his boys by then and clan affairs to oversee. Only twelve years old, Kenna found plenty to occupy her time. All of it dangerous.

She looked down at the wide ledge at the base of the tower wall. Beyond it, a high cliff dropped to a gray-blue sea.

"This will hold my weight. Don't give it another thought." The assurance was more for herself than for the nun.

One end of the line was tied to the frame of the bed that she'd slid to the window.

Her captive's muffled complaints grew more alarmed when Kenna dropped the coiled line out the window. It didn't quite reach the ledge, but the distance remaining looked to be a manageable drop. She cast one final look back at the nun.

"Wish me well."

Kenna climbed out and the bed shifted. On the outside, she almost lost her grip as she dropped a foot and jerked to a stop, banging hard against the side of the stone tower.

"I can do this," she whispered, holding on tight. The shoes were too big and one slid off. She kicked off the other one, too, and started down. Her descent was slow. The wind buffeted her against the rough stone. Her hands were burning from the knotted rags and rope. As she descended, the ledge between the tower and the cliff seemed to shrink by half. Her legs wrapped around the makeshift line. Kenna snaked her way down, focusing on her next handhold and forcing back any hint of fear.

Her plan had been made hastily. She would meet Emily outside of the walls and once they were clear of abbey land, they'd find shelter for the night and get word to the castle tomorrow. This was all MacDougall territory. Any of the crofters would surely help them. And away from Alexander, Kenna would be able to think straight.

The thought of her husband finding them gone was a satisfying one.

The Macphersons would not rest until they had their ship back, but they would need to find another way of going about it. Kenna would speak to her father when he arrived at Craignock Castle. That would be their first communication since the wedding—with the exception of exchanging two letters: him ordering her to return to her husband, and her refusing his directive. She did it politely, but it was still a refusal. Even so, he'd want to get involved in this. She was certain he'd known nothing of Emily's dowry, but perhaps the MacKays could do something to renegotiate the marriage terms with the Lowlander.

Almost at the bottom, Kenna gasped as the rope suddenly lifted and she slammed hard against the building. Cursing, she looked up and found Alexander leaning out of the window above her.

"Are you mad, woman?" he called down.

Kenna had heard no shouting, no call to his men for help. Perhaps his pride wouldn't allow it.

Then he began to pull her up, and panic seized her.

She loosened her grip and slid down, quickly reaching the last knot. She had to jump, but the drop to the ledge seemed so far now. And with every second, the distance was increasing. But she wouldn't be hauled in like some salmon on a line.

Below her, the narrow ledge waited. She could do this. Once down, she was fast enough to get away before he came down the abbey steps and out through the courtyard. So long as Emily was already clear of the gates, their plan would work.

The rope shifted, and she hit the building again, jarring her shoulder.

"By the Virgin," she prayed. "Don't let me break a leg."

Her landing was far from graceful. She landed on a rock, rolling her ankle and sending her sprawling.

"Shite, shite, shite," she cursed, feeling pain shoot right to her hip.

Breathless from the impact of the fall, she tried to gather her strength. A dark image appeared above her.

She blinked. "Oh, Satan's hairy arse."

Using her makeshift rope, the beast was speeding down the side of the building. He appeared to have wings, and she guessed he'd be on top of her in seconds.

Kenna scrambled to her feet, but the pain in her ankle told her she wouldn't be outrunning him. Her second choice was the cliff. She peered past the edge at a small opening of water among the rocks. She could certainly break her neck going that way.

He landed beside her with the ease of a cat.

"Where do you think you're going?"

Her heart pounded violently in her chest, but she refused to look at him. Stretching a hand instead toward the colorful western sky, she replied casually, "This is far too beautiful an evening to stay locked up in a tower room. I decided to come out for some air."

"Air? Is that what you are after? Well, I'll give you air, then."

He grabbed her hand. She spun around, shoving at his chest. There was no escape. Instead, he snaked his arm around her and pulled her hard against him.

Suddenly, the ledge was behind her, and they were flying. Alexander never let her go.

No experience in her past could match the feeling in Kenna's stomach. A scream that she later realized belonged to her echoed off the craggy bluffs speeding by, but there was no crunching of bones at the bottom. No spattering of brains on the rocks. Just a quick cut downward through the surface of the pool, the shock of cold water, the sharp taste of brine in her mouth, and then the rapid ascent to sunlight.

Clutching at him, Kenna gasped for air, coughing up seawater. She couldn't catch her breath. Her heart was still lodged in her throat. The water was cold, but the air was colder on her face.

He pushed the hair out of her eyes and pulled her to him.

Her coughing subsided and Kenna's gaze fell on the muscles of his neck. She glanced up past the droplets of water clinging to his lips and then to his eyes. Their gazes locked, and his arms tightened around her as his kicking legs kept them afloat.

Alexander Macpherson had the bluest eyes she'd ever seen in her entire life, and they were staring intently at her now.

Kenna felt a jolt deep in her belly; she read hunger in that face. Flustered by the way her treacherous body responded to him, she still could not bring herself to push him away.

"Was that air enough for you?" His voice was low and washed over her like silk.

Her gaze flitted upward toward the top of the cliff.

"And you say I'm crazy? You're absolutely out of your mind." Her hands encircled his thick neck. She wanted to strangle him. "*Your* life might not have any value, but mine does, and I have no death wish. But more important, know this. I successfully escaped from you in this world; I have no desire to have you follow me into the—"

He crushed her lips beneath his, silencing her. Kenna's hands fisted and wedged between them. But her cheating body wouldn't muster the strength to push him away. It had been so long since she felt that delicious spark she'd only ever felt with him. Shock waves shuddered through her. His strong body pressed against her own. She wanted to be even closer. With an inaudible sigh, Kenna gave in, leaning into him, into the kiss. Her hands clenched his shirt as she welcomed the feel of those hard lips.

She knew the moment a sense of urgency seized him. His hands wrapped tighter around her, one clutching at her back, the other cupping her bottom. The pressure of his lips increased and Kenna melted deeper into the kiss. His tongue was soft and hard and she instinctively opened to him when he started sampling, tasting, learning the texture of her mouth. And her tongue responded to his, tentatively at first, but becoming bolder by the moment as his taste, his scent, the pressure of his body dazed her mind. She had never experienced this kind of heat, the raw desire growing within her.

His breath was ragged when he abruptly ended the kiss. He stared into her eyes, and she burned with embarrassment for she couldn't hide how much she'd enjoyed what had just happened.

Taking her hand, he swam to the edge of the rocky pool.

Nothing more was said. So what was she feeling? Disappointment that he'd ended it too soon? Confusion over her body's reaction? Embarrassment because of her response? Her anger was gone. Kenna's mind churned to make sense of what just happened, to get a grip on her whirling emotions. He didn't like her. She hated him. Why would he kiss her? Why did she respond that way?

Alexander climbed onto the rocks, pulling her up behind him. She forced back a gasp of pain as her ankle refused to support her weight. The dress, soaked with cold seawater, sagged on her body. Looking down, she was mortified to find that the linen blouse was molded to her breasts, her nipples poking through the cloth. Pulling the dress up the best she could, she followed him, trying not to limp. The rocks were wet and slippery and he caught her around the waist as she slipped. Alexander half carried her to a stony stretch of beach.

Just as they reached it, Kenna was surprised to see four riders, leading two additional horses, appear at the far end of the beach. Her cousin Emily was one of the riders, and her horse's bridle was held by James Macpherson. She sent Kenna a despairing look.

"The abbot and Diarmad are on their way to see the MacDougall," James told them. "We should get on the road, as well."

Kenna stood in the cold sand, staring at them and shivering. Darkness was only a couple of hours away.

"Now?" she demanded. "You have no right to endanger Emily's safety . . ."

Whatever else she was going to say withered on her lips as Alexander stripped off his shirt and walked to his horse.

His waist was narrow, his shoulders wide. His skin was bronzed from the sun. Kenna watched the muscles ripple across his powerful back and suddenly felt warmer. He wrung out his shirt and pulled it back on.

One of their men dismounted and brought a horse to Kenna, ready to help her. She shook her head and stepped back.

"Nay, I am not going anywhere."

"You heard James," Alexander said, climbing onto his horse. "We're getting on the road. Now."

"I cannot travel like this," she said. "My dress is soaked. I have no shoes. I need to change my clothes."

"You missed your chance for all that." He tossed her a tartan blanket. "You can fashion an *arisaidh* of sorts from this, I imagine."

It was the same plaid that Alexander wore. She threw

it back at him. "You'll never see me wearing that. I want a dry dress."

"Take yours off. I'll wring it out for you."

She sputtered and then stared at him in disbelief.

Alexander motioned to the others. "Go on, all of you. We'll catch up."

Emily sent her a desperate look over her shoulder as they rode off.

The evening sun broke through a cloud. Beams of light framed the man and the massive charger. But Kenna would not allow herself to be intimidated by the two beasts.

He grabbed her mare's bridle.

"I'm cold, truly," she said. The wet blouse felt like a sheet of ice against her flesh.

Alexander's gaze strayed from her face to her breasts. He reached down for her. "I know how to warm you. You'll ride on my lap."

She reached for her belt and was happy to find she still had her dagger after the fall. She took it out and flashed it at him.

"You ever try to hold me that close again," Kenna threatened, climbing onto the mare, "and you'll have more holes in you than a tinker's vow."

Chapter 4

Would you have me speak after my custom,
as being a professed tyrant to their sex?

Alexander wished his horse could match the speed of Kenna's tongue.

She cursed. She complained. She called him all sorts of names. She repeated how brilliant it would be once she was back at Glosters Priory, so she never had to lay eyes on him again.

He would have believed her if it were not for their kiss. He'd surprised her, and her response had been enthusiastic, in spite of herself. It killed him to end it so abruptly. But he had his answer.

Alexander led their group. Kenna and Emily rode behind him. James and their two men brought up the rear. They were still on MacDougall land, so they could not stop at an inn or at any crofter's cottage where Emily might be recognized, either. The full moon had risen over the distant Trossachs. The temperature continued to drop and the air was downright cold. He was relieved that Kenna had accepted a blanket from James when they'd caught up to them. He wanted her to learn a lesson for acting so foolishly, but he didn't want her catching her death.

Kenna spurred her horse ahead until they were riding abreast. "Why the devil are you moving so fast? We can't keep pace."

A moment before, she had been complaining that he'd been going so slow that they were in imminent danger of being attacked by lame bandits who might be lurking about on foot.

"Slow. Fast. Climbing a tower wall. Kenna MacKay, I don't believe you could ever have any difficulty keeping pace with me." *And that includes in bed making love,* he added silently.

His compliment silenced her for a couple of moments, and he took the opportunity to study her. The blanket was partially draped over her head and wrapped around her shoulders. But most of her curls were dancing in the wind, as free as her spirit.

The day had been a long one for Kenna and Emily. Diarmad told him how he and his men had followed the two and their escorts from Craignock Castle through the countryside and how, at a crofter's cottage, Kenna had delivered a bairn and most likely saved the mother's life.

She was obstinate and independent to a fault. But Alexander was impressed all the same. Of all the women he knew, there were none who could go through that and a kidnapping and an escape attempt and a long ride in a torn wet dress looking like hell and still keep their head up and ride beside him like royalty. None but his mother, Fiona Drummond Macpherson. He'd heard plenty of stories from his father. Alexander wondered if the two women had any idea how close in spirit they were.

"We're hungry and thirsty," Kenna said finally. "We should stop."

"I know a place not too far from here where we'll set up camp for the night. We'll eat then."

She looked around at the rolling heath of gorse and scrub pine. Below them, a river disappeared into a forest of tall pine. "I don't want to be sleeping out with wild animals. We should ride straight to Oban."

He shook his head and smiled. "I don't care what you want or don't want, wife. Have you forgotten that you're the prisoner here?"

"Nay, ogre. I've forgotten nothing. And your lack of consideration for anyone but yourself makes me think of strangling you with my bare hands."

"I like the sound of that. Do your worst, lass."

"Really?"

"The last time you tried to strangle me, you ended up kissing me. So I won't object."

Her eyes flashed like the blade of a dirk in the light of the moon. He remembered the weapon that she kept at her belt. She reined in and rode with her cousin for a few moments, but he was happy when she came up beside him again.

"Emily wishes to ride straight to Oban, too," Kenna pressed.

"We're staying overnight in the forest."

"Consider her reputation, blackguard."

Alexander slowed the pace of his charger and glanced over his shoulder at the other woman. "We need to stop soon. This darkness can hide many dangers."

"There's no worse outlaw out here than you," Kenna needled him. "Show some courage, Alexander. I'll protect you."

"I've heard enough. We're stopping now."

Turning down the hill, Alexander led them into a wooded glen beside the river. He dismounted on a flat area covered with soft pine needles. He could hear the burbling water through the gloom.

Everyone had climbed down from their horses but Kenna. She was leaning down and speaking to Emily. It was not hard to read her thoughts. In a moment she would be taking off into the night. He approached them and took hold of the mare's bridle.

"I'm warning you, lass."

"Warning me?"

"Aye, that I am. I'll be coming after you if you make a break for it. And I'll be catching you. And then there will only be the two of us in these dark woods."

"You cannot scare me."

"The sky will be our blanket, wife. The soft earth, our pillow." He let the suggestive words linger between them. "Would you like me to explain more?"

"I don't care to hear any more of your dreams. And so you know, it's a nightmare, to my thinking. Nay, I'm going nowhere."

It wasn't his imagination. Her voice had thickened.

"Climb down, Kenna."

"I'm tired of you ordering me about. I'll get down when I'm ready." She tried unsuccessfully to jerk the mare's bridle out of his grasp.

Alexander saw Emily's jaw drop open, looking from one to the other.

"Emily, will you be kind enough to help my brother with the food we brought from the abbey? I need a moment alone with my loving wife."

The young woman nodded and hurried off.

"Don't take orders from him, cousin," Kenna called after her.

"Would you like me to help you down, lass?"

Still holding the horse's bridle, Alexander reached for Kenna's ankle. Her cry of pain was totally unexpected.

"What have you done?" He felt her calf and ran his hand down the silky skin to the swollen ankle. She winced again but didn't cry out.

"Nothing."

"It was that mad climb down from the tower window."

"You shook me loose from the rope. It was your fault."

Alexander would have liked to argue who was at fault, but he guessed that would take all night. "Let me help you down."

"Nay, villain. Go away. I can manage by myself."

She threw off the blanket and swung her leg over to the other side of the mare. She was sliding off when Alexander came around and caught her by the waist, helping her land gently on both feet.

"Let go of me. I tell you I don't need your help."

She took a step and winced.

He swept her up into his arms, holding her against his chest. Her mouth was so close. He stared at her lips. He wanted to taste her again.

"Both ankles or one?"

"One," she whispered. "Put me down. I can walk perfectly well."

James had already started a fire. Emily had a blanket

spread next to it. Alexander carried the squirming bundle and deposited her there. He crouched down and reached for her leg. She pushed the skirts over it.

"Leave me alone. I'll see to it myself."

"Not till I make sure it's not broken." He reached for her leg again.

She tried to kick him with her good foot.

"Why must everything be a struggle with you?" He leaned across her lap and took hold of her leg. She punched him in the back. He pulled the skirt up and in the light of the fire saw the dark bruise on the ankle and the side of her foot. There was no blood, no protruding bones. He touched her shin above the ankle. "Does this hurt?"

"I'm a healer. I know what's wrong, what to do. I don't need your help," she growled at him.

"Does this hurt?" he asked again, pressing his fingers along the bone again.

"It does not."

"How about now?" He gently flexed her toes.

"So you think you're a physician now?"

"Answer me."

"Nay, it doesn't hurt. And I'm able to put my weight on it. My ankle is tender, but nothing is broken."

She had beautiful feet. Dirty, but beautiful just the same. "I need to wrap it."

"You don't need to do anything. I told you I can see to it myself."

She squirmed, trying to push him away from her lap. Alexander looked up and found James and Emily looking at them as if they were watching a pair of jesters. He let the hellion have her way and stood up.

"Will she allow you to wrap her leg?" he asked Emily.

"I believe she will."

"It must be tight." Alexander walked away to the line of surrounding pines. Touching her foot, wrestling with her on the blanket, and he was aroused. On the surface he may have been arguing with her. But in truth, he couldn't stop from imagining the pleasure there would be in stripping her of her wet clothes, washing her feet, her legs, every inch of her.

The problem was that he hadn't had a woman since their damned wedding. And the mistress of the French ambassador didn't count. He couldn't remember.

He'd ended up in the wrong bed that first night, but he had sworn to be true to her. And he meant it. Kenna might have run away from him, but they were still married.

Alexander walked into the woods, trying to focus his thoughts on his ships, his plans for the clan, lectures from his father on everything from hunting to horses.

Anything but her.

He thought of his duty as master of the Macpherson fleet. Every month, Spanish ships were returning from the New World bulging with silver and gold. They were sweet fruit waiting to be picked, and he had been picking them. His brother James was following another path. Like their uncle Ambrose Macpherson, James had chosen to pursue the life of a diplomat. Colin, the youngest, was overseeing with his wife, Tess, the Lindsay clan affairs, but he was also ready to take charge of the Macpherson fleet when Alexander succeeded his father.

In the days prior to his marriage to Kenna, Alexander's father had reminded him that it was time to assume the mantle as the next Macpherson laird. He would have done it already if Kenna had stayed. But when she left, he had asked his father to wait while he figured out what needed to be done.

An annulment was one answer. They had influence enough with the bishop. But six months ago, he couldn't do it. And he couldn't do it last month, though he made Kenna believe that he'd requested it. It was a matter of loose ends, unanswered questions, wounded pride, and Macpherson and MacKay clan welfare. Walking away from this marriage meant defeat. He wasn't ready then. He wasn't ready now.

Insane as it might seem, he still had hope. They might

still make a marriage work.

Alexander found himself standing at the river's edge. With the heavy rains of the previous four days, it was a raging torrent. Branches and timber raced by, carried by the speeding current.

If someone fell in . . .

If someone who was a good swimmer decided to run away . . .

Kenna could be halfway back to Craignock Castle by the time anyone realized she was missing. Alexander marched back to where they'd made camp. Perhaps a time would come when he'd stop worrying if his wife was going to run away or not. But tonight was not it.

Six horses stood tethered at the edge of the clearing. One of his men was looking after them. Alexander knew another would be keeping watch in the darkness. Everything seemed peaceful around the fire. James and Emily sat with their backs to him, speaking quietly. Kenna, sitting against a tree, had a blanket wrapped around her. Her foot was now wrapped in strips of cloth. She watched him suspiciously as he approached.

"Do you need to go anywhere, do anything?"

She looked up, pretending all innocence. "Go where? Do what?"

"You know." He motioned to where he'd walked from. "Do you need to relieve yourself, woman?"

"Now?"

"Now."

"When I'm ready, I'll go."

"If you need to go tonight, you'll do it now."

She glared at him. "What are you about?

He crouched down, looking into her eyes. "Don't tell me it hasn't crossed your mind. Walking into the woods? Disappearing?"

"Without Emily? Without a horse? Limping on a bad ankle?"

"An abbey tower couldn't hold you."

"In that case . . ." She smiled, peering around him at the woods. "I believe you should stay awake all night and worry about it."

"I'm not worrying about it," he said.

"Good. Then go away. You're blocking the heat of the fire."

Alexander walked back to his horse and retrieved a length of braided rawhide. No one, including James, said anything when he returned to Kenna a moment later.

Her eyes widened. "What are you going to do with that?"

She tried to squirm away when he looped the cord around the tree and reached for her hands.

"Get away from me."

In spite of her size, she was far stronger than he'd imagined. But Alexander had her hands tied behind her back before she could cause him permanent bodily damage.

"You won't get away with this. I'll kill you in your sleep."

"Which reminds me."

He reached inside her belt and found the dirk. But he took his time. Their faces were just inches apart as his hand rested intimately against the warmth of her belly. A flush rose into her cheeks. He saw her gaze move down to his mouth, but then her eyes narrowed.

"You come this close to me again tonight," she told him, "and I'll make you my wife."

Shaking his head, he took the dirk and walked away.

~

Sir Ralph Evers followed his squire down the winding torch-lit stairwell from a tower chamber. "Anything out of him?"

"Nothing, sir. Can't get him to say a word. Redcap says he thinks there ain't much more the old codger can take."

Ducking under the low round arch of the doorway, Evers stepped into what was once an attractive Great Hall. Now scores of men huddled in groups or lay on the filthy, blood-soaked rushes that covered the floor. Some were bound; others were too whipped to make a difference.

"The stench is getting worse," Evers said, letting his gaze

sweep across the room, searching for any remaining hint of defiance.

"Aye, m'lord. Got dead 'uns mixed in."

"Good. Keep it that way. It will remind the living ones that they're next."

The man motioned to a dead body near them. "This one, soon as he saw the end a-comin' for him, had a bushel full to pass on."

"Anything of interest?"

"Aye. Swore that Cairns talks to the dead. Knows all their secrets. Says the codger talked to his dead wife. And their lad that drowned in the river. Claimed the old man told him things only his dead kin could know."

Evers nudged the corpse with his boot, hoping there was some life left in him. He had more to ask him. Vacant eyes stared back.

This was the same thing he'd heard from others since Maxwell brought in the old man.

In a murky, torch-lit antechamber beyond the Great Hall, Redcap had strapped Cairns over a barrel. Blood was pooling around him on the floor. In the burly torturer's hand a whip dripped red.

Seeing Sir Ralph Evers enter, Redcap Sly shook his head in disappointment before kicking the heap of skin and bones.

"Tell his lordship the secret behind yer trickery and ye might receive his mercy."

There was no answer. The old man's breathing was labored. This room reeked worse than the Great Hall.

Evers glanced one more time at Cairns. Like all the others, the man was a fraud.

"Finish him," Sir Ralph ordered.

Redcap Sly ran a hooked blade across Cairns's throat. Not even a scream of pain followed. Nothing.

Cairns's body slid to the floor. Lifeless eyes stared up at Evers.

Evers turned to leave but stopped at the sight of a collection of items on a block of wood. Prayer beads, acorns, a hand-carved whistle, small knives.

"Any of these belong to Cairns?" he asked.

"The small pouch there. A paltry piece o' stone in it. Hanging around his neck, it was."

Evers snatched up the pouch and walked out. He had stayed long enough in this Borders hellhole. It was time to cut loose and move north. In the Great Hall, he paused by his captain in charge. "Finish them all. We're moving north at dawn."

Stopping beneath a torch ensconced on the wall, Evers pulled open the pouch. He reached in, only to jerk his fingers out.

The stone burned him. He shook it out of the bag, and it dropped to the floor. He crouched down.

Just a light-colored stone with markings carved on it. He

picked it up. It was still hot to the touch.

He turned as the sound of cries and pleas filled the hall. His men were moving among the prisoners, putting an end to their miserable lives.

A movement near him drew his eye. A man stood beside the dead Scot he'd passed before.

It was the dead Scot. No chains. No shackles. Just staring at him.

Before his unformed question could take shape, Evers had his answer. One of his soldiers walked by and stepped through the specter. No living man. A shadow. A ghost.

Beyond him, others were sitting up, rising from their bodies, standing, staring at him.

Evers strode back to Cairns's corpse.

"I know you cannot deny me in death what you refused me in life. Speak."

A dark wisp, Cairns's spirit hovered over its shell.

"Tell me about this stone. What is it? And are there others like it?"

And Cairns told him about the four who walked away from a shipwreck fifty years ago. Each carried a piece of an ancient tablet. The first talked to the dead. The second, a healer, could bring a man back from the edge of death. The third knew the secrets of anyone's past. And the last, a prophet, saw into the future.

Chapter 5

I charge thee on thy allegiance.

Kester, the MacDougall's captain of the guard, had his hand on the hilt of his short sword, awaiting the laird's command. The abbot kept his gaze on Emily's father, knowing that the next few moments would determine his fate. He sent a prayer skyward to Saint Andrew.

The abbot could wring his hands, deny his involvement, and bow his head until his neck ached. What the Macphersons had dared to do was inexcusable. But he himself had done nothing wrong. He was but the bearer of bad news.

Still, that could be enough to make him an accomplice in the eyes of the MacDougalls.

The Macpherson warrior had left him to his fate outside the gates of Craignock Castle. Watching the man disappear into the night, the abbot realized Diarmad was not about to allow his own head to adorn a pike when there was a cleric to sacrifice.

The MacDougall, three clan elders, and the captain were conferring in the laird's private chambers when the abbot had been led in. It was late. Coming through a subdued Great Hall, he'd felt dozens of eyes following his every step. Trenchers of food had long ago been emptied and taken away. Dogs gnawed on scraps and bone beneath the long tables. They'd probably be gnawing on his bones tomorrow, the abbot thought.

After hearing the cleric, Graeme MacDougall didn't say a word, but sat with his fist wrapped around the cup of ale as if he were choking someone's life out of it.

The abbot did not move. He barely breathed.

"Where are the men who escorted the lasses?" one of the elders finally demanded of Kester.

"They came back after the two went missing. I sent them out again with the search parties. We knew nothing of this. Just assumed Lady Kenna wandered off, with Lady Emily in her wake. We had no suspicion of foul play till this moment."

"Where are they now?" the other elder asked.

The abbot shifted his gaze from the laird. "I don't know. On the way to Oban, I should think. They were to leave immediately after I started here."

"What route were they taking to Oban?"

"I don't know."

"How many of them are with the lasses?"

"Five that I saw. But there could be more. Many more."
The abbot decided to not mention that Diarmad had accompanied him to the gates of Craignock.

"Are all three Macpherson brothers with them?"

"Only the two eldest . . . that I saw."

The elders began to speak all at once. The abbot said nothing, waiting for the laird to speak.

"Were any of their ships sitting off the coast?"

"We can go after them."

"If they had enough men, they would have laid siege to Craignock."

"They must have only a few ships."

"We set a trap in Oban."

"Nay, they're laying a trap for us."

"Laird, I told you it would bring disaster taking the Macpherson ship. If you'd only—"

"Enough!" The laird slammed his cup on a table beside him, sloshing ale on the scarred wood surface. He addressed the abbot. "Emily and Kenna. How do they fare?"

"Very well, m'lord. They're being kept together, and they were in good health and spirits when I took leave of them."

The MacDougall looked down, twisting a large gold ring on his finger. The ruby inset glittered in the torchlight.

"And how did Alexander Macpherson react when he

realized he'd kidnapped his own wife?"

"They were both astonished, m'lord." Saying less was the best course, the abbot decided.

"You say we can have Emily returned tomorrow?"

The old man nodded. "They're only after their ship. On that, Alexander was perfectly clear."

Before anyone could speak, the laird waved a hand, requiring silence. He and Kester exchanged a look. "No action will be taken against the Macphersons. The ship will be returned. We will have my daughter back."

The abbot breathed more easily.

"Word of this is not to leave this chamber," the laird ordered. "It that clear?"

"Aye, laird," an elder replied. "But what about Sir Quentin Chamberlain? What of Emily's dowry?"

"I negotiated my daughter's marriage contract. I will make whatever adjustment we need to make in her dowry. I always had my doubts that the Macpherson ship would have worked out, anyway. And I'm certain Magnus MacKay would have objected to it, too."

The other clan elder spoke up cautiously. "But what if Sir Quentin learns Emily has been in the hands of these Highlanders?"

"There is no reason he should know of it. We don't expect him for another sennight," the laird told them. "And you will spread the word that my daughter has gone to

Glosters Priory with Kenna for a few days. They will be back soon."

It all seemed settled. There was some grumbling, but not one of them was brave enough to speak out. A serving lad appeared and whispered in the laird's ear. Mac-Dougall nodded and then directed him to take the abbot to the Great Hall and find him some supper.

Satisfied that disaster had been happily averted, the abbot followed the lad out into the corridor, only to find Diarmad waiting to enter the laird's chamber. The warrior nodded at the stunned cleric.

Pausing at the top of the stairs, the abbot stared at the broad back of the Highlander. And before the door closed, he would have sworn he heard laughter.

Chapter 6

What we have we prize not to the worth
Whiles we enjoy it, but being lacked and lost,
Why, then we rack the value, then we find
The virtue that possession would not show us
While it was ours.

Dresses the colors of spring glimmered with needlework of gold. The jewels the women wore caught every ray of light, blinding with their brilliance. Their faces were bright as the moon. Their voices soft. Their movements deliberate and refined. They crowded the Great Hall, standing in groups, whispering and sending scornful glances in Kenna's direction.

The men in the hall formed a single line before her, their faces hidden behind masks. Her father stood beside her, nodding when it was time for each of them to approach and present himself. She looked down at her wet dress, torn in places, stained nearly black at the hem. Her feet were bare and filthy. Strands of hair fell across her face.

"Choose one," her father ordered.

"But I'm already married," she told him. "I'm married to Alexander."

"He cast you off. Sent you back. He doesn't want you."

Her throat tightened. Sadness clamped down on her heart, but it was no surprise. She'd fought him, deserted him, and said so many false things . . . all the while knowing that he was the only man she would ever want.

"Choose one for your husband and do it now, Kenna. We will not move until you have done so. I've grown tired of this foolish independence."

Kenna tried to prove him wrong. She needed no protection from him. She tried to take a step. Her feet wouldn't budge. She tried to raise her arms. They were bound to her side. She was a captive.

The next man in line approached. "Will you have me, lady?"

She could see nothing of his face, but only the crown sitting askew on his head. "Nay. You are just a prince's fool."

The next one approached. "Will you marry me, great lady?" he drawled each word as if they were a collection of yawns.

"You are duller and more false than a January thaw."

The next man was too cheerful in his question.

"Nay," she dismissed him. And the one after. And the dozens after that.

She did not want another husband. He might have sent her back, but they were still married. Alexander told her that. It was not too late.

The last man in the room finally stood before her. Before he could ask for her hand, her father spoke first.

"Take her. She is yours."

Kenna struggled against her invisible restraints. "I won't belong to another, Father. I'm already married."

Tears blurred her eyes. She shook her head, trying to get away as the man approached. She struggled to push him away. But her hands would not move. They were tied, bound now behind her back.

Startled, Kenna opened her eyes and gazed up at the blue sky through an opening in the trees. She was outside. There were no lines of men. Her father wasn't there. There were no clusters of women ridiculing her for the way she looked.

It was odd to imagine she'd come to think of Alexander as her escape. Six months ago, marrying him would have put an end to Magnus MacKay's authority. But was she happy with the arrangement?

She wasn't. Especially not after the talk with her father. Alexander lay sleeping on his side an arm's length away. They were sharing the same blanket. She looked at his unshaven face and long lashes. No man had the right to look as attractive as he did. Her gaze moved down his face, and she recalled the havoc the touch of his lips caused in her body.

In her dreams she'd wanted him to come for her. During her months at Glosters Priory, Kenna dreamed he would pursue her, know her, accept her for who she was, and fall in love with her. Then she would go with him to the farthest corners of the world. But he'd never come. He'd sent a messenger instead.

Perhaps she'd been too impulsive, burning the letter without reading it. But it was his fault. A man shouldn't send a letter saying, *Sorry, dear. I drunkenly bedded a wench on our wedding night,* or whatever else he wrote. If that in fact was the content of the correspondence.

Anger rose in her. Her hands were still tied behind her. Her shoulders and arms were sore from sleeping this way.

She glared at a bird singing loudly on a branch above them.

"Fly away, bird, or I'll be plucking your feathers the moment I'm free."

Kenna struggled and managed to sit up. Aches in the rest of her body matched the pain in her arms. She was getting too old to be jumping off towers and cliffs on the same day. She looked for her cousin. There was no sign of her.

"Emily?"

She couldn't see James Macpherson or the other men traveling with them, either. And the horses. Where were the horses?

Everyone was gone. They were alone.

"Wake up, mammet," she growled at her husband.

He mumbled something in his sleep and rolled onto his back.

"They're all gone, Alexander. Where did you take Emily?"

The coals in the fire were still smoking. They couldn't have been gone too long. Kenna stood up. She couldn't take more than a step away from the tree, for the cord restraining her hands was still tied to it.

"My husband," she said scathingly.

She assessed the object of her anger and balanced her weight on the sore ankle before delivering a kick to his hip with the other. "I said wake up, you puny—"

The breath was knocked out of her as she hit the ground. One moment she was delivering a kick and a curse and the next, she was down on the blanket with Alexander's weight partially covering hers.

"My wife. I can't put into words what a joy it is to wake up to your caresses and endearments."

This was too close. He could surely feel the thrum of her heart. "Untie my hands, you villainous pignut."

"Must I?" He pushed the hair out of her face and gently cupped her cheek. His thumb caressed her bottom lip as he looked into her eyes.

Kenna forgot to breathe and his knee slowly slid upward between her legs. She lost track of the terms of abuse she was planning to deliver. The weight of his body felt perfect. A delicious tingling spread to unthinkable places.

"I like you when you're submissive like this."

Her knee was intended to connect with his groin, but he was too quick. He rolled them until she was straddling his lap.

"You don't need to unman me. Speak to me. You can be on top. I won't argue."

"Untie me, you qualling measle," she demanded. "Everyone's gone, including Emily. What have you done to her? Where did they all go?"

A moment later, she was free. He moved across their camp. She stretched her sore arms and limped after him. The others were definitely gone.

Alexander disappeared into the woods. Kenna noticed a bag left by the fire. She rummaged through it. Another blanket, some dried meat, and oatcakes.

He came back carrying a sword in its sheath. He

strapped the weapon to his belt.

"Where is everyone?" she asked again. "Where is Emily?"

"James must have taken her, and not too long ago."

"But why? Where are the horses? We have to go after them."

"They've taken those, too," he said.

"Why? There has to be a mistake."

"I don't think so." He looked around the camp. "We've been abandoned . . . for some reason."

She threw up her hands in frustration. "But why would anyone do such a thing? Are they insane? Weren't they afraid I might cut your throat while you slept?"

"The thought must have crossed their minds. James left my sword where the horses were tied, out of your reach."

He crouched by the fire, pawing through the food.

Kenna couldn't believe how calm he seemed in light of everything. Deserted with no shelter and still on Mac-Dougall land. After what the Macphersons did yesterday, she wouldn't be surprised if there was a price on Alexander's head. "Emily wouldn't go with them without putting up a fight. She must have been kidnapped."

"She was kidnapped. Yesterday," he reminded her, looking amused. He took a bite of dried meat. "But from the looks of things, she didn't put up a fight or call for help."

"Maybe she did. You sleep like the dead."

"And what about you? Did you hear her?"

Kenna hadn't. She recalled last night before falling asleep that she'd found it peculiar that Emily appeared to be so comfortable with James Macpherson. Would her cousin do that? Run away with a Highlander? Would she abandon her? No, none of that made sense.

"Emily has a reputation she protects fiercely, never mind an upcoming marriage. I wouldn't even be here if she hadn't refused to be alone with you and your brother."

"Her reputation is safe. The abbot saw you two were together. That will be enough until we hand her over to her father in exchange for our ship."

"The MacDougalls won't return your ship unless I'm returned. Don't forget—I was kidnapped, too."

"You overestimate your value. You were taken by your husband."

"That's still kidnapping."

"Not in the eyes of the Macphersons or the MacKays. Your father suggested many times that I should ride over to Glosters Priory and reclaim my wife."

Her father would say that. Magnus MacKay had only two things he valued: keeping his sons safe and protecting his clan's future. He needed the Macpherson warriors. And Kenna was just a marker in the exchange. As far as he was concerned, she had no voice in what was to become of her life.

"I'll not be a sack of grain to belong to the highest bidder."

"That's exactly what I told your father. I said Kenna is more like a Scots Grey or a bearded collie."

"So I'm a chicken . . . or a dog?" She could hurt him. She wanted to hurt him. She wanted to hurt someone. She moved toward him, hand outstretched. "My dirk. I want it back."

He pushed to his feet, backing up. "Only a fool would hand Kenna MacKay a weapon when she's this unsettled."

"And a bigger fool would think he's safe in the wilderness, no matter what scheme my father or your brother has been devising to bring me to my knees. It won't work."

Kenna was surprised to see the hilt of the dagger stretch toward her. She paused in taking it, searching his face for any sign of a trick.

"James might have had the best of intentions, but there's danger here."

She took the weapon and tucked it in her belt. Limping into the woods, she realized this was the first time he'd trusted her.

Kenna tried to not place too much importance on it.

Right now she needed privacy, which she found under a tree close to the river.

The two of them left alone. What was everyone thinking? What did they hope to accomplish? That all their past trouble would just vanish? Alexander and Kenna couldn't string two sentences together without fighting.

She stood up and shook out her skirts. The dream she'd had wouldn't leave her. And what if she did somehow clamp her mouth shut? Cut back on insults that seemed to come so naturally when she spoke with him?

Remembering Alexander's weight on her made Kenna's heart race, even now. She wasn't immune to his looks or to the way he had with women. He knew exactly what to do, what to touch, how to make her skin tingle and have her breaths catch in her chest. And he'd returned her dirk.

She touched her mane of hair and cringed at the thought of how bad she must look. No better than a fairy woman, the *Bean Nighe* even. A nightmarish sight, to be sure. Her wild hair. Her ruined dress. All she was missing was webbed feet, a great tooth protruding from her mouth, and breasts hanging to her knees.

Kenna walked to the river and stepped out onto some rocks. The surging waters ran deep and fast all around her. The current was too strong. She leaned down and washed her hands and face. The sane decision would be for Kenna to walk back in the direction they'd come. She could take shelter in some crofter's cottage while Alexander moved north. His brother and the men would come back for him once they had the ship.

A movement across the river caught her attention. More than a half dozen men emerged from the trees at the water's edge. They carried bows and English halberds. All were armed with short swords. She crouched low on the rocks. Perhaps they wouldn't see her.

She was wrong.

"We can ford up stream," one of them shouted in English, moving quickly upriver. The rest followed on his heels.

Her first thought was to warn Alexander. There was no way the two of them could fight off so many.

She stood up and turned to see him coming toward her.

"Kenna."

She recognized the urgency in Alexander's hushed voice. He must have seen them, too.

"Go. Run," she told him. His fate would be much worse than hers, she imagined. With her bad ankle, she would only slow him down.

"We go together," he said, lifting her by the waist and plunging them both into the rushing current.

~

Gold and revenge. They were the only things that gave a man real pleasure. And, of course, a good fire.

Sitting on horseback beside Sir Ralph, Donald Maxwell felt, even at this distance, the heat of the flames rising above the roof of the burning tower house. He breathed in the smell of scorched wood and thatch and flesh.

He'd gotten back to Evers too late to take part in this raid, but what he had learned was worth three days of hard riding.

"The healer was the wife of Magnus MacKay, a laird far to the north." Maxwell turned in his saddle and nodded toward the blue mountains in the distance. "She's the one Cairns told you about. She had a carved stone, and it passed on to her daughter Kenna when the lass married the son of the Macpherson laird, half a year since."

"Where is she now?"

"I sent a raiding party to bring her back. The lass has been in a priory—"

"I don't care where she's been or who she's married to. I want the stone."

"My men know what you want. They'll bring it."

"Where is she now?" Evers asked again.

"Near Oban."

"Good. Send word to them. They're to come back with the stone or not come back at all."

Chapter 7

Speak, Count, 'tis your cue.

"You think I'm a child . . . or a fool."

Emily paced the room James Macpherson had taken at the ferryman's inn for her. Her meal, barely touched, sat on the table.

James shook his head. "That's not it at all."

She huffed and stared out the tiny window at the windswept gray waters of the sound. Along the coast, Oban's cottages huddled together out of the salty winds of the sea. She could chew his head off. She'd fallen victim to the Highlander's crafty charm. She *was* a fool, she thought angrily.

Because of her gullibility, Kenna was in danger.

"You told me they could mend their differences with a few hours alone."

"I meant it. There's a great deal they need to discuss, and they've never had a chance to do that."

She waved him off. "I believed your tales that Alexander hasn't been the same since Kenna left him."

"Anyone who has spent any time with my brother will swear to that."

Emily continued to pace. James had played to the romance in her heart, knowing she'd soften at the prospect of her cousin out of the priory and happily settled into marriage. She would not be caught again in his snares.

"You led me to believe that it was up to us to give them another chance."

James Macpherson nodded. "And that's what we've done."

Like an obedient sheep she'd followed his lead as the sky lightened along the eastern horizon. Trusting him, she'd crept silently away. She'd rode on, leaving Kenna and assuming the Macpherson men would do right for Alexander and her cousin.

"You lied to me."

"I may have omitted one or two things," he replied.

She stopped, facing him. "You told me you left them a horse."

"True, that was a lie," he admitted. "But if we'd left them a horse, they would have arrived here ahead of us. Sharing a mount, there'd be no time to talk. We needed to slow them down."

"And now she's in danger of English raiders."

"Alexander can take care of them both."

Arriving at the inn, James heard talk of raiding parties being seen farther north than ever. Some were rumored to be in the same area where they'd left Kenna and Alexander.

Now James intended to go back for them.

"There's no point in waiting any longer for my kinsmen. I'm coming with you," she announced. "As it is, Kenna will never forgive me. If anything happens to her, I'll never forgive myself."

"That's out of the question. You're not coming with me. You're going back to Craignock Castle as soon as your father's men get here."

All the politician's charm dropped away when James issued a command. And what he was telling her now was certainly an order.

Emily matched his glare. "What about my exchange for the ship? Where is it?"

"Well, that business is settled. I suggest you rest. I suspect the MacDougalls will arrive any time now." James edged toward the door. "I'll watch outside for them."

Something was wrong. He'd fooled her once. She wouldn't allow it to happen again. Emily moved to the door, blocking his exit. "You really take me for a fool."

His expression hardened, but the arresting gray eyes avoided meeting hers.

"Talk, James Macpherson, or by God I'll put on a show that will make my cousin Kenna proud," she threatened.

"You're two different people. Be happy with who you are. You're much easier to reason with."

His words were intended to be a compliment, but Emily didn't perceive it that way. She took a threatening step toward him, her tone sharper than before. "What is this business that is settled?"

"Now, listen to me. None of this involves you. Let me go by."

"I'll set the inn on fire if you go out this door." She poked his chest. It was like jabbing a rock. She did it again, enjoying the thrill of standing up to him. "I'll scream 'murder.' I'll steal a horse and ride back to where you deserted my cousin."

"I didn't think it was necessary to keep you in the dark. I don't know why I should be the target of your wrath. Your father could better explain when you return to Craignock."

Father. Kenna's words came back to her. They were nothing but brainless, senseless property in the eyes of their fathers.

"My father will never see me again unless you explain." She rose up on her toes, looking him directly in the eye, making certain he understood she meant every word.

He stared back long enough that Emily felt a kick deep

in her belly. Something changed in his gaze. Their faces were a hand's width away, and time froze in the room. They both felt it. The argument was forgotten.

James broke the spell and moved to the window. The sea breeze pushed through his dark red hair. Emily studied his broad shoulders. Her gaze moved uncontrollably down his back to the narrow waist and along the length of his kilt to powerful calves that disappeared into boots. The warmth rising into her face was unexpected.

"The ship," he said finally. "The Macpherson ship was never part of your dowry. That was only part of the plan. It was a ruse to bring Alexander to Craignock."

Emily covered her burning cheeks with cold hands. She was embarrassed by the thoughts rushing through her a moment ago. Sir Quentin Chamberlain. She repeated the name in silence. Her future husband.

"I'm relieved about that," she managed to say. "But I'm certain there's a great deal more you haven't told me."

"Our ship was never actually taken. The kidnapping was simply to bring Kenna and Alexander together. If they reconcile, then that puts the MacKay and Macpherson clans back on their arranged path. We accomplished exactly what we intended. The only complication is the English."

She pressed her fingers to her temples, trying to shut out her momentary lapse of judgment and focus on what was at stake. "Alexander knew nothing of all this?"

"Nothing. Those two are so bullheaded that if either one knew, then the plan was doomed. And we carried it off brilliantly, when you think of it. I don't believe Alexander or Kenna suspected a thing."

"So this is not another Macpherson prank?"

"Absolutely not," he said defensively. "The clans stand to lose a great deal if those two go through with an annulment. We had to try, and your father was most agreeable in allowing us . . . allowing me to use your wedding for the plan."

"My father . . . allowing you . . . and use my wedding," Emily repeated. Her head was beginning to pound. "Why wasn't I told?"

"Very few people know the truth. We couldn't chance failure."

"Failure? What kind of success would it be if Kenna stabbed one of your men at the river yesterday? And you know that was a strong possibility. Because I wasn't told, I didn't stop her from climbing down the wall at the abbey, where she could have fallen on her head and died. And that was a possibility, too."

"Well, there's still the distinct possibility that she's already stabbed Alexander and he's strangled her in return," James offered. "But these were hazards our families were willing to take."

"Our families. *Our.* Including the MacDougalls. And

you still don't believe there was anything wrong in keeping me ignorant of the plot? You had so many chances to explain."

Before he could answer, a knock on the door drew their attention.

"A company of MacDougall warriors," a Macpherson warrior called out. "They're at the tavern on the harbor."

~

The current was strong. The rushing water broke Alexander's hold on Kenna as soon as they were dropped at the first bend of the river. She was carried ahead, bobbling under and above the racing stream. Alexander's ribs and legs banged against submerged objects as he sailed by them. The sword at his belt threatened to pull him under or snag on branches lodged in the rocks, but he wasn't about to let the weapon go. He tried to stay afloat and avoid smashing into the boulders. Suddenly, he could no longer see her.

"Kenna!" he shouted over the roar of the water.

Urgency seized him. He knew she was a good swimmer. That much he'd learned when they jumped off the cliff at the abbey the day before. But neither knew what the next bend in the river would bring. She could bang her head against a rock and go under.

"Kenna!" he shouted again, swimming with the current and scanning both shores for some sign of her.

The river became narrower and deeper, and he felt himself drop down a number of levels. Where the current passed between large rocks, the flow of the water was stronger and faster.

With its roots pulled loose from the bank, a tree stretched across the river ahead. He was relieved when he spotted a slight figure holding on to the very end of one limb.

"Kenna!" he shouted, gliding in long strokes toward her.

She turned and stretched out a hand toward him. The water was pushing him away from the tree. In a moment he'd sweep past her. He swam across the current, trying to close the distance to her. But the river had a mind of its own, pushing him away.

"Stay there! Work your way to the shore," he shouted as the water carried him past her. "I'll find you."

To Alexander's dismay, she let go of the tree and disappeared beneath the surface.

"What are you—" The breath was knocked out of his body as he slammed against a large boulder. He felt his left arm go numb as his shoulder struck another half-submerged rock beside it. He hadn't been watching, hadn't seen it coming. He was nearly on top of another boulder and he winced, awaiting the next smashing blow.

"Don't worry. I have you." Small arms wrapped around him from behind. She stretched her legs out, planting her feet against the boulder and pushing them away from the obstacle. "Lean against me. I'll pull you to shore."

Alexander was relieved to have found her. At the same time he wanted to laugh out loud. He coughed out a mouthful of water.

"*I'll* carry us to shore," he corrected. "I'm saving *you*."

"Say what you will," she cried in his ear. "But let's not waste any of your strength. If you panic, I'll have to drown you and go off on my own."

Alexander heard her grunt as she managed to swing him around and wedge the two of them against another fallen tree limb. He glanced toward the shore. There appeared to be an eddy beyond the tree. They were not far from the water's edge.

He turned in her arms. "Hold on to me."

"I am holding on to you," she shouted. "If I let you go, you'd probably crack that thick head of yours on one of these rocks."

"Have it your way. I'll hold on to you." He looped one arm tightly around Kenna's waist and used the other to work his way along the tree toward the shore.

Alexander's shoulder throbbed. The two of them managed to work together until their feet touched the riverbed. A moment later, they dragged themselves out of the water.

Once ashore, Kenna sank to her knees on the muddy bank. Alexander reached for his belt and found the sword still attached.

"You can drop that weapon."

They looked up. A soldier stood a few steps away, short sword raised.

He turned his head, calling to someone beyond the line of trees. "Over here, lads. Come see what the river coughed up for us."

Chapter 8

And in her eye there hath appeared a fire.

Kenna could see one man, but how many more were beyond the trees? Jumping back in the river no longer seemed a viable option. The soldier was too close.

By the Virgin, she wouldn't allow the English to take them. Still on her hands and knees, she stole a glance at Alexander. His expression told her he had no intention of surrendering, either. His hand moved to the hilt of his sword. She reached for the dirk and gathered every ounce of strength left in her body. She leaped for the Englishman, dragging one leg behind her.

The soldier's eyes widened, and he swung his sword in her direction. Alexander was on him before the man could even utter a cry for help. Cut down, the soldier crumpled at her feet.

"Wait here," he ordered, pushing her behind a tree.

His eyes met hers for only an instant. He was a warrior

ready for battle, and he would protect her to the last breath left in his body.

"As soon as I've led them away, go back in the river and let the current take you as far as you can go."

Voices. She peered out as soon as Alexander plunged into the undergrowth along the bank. Four men came out into the clearing, the first one nearly stumbling over their dead comrade. Seeing Alexander in flight, they leaped after him and the chase began.

She picked up the short sword of the dead soldier. It was no heavier than the ones she used in practice with the MacKay warriors. The river was only steps away. She turned and followed the shouts. There could be more of them ahead, but she couldn't leave him here. She wouldn't let him die. They'd exchanged vows of marriage, regardless of the mockery they'd made of it for the past six months. Kenna wouldn't be able to live with herself if anything happened to him because of her.

The sound of fighting brought her to a clearing. Three men were down. Alexander was deflecting the blows of the last one, a huge soldier swinging a massive sword.

Blood covered Alexander's shirt. His left arm hung limp and was clearly no use to him in the battle. The Englishman drove him back and he stumbled over a root. As the soldier raised the weapon over Alexander, Kenna shouted, rushing in. But she stopped short as someone grabbed a fistful of her hair from behind, yanking her backward. Then she felt the edge of a blade against her throat.

"Drop it."

Alexander's sword ran upward through his foe before the blow could fall, and the giant collapsed on her husband's body.

"I said drop the sword."

The man was a Scot, a Lowlander by his accent. Kenna wondered how many more of them were left.

She dropped the sword at her feet as Alexander shoved the dead body away and stood up. He saw her and whoever it was holding a knife to her throat.

"I'm taking the woman," the Lowlander threatened. "If you follow, she's dead."

"You're not taking her anywhere," Alexander told him. "She means nothing to you and she belongs to me."

"If she's the one we're looking for, she means a great deal to me."

He started to back away. Kenna stumbled and the man jerked her upright. As he did, she pulled the dirk from her belt and stabbed backward at him, hitting him in the thigh and again in the belly. She felt his grip loosen.

Wrenching herself free, she turned to face him. But before she could strike again, he suddenly stood up straight, a peculiar look on his face. Dropping his knife, he reached back over his shoulder.

When he fell dead on his face at her feet, she saw the hilt of a short sword protruding from his back. Behind him, a boy stood looking at them, his face flushed with anger. He couldn't have been more than eight or nine years of age.

"There's more of them nearby. I seen 'em. Follow me."

He started off in a direction away from the river. Alexander joined her and took her hand. He was covered in blood, but she didn't know how much of it was his.

"The lad's our best chance," he told her.

He was badly hurt. Fresh blood was seeping through the shirt on his side. His steps dragged, but they kept the boy in sight.

Kenna wrapped an arm around him, encouraging him to lean on her. Then, just ahead, water shimmered through the trees. By the time they reached a stony beach, the boy had shoved a small skin-covered fishing boat into the water.

"Is he going to die on you?" he asked, as Kenna helped Alexander climb inside. Blood dripped onto nets in the bottom of the boat.

"Nay, we'll have no dying today," Alexander answered. "You're a brave lad. What's your name?"

"Jock." He pushed the boat away from the shore and climbed in. He nodded at the brooch on Alexander's kilt as he fitted the oars into the pins. "You're a Macpherson.

I've seen the crest on yer ships' flags."

"Aye. And I can see you're a smart one, at that."

Kenna searched the shoreline for any sign of anyone following them. None that she could see. A dense fog was rolling in from the northern hills out over the water. When she offered to take the oars and row, the boy bristled and then turned back to Alexander.

"You're too far south and with none of your people."

"True. But how about you? You are too young to be out on your own. Where's your kin?"

"Down the loch on the south shore. Knipoch. Before those accursed English came, my cousin and me fished up and down the bay. But one of them fen-sucking devils cut him down, day before yesterday." He looked with loathing back toward the shore they'd left. "So I been watching them. Staying just ahead of 'em. Warning the crofters and the fishing folk when I know they're coming close."

Kenna was relieved when the fog rolled in, enfolding them, shielding them from men or beast that might be lurking on the shores. The wound in Alexander's side continued to bleed. She tore out a section of her shift and pressed the fabric against his wound. He pretended there was nothing amiss, continuing to talk to the boy.

"How many have you seen?"

"All told, more than twenty. That's as much as I can

count," Jock explained without apology. "But they move in packs. Five or six, usual. Don't know if there's more inland."

"That was a Scot helping them."

The boy spat over the side. "Aye, devil take him. Word is a filthy Lowlander called Donald Maxwell leads 'em. Has other renegades fighting for him. But he has English gold, they say. It's his people what's doing the burning and killing, blast 'im." He paused, glancing at Kenna. "And asking about a woman."

"What woman?" Kenna asked.

"They're offering English gold for the wife of Alexander Macpherson. A MacKay woman." Jock looked at her. "They're looking for you."

~

At the first bend of the road south of Oban, James found the MacDougalls waiting for them. Ten of them, all on horseback. Emily sat astride her horse in front. He'd been restless to leave, but he should have known that she wasn't finished with their argument.

The calm and compliant Emily MacDougall that he'd met at Alexander and Kenna's wedding six months ago and again yesterday was gone. She was still beautiful to look at, pleasant to speak to, and there was an aloofness about her that kept James safely at arm's length. Before, her spirit was subdued. Not the woman for him.

Now, a day later, James didn't know what to do with this hellfire. Actually, he knew exactly what to do.

He spoke directly to Kester, the leader of the men sent to escort the laird's daughter back.

"If I'm not mistaken, you're taking the wrong road."

"We're coming with you," Emily answered instead.

He addressed the warrior. "You have orders from the laird. I suggest you escort Lady Emily directly to Craignock Castle."

Emily nudged her mare forward and positioned herself between James and Kester. "You will speak directly to me when your conversation involves me."

James studied her. The clear voice, direct look, the confidence. If there were a low-hanging tree in sight, he would have thought she'd struck her head once or twice, for she was even bolder than the woman he'd spoken to earlier at the inn. And if he thought she was beautiful before, Emily MacDougall was magnificent now. The protective shell was shattered. The real woman now sat before him.

Fighting the urge to sweep her off her horse and drag her back to the inn, James looked off at the whitecaps checking the gray-green firth. The MacDougall men outnumbered them two to one. In any event, making love to her now might not be the most political of strategies.

He addressed Kester. "I'd like to have a private word with you."

The aging warrior glanced at his mistress first and agreed only after Emily nodded her consent.

James rode back around a small grove of scrub pines. Kester followed.

"I'll not play games here. My brother and his wife may be in danger. I need to get to them as fast as I can," the Highlander explained. "Graeme MacDougall and I agreed to the arrangements. You must take the laird's daughter back."

"Aye, m'lord. I agree with everything you say. But Lady Emily makes sense. She wants to travel the same road you're taking. It leads to Craignock and to the abbey. And this way, our swords will be at your service until you reach your brother."

"I don't need your swords. And I don't need the worry of a woman traveling with us."

"We can keep her from harm," Kester said. "And she's going to do it anyway, with or without your leave."

James fought back his anger. "Who do you answer to? Isn't it your responsibility to get her back to prepare for her wedding?"

"I need no reminders from you who it is I serve. I've known this lass here since she was a wee bairnie. In some ways I know her better than the laird himself does. And I know it'll serve no purpose in crossing her when she has her mind set on a thing."

"Even when she's wrong?"

"She never is. It's her nature to think things through. She's not one for foolhardy decisions. Unlike her cousin, Lady Kenna, she leans toward caution. If she says, 'We travel this path, Kester,' then I follow."

The man was a fool. He didn't see that this stubborn, troublemaking sprite was different from the docile lass he knew. James had no time to worry about any of this now. If Kester wanted to put Emily's life in danger by traveling into a region rumored to be crawling with English soldiers, it was his choice. As for himself, he and the Macpherson warriors would not wait.

"Have it your way. You must answer to the Mac-Dougall. I did my best to warn you."

The two rode back around the bend. The Macpherson men were the only ones waiting.

"Where is Lady Emily?" Kester asked.

"She took the men and rode ahead. She said we can catch up to them when you're done talking."

~

Sir Ralph Evers looked across the Tweed River at the massive stone structure with the clusters of cottages and shops huddled close to its walls.

This abbey had history. A Scottish king had died within sight of this place . . . and the coronation of an infant king had quickly followed within its walls. More important, this abbey was known far and wide to be the richest of any in Scotland.

Evers assessed his prize. The place was braced and ready for an assault, but it would do no good. They would take the abbey if he had to burn the place to the ground.

"I want every jewel and every pound of gold in their vaults," he said.

"We'll take possession of the abbey, m'lord, but these monks are a hard lot," his captain warned.

Maxwell agreed. "They'll never tell you where the vaults lie, where the gold is hidden."

"Take the abbey. Kill the abbot." Evers turned an icy gaze on his men. "Then bring me his body. He will tell me everything I want to know."

Chapter 9

What fire is in mine ears? Can this be true?

The north shore of the narrow loch rose quickly to rugged foothills covered with gorse and dotted with rock outcroppings and twisted trees. In protected places, dense groves of tall pine spread out, green and dangerous. Good places for lookouts to hide.

Kenna's gaze swept from the stony beach to the wooded hillside. Thick mists clung to the high grassy elevation beyond. A soft rain was falling—chilling her and adding weight to the dress still soaked from her time in the river.

"You can't be taking the road to Oban," Jock warned them. "To be sure, the English will be waiting for you."

Kenna and Jock helped Alexander out of the boat and through the shallow water to shore. She had questions for the boy about this Donald Maxwell but doubted he knew more than he'd told them already. She definitely didn't know the man. Never heard his name. She didn't understand why anyone—especially a renegade Scot—would be working with the English to find her. Unless it was ransom they wanted. But why not Emily, rather than her?

In all the years of running wild in the Highlands, she'd never thought even once about being kidnapped.

Jock was staring at Alexander's shirt. The wound was bleeding badly again. "And the hills are too high for climbing."

"The fishing huts are just through these trees?" Kenna asked.

"Aye. Tumbled down, mostly. Put up before Noah and his animals, they say. Some folk who fish here in season use them now and again."

She had to get Alexander under cover where she could see to his wound and do whatever she could to stop the bleeding.

"I can take you to my folk at Knipoch."

"Nay, lad. We'll be fine," Alexander managed to say. "From here, we'll follow the loch down to the sea. I'm thinking we're not a day's walk from Oban."

"Aye, that's about right."

Alexander reached into his sporran and held out some coins. Jock backed away.

"I didn't help you for gold. And I'd never give you over to no English pissling or Lowlander, neither. I'll not say a word to anyone, not even to my kin."

"We know. Take it, lad." He gave the coins to Kenna, who put them into the boy's hand. "Be on your way now."

Kenna pushed the boat off, and Jock rowed away into the fog. Trudging out of the water, she found Alexander sitting on a boulder. He looked pale, his face drawn. Blood was running through the cloth he held to his wound and dripped steadily from his fingers.

Panic arose in her, causing her heart to drum loudly in her ears. She'd never been squeamish at the sight of blood, but now she felt vaguely ill and wet and cold. She'd sewn up many wounds at the priory. She'd looked after many men. But none were this badly hurt. And none had been Alexander.

She glanced out into the fog. Perhaps it wasn't too late to call Jock back. They should have gone with him to Knipoch. But she understood Alexander's thinking. He didn't want to lead the devil to the door of helpless fisherfolk.

Now was the time to be strong. She'd use whatever shelter they could find, and she'd tend to his wounds. They were too exposed here. There was no assurance that those pursuing them didn't have a boat. They needed to get away from the beach.

How the feeling between them had changed, she thought. Whatever had kept them apart was behind them now. At this moment, all that they had was each other. Alexander saved her life fighting the English raiders. Kenna was his only help now.

"Don't forget your promise," she told him. "No dying on me today."

"If you start fretting and whispering sweet nothings in my ear, wife, I'll know I'm a dead man." He stretched his right hand for her to take. "Where's the she-devil I married?"

"Right here. Though I don't know why I shouldn't be running even now." Kenna helped him to his feet. "I'm staying to help you for only one reason."

"And what would that be?"

"I'll not have some weedy, plume-plucked Englishman killing you. I'm the only one who has the right to do that."

"There's my woman," he said, leaning on her heavily as they walked.

Kenna led him inside the protective line of trees. Three low mounds of earth and stone, with doors cut into the sides, sat in a circle. The cottages. Two of the roofs had caved in. Near the third, a number of drying racks for fish had been erected, but they too were in various stages of ruin. She looked and listened for any sign that other people might be around, but only the sound of seabirds and a small stream tumbling toward the loch disturbed the silence.

The best hut had a patch of skin fashioned as a door. Pulling it aside, Kenna peered in. Several piles of dry seaweed and straw used as bedding were visible. A fire pit contained charred wood, and the place was dry and reasonably clean. No one had been here for quite some time, but no animals were taking shelter in it.

Wincing, Alexander stooped and followed her in. He lowered himself onto a log by the doorway and leaned back against the stone wall.

"Now tell the truth." The short walk took too much out of him. His words were drawn out and he had to pause to catch his breath. "Are you truly a healer? Or are all those rumors coming from Glosters Priory . . . are they just tales to justify your stay there?"

"Just hush and save your strength."

"Oh, do you have plans for me?"

Kenna removed a slab of wood from the only window, allowing in air and light. She quickly searched the cottage for anything that might be left behind. Kicking at the bedding, she raised some dust but found a battered wooden bowl by a wall behind one of the piles of straw. Anything else of use had been taken. She hurried out to the stream to wash and fill the bowl with water.

By the time she returned, Alexander had pushed the tartan off his shoulder and was struggling to remove his shirt. She went to him, pushing his hands away. The cloth was plastered to the wound. She peeled the shirt gently from the skin and pulled it over his head.

The shirt slipped from Kenna's fingers to the floor. Tears burned the back of her throat. The wound in Alexander's side was a ragged stab. The gash was as wide as her hand, and it went deep. He'd lost so much blood. There was nothing she could do.

She sat back on her heels and stared at the wound. She didn't want to look into his face. She didn't want him reading her thoughts.

"Drink this." She held the bowl to his lips.

"So those tales were all lies," he teased. "You're no healer. You have no talent. They kept you there to tend the sheep and milk the goats."

"The nuns at the priory would have welcomed me even if I had no . . . no . . . no aptitude."

He labored to speak. "Or perhaps Magnus MacKay had to send . . . gold to the priory . . . to put up with you, since you obviously can't take care of a wee scratch like this one."

Alexander couldn't quite muster a smile. His tolerance for pain was impressive, but she saw his vitality draining out of him with every passing moment.

Kenna's gaze searched the hut again. There was no chance she could find a needle or thread. And she knew nothing of the damage done inside of him. But she had to save him, help him somehow.

His eyes started to drift shut. She was losing precious time. The light from the window fell on the straw across the hut.

"Help me. Walk with me to that bedding."

His eyes fluttered open. "Are we finally to make love, wife?"

"Nay." She pressed her lips against his fevered brow. "It'll be easier for me to desert you if you're away from the door."

With her help, he managed to get to his feet and took the faltering steps. "But I'll come after you. In this life or the next."

"Why? Still for the good of the clan?"

"Nay, lass. I'm getting used to you . . . as you get used to a wart."

He sprawled out on the bedding—his breathing as labored as if he'd climbed a mountain. She rolled him onto his back.

"Not a bad response for an ape. You're learning. But I've always been a good teacher."

No answer. Blood continued to run down his side, disappearing into the straw beneath him. Fetching the bowl, she tore off another piece of her shift and dipped it in the water, cleaning around the wound.

He closed his eyes. His breathing became shallower.

Kenna couldn't stop the tears. She knelt beside him, her hand on his heart.

"Don't do this. Do you hear me? You can't die on me."

His eyes remained closed. There was not even a hint that he could hear her. The beat of his heart was growing weaker.

Prayers, calls for guidance filled her thoughts. She searched her mind for distant memories of days when her mother was alive. Many times, Sine MacKay went away to heal a child or see to a sick cottager or a wounded warrior. Staying in the shadows, Kenna often followed her, watched her as she performed miracles. Sine always wore the stone fragment. She always held it as she prayed.

The skin near Kenna's heart was growing warmer. Thinking of her mother, she reached for the leather pouch hanging around her neck, feeling the piece of tablet within. This was as far as she'd gone in relying on the stone before. But it wasn't enough. Her husband was dying. There had to be more. Kenna opened the pouch and dropped the stone into her palm. Her fingers closed around it.

Power surged up her arm, but she held on to the relic. Heat released in bursts through her body, the intensity of it seizing control of every limb. Alexander disappeared and other images danced before her eyes.

Her mother's face. Others whom she didn't know. Women and men with black and brown faces. Old and young. They spoke to her all at once, but the words came at her in unknown tongues. They flowed around her like a melody to decipher. The music became louder. Kenna's struggle became desperate. She needed to understand what she had to do.

Kenna reached out and her fingers brushed against Alexander's skin. All at once, like the cessation of a summer storm, the voices and the words became orderly. She closed her eyes and a sense of calm filled her. Fear gathered in a diminishing space and then suddenly was gone. The music of the words became clear, understandable. She knew what to do.

The stone slipped from her fingers onto her lap, and Kenna laid both hands on Alexander's chest. The skin was cold, his heartbeat faint.

She flattened one palm on the skin below the bleeding wound at his side. Slowly, she moved her hands around the gash, circling it. Two shafts of light, one coursing up from her feet and another down from the top of her head, combined into one. It swirled around her heart and flowed out through her arms and hands. Her fingers vibrated on his skin, conducting the force from her body into his.

As the power flowed, she saw in her mind's eye where

the sword had cut through and ripped the flesh within. Kenna felt where the pain was sharpest and the damage worst. She followed the path of the blade through the sinew and muscle. She saw things in her mind that were beyond reason.

With a feathery touch, she placed her hand over the wound. She closed her eyes and willed her mind and heart to pass on the restoring light.

The voices became one: *Heal this man. Heal this man.*

Her hand warmed, then it iced, and then it grew warm again. She didn't know how long she sat still, allowing the power she'd unleashed to run through both of them, to heal him.

The voices became encouraging whispers.

Finally, when Kenna opened her eyes, the bleeding had stopped.

The wound was closed.

This was no traditional treatment, nothing she'd been taught by the nuns. Everything she'd known before changed at this moment. No longer would she be limited by the experiences of those healers around her. And whatever this power was—be it magic, dark arts, or witchcraft—Kenna welcomed it. It was a gift from her mother. And it was saving the life of her husband.

She pressed her palm against Alexander's heart. The beat was stronger, his breathing regular.

The sword wound wasn't the only injury to his body. Kenna's fingers traveled over his chest, up his shoulders, down his left arm. She found exactly where each blow had fallen. Using the same touch, circling the injury, feeling the rush of light through her, focusing the heat and cold and heat, she used the power in her.

She unclasped his brooch and belt, removed the sword, and laid it at his side. She pulled off his boots. His kilt, still wrapped around his waist, was wet from the river and soaked with blood. Leaving the tartan draped across his midsection, she continued to search for points of pain. Her hand traveled down one leg and up the other, past the worst wound and to his chest and down the arms and to the fingertips.

Even as she searched, she could hardly ignore the powerfully defined muscles, the skin so soft that she wanted to press her lips to it. His chest was broad and magnificent, and a slant of soft hair that thinned as it moved down to his navel disappeared beneath the fold of the kilt. His legs were long and muscled.

Kenna couldn't stop touching him, memorizing every dip and valley, every scar. The fluttering deep in her belly made her pull back her hands. She sat back on her heels, studying the body of her husband, realizing that this was no longer a journey of healing but one of passion.

She slipped the tablet back into the pouch.

"Kenna."

She jumped. His eyes were open. He was watching her. Her face burned with embarrassment. She didn't know how long he'd been awake.

"The bleeding . . . the wound at your side . . . it's better."

"Pain," he whispered.

"Where? Tell me."

"Come closer."

He hadn't moved. She inched closer. "You need to rest. Your body needs time to recover."

"It's too much. I'm suffering."

"Where?" she asked, her knees brushed against his bare skin. He closed his eyes, his fingers moving weakly across the bedding. Kenna took his hand. "Show me."

Alexander took her hand and brought it ever so slowly to his chest. She flattened her palm, his hand covering hers. He guided her hand down to his stomach, moving it lower.

By the time Kenna realized his intention, it was too late. Her hand was under the kilt. His arousal was silky and hard. She jerked her hand away.

"You are the devil, Alexander Macpherson."

His eyes were closed, but a smile tugged at his lips.

"That's where you need to be healing me next."

Chapter 10

May I be so converted and see with these eyes?
I cannot tell; I think not: I will not be sworn,
but Love may transform me to an oyster;
but I'll take my oath on it,
till he have made an oyster of me.

Emily was no hunter or tracker, but she knew many men had come through the place they'd camped. When they arrived at the riverside clearing at dusk, she felt the claws of panic scratching at her normally calm façade.

The rawhide that bound Kenna was still attached to the tree. Scraps of the food she and James left for the two were scattered on the ground by the cold ashes of the fire. Everything else was gone. For the first time the full danger Kenna might be in hit her hard.

The Macpherson and MacDougall warriors spread out into the woods and along the river, searching.

The harmless hoax had turned sour. But angry as Emily

was with James before for keeping her ignorant of the affairs, she couldn't be angry with him now. She could see he felt a hundred times worse. His plan had put them all in this predicament. She knew the last thing he wanted was to put his brother and Kenna in danger. Emily saw him stride out of the trees and speak with Kester for a moment before heading toward the river. He was all concentration and didn't even seem to notice her as he brushed past.

She stayed out of the men's way as they used what daylight remained to check footprints and whatever else might help them decide what happened to Alexander and Kenna.

There were no bodies, dead or wounded, and no blood that she could see. Emily told herself that had to be good news. Her hope was confirmed sometime later when Kester joined her.

"The raiding party, if that's who came through here, went down both sides. But there's no sign of any woman's footprint below this point. No one went upriver," the MacDougall leader told her. "They went in the river."

"Kenna is a good swimmer, but the current is strong. Do you think they got away unharmed?"

"That's my hope. James says Alexander could swim from here to Oban, if need be. But as you say, m'lady, the current is strong. Still, I don't see anyone else jumping in after them."

Emily watched as James Macpherson came back into

the circle of his men. He was impressive even in times of distress. On the way here, she'd ridden recklessly to keep up after he and Kester caught up to them and James galloped ahead. Chasing after him had been exhilarating. Still, she felt a twinge of guilt, knowing the excitement wasn't about the ride but the rider she was pursuing.

"And you knew about all of this, too, about Kenna and Alexander. About trying to trick them to get back together."

Kester looked away. "Aye. That I did."

The old warrior was as close to her father as any brother. He was also a man that Emily could always talk openly with. She could seek his opinion on things she could never say to her father. From childhood, she'd known she could trust him to keep her secrets. She wasn't about to be angry with him now.

Snippets of discussion reached them from the Macpherson men. They'd follow the river to the loch west of here that led to the sea. They'd try to catch up to the raiding party or Alexander and Kenna. James told one of the MacDougalls that she needed to go back to Craignock Castle. She heard the word *wedding* mentioned several times.

Her cousin's objections about Sir Quentin came back to her.

"You were there when they negotiated my marriage," she said to Kester.

"Aye."

"Why him?"

"You know why, lass. The MacDougall believes it's a good match. You're an only child. Many of the elders of our clan have been after your father to marry again, to produce a son. But he's not interested." Kester paused. "The world's getting smaller all the time. As you can see, the English feel free to roam about here, taking what they please. Raiders from the sea are a threat like never before. Your father thinks the safety of our people lies with you and your future husband."

Two summers ago, Emily's mother died. While she was sick, Emily had heard many a heartfelt lecture on duty and responsibility.

"But why *him*?" she repeated. "Why Sir Quentin? Why not . . . why not someone I know, at least?" And someone with a dozen more qualities that Sir Quentin seemed to be lacking.

"You've never shown any interest or made it known that you wanted to choose. I, for one, never saw you show any fondness for any particular lad. So your father took the first good offer."

"I had a choice?" she asked, stunned. "I had a choice in whom I was to wed?"

"Of course. You had a choice of 'aye' or 'nay.' You're Graeme MacDougall's only child, lass."

Emily's gaze drifted to James Macpherson. He was issuing orders to his men. "Do I still have a choice? Is it too
late?"

"Your father wants you safe. He wants the clan safe.
He may not be thrilled for you to speak up now. But so
long as you keep those things in mind—if you're asking
me—it's never too late."

~

He was dreaming. Alexander knew it, but he still could
not shake off the blurred chaos of events disturbing his
sleep. The force of the river. The panic at losing sight of
Kenna in the wild rush of the current. The fight with
the soldiers. The short sword jabbing into him. The claw-
ing dread at the thought that the Lowlander might take
Kenna away. Jock wielding the oars that weighed nearly
as much as the lad himself. The fog rolling in around the
boat as they moved across the loch's black waters. The
look of fear in his wife's face.

Alexander blinked back the mist from his mind and
opened his eyes. A thin band of moonlight streaked in
through the window and lit the stone wall of the cottage.
He remembered where he was. He took a deep breath
and tested his shoulder. It moved. He fisted his hands and
held them up before his eyes. They were whole. He re-

membered the wound in his side. It wouldn't stop bleeding. He touched it. There was no fresh blood, and the hole made by the raider's sword was closed. It felt more like an injury weeks old. He shifted his weight. Soreness, but more of a nuisance than anything. Nothing like the sensation of a hot poker boring into his side.

He wondered how long he'd been unconscious.

The last clear memory he had was Kenna fussing over him as he tried not to pass out. Everything after that was a jumble, a hazy hodgepodge of visions from his past, of touches both healing and sensual. There were moments when he didn't know if he was dead or alive.

The life Alexander led up to now was full and adventurous. He could think of very few moments that he would do over. His wedding night was one. And he regretted not going after Kenna the next day. Or the day after. He should never have allowed so much time to go by with the two of them apart. They'd been strangers at the kirk steps, but they were well suited for each other. She was fearless and independent. She was unlike any woman he'd ever met.

He recalled something else. Pain. He'd been here in this same hut and he'd felt the worst pain. He was dying. And wanting Kenna had been his final wish.

Alexander turned his head. Kenna was sleeping an arm's length away. She hadn't deserted him.

His sword lay between them, close enough for either to reach. He wondered for a moment whether it was there for defense against the danger lurking outside or a message to him.

He was alive, and he wasn't about to be deterred.

He rolled toward her, admiring how beautiful she looked in spite of everything she'd been through. She was fast asleep, one hand tucked beneath her chin. Her lips were parted, her breathing uneven. She was fighting demons in her dreams, as well. The laces of her dress had loosened, and the curve of one breast showed above the linen shirt she was wearing beneath it. He immediately went hard. It was good to know everything was in working order.

He reached for the sword to move it. Her eyes flew open. She grasped the weapon just as he did.

"What are you doing?" she asked breathlessly.

"Good morning, wife," he replied instead. "Or is it night? It's still dark, it seems. How long have we been here?"

She pushed up onto one elbow. A blanket of curls swept over one shoulder. The neckline of the dress pulled further apart, giving him a better view of the tops of her breasts. He wanted to taste them. She seemed to be struggling to wake up.

"May I?" he asked, moving the sword behind him.

She slowly sat up and got onto her knees. The dress

slipped off one shoulder. He was relieved he still had his kilt covering him. He didn't want to frighten her.

"How are you feeling?" she asked, peering at his stab wound.

"Better than you know."

Kenna didn't appear to trust his words. She pushed his shoulder, rolling him onto his back. As she leaned over to inspect his side, her hair trailed across his stomach, caressing him with its silky softness. Her touch was as arousing as any dream.

Alexander took a deep breath. Control, he told himself.

"How long have we been here?"

"Since yesterday. It hasn't been a full day." She sat back on her heels again. "I want to wash the wound. I'll be right back."

Alexander couldn't tear his gaze from her as she picked up a bowl and went out into the darkness.

"Wait," he called out, but she was gone.

He struggled to get up. He had to go after her. Danger could be right outside the door. He felt weak. By the time he managed to sit up on the bedding, she was back.

"You shouldn't go out unprotected," he snapped. At least she wasn't limping, he noticed. "Where's that dirk you're always waving about?"

"Right here, to use against you when I need it." She

crouched down beside him, holding the bowl to his lips. "Drink this. We have no food, but this should quench your thirst."

She was the only thing that could quench what he was feeling. As he drank from the bowl, he felt her sleeve. "This is wet. Why are you still wearing it?"

One eyebrow went up as she took the bowl away. Alexander watched with interest as she reached under her skirt and tore another strip from her shift, but not before he had a good view of the cream-colored skin of her legs. He imagined them wrapped around him.

"Let me wash your wounds."

"And I'll help you out of this wet dress."

"You must be dreaming." Her voice had suddenly grown husky.

"I *was* dreaming, and you were quite happy in my dreams. Sitting naked on my lap, riding me while I suckled your breasts. You couldn't get enough of me."

Even in the dim light he could see the blush that crept into her cheeks.

"This is no way to talk to me, you saucy ape."

"I think you like me the way I am." He reached up and ran his finger along the silky softness of her neck. She didn't pull back from his touch. He slipped an arm around her and brought her mouth to his. She immediately opened up to his kiss, and he felt his loins tighten.

Too soon she drew back, breaking off the kiss. She dipped the cloth into the water again and gently dabbed at his side.

"I want my wedding night, Kenna."

"You're not going to get it. We're going our separate ways once we reach Oban."

Leaning back, Alexander smiled. "Devil take me if we do."

He ran his fingers like a comb through her hair.

"You're distracting me," she said, inching closer without moving her gaze from the wound.

Alexander knew women. And right now he knew Kenna. He untied the top lace. He heard the breath catch in her throat.

"Let me finish," she whispered.

"You just keep on with what you're doing." He pulled the next pair of laces free, and the next.

She shifted her weight from one knee to the other. He saw her hand tremble as she dipped the cloth into the bowl again before placing it against his skin.

"You forget I have a cut on my shoulder."

She moved closer to check, and Alexander caught her by the waist, drawing her near. Their gazes locked in a moment of challenge.

"You lied to me."

"And I will lie again." Alexander spread the neckline

open until the tops of her breasts were exposed. She shivered as he trailed his fingers along her throat and chest, slipping his hand inside the fabric. He cupped one of her breasts, lifting it and stroking the hardening nipple with his thumb.

A soft gasp escaped her. Her eyes were wide and uncertain as she stared at him. The wet cloth slipped out of her hand.

"I'm not done cleaning the wound."

"I know," he whispered back, kissing her neck. "I'm not done with you, either."

He pressed his lips to the top of each breast. He pushed the clothes down and suckled her nipple.

She cried out his name, and her fingers gripped his hair.

Alexander's hand moved up her leg and beneath the dress. Her skin was like silk, her legs strong and smooth. His fingers reached the juncture of her legs, and she gasped again. She was moist, ready for him.

"Wait," she whispered.

He stopped, hearing the same noise. He reached for his sword.

Someone was coming.

~

Twelve wagons, laden with boxes of abbey treasure, sat in a line on the river road, while sparks and glowing embers rose from the fiery structure, lighting up the night sky.

"But Sir Ralph," the duke of Hertford's messenger stressed, following Evers and Maxwell down to the river's edge. "His Grace sent me specifically to tell you that anything taken from the abbey was to be sent to him for shipment to His Majesty."

Maxwell watched Evers crouch by the slow-moving water, peeling his gloves off and washing blood and soot from his face. The monks had put up a good fight, but they didn't have a chance once the invaders smelled blood.

When it was over, Maxwell had stood in the shadows, the hackles rising on his neck while Evers spoke to the empty air above the body of the dead abbot. Then he'd followed the Englishmen directly to a crypt in a chapel where he opened a secret passage into the abbey vaults.

So now it all belonged to Evers. All of it.

"It's a dangerous job you have," Sir Ralph said, standing and facing the messenger. "Riding through the countryside of our Scots enemy. Many messages must go astray and the messengers lost to our foes."

Evers stepped back as Maxwell drove his knife through the man's throat and upward into his skull, lifting him until the messenger was at eye level with him. Even in the dark, he could see the life disappear from the man's young face, and he let the body drop into the murky water. The chain shirt pulled the body under, and only a few bubbles remained. Soon those were gone, as well.

Sir Ralph nodded his approval. "Henry and Hertford be damned, Maxwell. I'll send word we found no treasure here."

Chapter 11

Time goes on crutches till Love have all his
rites.

Kenna stood in the shadows next to the skin flap, dagger
drawn, holding her breath. Waiting. Alexander pushed
himself to one knee by the straw pallet and wrapped his
hand around the hilt of the sword. Moonlight poured
over him from the small window, making him the immediate target of whoever came through the door.

She'd made no fire. They'd done nothing that might
bring anyone to this hut in the middle of the night.
Kenna tried to remember what Jock told them about the
marauders. Five or six or more in each raiding party. Too
many for the two of them to handle.

Footsteps. Right outside the door.

Her heart drummed. Cold sweat prickled along her
spine. She and Alexander exchanged a look. At the very
least, they'd both die fighting.

The flap pulled back. A head appeared. Kenna stopped herself at the last moment from jabbing the dagger into the intruder's neck. It was Jock.

She grabbed the back of his shirt and tossed him inside. He rolled onto the dirt floor.

"I'm alone," he chirped. "No one else."

She peered into the darkness, listening for any other noise. She was too tense to take the boy at his word. She let the skin flap fall back in place.

"Coming back was dangerous." Her tone was sharp. "I could have killed you. What are you doing here?" She cringed, thinking how easily she could have hurt the boy.

He stood up and pulled a satchel of rough woven sacking off his shoulder, giving it to Alexander. "I brought you food."

"Someone could have followed you," Alexander told him.

Her heart still hammering in her chest, Kenna looked out the tiny window. The moon was bright, but she saw no movement except for the soft breeze through the branches of the pines.

"No one followed me," Jock grumbled. His gaze went from one to the other, searching for an ally.

The Highlander wasn't satisfied. "Anyone could have seen the boat from the shore. They could be out there now."

"Nay, I landed a ways down the loch and pushed the boat out into the tide. No one will know where I came ashore. I'm not helping them to find you. But they're coming."

"Where are they? How many?" Alexander asked, taking a deep breath and standing.

"Their groups are getting bigger. They're combing the loch on both shores, north and south."

Alexander pulled his shirt on and arranged his kilt. Kenna had washed much of the blood out of his clothes after he fell sleep.

"They could be here any time." The boy's gaze flitted from the Highlander's face to the wound in his side.

Kenna straightened her clothing. She tucked the dagger into her belt and went to her husband to help him strap on his sword.

"You should be with your kin," she said. "Not here. How will you get back to them with your boat gone?"

"None's left." Jock's voice lost its tough edge.

They turned to the boy.

"What do you mean?" Alexander asked.

"As I rowed past the point below here, I saw it. The village was already burning," he said softly. "The flames was shooting high in the sky. I didn't know what to do, so I beached and hid in the trees. When the bastards moved on, I come out, but I couldn't find my sister and her bairnie nor none of the cousins. One of the old folks hid himself under a log in the glen and come out too while I was there. He said the others took to the boats and others to the hills, aiming to work their way north, he figured. He was too old to run, he said. Them devils killed the ones that stayed."

"Were they Scots or English?"

Jock spat on the floor. "Mostly Scots. Maxwell men."

"Who is this Maxwell?" Kenna asked.

"He's the youngest son of a laird down by Loch Lomond," Alexander answered. "Fought in France. Switched sides a few times, they say, fighting for whoever paid the most gold. Cast off by his family. Bad reputation as long as I can remember."

She wanted to ask why Maxwell would be after her, but with the lad here, she decided to hold her questions.

"You should go after your family. You won't be safe traveling with us," Alexander said to the boy.

"I'm going north, same as you. And with those devils about, you canna go along the loch shore. You've got to go over to the hills to Oban. I know the way." He touched the hilt of the dagger at his belt. "And with me, you'll have an extra hand for protection."

Normally, his size would have made Kenna laugh. He was no bigger than her brothers, but she knew what the boy was capable of. Alexander was standing up straight, looking strong, but she guessed he was still hurting.

"You should eat something before we go." She divvied up the food. Jock shook his head at the offer.

"You're still alive," he said finally to the Highlander. "Didn't think you would be."

"So now we have the truth. You came back to woo my wife."

The boy cast a wary eye at Kenna. "You healed him?"

Kenna heard the hint of accusation in the boy's question. She was still trying to fathom what had happened. One moment, she'd thought her husband was going to die. The next, she was able to close the wound and stop the bleeding. Her mother's gift had to be responsible for Alexander's recovery. But how? Kenna could come up with no logical answer.

She thought back to her childhood. To her mother. Sine was respected as the laird's wife. She was valued as a healer like any physician. There'd been no rumors of sorcery. If the stone was the source of a healing power, Sine MacKay had shown no clue of it.

Kenna needed time to think. She had to remember what exactly had happened yesterday. Perhaps Alexander's injury wasn't as bad as she'd thought.

Ignoring the boy's question, she gathered up the blood-soaked rags and kicked the straw bed. It was best if no one guessed they'd spent some hours at this hut.

"How did you do it?" Jock persisted.

"My husband is a warrior. He has scars from many wounds." She looked around the cottage.

"Did you sew it closed?" the lad asked. "It's not bleeding no more."

She saw Alexander reach under the shirt and touch the wound, but he said nothing.

"Finish eating. We need to go," Kenna ordered. "We haven't much time before dawn."

~

Emily. One moment stubborn and fiery, the next docile and agreeable. She knew how to get what she was after, but James saw that she was careful of not pushing him too far. The two sides of her were contradictory. And yet, the mix of the two was so alluring. Too alluring.

She had to go, he told himself. She was about to be married. He didn't need the complication of a hardening cock every time he looked at her. He needed to distance himself from her, but he also needed to consider her safety. He could not send her directly to Craignock with Kester. The way south could be dangerous, what with the night and the marauders lurking about.

That's what he kept telling himself.

So she stayed with them as they moved at a snail's pace

along both sides of the river, searching for some sign of Alexander and Kenna. She kept away from him, but not so far away that James could forget for a moment her maddening presence.

At the first light of the day, they found bodies by the river and in a nearby clearing. James went from one bloody corpse to the next, relieved not to find his brother among the dead. He directed his men to spread and search the surrounding glen. If any of the raiding party remained in the woods—if Alexander or Kenna lay wounded somewhere—he didn't want to miss them.

Kester confirmed James's conclusion a short time later. "They were here. The two of them. Tracks of a bare-foot woman and a man, in the mud by the river. One raider lying dead where he must have confronted them on the bank. Alexander cut him down before the fight moved here into the clearing. Had his hands full, it appears."

James looked around at the dead. "They'd need more than this to kill my brother."

"Aye. But where are they now?"

"I dinna think they took Alexander prisoner," one of the Macpherson men said. He pointed west. "The trees give way to salt marsh not far from here. There's a loch beyond, but there's no cover for them and no sign they went that way."

"They must have continued following the river," James told them. "They'll be heading to Oban, where Alexander believes the exchange for the ship was to take place."

"Aye," Kester agreed.

James noticed Emily standing at the edge of the circle. He exchanged a look with Kester.

It was time.

"Can I talk to you alone for a moment?" she asked.

James nodded and followed her until they were out of earshot of the others.

Three days on horseback, one night sleeping on the hard ground, and the next night searching along this river. Her clothes were rumpled and dirty. Her blond hair was a jumbled mass of windblown curls. Her blue eyes had dark circles under them. But she still looked beautiful. Damn it.

She had to go now.

"Kester will accompany me back to Craignock Castle. You can keep the rest of the MacDougall men."

"That won't be necessary."

"You're not only searching for your brother. My cousin is missing, too."

"She is my sister by marriage," he said, feeling a prickle of annoyance. "I have no intention of fishing Alexander out of this river and letting Kenna drown."

"I didn't think you would. I meant nothing of the kind.

I'm trying to help. Nothing more."

"We can find them without MacDougall help."

"You're being pigheaded."

"No more pigheaded than you forcing yourself on us at the most inconvenient time."

"I didn't force anything on you. We were traveling in the same direction."

"You should be at Craignock Castle right now."

"I've been no trouble. I didn't complain once."

"You slowed us down."

"I kept up with you. You're just being difficult. And I'm the one who should be angry about the lies you told me."

He stared at her flushed face, the stubborn tilt of her chin, the full lips that begged to be kissed. "Enough. I have no time for this. You can complain to your father. Take your men and go. Safe journey."

He was about to walk away, but she reached for his arm. A hesitant touch.

"Wait. I don't want us to part ways like this."

The other Emily was back. The soft-spoken beauty. James told himself to walk away before she tangled him completely in her net, but his arm burned beneath her touch.

"You have to go back to Craignock Castle," he managed to mutter.

Her hand dropped. "I'll go. Kester and his men will deliver me safely back to my father."

Her gaze moved over his face, his neck, focused on his lips for an extra heartbeat before meeting his. Then she took two faltering steps back.

"I am eager for my marriage." It was a lie. It came through to him clear as a bell. "And I'm keen to finally meet Sir Quentin. I've heard that he's kind and generous. Absolutely the man of my dreams."

James felt the frustration rising within him. She took another step back.

"He needs an heir. So the next time you and I meet, if that time ever comes, I'll be holding his bairn at my breast."

James gripped the hilt of the sword. Say nothing, he told himself.

"Farewell, James," she whispered before running across the clearing to where Kester waited with her mount.

Chapter 12

Just to the gate of hell I will go;
and there will the devil meet me,
like an old cuckold, with horns on his head.

Before they'd reached the top of the first hill above the loch, the ache in Alexander's side had given over to a sharp, piercing pain. With every awkward step, a molten blade sliced through his belly, taking his breath away. Leaning on a stout stick he'd picked up, he did his best to avoid Kenna's looks of concern. He would not slow them down.

They continued to climb steadily through the hills and valleys, traversing open meadows as quickly as they could and staying close to the heavy pine forests when possible. Past midday, a steady rain began to fall. The whirling mists that hung about were a godsend. It would be difficult for anyone to see them. At the same time, he couldn't see what lay ahead.

The hills were steep and the waist-high gorse heavy. Before they left, Kenna cut in two the sacking that Jock brought from his village, and tied the pieces to her feet. Alexander didn't think they could provide much protection from the sharp rocks and brambles.

As the day wore on, he found himself stopping more and more, leaning on his stick and breathing heavily. The yellow flowers and their fragrant scent reminded Alexander of the hills around Benmore Castle. The highlands around the Spey were covered with it. The gorse was just coming into bloom when he left. He brushed aside the thought that he might not see his home again.

The pain was growing fiercer with every step he took. Once, wading across a rushing stream, Alexander became dizzy, nearly losing his balance, but Kenna was beside him in an instant. Somehow, they kept moving.

Later—how much later he didn't know—as they climbed a slippery track, he stopped to catch his breath. Trying to focus on the hill ahead, he saw Jock scramble up through some boulders at the summit. Alexander looked back across the mist-enshrouded valley. There was no sign of Maxwell's men, but he knew they had to be coming. And he knew he was making it easier for the pursuers to overtake them. What was worse, it appeared that the rain was easing a little. The mist was dissipating.

"Do you need to rest?"

"Nay." He started up the incline and stumbled over a rock, wincing with pain. She took hold of his arm.

"We need to stop," she said.

"We can't," he replied. "They're following us. Traveling faster. With the rain stopping, they'll find us." And I don't know how much protection I can offer, he finished silently.

"Let me help you."

"Stop fretting over me."

"Fretting? It'll be a cold summer in hell before I fret over you. Now put your arm on my shoulder."

At the crest of the hill, the boy was waiting. Outcroppings of stone were visible as far as he could see in either direction along the ridge.

Alexander eased himself down onto a boulder and turned to Kenna.

"We part ways here," he told her. "You and Jock will go on without me. You can find your way to Oban by midday tomorrow if I'm not slowing you down."

"I'll do as I want." She took his hand in hers. "I'm not leaving you here."

"Kenna, I'm telling you to go. You'll find Macphersons in Oban—or those who know us. Send back whoever you find there. I'll be waiting."

"You've lost your senses. You might as well order these rocks to walk to Oban."

It was impossible to imagine her more disheveled or more beautiful. This was the way he'd always remember her. Temper bringing color to her cheeks. She was ready for battle. A knot tightened in his throat. His wife.

"These last days," he said, "in spite of anger, injury, or danger, you've stayed beside me. You've done your duty. But now you need to be reasonable. For both of our sakes."

She snorted.

"We can't fight them here if . . . *when* they catch up to us. You need to go and get help."

"We both know that I can't get back here quickly enough. We stay together."

"Listen to me, Kenna. Any fool can see that you care for me, but—"

"You're a fool if you think I care a straw about you."

Her eyes and her actions contradicted the words. And her response to him in the fishing hut before Jock arrived and interrupted them told him all he needed to know. They were together, and they had to learn how to maneuver the rough waters. But she needed to listen to him now.

"If you don't care, why are you still here?" He brushed a streak of dirt from her cheek.

"Why?" Kenna pushed his hand away. "Because you carry a sword. And you've shown that you're worth having around in a fight."

"You're not too bad yourself. Lethal, with that dagger of yours."

"A good thing to keep in mind. I may still use it on you."

"Too late. I know you won't make me bleed. Not after saving my life."

"You're a greater simpleton than I thought," she said. "And you must be too muddleheaded to remember. I warned you yesterday and I'm warning you today. I'll not have some Lowland dog wearing English fancy pants killing you. I'm the only one to do it."

"Do you think I could forget such sweet talk?" He smiled, respecting her hardiness. "It's time you followed your husband's orders."

"You must take me for the mother of fools."

"Not yet. But if that's what we're blessed with, so be it."

"Now you listen, Alexander Macpherson. I decided yesterday that I'm staying with you until we reach Oban, no matter what comes of it. So stop giving orders. You're not in charge here. I am."

"Is that so? Has the world turned upside down? And do you have a satchel with you to carry my balls in?"

"Don't be an ass."

"You're going to Oban."

"Aye, with you."

Kenna walked away and waved to the boy, who had

been keeping his distance.

Alexander wasn't done arguing with her. But he couldn't keep up the pretense of strength. He felt hollow, exhausted. His body was giving out. He had no open wounds now that he was aware of, but his gut felt like it had been ripped asunder and stuffed with hot, writhing eels. And each time he moved, it was getting worse. He realized that his mind was wandering. Perhaps he was finally dying.

He heard Kenna's voice, but he wasn't sure if any time had passed. She sounded distant. Or maybe she was inside his head. He couldn't tell the difference.

"Jock, do you know where we can get out of this weather?"

"No hut that I know of. Wait—there is a place. Over that way. But I don't think . . ." The boy's voice faltered as if he had misgivings about what he'd admitted.

"Tell us," Kenna ordered. "Where? How do we get there? How far?"

"A cave, of sorts. It's in the dark wood not far from here. But no one goes there."

"Even better. Take us to it."

"It's not a good place. Ghosts and fairy folk live there. It's where they bring stolen bairns and lost children and roast 'em over a pit. The cave has bones piled high as the moon. They say the witches gather there on . . ." He stopped.

"Take us there now, Jock," she ordered quietly.

Alexander twisted at the waist as a searing bolt tore through his belly. He wanted to stay here. He wanted them to go. He wanted Kenna safe and far away.

"Come and help me." Kenna's voice rang in his ear. "*Now.*"

He looked up into her eyes. She looped his arm over her shoulder. Jock was at his other side, trying to lift him off the rock.

"I know you're in pain. But you need to help us."

"Go to Oban," he ordered.

She touched his cheek and looked into his eyes. Her words were a whisper, intended only for him. "I need to help you heal. But we're too exposed here in the open. The fog can lift any moment. We will be seen from below. So if you're worried about me, if you care for me at all, stand up. Help us however you can."

Alexander cared for her . . . far more than he'd ever shown. Holding onto them both, he pushed to his feet. He didn't know where he summoned the strength. The hills around him were a distorted haze that wavered with every movement of his head. He forced himself to move his feet where Kenna and Jock guided him. As they went, she continued to whisper words of encouragement.

They descended from the crest a short distance and then followed the ridge until they entered the darkness of a forest. The scent of pine filled his head and the bed of needles beneath his feet was soft and inviting. How long they traveled, he had no idea, but suddenly the boy stopped dead.

"Come on," Kenna said.

"This is as far as I go. I'll not go closer."

"I can't hold him up on my own."

"I'm sorry. That's the place. There. At the edge of the clearing, where the ground drops off, you'll see the entrance."

Alexander focused. Just below them, huge slabs of rock stood in a circle. He'd seen other places like this. From the old religion. Through a break in the trees beyond it, the vista opened onto another rugged valley below.

"Then wait here and keep watch," Kenna ordered.

Jock shrugged and backed away. "There's danger here. Souls of the dead, fairies, ghouls."

"You need to be a man now," she told the boy. "Those curs following us are the real danger. Understand me?"

Alexander did all he could to help her, and somehow he and Kenna lurched across the circle. Suddenly, the misty rain gave way to the cold dampness of a cave. The smell of the grave invaded his senses. They pushed deeper into the half-darkness. Never in his life had he felt less prepared or less capable of dealing with whatever lay ahead.

"This is far enough away from the entry," she whispered.

She helped him sit, and Alexander leaned back against the damp rock wall. He wanted to close his eyes, but the thought occurred to him that he might never open them again.

"You got your way," he murmured. "You brought me here. Now go to Oban and send someone back."

"Hush." She knelt beside him and caressed his brow. She pulled his tartan off his shoulder and moved the shirt away from the wound. Her fingers touched his skin. Warmth instantly replaced pain. As she prodded the flesh below the wound, he felt a stirring in his loins.

"Would you tease me like this when I'm not ready for you? Go to Oban. I'll be waiting for you here when you come back with help. Ready and rested."

"Close your eyes. Let me do what I must."

He wanted to watch her. But his body was spent. He drifted off, vaguely aware of the feathery touch of her hand and how the pain dissolved wherever she stroked.

Hovering somewhere between reality and dreams, Alexander saw the two of them together in an open meadow. Kenna's hair was a cascade of curls on the green grass, her eyes shining with desire. He kissed her lips, and her arms encircled him, drawing him deeper into the embrace.

He wanted her. He wanted to make love to her. He touched her face and ran his hand down her neck and breast, along her stomach and legs until he reached the hem of her skirt. He slid it up.

"Is it time, lass?"

"It's time, Alexander."

"We've waited so long. Too long."

"Wake up, Alexander."

He blinked a few times, and the cool darkness of the cave returned, replacing the warm sun of the meadow. He turned his head in the direction of her voice. Kenna's face came into focus. She was crouching beside him.

"We need to go. I just went out to check on Jock. The boy's gone."

~

How does a king conquer a country? He raises an army.

And how does a king raise an army? thought Evers. He calls on his dukes and his earls, who call on their barons and knights, who drag their peasants from their plows and their scythes and their flocks and their herds. They put a lance or a bow or a sword in their hands and tell them, "Do your duty, for God and King Henry."

But how long will duty keep them at their killing task?

And how do I raise an army? I start with duty. I tell them,

"For God and country, and good Sir Ralph."

And how do I keep them when duty grows old and the harvest at home is ready to take in?

Gold.

The fields and the flocks will wait while I have gold to share. And share it I will, with Englishman and Scot, if they will fight for me.

Gold. I know now it is only a means to the end.

Aye, before I am finished, I will be king of Scotland.

Then perhaps greater still.

And in the meantime, we will enjoy this hunt a' force. We have good game in this woman who carries the healing stone. She is no doe, but a hart of ten, and the antlers are sharp. That is what makes the game worth playing: the risk of loss elevates the stakes . . . and the gain. And how is a kingdom won without the hunter's skill?

I will take that stone, as the chess player takes the queen. For then I am master of the game. I will have that piece. Even now, I drive her into the corner where she will fall.

I have heard the horn calls from my hunters in the west, and I know I have flushed out the hart. The chase was good, and the prey is now cornered. At bay. The hounds close in on all sides. There will be no escape.

My arrows will find their mark, and I will break the body of the slain hart. The choicest meat will go on the stick.

And the second stone will be mine.

Chapter 13

Done to death by slanderous tongues.

The trees thinned as they made their way out of a woody glen and climbed to the top of another rise. In the grassy meadow that spread out below, a half dozen deer raised their speckled heads and then moved off.

Kenna shielded her eyes and looked to the west. The sun, now a disk of burnt gold, rested on a purple hill. Above her two hawks wheeled in great arcs, gliding effortlessly across the clearing sky.

She wished one of them would dive and pluck her off this hill and carry her away.

Or better yet, carry off Alexander and his questions about how she healed him.

Alexander had regained the vigor he had prior to his injury. Dogging her every step, he now wouldn't shut up, constantly badgering her with questions. Kenna remained silent, hoping he'd give up. But the man was tenacious, to say the least.

What was worse, she couldn't ignore the feeling she had when she'd touched him back in the cave. Once she knew he no longer suffered, her curiosity took charge. The heat racing through her that had nothing to do with the stone, nothing to do with healing him. When she touched him, something thrilling vibrated deep in her belly, resonating in the very core of her womanhood.

She wanted him. It was as simple as that. Running her hands over his skin, feeling the ripples of muscle on his arms and chest, the lines that cut downward along his abdomen. As much as her brain wanted to keep him at arm's length, her body wanted him closer. Much closer.

"There must be something you can tell me to explain it. There must be rational explanation to whatever it was that you did to me."

She wished she *could* explain. Hovering over him in that cave, Kenna had hoped there was reason for the way her hands warmed. She yearned to know why her mind knew instinctively where he hurt. But she couldn't find a logical reason.

She no longer doubted the magic of the stone. And she was afraid.

Descending the hill, she could see a loch in the distance. It didn't appear to open out into the sea. It grew narrower and then disappeared into a forest glen. She directed her steps toward the upper end.

"If it's black magic, or white, tell me. I deserve to know if a coven of druids will be coming in the night to nail my heart to some oak tree. Where does the power come from?"

Kenna only wished she understood it herself. One thing she knew: the stone dangling between her breasts was a danger to her, and she was at a loss how to handle it. The relic was not only a gift, but also a curse. Women were tortured, hanged, and burned for the gift she now seemed to possess. She knew in her heart that she needed to use it for good, but how could she protect herself at the same time?

She had so many unanswered questions. Where did the stone come from? How did her mother come to have it? Why didn't she warn Kenna about it? Why had no one else used it since Sine's death? It was a fragment of something larger. But what?

And Alexander kept rattling off even more questions in her ear. But how could she answer him when she didn't know herself? And to whom could she go for answers? And besides, was it right to burden him with such an enormous secret as this, when it would accomplish nothing but put him in danger, too?

"Talk to me, Kenna."

She glanced up at the setting sun. "It will be dark soon.

We'll be sleeping in the open. Perhaps we should have stayed in the cave."

"Too late to go back there."

"Do you think Jock went back to his village?"

Alexander shook his head. "He's out here somewhere, looking for his kinfolk."

"I hope he finds them."

"Do you? The first thing he's going to tell them is that a witch is drinking Macpherson blood in a cave beneath the circle of stones."

"Jock is just a boy repeating old ghost stories that were told to him to keep him from wandering off in the dark," she said dismissively. "Who would believe him?"

"Probably the ignorant folk who told him the stories to begin with. The same folk who would stay far away from that place."

"There was nothing strange about the circle of stones or that cave." She plucked a yellow flower from a shrub as she walked. "We might catch up to him."

"We might," he said with a smile. "Unless you turned him into a toad and have him snug in your pocket."

"That's not funny." Kenna turned to him, tired of the not-so-subtle hints and accusations. "But since you're so afraid of me, perhaps it would be better if we parted ways right now. I can go east and you can go west."

"Afraid?" he scoffed. "I fear nothing. And I'm certainly

not afraid of you. I asked a reasonable question."

"Oh, was there a reasonable question hidden among the hundreds you've been spouting for the past few hours? I don't know how I missed it. Oh, I know: I wasn't listening."

"I have a right to know how my wife can heal without stitches or bandages or herbs."

"So you have a 'right' to know?"

"Aye, and you've had plenty of chances to answer. But why do you choose not to?"

"Because *I* don't understand what happened to you. I don't know how I healed you." She spoke the truth. To tell him the stone did it was no answer.

Her outburst stopped him. But only for a moment.

"I bled buckets yesterday. And you managed to stop the bleeding. And today, I felt as if someone were gutting me from the inside out. And you made the pain disappear." He put a hand on her shoulder, turning her around to face him. "How?"

Kenna shook her head. She couldn't. Not yet. Not until she figured out what it was that she possessed. They were married. But they weren't. He'd requested annulment. It wasn't fair to burden him into her secret.

"Your wound was not as bad as you think it was."

He snorted.

"It just took some proper care."

"And what is proper care?" he asked, sarcasm dripping from his words.

She shrugged. "The care that the nuns taught me at the priory. Wash the wound. Keep it clean. Try to close it to lessen the bleeding. Make the patient rest. You're strong and healthy, Alexander. It was your own doing, not mine."

"You didn't stitch up my side."

"I had no needle or thread. If I did, I would have sewn your mouth shut while I was at it."

"Then how did you close the wound? You stopped the bleeding."

"I pressed on it. Your body did the rest."

"And nothing else? No spells? No magic potions?"

"If I had a potion, I would have turned *you* into a toad. And I wouldn't keep you in my pocket."

She started walking. Kenna was troubled by more than withholding something from him that she herself didn't understand. She'd thought Alexander was healed last night at the fishing hut. But today, he'd been in agony. She didn't know what she was capable of or if she was using the stone correctly. Her memories of her mother visiting the sick failed to offer anything useful. Perhaps someone in her clan might know more. Someone close to her mother.

Kenna had to go home. Her search for answers had to start there. When she knew, she'd tell him.

"You shouldn't have mended me if you planned to leave me behind."

Alexander was beside her, keeping pace. After the short time in the cave, he was a different man. Looking at him now, one would never guess what he'd gone through.

"No more questions about how or why or what," she ordered.

"I'll ask whatever I want."

"Earlier, you told me to leave and go on to Oban without you. I accept your order."

"Too late. That was this afternoon."

She walked faster, but his legs were longer.

She was stuck with him for now and although she wouldn't admit it, she was glad. It would soon be dark, and Kenna didn't know these hills. It would be good to have him with her. She could *act* tough and fearless, but she wasn't foolish.

She searched for a distraction that might steer Alexander's attention away from her gift.

"Where do you think James is now?"

"On the way back from Oban, searching for us."

"What has he done with my cousin?"

"I know what he'd *like* to do with Emily." He sent her a sideways glance. "But I'm certain he handed her over to the MacDougall in exchange for our ship. It's worth more than any woman."

163

"Why do you try to be such a pig, when you don't have to?"

He had the audacity to flash a smile. "I have no idea what you're talking about."

"You just said that to rile me."

"Did I? Are you upset?"

Kenna held her breath for a couple of moments before letting it out. She wouldn't give him the satisfaction. "Your brother Colin."

"What about Colin?"

"He's my favorite of all of you."

"He's the devil's spawn," he sniffed. "He's a trouble-maker to his very core. He's the blasted fool who caused the trouble on our wedding night! By 'sblood, how could he possibly be your favorite?"

"He and his wife, Tess. I like both of them very much. He told me how they met on a deserted island. Tess fished him out of the sea after you threw him overboard off one of your precious ships. He said you were trying to drown him because he's so much more handsome."

"He said that now, did he?"

She nodded. In truth, Kenna had been fascinated by Tess's tale of growing up without knowing who her parents were. Colin had been responsible for bringing her back from the Isle of May in the Firth of Forth and helping her claim her Lindsay legacy. The romance of their tale was enthralling.

"You realize that the stories surrounding the Macphersons can be a bit daunting."

"Daunting?" he spat. "You find us daunting? You're joking. No person walking the earth can intimidate you."

She realized that Alexander only saw her as she wanted to be seen. Tough. No-nonsense. A woman with an independent spirit.

"Your mother is a bit daunting."

"My mother?" He looked at her as if she'd sprouted horns. "Fiona Drummond Macpherson? A woman you only met at our wedding?"

Kenna had been in Fiona's company barely long enough for a dozen formal sentences to pass between them. And that was when she was being welcomed into the Macpherson family. Fiona had done all the talking. Kenna had stared at her feet in guilt and nodded, knowing that she'd be running off that same night.

"Your mother's manners are perfect. She's educated. She dresses and looks and speaks like a kindly queen. She's respected, and not only in the Highlands. People know of her across Scotland. She's a legend."

"Aye, but she's also *my* mother. That should speak volumes on how flawed the woman is."

Kenna waved him off like a noisy fly. "That woman is the daughter of King James."

"And you find her daunting... an ancient, bastard daughter of a dead king?"

"Ancient?" she sputtered.

"Aye, the woman must be ninety years old."

Kenna punched him in the shoulder. "Your mother is not yet fifty, and she has the beauty of a lass!"

"By 'sblood, she's an ugly old crone. Are you certain you met the right woman during our wedding celebration?"

"Why do you do this? You must think your mission in life is to rile me."

She saw the raised brow, the crooked smile that dimpled one cheek. She looked into his eyes and felt a kick deep in her belly. She was far from immune to his charms.

Kenna looked away. The valley below now lay in deep shadow. Night was claiming the land.

"How could I ever live up to your family's expectations when you constantly strive to upset me?"

"Expectations? There are no expectations when it comes to Macpherson wives."

"Aye, there is. I have none of the accomplishments that are required to be your wife," she confessed. "You're the next laird. You wife will be the laird's right hand. For years I've heard stories about your mother and her intelligence and her virtue. Then I see her and find that all of them are absolutely true. She's everything that I'm not. I could never—"

Alexander took hold of her hand and flattened it against his chest, stopping her. "Kenna, my mother was spirited away to Isle of Skye to become a nun the night her own mother was murdered. Tess was a wild child before Colin met her. My uncle Ambrose's wife, Elizabeth, dressed as a man and painted with Michelangelo in Italy for a decade before she married him. There is nothing traditional in the accomplishments of the Macpherson women."

Kenna lost her voice, feeling choked up. She'd revealed too much, said more than she'd intended to. Her father's words never left her. Why did she do that? Why allow Alexander to see her as vulnerable? She tore her hand free and walked down the hill.

He caught up to her. "Wait. Now I understand. You ran away on our wedding day because you thought you wouldn't measure up in some way?"

Kenna shook her head, walking faster. It was difficult to explain the education she'd lacked, the motherly advice that she'd never had. It was impossible to talk about her childhood and not break down. She would never forget how little her own family thought of her value.

"Talk to me, woman. How can you expect me to trust you when you don't trust me?"

"I . . ." Kenna faltered.

Suddenly, a crowd of people carrying torches appeared in the lower end of the meadow. Kenna stopped as Alexander moved in front of her, his hand on the sheathed sword.

"Who are these people?" she asked in a whisper. "Friend or enemy?"

"Your guess is as good as mine."

The mob of men and women climbed toward them, dirty sunburned faces flashing in the torchlight. Many were armed with stout sticks. Kenna's mind raced with Alexander's warning. She imagined murmurs becoming chants. Words like *witch* and *sorcery* and *old religion* danced in her head. She moved closer to Alexander, her heart racing with fear.

A boy pushed his way through to the front of the mob. Alexander drew his sword.

"That's her," Jock said, pointing at her.

~

Craignock Castle burst with excitement when Emily, Kester, and the other MacDougall men rode up through the village to the gates. Children appeared from every direction, running alongside her as she passed shop windows and houses already decorated with banners and garlands of flowers—red and yellow and violet. The castle gate was open and jammed with carts laden with meat and fowl and vegetables for the wedding feasts, and lookouts called down greetings to her and to the others from the high walls.

Inside the courtyard, the castle folk rushed forward with cries of delight. Women pressed in around her, wanting to carry her off and bathe and dress her. The cook appeared, covered with flour and soot, ready to drag her into the kitchens and feed her. Clan elders tried to push past the others, eagerly shouting questions. Amid this mayhem, Graeme MacDougall stood on the steps leading to the Great Hall, silent and calm. He'd always known she'd be back safe.

Emily looked about her happily. Maggie the cobbler's wife and her twin bairns on each hip, Molly the scullery maid with her red face and lisp, Robbie the stable boy with his shy smile. So many others. These people were her clan, her friends, her family. A warm feeling washed through her. The look of joy mixed with relief on their faces was not feigned. They cared about her, loved her as their own.

And she cared about them. She always had. But as the daughter of the laird, she held a special place here, a position of responsibility. She would never do anything to endanger them, she thought, feeling a twinge of uncertainty gnawing at her.

She shook off the feeling. She knew what she must do. And she was happy to be back, even if it were for a short time.

Emily dismounted and handed off the reins of her mount. She turned and found Kester standing beside her. She looked up into his kindly gray eyes.

"Aye, do it now, lass. Seize your moment. Speak your mind."

Emily nodded and gathered her courage. Smiling and greeting the crowd as she passed through, she climbed the stairs.

"Father." She halted a step below the laird. To everyone else, he was a man of business, cool and analytical. He was known as the one to call on for tricky problems, to offer suggestions on which course of action to take. For all of Emily's life, Graeme MacDougall had been relied upon by both king and ministers, often called away from Craignock to negotiate something on behalf of the crown. But as busy as he was, he always had time for his daughter.

Today, she thought, he looked tired. And when he was tired, her father was not always his most receptive.

Emily inclined her head as he kissed her brow. "May I have a moment alone with you?"

"Aye, my dove. You go with the women now. We'll take a late supper in the hall and you can tell me and everyone about your travels with your cousin, Kenna."

He was speaking for the benefit of those around them, and Emily couldn't miss the warning glance he sent her. She'd learned from Kester what people had been told about her whereabouts.

"I need a moment alone with you ... now," she repeated in a lower tone.

"You must be weary from your travels."

"*Now*, Papa." She moved to his side and took his arm. She had to sway him, convince him that something that he'd done for the sake of the clan must be undone. In her entire life, she'd never tried to do that. Her father loved her, in his own way; she was his only child. But for Graeme MacDougall, the clan's welfare would always come first. "Please. It's urgent."

Emily was relieved when he nodded and they went inside. The MacDougall was a respected and reasonably even-tempered man in the eyes of other leaders at court and among the clans. Nearly all his life, he'd contended with others who claimed to be chief, and because of their rivalry, she had witnessed his occasional bouts of rage. She knew he was capable of it. But he'd never lost his temper with her. She never gave him any reason to. Today, she guessed, might be the first time.

She waited until they were alone in the laird's private chambers. His worktables, as usual, were strewn with sheets of parchment, bottles of ink, wax and quills that lent a smell to this room that Emily always associated with her father. On one wall, a French tapestry depicting a lady and a knight in a garden of trees. She had a rose in her hand and was holding it out to the knight. On the wall behind his favorite chair, another tapestry with the MacDougall crest. Above the image of the steel-encased arm flexed and clutching a cross, the clan motto: "Buaidh no Bàs." Conquer or Die.

She took a deep breath, embracing those words.

"So what is so urgent?" he asked, going to a sideboard and picking up a pitcher of mead.

"I need you to postpone my wedding by a month."

Her father stared at her, the color in his face rising.

"What happened?" he demanded finally. "Did one of those Highlanders . . . ? Did they force you—"

"Nothing happened," she interrupted. "But don't you think you might have thought of those possibilities before delivering me and Kenna into the hands of the Macphersons?"

He poured himself a cup of mead, all calmness again. "I knew nothing would happen to either of you. I was helping the MacKays and the Macphersons, kinsmen and allies. So tell me, how does your cousin fare? Has she put all that foolishness behind her? Is she ready to return to her husband?"

"I don't know how she fares. She is missing. I don't know where she is."

"Missing?"

Emily wasn't ready to drop the subject of her father's

participation in the scheme to get Kenna and Alexander together. Nor was she ready to forget about his willingness to keep her ignorant of it. But right now she needed him to focus on the impending date of her wedding.

"In part, that's why I need you to postpone my wedding."

"Rubbish. She'll turn up tomorrow or the next day. We can't postpone the wedding, Emily. Not after all these preparations. And what would I say to Sir Quentin?"

"Father, we *will* postpone this wedding ... or cancel it," she said forcefully. "The choice is yours."

"What did you say?" He fixed his gaze on her, one brow raised. He was no longer the solicitous father; he was now the hard-dealing laird.

"I'm giving you the choice out of respect," she said. "I'll not spend any more time preparing for this foolish affair. And you can tell Sir Quentin anything you like. Or you can lock me in the dungeon and drag me to the chapel and force me to marry against my will. But if that is your choice, you will end up with a far greater mess than you can possibly imagine."

"Are you threatening me?"

"I'll not marry right now. That decision is not yours to make. But you have the choice to postpone or cancel."

Her stomach was in a knot. She pressed her lips together to keep them from quivering.

Her father slammed his cup on the sideboard, sloshing mead onto the dark polished wood. "You dare to tell me what I have a right to decide and not decide?"

"Did you raise me to be bullied into decisions that affect my entire life?"

"What do you know about life?" he bellowed. "You're a mere chit of a lass."

"One who has no say in whom she marries? Am I a prize cow to be auctioned off?"

"Enough! I'm laird here. I'm your father. You will do what I see fit for you and for the clan."

Emily took a step toward him and matched his glare.

"I've been the perfect daughter. Submissive, agreeable, never a moment's trouble. I've not demanded anything of you until now."

"By the devil, you ride out with Kenna MacKay and return more like her than—"

"I'm not Kenna. I'm a thousand times worse."

"That's nonsense."

It was now or never. Her hands fisted at her sides. "You'll grant me my wish or I'll walk out of here now, and you will never see me again."

"Go on. This is all talk."

"Talk? I will bring disgrace on this clan like you'd never imagined possible. Kenna escaped to a priory. I'll move to a brothel in Glasgow where there will be more contenders to your laird's seat in a year and every year after that. I will become mistress to your—"

"Enough," he shouted. "That's enough."

"You can't keep me in chains forever. Sir Quentin will recognize my insanity the moment you drag me to the kirk steps."

Kenna saw her father's face change, as if he were seeing her in a new light.

"What do you want?"

"I already told you."

The descending sun was casting long beams of golden light through the narrow windows when Emily left the laird's chambers and hurried up the stairwell to her own.

She had a month. If she could not succeed, the marriage would proceed as planned.

Servants were waiting for her, but she sent them out, directing one to find Kester and send him to her. She sat for a moment by the open window. She had a plan, but she needed to act now. The sea air wafting in seemed to carry a scent of promise.

Her gaze fell on a small needlework pincushion her mother had made when Emily was just a child. She picked it up. An image of a shield divided in two. At the top, the motto of the MacDougall's. On one side, the arm and cross. On the other, a blue sailing ship. Emily stared at the ship now, wondering what her mother was thinking when she devised the image.

Buaidh no Bàs. Conquer or die.

Chapter 14

I have a good eye, uncle. I can see a church by
daylight.

Alexander followed the short, barrel-chested man called
Peter to a heather-covered hill overlooking the loch. The
red-bearded cousin of Jock lost half his hand only a few
days ago in a fight with the marauders. The stitches that
Kenna had used to close his wound glistened with oozing
blood, but the man would live to use that hand again.

And Peter was not the neediest in this camp.

"We've put the wounded down there at the water's
edge. The womenfolk are keeping the sick, the old and
young, in an old kirk beyond that brae."

The moon had not yet risen, but Alexander could see
dozens of people huddled around a few fires. There had
to be more refugees beyond what he could see. Alexander guessed most of them had to flee with only the
clothes on their backs. They were hungry, desperate, vul-

nerable. This made them unpredictable. He wanted Kenna away from here.

She had already gone to work with those needing her. As he looked from one group to the next, he spotted her at the center of a small cluster of folk. A tall lad in rags was holding a torch up for her, and she was cleaning and bandaging the head of a wounded farmer. A moment later, she followed an old woman to another dark shape by the water's edge. She bent down for only a moment and then stood up, giving directions to a bystander. Alexander watched her move on to the next.

"We've had no time to bury the dead. The bodies, bless 'em, are by them trees. There's a priest come into the camp today. Says he'll give them last rites in the morning. Don't know as it'll do them much good then." Peter spat on the ground and glared at the grove of trees. "But what do I know, being just a fisherman?"

Alexander glanced at the shadowy grove, but he quickly turned his attention back to Kenna. He wasn't about to lose track of her. So far, they'd been received with gratitude, and he'd seen no sign of hostility, but their position was uncertain. Right now, they needed her. But what would happen when they didn't? He was a Macpherson; she was a MacKay. They had to be considered outsiders, at the very least.

"Who are all these people? Where did they come from?"

"Some are from around Knipoch. But some are folk from other villages to the south. MacDougall land mostly. And there are others from inland," Peter said. "With them dirty English bastards and that treacherous Lowland scum doing their killing for them, it's safest to take to the hills."

Alexander nodded, fixing his gaze on Kenna.

"Jock arrived here ahead of you this afternoon. The lad said yer wife has a gift at healing. We were anxious for you to get here."

Kenna was directing those around her, and bits and pieces carried to them. Her voice was clear. In control. Confident. He'd seen many a surgeon work on the wounded, and there was common sense in everything he saw her doing.

Above the trees at the far end of the loch, the black velvet expanse of night sky was studded with stars. He felt foolish for the teasing he'd given her when they were walking. There had to be a logical explanation for how he was healed.

"My wife was trained by the nuns at Glosters Priory on Loch Eil, on Cameron clan land," Alexander told him. "She knows how to bind a wound and deliver a bairn."

"Did a fine job with mine," Peter replied, holding up his mutilated hand.

Jock had disappeared as soon as they arrived. Alexander wanted to find the lad and talk to him about exactly what he'd told these folk. He didn't want any ignorant nonsense circulating.

Apparently finished with the wounded for the time being, Kenna was led away from the loch toward the rise and the kirk beyond it. Alexander followed, with Peter hurrying to keep up.

"Does everyone know who we are?" Alexander asked. "My wife? Me?"

"Aye. Yer the Macpherson's laird eldest. You command yer clan's ships. Not many folk along the shore don't know you."

They reached the top of the hill as the moon appeared above the mountains to the east. The ruins of an old kirk nestled between two hillocks in a broad meadow. Not far away, a stream ran down toward the loch. The building must have been deserted long ago, he decided, from the overgrown look of the vines and other plants covering the crumbling walls and windows. The roof was gone, from what he could see.

Kenna and her entourage disappeared into the kirk, drawing looks from the scores of travelers who'd built fires outside the wall surrounding the kirk yard. Now those faces turned toward Alexander.

"Word spread before you arrived," Peter told him. "Alexander Macpherson and his wife Kenna MacKay."

"Jock," he muttered as they started through the refugees' encampment. So much for the boy's promise. No wonder he was making himself scarce. Alexander wondered where he was hiding.

"Don't blame the lad. He didn't know his sister was injured until he found her lying here with a gash on her leg and a terrible burned arm." Peter motioned ahead to the ruined kirk. "Jock's young. He was desperate that we find yer wife. And we—"

At the sound of the rush from behind, Alexander whirled in time to knock away the arm holding a blade. As he smashed the assailant on the side of the face with his fist, a club whirred through the air, aimed at Alexander's head. The weapon landed low, striking him hard on the shoulder and sending him tumbling backward. He was on his feet before they could reach him.

The two remaining men hesitated, and Alexander knew from their faces this was not going as they'd planned. Another man—the one with a short sword—was shaking his head and trying unsuccessfully to rise.

He faced them, and the two began to spread out. From their clothes, he knew his burly attackers were fishermen. They carried small clubs and dirks. Behind them, Peter was on one knee, clutching his injured hand.

"Do I know you lads?" Alexander asked coolly, his hand on the hilt of his sword. "Because I like to know the men I kill."

"Ne'er mind about that," one growled, raising his club menacingly. "We know you... pirate. You and yer MacKay bitch."

The two rushed at him, clubs swinging. Alexander took a glancing blow to the head as he ducked under one club. Coming up quickly, he slammed his fist into a furious face, driving one fisherman into the other. The two tumbled to the ground. Following, the Highlander landed a kick to the head of one, knocking him cold. He turned to drop a knee on the throat of the other, who was moaning.

He glanced up just in time to see the third assailant, standing now with his sword in hand, take a blow to the side of his head and topple like a straw man in the wind. Peter was behind him, glaring fiercely at the three.

"I'll take it from here, if you don't mind," the wounded fisherman growled, picking up a club. "I know these birds only too well."

As Alexander stood, Peter solidly rapped the head of the moaning attacker, silencing him for the moment.

Kenna appeared, pushing through the crowd that had formed a larger ring around them. She looked from Alexander to the three fishermen and Peter, and back at her husband.

"Have you finished introducing yourself around?" she asked tensely.

Alexander glanced at the crowd. No one else appeared ready to fight. "I believe I have, wife."

Kenna took him by the arm and pulled him toward the ruin. The crowd parted for them.

As they started across the kirk yard, Peter could be heard shouting at the others. "So this is the way to thank the MacKay lass for helping yer kin now, is it?"

Alexander turned to see him kick one of the men who'd started moaning again.

"Yer lucky the Macpherson didn't cut yer throat, you cod-faced dolt. And nay, I'd not blame his wife for not sewing you back up if he did."

Inside the kirk, Alexander saw that a small fire had been lit at the far end of the church nave. Near it, a number of sick folk lay on blankets, and those seeing to them hovered around. Kenna took him across the chancel through an open doorway into what must have been the vestry at one time. Now, only three walls and part of a fourth remained, and ancient charred timbers from the former roof stretched across the room.

The rising moon cast shadows across the stone floor, and Alexander looked up at the broad night sky above.

Kenna led him to a timber in the corner against a wall.

"How many times do I have to fix you?"

"I believe we took an oath that calls for . . . a lifetime's worth."

She shook her head and pressed a flat hand against his chest.

He sat down. They were eye to eye. Alexander wondered if this would be the good time to apologize for his earlier ribbing.

Kenna looked exhausted. She used a rag and dabbed at his forehead and the side of his mouth. He wished there were a way he could carry her away from all this, take her somewhere where it would be only the two of them. To a place where he could take care of her and show her that he was a husband that she'd want to keep.

"That was the same oath that we're getting annulled. You're far too much trouble."

"Aye, I'm some trouble. But I'm worth it."

"For a brigand and an ape, you do have a fanciful imagination."

"Admit it, Kenna. You like me."

He pulled her by the waist until she stood between his knees. Her eyes rivaled the stars above. Her mouth was inches away.

"You're a curious beast, to be sure." She traced what had to be a bruise by the line of his jaw. "But you have very little charm. Nothing that entices me nor tempts me to change my mind."

He drew her closer until her breasts were crushed against his chest and kissed her with a lashing assault of lips and tongue. There was no hesitation on her part. She moaned deep in her throat and her arms encircled his neck. Her mouth opened under the pressure of the kiss, her tongue dancing with his in a seductive promise of more.

He wanted to tear open her blouse, taste the sweetness of her breasts, feel the weight of their fullness in his palm. He ached with desire for her. He wanted to bury himself deep inside of her. She ground her body against him, and the urge to yank up her skirts, to lift Kenna onto him, was the only half-conscious thought racing through the flashing heat in his head.

And then, from somewhere, a rational thought intruded.

To take her here, now, would mean there would be no annulment. The choice he wanted her to make, the choice to stay with him, would be gone. And she would blame him for the rest of their lives.

Bloody hell, he cursed inwardly. Bloody, fucking hell.

He ended the kiss, wrenching his mouth away. She was breathless. Alexander stared at those swollen lips, at those half-closed eyes, clouded with passion.

"I'm telling you now, lass, sex between us will make the Highland storm seem tame, make the summer lightning only a pale flash of light. And you don't even know where my fancy can take us."

"So my reason, my sanity even, depends on *never* making love with you." Her eyes, clear and focused now, flashed with mischief.

"Nay, your reason will never be trustworthy until you experience the bliss that I bring to our marriage bed."

"A wee bit full of yourself, I'm thinking."

Before she could object, he turned her slightly in his arms, reached under her skirt, and slid his hand up to the junction of her thighs. She gasped as he touched her wetness. Holding her steady, he slipped a finger into the tight sheath and saw her eyes grow round. A soft cry escaped her lips.

"What . . . what are you doing?"

"Showing you something of what's to come."

He withdrew his finger and slid it in again. This time she rocked against his hand. He stared into Kenna's eyes. Her desire matched his.

"Bad timing, lass. And not the perfect place, but I want to give you this, now."

He rose to his feet and pressed her back against the wall, his body shielding hers.

Her body quivered when he pushed a knee between her legs and he touched her again. He teased her slick folds, and his tongue played the depth of her sweet mouth as he copied the action of his finger. Her breaths became shorter and shorter; her little gasps became whimpers. Suddenly, with a cry that Alexander swallowed with a kiss, she arched against his hand and shuddered with complete abandon.

Sweeping her into his arms, he sat down and gathered her on his lap. She clutched him about the neck tightly, and he could feel the tremors racing through her body as waves of pleasure continued to wash over her. Doing his best to ignore his own throbbing desire, he simply held her.

It was some time before he felt enough control to set her again on her feet and find his voice. "And this is only a sample, wife."

She took a deep breath. "Oh my. I've . . . I've never . . ." She stopped, smiled shyly, and stared at his chin. "Very well. I admit it. You're a temptation."

He heard Peter call for him from the nave. Kenna straightened her dress, and he waited until she gave him a nod before going out of the vestry with his wife behind him.

A hooded, ferret-faced priest was standing beside Peter. His eyes followed Alexander as they drew closer and then fixed on Kenna.

"The good Father here wants a word with you," Peter said. "Alone."

"I'll be over there, tending to those who need me." Kenna motioned with her head toward the sick.

Alexander watched her go, in no hurry to recover from

what had just happened. To him, Kenna's magic—if that's what it was—ran far beyond the power of healing. Her true gift lay in the power she had over his heart.

"What is it, priest?" Alexander demanded when Peter walked away.

"I need to speak with you privately." The man looked at the women working at the far end of the ruin. "What I have to say, what I have to offer, is for your ears only."

Alexander wasn't letting Kenna out of his sight. "Whatever you have to tell me, you'll tell me here and now."

The priest visibly bristled; then he shrugged.

"I know who you are, Highlander, and I know why you're here," he said, glancing in Kenna's direction.

"So, what of it?"

"My church and living in the Borders were destroyed by the English marauders, so this is my flock now, such as it is."

"And what can I do for you?"

"It's not that. It's I who can be of service."

"Go on."

"I had a servant traveling with me. He's gone. Tonight. Taken one of my horses, the scurrilous villain. I believe he's gone back south to find that Maxwell rogue. I believe he means to lead him back here to you."

Alexander looked over at Kenna, who was crouched

over a sick woman. He needed to take her out of this place. He looked back at the priest.

"I still have one horse," the priest continued. "I want you to have it. Take the woman and get clear of here. Go to Oban and farther if you need to, but get away from us. And go tonight."

"I can buy the horse from you," Alexander told him.

"Whatever suits you, Highlander."

Alexander nodded. "You have been of service. But what of you? Why stay?"

"As I said, this is my flock now. They need me. If Maxwell comes and you're gone, he may leave us alone." The priest shrugged again and looked away. "If not, we're in God's hands."

~

Donald Maxwell sliced a chunk of meat from the mutton roasting over the fire pit and tore at it with his teeth. The cotter's fat wife huddled in a dark corner with her two terrified children.

They had reason to be afraid. Their stupid oaf of a father lay dead on the dung pile by the sheepcote. Why Highlanders always believe they must fight would always be a mystery, he thought. Not that it would have made a difference.

"Ale, woman. And be quick about it."

The two English riders stood eying the mutton hungrily, but Maxwell was not about to offer them any. His own men nearly filled the cottage, sitting and standing around in the flickering shadows cast by the fire.

"Go back to Sir Ralph and tell him this: the noose is tightening."

He paused as the cotter's wife handed him a horn cup full of ale. Taking hold of her wrist, he dragged her into his lap, eliciting a burst of laughter from his men as she struggled for a moment and then stopped. Maxwell's knife rested against her throat. He looked up at the messengers.

"Tell him that the MacKay woman and the Macpherson have taken to the hills, but they're exactly where we want them. My men are on their trail, beating the bushes and driving them to me here, where I wait, in hospitable Oban."

Chapter 15

I do love nothing in the world so well as
you—is not that strange?

He'd ignored completely her demand for more time . . .
simply scooped her up in front of him and then kicked
his heels into the sides of the gray steed. In moments, the
loch and the camp and the fleeing refugees were far behind them.

Several broken bones, some horrific burns, many open
wounds, a woman nearing childbirth, and two children
hot with fever. Jock's sister and his cousin. Kenna had
tended to them and used no magic. Not intentionally.
She didn't take hold of the stone tablet in the pouch even
once, but there were whispers by some of the wounded
that her touch alone felt warm or lessened the pain.

She didn't understand it, but she was too tired to think
it through. She'd been led from one person to the next for
hours. She examined them and decided what was wrong.

If there wasn't enough time to do it herself, she passed on the same instructions she'd been taught by the nuns.

There were some she hadn't been given time to look after at all. And there was no reasoning with Alexander. He wouldn't listen. He simply said that she was no good to anyone if she was a hostage or dead. That was what would happen if they were still here when Maxwell's men caught up with them.

He would allow no discussion, hinting that he'd drag her away tied and gagged, if need be. After the last few days, Kenna knew he'd go through with the threat. And she knew she was too tired to fight him.

Kenna left instructions. Many helpers stepped forward. She hoped it was enough.

Now, riding through the rolling countryside, she felt the complete weight of exhaustion descend on her. Wrapped in Alexander's protective arms and lulled by his warmth, Kenna dozed, hovering in that shadowy limbo between consciousness and sleep.

She dreamed of blood and severed limbs and her frustrating inability to sew the wounds quickly enough. Then as a turn or a bump would lift her into wakefulness, Kenna's thoughts would hearken back to the memory of Alexander's every touch. Of the two of them locked in a sensual rhythm against the wall. Of her complete surrender to him. Of the excruciating pleasure building within her before that final blaze of glorious release. She'd never thought such a thing possible. Now *that*, she thought with a smile, was real magic.

She didn't want to go back to sleep. She wanted to experience again and again in her mind what had happened between them. But the rocking rhythm of the horse lulled her.

A stirring deep in her belly made Kenna open her eyes. They were riding through a wooded glen and then out into the predawn light of rolling moorland. Patches of purple flowers covered the hillsides.

Alexander's hand was on her breast.

Kenna leaned back against his chest, looking up at him.

"What are you doing?"

"Enjoying myself and answering your demands."

"Demands?" She removed his hand. "While I sleep? We've exchanged no words since we left the camp."

"Your body spoke for you," he whispered in her ear. "Nestling into my chest, running your hands along my thighs, making small noises in the back of your throat. I'm a man. There's only so much I can take."

"You're talking nonsense." Kenna tried to shift her body, but she had nowhere to go.

"You're not helping."

"I'm not doing anything. This is all your imagination."

He wrapped an arm around her waist and pulled her firmly back against him. She could feel his arousal against the small of her back. A delicious heat rushed through her body, surprising her.

"I know you feel that, and you're responsible," he said flatly. "So sit still or your first time will be up against a tree or on the hard ground with a heather branch stabbing in your ear and rocks jabbing you in the—"

"You wouldn't."

"Don't tempt me, wife."

The words didn't frighten her. After last night, she was looking forward to their first real night of lovemaking, in spite of the vaguely alarming hints that the MacKay women had whispered in her ear about what happened in the marriage bed. She was feeling the same reckless impulse that she felt when faced with any adventure. Annulment or no annulment, she was ready for more. But they were on strange land. She would be happier in a secure place for that special moment, with at least a roof over their heads.

Her gaze drifted up to her husband's face again. The angry words they'd exchanged less than a week ago sounded so hollow now. If they stayed together and lived as man and wife, they'd have many arguments, to be sure. He was as pigheaded as she was.

One thing, more than any other, made her uneasy: the

broken tablet, her inheritance from her mother.

Descending into a hollow in the moor, they were enclosed by a pocket of early morning mist. Kenna could see only a few paces in front of them, and it occurred to her that this was life. *We only see a few paces ahead, if that.* There was no telling what would come of her or Alexander or the stone tablet, and the gift and the curse that accompanied it.

"About the questions that you were asking me before we were taken to the camp."

He looked into her face. "You're a talented healer. I saw what you did for those people. I was . . . I am very proud of you. The nuns trained you well."

She shook her head. "But what I did for you . . . what happened in the fishing hut and later in the cave . . . I needed more than what I was taught."

She paused, looked down at her lap, trying to decide how much she should tell him now. They were on the road. He had enough on his mind to get them to reach safety.

"Will you trust me?" she asked. "Will you wait until I understand better myself what happened there, before I tell you everything?"

"You mean you don't understand it yourself?"

"I don't understand *all* of it." It was the truth. "Will you give me time? Trust me for now?"

"You saved my life," he reminded her. "Twice. I can wait."

That was all he said, and Kenna felt a weight lift off her for now.

They continued to ride in and out of patches of mist, past unearthly rock formations, and over heather- and gorse-covered hills. As the land began to rise steadily, they entered more woods.

Kenna looked around her in awe. The branches of ancient oak trees entwined into a canopy above them. As they rode through a clearing, she realized that the first rays of the sun were casting shadows in front of them.

"We're riding west," she said. "We're not going north. Aren't we going to Oban?"

"There's a trap set for us there."

"A trap? How do you know?"

"That priest. What kind of man doesn't give last rites to the dead until it's convenient for him? By 'sblood, I've seen many a priest with as fine a horse as this, but never one so willing to part with him. And the bloody weasel never even bickered on the price. Nay, there's a trap set, no doubting it."

"He never went near the sick or injured while we were there," Kenna told him. "I didn't even know there was a priest with them until he came to see you."

"Also, he's a Lowlander."

"And you think he's working with Maxwell."

"He said a half dozen times before we left that the only safe place for us is Oban."

The fog in her head cleared. After everything they'd been through, to trust any stranger was foolish. She was relieved Alexander had been aware of it.

As they rode on, they left the forest behind, and Kenna looked around at the unfamiliar terrain. Behind them lay the mercenaries pursuing them. Ahead of them and to the south was the coastline that Jock warned was crawling with English raiders. To the north lay Oban and a possible trap. They were being driven into the nets of their enemy.

"Where are we going? Where can we hide?"

Alexander didn't answer.

"Tell me."

"Where those bastards will *not* catch us."

The sun was still low in the sky behind them when he reined in and dismounted. She could see nothing but a series of rolling hills. Alexander reached up to help her down.

Kenna hoped their destination was near. The shoes given to her by one of the women at the camp were too small and hurt her feet. She didn't want to walk far. She slid off the back of the horse.

Alexander stripped the gear from the mount and

slapped the animal on the flank. The horse ran off, disappearing along the pathway leading north. She pulled her hair back and tied it into a knot. Shaking out her dress as if it weren't torn in a dozen places and stained from waist to hem, she faced her husband.

"Where do we go from here?"

He took her hand and smiled, pulling her uphill through thick shrubs that caught and pulled at her skirts.

"Any time now," she told him. "Please feel free to tell me where we're going."

"You'll see soon enough."

"Thank you. Perhaps I'll write a poem about that. I'll call it 'Soon Enough.'"

She followed him, weaving through outcroppings of square black rock and thorny shrubs. No physical effort or discomfort, however, could erase the smile she felt had been branded on her heart. Looking at him ahead of her, Kenna could not help but admire the powerful width of his shoulders and the possessive hold he kept on her hand.

As if reading her thoughts, he glanced back. "I never imagined you would be such a woman as this."

"Before I commit to this conversation, I want to know if you are insulting me or complimenting me."

"Complimenting, of course."

"Oh, of course. Well, you must know I'm not accustomed to hearing compliments from you. But go on—say nice things about me."

His laughter made Kenna's insides go warm.

"To begin, I don't know many women who would make this journey without even a wee complaint."

"It's a relief that you are so aged that you don't recall all the complaining I did the first night you kidnapped us."

He waved that off. "Nay, I heard nothing unreasonable. And you're as brave as you are bonny."

"Oh, aye, I'm feeling like a rare beauty right now. But I will accept your assertion that I'm brave."

"Thank you, wife."

"Still, I think you're a bit touched in the head. What were you doing picking a fight with those men outside the kirk? The day before, if you recall, you were nearly gutted like a pig."

"I had no choice, lass. They started it," Alexander corrected it. "But back to you. Since our marriage, I've seen that your intelligence—"

"Stop right there," she ordered. "This is already sounding like an insult."

"Nay! How is that?"

"I'm not brave and intelligent as a reaction to you. I am the same woman that I was long before I met you."

"Are you trying to say you had a life before meeting me?"

"Aye, and I'll have a life after, too, once I find a cliff high enough to push you over."

"How about this one? High enough?"

Kenna gasped as they suddenly broke through the line of shrubs and came to a halt at the edge of a cliff. Jagged pillars of black rock dropped away below and the gray-green sea boiled at the bottom.

She looked up and her breath caught in her chest. The sea and a long stretch of land across a broad strait spread out before them. Fishing boats, looking tiny in the distance, bobbed among the whitecaps. Almost directly across the firth, a ship lay at anchor.

"What is this? Where are we?"

"I told you—we've arrived."

"Arrived where? Is that one of your ships in the distance?"

"Aye. The one MacDougall stole from us. The trade for Emily must have worked. I was hoping it would be here, though I feared we might be early."

"Will they come for us?"

"Aye, lass. But judging from the wind and the tide, it'll take them most of the day to get here. But they will."

Kenna looked around her. There were no buildings, nowhere for them to take shelter. The two of them seemed insignificant against the cliffs. "But we're only a speck on top of this cliff. How will they even know that we're here?"

"You're right." Alexander's face clouded over. "Our best course of action would be to swim out to them."

"That ship is too far from here! We'll drown long before we reach them."

"We'll not drown." He stretched out a hand to her. "Come on; let's get started."

She backed away and planted her feet. "You're not doing that to me again. We're not jumping. Did you see those rocks down there? We'll never reach the water."

"Suit yourself, lass. But I'm reconsidering what I said about you being brave and uncomplaining." With a shrug, Alexander stepped to the ledge and jumped.

Kenna screamed and rushed to the edge. Dropping to her hands and knees, she peered wildly over the rocks. There, perched on a narrow ledge about twice his height from the top of the cliff, Alexander stood looking up at her.

"Jump," he said.

Kenna eyed the space where she needed to land and, without a moment's hesitation, dropped into his waiting arms.

"Very well, Kenna MacKay. I'm convinced. You *are* brave."

"But we can forget about the 'intelligent' comments. I don't believe I just did that."

Keeping a firm hold on her hand, Alexander led Kenna

a short distance along the ledge, then dropped to his hands and knees and crawled through a low opening in the face of the cliff. Kenna followed him into the half-darkness of a cave. The damp, cool smell of earth filled her senses.

As she stood up, Alexander pulled a flint from his sporran and proceeded to light a torch that was leaning against the wall of the cave. The narrow space lit up. As Kenna's eyes adjusted, she saw that the cave sloped downward for a few paces beyond where Alexander was standing and then angled off.

"Where are we?"

"Sailor's call it Hermit's Rock. We're south of Oban."

He took a pile of dry wood from an alcove and went to the cave mouth. In a few moments, he'd started a fire.

"A signal?" she asked as he stood back. Smoke from the blaze billowed out.

He nodded.

"Won't that give our whereabouts away to Maxwell and his men?"

"The signal is only visible from the water. By now, either James or Diarmad is in command of that ship. They'll see it and come for us."

"So you've done this before."

"This is one of many places we know to use in case of trouble."

"But what about those fishermen who attacked you at the camp?" she asked. "There are fishing boats out there. Won't they know we're here?"

"The fire at the mouth of the cave is not only a Macpherson signal. Others will see it, but they won't know what it means. My brother and Diarmad know we ran into trouble, or we'd have been in Oban yesterday or the day before. That's why that ship is anchored there. They're waiting for our signal. Now, I'm relying on them to be the first to reach us."

Kenna looked around the cold empty place and the passage leading into the darkness. The walls of the cave were squared-off blocks, as if they'd been hewn from black stone by an army of giants.

"What do we do now?" She rubbed her arms. "Wait here? We still need to get down that cliff somehow."

"I told you that we've used this in the past. We won't wait here." He took her hand and led her toward the back of the cave. His torch threw wild shadows on the rugged walls. "But I'm hoping it will take them a very long time before they reach us."

The glint in his eyes made her stomach flutter. "Why?"

"No more talking, lass. I'll show you."

Chapter 16

I love you with so much of my heart that none
is left to protest.

"Is this a crypt of some kind?" Kenna asked, stopping and gesturing to a low opening in the cave wall. A thick oak door with a sheet of beaten metal stood open.

The tunnels had taken them downward in a series of gradual steps, and she could feel heat emanating from the doorway.

"Nay, they say this was where the hermit lived. Let me show you."

Alexander let go of her hand and ducked through, holding the torch up ahead of him.

She passed through into the low, square, musty chamber. The room opened up, but there were no windows, no other doors. Alexander's head brushed the low ceiling. Kenna's attention was immediately drawn to two things: pictures etched into one of the walls and the heat.

Some of the engraved images she could identify: whales and fish and birds and elk and trees and men with spears. Some were complex labyrinthine designs that she'd never seen before. In the center of one wall, she saw what appeared to be a cross.

The heat in the chamber was intense, and Kenna had started sweating the moment she'd entered. The tablet hanging around her neck wasn't easing her discomfort, either. The stone was hot against her skin.

She reached out to touch the engraved cross . . . and pulled her hand back immediately.

The pain was sharp and instantaneous, like putting a hand into fire. She recoiled, stepping back against Alexander's chest.

"What's wrong?" he asked, steadying her.

"Nothing." She hid her hand in the folds of her skirt. Talons of fear wrapped around her pounding heart. "Who made those drawings? What do they mean?"

He went near them, reached up and traced a spiraling design with a finger. "I don't know. I don't think anyone knows."

The tablet was becoming hotter, burning her skin through the pouch. The air in the chamber was heating up, as well, suffocating her with its heavy dryness. She realized she was sweating, but Alexander didn't seem to notice the scorching temperature of the wall or the increasing heat of the air.

There was something unsettling, something powerful, and she didn't like it. Perhaps dark magic was at work here. On an opposite wall a generous supply of flints, candles, torches, blankets, and other things had been stored.

Kenna moved toward the door of the chamber. She had to get out, get away from whatever it was in that room that was responding to the tablet she carried.

"We don't need to wait here, do we?"

"Nay, there's more I want to show you."

Kenna practically ran out of the chamber ahead of Alexander. Outside, she leaned against the cold, damp wall of the dark tunnel. The heat started to subside. She could once again breathe. Alexander was still in the chamber. She heard him rummaging through the supplies.

Kenna looked more closely at the heavy door. The metal sheet over the thick oak was covered with designs and images that were similar to the stone carvings inside.

She hesitantly reached out to touch the door. Again, her hand burned. She stepped back.

"So, finally, something that Kenna MacKay is afraid of." Alexander came out of the chamber, carrying a few things under one arm and holding the torch high.

"Not afraid," she grumbled, looking away. "Maybe just a bit uneasy."

"Nay, this is a first. You're frightened." He laid the torch against the cave wall and lifted her chin until she was forced to look into his blue eyes. "What's wrong, lass?"

"I don't like places like this. Crypts, dungeons, and such. Wee, tight places. I can't breathe in them." It wasn't a lie. She didn't like enclosed spaces.

"That's a good thing for me to remember, for all the times in the future when I have to punish you."

She snorted and pushed his hand away.

"Just be warned, love. Benmore has many cellars and dungeons."

"You're a blackguard, Alexander Macpherson. I see no humor in this." Kenna turned around to go back the way they'd come, but he took her arm.

"Not that way."

"Another crypt?" she asked.

"Nay. You'll like it where we are going. Trust me."

"'Trust me,' he says. Right after he tells me he plans to shackle me in Benmore's dungeons. And why shouldn't I trust you?"

"I made no mention of shackles. But I've heard rumors that some like it that way when they make love, so if that's your preference . . ."

Even as an unexpected thrill ran through her, she opened her mouth to respond. But nothing came out. Realizing she must look like a fish out of water, she closed her mouth.

His laughter brought an end to her speechlessness.

"There is something definitely wrong with you, pirate," she snapped, punching him in the chest.

But in the next moment, Kenna was gasping for breath at the suddenness of his embrace. Tight against his body, she could feel his arousal hard against her. He kissed her and drew back.

"As I think you can tell, Kenna, there's only one thing on my mind right now. And that is making love to my wife." He pushed the pile of supplies into her arms and picked up the torch. "I say we waste no more time."

He didn't look back at her as he started down the passageway. She followed, but she thought she might collapse under her weight at any moment. Her head was in the clouds. Her mouth was dry. Her heart raced like she'd been running up Ben Nevis. Her skin tingled . . . everywhere.

Kenna knew her heart. It was time.

The tunnel seemed to be winding downward for miles into the earth. The air was growing damper, the smell of the grave infused in every breath. The sharp-edged blocks of stone that formed black walls grew so tight in places that they needed to squat and turn sideways to squeeze through. Alexander occasionally looked back to make sure she was still with him.

Suddenly, the passage widened, and a cool breeze

swept through her hair. Like some starving beggar who finally sits at a table, Kenna filled her lungs with the fresh air and hurried to keep up with him.

"Is there another opening?"

"Aye, but not an easy one that anyone can find or enter through."

As they started climbing down an odd, stair-like rock formation, Kenna saw light at the bottom. The scent of the grave disappeared, supplanted by the smell of water. Reaching a platform of rock, she stood in amazement. From two dark openings, water flowed into a broad pool. A warm, steamy mist rose from the black surface, creating an otherworldly scene. Alexander took her hand and led her along the path that hugged the shimmering black walls.

Kenna's breath caught in her chest the moment they entered the next cave. Perfectly cut black pillars arced upward to a cathedral-high ceiling. Beneath them, the water cascaded into a small lake that dropped off again farther along. She could see daylight flooding in from the top of a cave opening. Here, the walls rang with the melody of the waterfalls. The water, no longer black, had taken on a turquoise color and weaved through mist-covered rocks.

She dropped the bundle she was carrying and walked to the edge of the pool.

"What is this place? It must be heaven."

"An *uaimh bhinn*, a cave of melody," he told her. "Many springs join together here from the hills."

Kenna smiled, breathing in the freshness of the air. She dropped to her knees beside the turquoise water lapping the smooth stone surface. She splashed her face with it. It was warm—a perfect temperature. She marveled at the crystal clarity of it.

"I've never seen anything like this. Thank you for bringing me here." She glanced over her shoulder at him. The way he stood watching her made her stomach tighten in anticipation.

Kenna sat, swinging her legs around and removing the tight shoes. There were blisters on her feet. She dipped them in the water and shivered with pleasure.

Alexander moved to the edge of the water, standing above her.

"It's lovely here."

"Aye," he responded, never taking his eyes off of her. "It's lovely, indeed."

Kenna's eyes and Alexander's locked. She remembered his words when they'd left the hermit's chamber. He wanted her. This was the place he'd brought her to make love. She let her gaze sweep across the water and the walls of the cavern. And she wanted him, too. She wanted him to hold her, to run his hands over her skin, to kiss her.

"Would you like to go in? You can swim and wash."

"With you here, watching?"

"With me, going in with you."

Something inside her tingled at the thought of his eyes on her. She recalled his hardened manhood pressing against her so intimately. Her face warmed.

"I would like to swim." She gestured to the underground lake. "There's plenty of room for us to go in . . . separately. That might be best."

"As my wife wishes." Alexander unfastened the leather belt holding his sword and laid the weapon on the ground beside Kenna. She glanced up at him hastily, startled by the suddenness of the act.

"What are you doing?" she asked.

"What do you think I'm doing?" He grinned mischievously, undoing the brooch that held his tartan over his shoulder. It fell with a ringing sound beside the sword. "I'm going for a swim."

"With me here?" she blurted.

"With you here," he repeated seductively.

"I thought you just agreed to find your own place to swim."

"I agreed to go in separately. I'm going in now and then you can join me."

"I don't want to swim with you." She watched as he kicked off his boots, exposing muscular calves.

"Shall I convince you otherwise?" He reached for her but she scrambled to her feet and stepped back. "Would you prefer that I carry you in?"

She shook her head. "You go in and swim off... that way. I'll find my own place to swim. Now, away with you, beast."

"Once again, I'm going to prove to you that I can be reasonable. So I'll do just as you say."

He pulled up his shirt from the belted kilt, and whatever she intended to say trailed off as Alexander peeled it off and dropped it on the ground. She stared at his muscular chest. She'd seen it before, tended to it when he was injured. But this was so different.

Like a god he stood framed by the glowing light of the cave opening behind him. He was magnificent—she could not deny it. The wound at his side had already healed into a thick scar. Kenna ached to reach out to him, to run her fingers across the rippling lines of his powerful warrior's body. As if the wind had been knocked from her, she stood motionless. Breathless.

"I'll even swim away so you have the privacy you seek." He slowly unhooked the thick leather belt that held his kilt in place.

Her throat was as dry as an old bone. She took another step back and watched.

"Would you like me to undress you before I go in?"

Wide-eyed, Kenna shook her head, trying to keep her gaze on his chest and not below.

Something dropped to the ground. It had to be his belt and kilt. He smiled and walked slowly into the water. She waited, waited, only a moment before letting her gaze sweep down over Alexander's back and buttocks. Magnificent? Naked, he was glorious.

"Don't wait too long or I'll have to come after you."

He dove headfirst into the water and a few seconds later Kenna saw his powerful strokes take him across the lake to the cascading falls.

Kenna recalled all the scrubbing the MacKay women had subjected her to on the day of her wedding to prepare her for the marriage bed. There would be no seductively transparent silk for a nightgown, and right now she had to smell like . . . Lord knows what. Kenna had no idea what Alexander found attractive in her.

She could no longer see him.

Kenna unlaced her blouse. Walking to the bank, she quickly stripped off the dress, pulling her arms free and pushing the garment down over her hips. Her shift was a mess for all the material she'd ripped from it. But she left it on. Imagining herself naked while Alexander might be watching was too embarrassing. She removed the pouch from around her neck and tucked it into the folds of her dress.

A moment later, Kenna broke the surface of the water and ran her fingers through her wavy mass of hair. She sighed with pleasure. She was about to make love to her husband for the first time. As she floated on her back in the warm spring water, Kenna pushed aside all thoughts of the stone and the chamber above. Soon she'll tell him. But not now. Not this moment. He accepted her decision to wait. She loved him for it.

She turned and dove into the deeper water, swimming submerged in the cleansing spring-fed currents.

~

Alexander had been watching her from the moment the first lace was pulled free.

She was a vision. Like some water nymph, like some unearthly being, some goddess, she graced these waters with her beauty, with her very presence. He saw her rise out of the water for a moment, and his eyes were drawn to the shift clinging provocatively to her breasts. Alexander stopped breathing.

~

Kenna floated into the deep current. She looked in the direction Alexander had disappeared. There was still no sign of him. Suddenly, from beneath her she felt strong hands grip her waist and lift her out of the water.

She gasped, but even as she did, she knew it was her husband. He drew her legs around his waist.

"Do you really need to sneak up on me?"

"I couldn't stay away any longer."

He brushed the dark tip of her breast through the shift. She shivered involuntarily as her nipple hardened.

"What are you doing?" she asked as he started carrying her into waist-deep water. "I haven't had a chance to swim."

He stopped her complaint with a hard and thorough kiss.

"Unless you stop me, I plan to have you before I lose my mind. It has been too long, and I'm going to make love to you . . . right now."

She could not calm the violent pounding of her heart. Something within her thrilled to know that she could affect him like this. Kenna looked into his intense blue eyes.

"You say it's been too long."

"Aye, lass."

"How long?" she asked. "How long has it been?"

"You know how long it's been."

"Do I?"

"Aye. Six months. Longer. I've been faithful to you

from the moment we exchanged our vows."

She met his gaze. At that moment Kenna realized that he wasn't holding anything back. She believed him.

"It's been long enough, wouldn't you say?" he whispered, his voice husky with desire.

She didn't trust her words. She wanted him. Kenna nodded and brushed her lips softly against his.

Alexander's mouth took hers, just as his hands pulled her hard against his chest. Suddenly Kenna wanted to lose herself in him, drown in him. Her fingers locked in the strands of his wet hair and she pulled him even closer.

"Tell me what to do."

"This first time? Nothing but hold on to me. I can't bear to have you touch me. As it is, I may come apart before I even get inside of you."

Inside of you. The words clicked in her mind. She wanted him inside of her. Deep inside.

As he held her close and moved through the water, she ran her fingers along the muscles of his chest and neck. She saw his gaze wander down over the transparent material clinging to her body. She pulled herself higher and trailed her head back as he forged through the water. He kissed her chin and ran the tip of his tongue down the hollow of her throat.

When he could stand, he swept her up in his arms and carried her. Once ashore, he placed her on her feet, and she stood at the edge of the water as he picked up a blanket and spread it on the smooth rock. Her eyes focused on his manhood and she hesitated. He was huge, intimidating. She wondered how they could possibly fit together.

Before her doubts could become actions, she was back in his arms. He kissed her deeply, and Kenna shivered with excitement when he traced the swells of her breasts. She pulled back and followed the movement of his fingers and saw her nipples again come to life beneath his touch. He pushed her wet shift off her shoulders until it was held up only by the tips of her breasts. She thought she would die of the anticipation that inflamed her, so she slipped the chemise past her breasts, letting it drop to the ground. Now there was nothing that separated her body from his gaze. Nothing that separated her burning skin from his.

"You are so beautiful." His mouth descended on hers, crushing her lips with his bruising passion.

A hot, liquid yearning began to flow deep within Kenna, rising from her very core and searing her flesh with its heat. Wrapping her arms tightly around his neck, she felt Alexander's hands move down her bare back and take hold of her buttocks, lifting her against him. She moaned at the feel of his arousal pressing against her flesh.

"Husband and wife. Say it after me."

"Make me yours, Alexander."

He laid her down on the blanket and before she could move to make room for him, his mouth closed over her breast. Her mouth fell open with a gasp as he circled her hard, erect nipple with his tongue before tugging at it with his lips and teeth. She paused, paralyzed with excitement, and watched him through half-lidded eyes until she could barely lie still another moment.

He buried one hand in the heavy silken spill of her wet hair, tugging it back, exposing the stretch of her neck. He ran his tongue and lips over the skin of her throat while his other hand cupped her breast, his thumb stroking the aroused nipple.

"I wanted to do this to you from the moment Diarmad brought you back to me in the abbey."

"I was tied. Such wicked thoughts," she groaned as his hand slid down her stomach, over the downy mound, and between the folds of her womanhood. She shook from the vibration of her body's response. Her hips curled against his hand, and one leg lifted and wrapped itself around his waist and his naked buttocks.

Her blood pounded in her brain. Her body and skin were on fire, and she felt her breaths growing shorter as he continued to stroke the sensitive spot within her. Kenna threw back her head and moaned as he probed deeper and deeper into her intimate heat, and his mouth once again suckled a breast.

Sensation began to crowd out her consciousness. It was like gliding along on some fast-moving cloud, or running in a dream down some endless hill, feeling the excitement rising and never wanting it to end. But there was an urgency that told her that complete fulfillment was near at hand. Still, she didn't want it to finish. No matter how rapturous whatever lay beyond could be, she didn't want to cross that line—this time, not without him.

Blindly, she reached out for him, her fingers groping down his body until she found the long, hard shaft. The skin was hot, and he throbbed to her touch. Her hand curled around him and slid the entire length until her thumb caressed the satiny crown.

"Nay, Kenna," he groaned tearing his mouth away from her breast. "Not yet."

But in spite of his voiced reluctance, he hardly resisted as she brought the broad tip to her moist folds and pressed herself against it.

"Now, Alexander," she whispered, looking into his passion-glazed eyes. "Take me now."

Driven with the urgency to have him inside of her, she moved with him as he centered himself over her and took hold of her hips.

"You belong to me now . . . and forever."

She drew his head down, kissing him with all the passion she had in her.

As he drove into her, Kenna stiffened at first, stunned by the tearing pain of his entry. She kept her eyelids pressed shut and bit her lip to keep from crying out as he ceased to move for what seemed like an eternity. But then, gradually, she felt him begin to move, slowly at first, and then faster and faster, until her mind cast off all memory of pain, all memory of innocence, and the white-hot lights of some blazing heaven opened and consumed her.

~

"*The Macpherson ship is sailing past Oban. It's heading north.*"

Maxwell drove the point of his dagger deep into the rough-hewn table.

"*Are Alexander and his wife aboard the blasted thing?*" he *barked.*

Not an hour earlier, he'd received word from his priest's man that the two had left the camp. They'd even been given a horse by the priest and sent north to Oban, where Maxwell waited to spring the trap. But the bloody Highlanders had yet to be seen.

"*We don't know. No one saw anything. But Macpherson and the woman must have boarded somewhere, for that ship's just been sitting there a-waiting.*"

"How about the younger one... James? Where is he now?"

"He ain't moved since coming north to Oban. He's still at that inn a stone's throw from the harbor. The livery boy says, word is that he's waiting for more fighters to arrive before coming after us."

Maxwell stood up, yanked the dagger from the table, and stalked to the fire. He wouldn't be so stupid as to wait any longer. He wasn't about to waste men fighting James Macpherson after the Highlander gathered more men. And he had no way to attack that ship or put up a chase, either. It was one thing to burn a village and scare gutless tenants; it was another to fight and lose. And for what? He wasn't being paid to fight Highlanders, only to get the woman.

Evers was pushing north. Maxwell wasn't going to wait around to be chastised for what he should or shouldn't have done. There were too many coves south of Oban where those two could have been picked up. Damn them all.

He turned to his men. "We still get them to come to us."

"How?"

"If they're sailing north past Oban, then there are only three places they could be going. Benmore Castle, MacKay land in the godforsaken north, or Glosters Priory on Loch Eil. We don't have enough men to be going in all three directions."

Maxwell's men waited for him to continue.

"But we do have enough men to snatch away the ones that

matter to them," he said. "We take the right people, and the bitch will come willingly . . . and give us anything we want in exchange."

Chapter 17

Is't come to this? In faith, hath not the world
one man but he will wear his cap with suspicion?
Shall I never see a bachelor of three-score
again?

A Highland clan would fight ten years over a shaggy-haired cow and a hundred years over a barren, windswept sea marsh that no one really wanted. A broken promise over a political alliance could set two clans off, and a reneged-upon marriage contract could start bloody feuding that would cost the best warriors of a generation. Bullheaded in their ways and passionate in their opinions. There was no other way of describing a Highlander.

James Macpherson shook his head and looked into the horn holding the ale. What a bloody race he belonged to, he thought.

"And all those bloody lairds and clan chiefs are no better than the most ignorant slop boy," he muttered. Realizing he'd spoken his thoughts aloud, James looked again at the ale. Stronger than one might expect, he thought.

James had spent enough time acting as negotiator between leaders in the Highlands to know that regardless of how well they dressed or how small the issue at hand was, getting them to agree on anything was nearly a miracle. Except for one thing: when the word went out that an enemy threatened Highland soil.

Edinburgh had just been burned by the English navy while the Lowland court of King Jamie ran for cover into Fife. Sir Ralph Evers was pushing north with his army. His treasonous Lowland lackey, Donald Maxwell, had made raids almost to Oban with his men.

The time had come for the Highlanders to step up and defend their land.

James pushed his trencher of food away and looked down the long table at the inn's boisterous revelers. Focusing was becoming a problem, and he held on to the table to slow the room from spinning.

He and his men had reason to celebrate. Upon reaching Oban, he'd received word from Diarmad. The Macpherson captain was picking up Alexander and Kenna at Hermit's Rock and taking them up to the River Spey, where they'd go overland with a Macpherson escort to Benmore Castle.

And Diarmad would be back soon with enough men to stop Maxwell here.

James knew his older brother would be angry to miss out on a fight, but he had gone to a lot of trouble to get that marriage back on the right foot. Neither appeared to have killed the other during their days together, which was excellent news, and James wouldn't let anything slow them down until they were delivered to Benmore. Diarmad was also sending word to Magnus MacKay that his daughter was en route to the very place she was supposed to go to six months ago.

James tried to focus on the half-eaten trencher of food before him. He couldn't.

"Brilliant work," he muttered, congratulating himself. A month ago, he'd met with his own father, Alec Macpherson, and the MacKay laird. The marriage had to work. Both clans needed it. It was left to him to make whatever arrangements needed to be made. His job wasn't to negotiate an intricate treaty but to play matchmaker for two of the most pigheaded people he knew.

"Marriage," James snorted. He'd never been married himself. Never considered it. And the only time he'd ever met a woman that might even tempt him, she'd been promised to someone else. And a bloody Lowlander, at that!

"You say 'marriage,' love?" a wench asked in slurred

tones, dropping herself onto his lap. "I'm available, if yer askin.'"

She laughed and shouted across the table at some blurred shapes. "Ain't we available for marryin', Jeannie?"

James's head wobbled but he managed to shove the woman off his lap.

He knew nothing about matchmaking or marriage, so he'd sought out advice from experts. According to his mother and Tess, Colin's wife, the secret to love appeared to be spending uninterrupted time together. James had been able to arrange that. The plan was brilliant.

All around him, the tavern where he was staying bustled with Macpherson men and some Campbell warriors who'd already come across from Mull to join them. The food wasn't sitting well in his stomach. He pushed unsteadily to his feet.

James needed a bed—somewhere to put his head down and close his eyes for a few hours. That would mean somehow making it up the rickety stairs to the bedchamber he was sharing with a half-dozen Macpherson men.

One of his men suddenly loomed up in front of him.

"James, you look about ready to lose your innards."

A woman's voice, shrieking with laughter. "He just promised to marry me, and won't that be a great surprise to my old man!"

James pushed his way past them and lunged for the closest door. Behind the tavern, he stumbled and then doubled over, his stomach emptying, even as the ground rolled like a stormy sea.

He wobbled, trying to stay on his feet. Something was wrong. He hadn't drunk anywhere near enough to feel this way. Nay, it wasn't too much food or ale. It was something else.

The realization came too late, and James Macpherson fell flat on his face.

In a final moment of awareness, he heard the slurred sound of hushed voices and a set of boots beside his head before the world went dark.

~

As the ship pitched again, Kenna braced herself against the bulkhead in the near-darkness of the tiny cabin.

She had very little space to clean up, and getting out of her wet shift and soiled dress had been a struggle with the Macpherson ship rising and diving into every trough in the sea. The row of holes in the wooden wall let in little air and even less light, but she could hear bits and pieces of Alexander's discussion with Diarmad next door in the larger cabin beneath the stern deck.

Sailors from the Macpherson ship had arrived at Hermit's Rock too quickly. Alexander and Kenna where still wrapped in each other's arms after making love and swimming and making love and . . . it was all such a blur. Hearing their voices when they came hallooing into the cave had quickly snapped her back to reality. Her face still burned in the darkness as she recalled the smirks and knowing sidelong looks the men exchanged. Alexander didn't help things, either, by treating her so tenderly in their presence. Not too many days ago, he'd been ordering Diarmad to throw her from the abbey tower into the sea, and they all knew it. And none of this improved during the long row to the ship.

A young lad had followed them into the cabin when they arrived, carrying in a pitcher of fresh water, a washbowl, and dry cloths. Showing her the tiny space where she could get cleaned up and change, Alexander had motioned to a chest in the cabin, telling her that she'd find dresses and some linen undergarments there. Kenna immediately bristled at the thought of some other woman's clothing in her husband's cabin.

That was a conversation they'd be having in the very near future, she thought.

Ignoring the chest of clothing, Kenna eyed her own ruined garments. They were disgusting. She couldn't put them back on. Seeing a line of pegs on the bulkhead and what hung there, she realized she wouldn't have to.

Alexander stopped talking the moment Kenna stepped into the room. His gaze traveled from her bare feet and legs to the woolen jerkin that covered a coarse shirt and hung below her knees. She'd also found a rope that she wrapped twice around her waist to hold everything in place. There was nothing she could do with her hair—that untamed wilderness of brown curls had taken on a life of its own. His eyes fixed on her face.

"You look . . . beautiful."

Diarmad looked from Alexander to Kenna and back at Alexander with an expression that clearly said, *You've gone mad. Stark raving mad.*

She smiled at her husband and strode to the table where the two had been bent over a map. Diarmad moved to the far side of the table. Kenna knew the man still had to be thinking of the scratches and bruises she'd given him when he'd kidnapped her.

"What's this about?" she asked, noticing the small flat stones arranged on the map. One was sitting on what she thought must be MacKay land.

"Diarmad has learned a few things about this English commander named Sir Ralph Evers, who's pushed his men all the way to the Highlands. And there are rumors about *why* he's going so far north."

Kenna had never heard the man's name. "He's responsible for all the destruction?"

"It appears to be so."

"And he has an army of his own?"

"Small and fast moving, they say. And not entirely made up of English fighters. Outlaws and rogue Scots, all mercenaries, make up more than half of his command. And from the looks of things, he's cut his ties with Henry Tudor. There's something bigger he's after."

Kenna felt the weight of the pouch around her neck. None of this made sense. There was no logical reason why there would be any benefit in coming after her, unless it had to do with the tablet. But if that were true, then it meant others had to know of its value.

She felt the heat rising in her face. There was no way to hide her emotions. Alexander's gaze never wavered from her. He saw everything. She'd already hinted to him that there was something she was holding back.

"And Maxwell works for him," she said.

"Aye, that bloody Lowlander leads one of three fronts that Evers is pushing into the Highlands," Diarmad explained. "Maxwell is moving in the west. Another command is moving northward up the eastern coast. Evers has split the country."

Kenna was tired of speculating. "What do they want from me? Why is there a price on my head?"

Diarmad exchanged a look with Alexander and then continued. "There are rumors."

"What? What's being said?"

"Something happened to Evers when he was fighting in the Borders. He'd been doing his king's bidding. Burning monasteries. Raiding castles. Torturing and killing anyone he pleased. They say there was an old man named Cairns who died at Evers's hands. The rumors are that the old man had a gift."

Kenna's heart drummed so hard in her chest that she feared the two men must hear it. She focused on the map to avoid facing her husband's scrutiny.

"What kind of a gift?" Alexander asked.

"It sounds daft, but they say Cairns talked to the dead. The local folk swore to it. If it was witchcraft, no one complained. The old man never brought harm on anyone."

"And Evers changed after he killed Cairns?" Alexander repeated.

Diarmad shrugged. "After Cairns died, Evers stopped following the king's orders. He went where he pleased. Stopped ravaging the Borders and pushed north. Sent out raiding parties looking for specific people that he wanted. Word went out about bounties offered."

"Who were they looking for?" Kenna felt her voice had crept out of a deep well.

"A woman in clan Munro. And another who's a Mac-Donnell."

"And me," Kenna said. It wasn't a question.

Three women and Cairns. Could it be that the piece her mother gave her was one of four fragments of a larger stone? Did Cairns have one of them?

Diarmad nodded.

"Do you know the names?" Alexander asked. "We should warn their clan."

"Nay. That's all I know of them. But I sent out word to the clan chiefs in both places."

Kenna had to stop herself from pulling the pouch from under the shirt. "He put a bounty on me. He knew my name."

"They say that your mother was the one they were looking for. Once word came back that she had passed away, Evers sent his men in search of you."

"What could your mother possibly have had that is so valuable to him?" Alexander asked.

Kenna shook her head and focused on the map. Three women and an old man living in different corners of Scotland.

Questions battered her mind. How did her mother come to have such a thing? And why Sine and not her sister, Emily's mother? Sine was the elder. Did *their* mother possess it before Sine? Where did it come from originally?

And Cairns and the other two. How did they come to

have a fragment, if that's what it was? What connected them? She had the power to heal. If the old man could speak to the dead, what powers were trapped in the other fragments?

Cairns must have had many of the answers. But he was gone now, and Evers appeared to know what he knew.

Alexander broke into her thoughts. "Think, Kenna. Did your mother give you anything before she died? Pass *anything* on to you?"

She held back what she knew because she didn't know the entirety of it. Because she wasn't certain of the source of its power. Now she had to hold it back because of the danger it entailed. She would never bring that kind of peril into the life of the man she loved.

Kenna fought back the tears and shook her head.

Chapter 18

I have drunk poison while he utter'd it.

James's stomach heaved and he rolled, lifting himself on his hands and knees in time. Remnants of vile burning liquid spewed out. As the retching subsided, he became aware of noises—the sound of wind and drums—pounding in his head.

The last thing he remembered was ... what? He was at the inn in Oban. Nay, he went outside. The stamp of a horse hoof near his head. That's it. He made it outside the inn. He was on the ground.

But where was he now?

The damp smell of oat and earth invaded his senses. Still on his hands and knees, he pried open his eyes and stared at the packed-dirt floor and his own vomit. Near him, beyond the shadows that enveloped him, a thin ray of moonlight stretched down from a barred window high up a stone wall.

He sat to one side, trying to stay upright. The world outside his head began to spin. His stomach heaved again, but there was nothing left. The dry retching left him panting and sweating. He needed water.

As his situation became clearer, cold fear pushed into the fogged recesses of his brain. He'd been drugged, poisoned, and thrown into this hole. It had to be Maxwell. The bastard. Fear gave way to anger. He reached for his sword. Gone, of course. He felt for the dirk in his boot. Nothing.

Taking a deep breath, James pushed to his feet. The cell swiveled and tilted. He reached out and found a rough, wood wall and held on until the room began to steady itself.

His throat was parched, tight. A hot flush washed down his back and the accompanying weakness nearly sent him back to the ground. James pressed his back against the wall. The dungeon floor rolled again, lifting and dropping like a ship in a storm. He didn't move, but waited.

How long he stayed there, he didn't know, but then a heavy door creaked and banged shut somewhere in the distance.

James tried to think of anything that he might remember after stumbling out of the inn. Hushed voices. Boots. And then nothing. He didn't know where they'd taken him or how far. It was night, but he had no idea whether he'd been unconscious for a few hours or a few days. Was he even still in the Highlands? And why take him and not kill him? From all he'd heard, this was Evers's way. For ransom, the English bastard would deliver him piece by piece, one limb at a time, to his family until there was nothing left.

His eyes scanned the cell. Two pairs of shackles hung from iron rings driven into a wall. A few sacks of last year's oats were stacked in a corner. Just like every other castle in Scotland, the dungeon served more than one function.

It was curious that his captors hadn't put him in chains. Perhaps they didn't expect him to regain consciousness . . . ever. Ransom would still be sought.

The small barred window was built high in the wall. There were two doors: One, a stout, oak half door that he guessed led to an adjoining room. A second door had air holes drilled through the wood at eye level.

James heard heavy footsteps coming down a passage. He slipped into the shadows, pressing his back against the stone wall near the door. He'd strangle any bastard who made the mistake of coming in here.

The footsteps stopped by the door. James stood motionless, making no sound. He hoped they'd come in. The man had to be staring in through the opening.

To his disappointment, the footsteps continued down the passage.

With every passing minute, James's stomach settled a little more. His strength was returning. The cell was too small to hide any surprises. His gaze moved once again to the barred window. Below it, the iron ring and shackles.

If he was going to get out, that seemed to be the only way.

Steeling himself, he darted to the wall, jumped high enough for his boot to find a foothold in the ring, and leaped as high as he could. The ledge of the window was just a few inches beyond his reach, and he tumbled back onto the packed-earth floor.

He gathered himself for a second attempt. His timing was better this try, and his fingers just caught the stone sill of the window. Hoisting himself up, he managed to get one hand fisted around the bars.

Even in the darkness, he could see that if he could pry open the barred window, he might be able to squeeze through. It was latched on the inside to keep pilferers out of the grain storage space rather than to keep prisoners in. That's what the shackles were for.

As he was thinking about how to break the latch, a woman's cry reached him from somewhere in the dungeons behind him. James glanced back toward the door. Again, the creaking and the bang, and footsteps approached.

"Why are you doing this? Where are you taking me?"

He knew that voice. He let go of the bars and landed softly.

"Why must I wear this? Remove this hood from my head."

A tumble and a sharp gasp.

"Get up." The voice was gruff and hard.

"Don't yank me so. You're breaking my arm. I tell you, you're hurting me."

James rushed to the door and peered through the air holes into the dark passageway. They were coming. He saw the back of a man's head as the group stopped near James's cell.

An iron latch scraped and lifted. A door very near screeched on rusty hinges. James moved to the smaller door, and through a tiny slit at the very top he saw a woman roughly shoved in. She hit the ground hard and the door slammed shut behind her.

She scurried out of his line of vision. He heard her crying softly.

James waited until the footsteps retreated and they were alone before he spoke.

"Emily?"

A sailor's woolen cap she'd nipped from somewhere. And an oiled leather pouch. And extra food.

And questions for Alexander's crew. Where was the square-rigged caravel taking them and how long before they reached there? How do they lower the dory that was lashed to the deck of the ship?

She was as bloody transparent as a puddle on a sunny day. She was planning to jump ship.

What a fool he'd been, making romantic designs regarding their first night in a real bed, of sorts, in the privacy of the captain's cabin. Like some dreamy-eyed whelp, in love for the first time, he'd been making plans for wooing his wife and been ignoring everything that needed his attention on deck. Like some lovesick lad, he hadn't stopped thinking of her all day.

And all the while, she'd been making other plans.

Alexander half expected Kenna to be gone—having dropped over the side and swimming for shore—by the time he burst into the cabin. She was still here. Dressed in the same clothes as before. She was wearing a dagger at her belt. Her hair was now tucked into a wool cap, and she was wearing boots he knew she'd borrowed from the second-in-command.

She was poring over the details of the map, and leaped back from the table, clearly surprised to see him.

"Just where do you think you are going?"

"I don't know what you're talking about."

He approached. "Don't lie to me. Everyone has been telling me, word for word, what you've been asking."

She moved, keeping the table between them. "So now I'm not allowed to speak to the sailors?"

"Of course you are . . . unless you have ulterior motives."

"Is that what they told you?" she asked, her violet eyes flashing at him. "That I have *motives*?"

"Nay, woman. If any of them said such a thing about you, I'd have thrown him overboard straightaway." He moved in one direction, and she countered, keeping him away from her. "That's what I concluded, knowing you so well."

She snorted. "You don't know me at all."

Alexander was relieved she was still here, but they were playing a game of cat and mouse. And what a fool he'd been to think she was done playing runaway games.

"Know you? I know the trouble you're about to get into before you even *think* of getting into it. Nay, wife. I know you very well."

"Oh, so you've suddenly become brilliant. I can name a half dozen village idiots with more brains than you. And stop calling me 'wife.' Word of our annulment could come any day, thank the Lord."

"Bloody hell, lass. Have you already forgotten that cave?"

She looked in the direction of the door. "No one knows anything about that."

"I know and you know and God knows. And that bairn growing in your belly knows, too."

"So you're a midwife now, as well." Her face flushed. "Bairns aren't conceived so fast."

"I suppose the Mother Superior told you that."

They stopped circling the table, and Kenna shook her head. "You can't keep me against my will. I'm telling you now that I wish to return to the priory."

Alexander had spent enough time with her to know there was something different about her at this moment. This wasn't the willful Kenna of before who would be difficult just for the sake of a good fight. Her eyes were red and puffy; she'd been crying. She avoided meeting his gaze. She didn't want to be touched. There was a catch in her voice when she said she wanted to go back to the nuns at Loch Eil. He tried to reach her, but she moved again.

"We made a promise."

"Promises get broken. You have to let me go. I have to get off this ship."

Alexander knew there wasn't another woman like this one in all of Scotland. She embodied physical courage and ability that many men lacked. And she had determination. If she'd really set her mind to go—if her heart truly wanted it—she would have been gone already.

Nay, perhaps a part of her wanted to leave, but the greater part of her wanted to stay. On that he would stake his life. He had to convince that other part to be reasonable.

"Let's talk about whatever it is that's bothering you."

She shook her head. "Nay, it's too late."

"It's never too late." Alexander stopped and planted both fists on the table, facing her. Her gaze darted into every corner of the cabin but not once at him. He saw the vulnerability she was trying to hide, and he saw the fear. She was as frightened now as he'd seen only once before . . . outside of the hermit's door back in the cave. It stung him to think he was responsible for it. He gentled his tone. "Whatever is wrong, it must involve me. You're angry with me. Tell me what I've done."

Her lower lip quivered, but she held her head up and shook her head. "You've done nothing wrong. Please, let me go, Alexander. It's for the best."

"Best for whom? It's the two of us, now and forever. Remember?"

As the tears broke through the shield she'd erected, the point of some invisible blade slipped between his ribs. Alexander breathed in sharply as the point touched his heart. In the next moment, he had her in his arms. He pulled off her cap and her hair tumbled down in shimmering waves. As he drew her head against his chest, he found himself mumbling what had to sound like nonsense. She remained in his embrace, no longer fighting him but crying softly. It was some time before he found his voice to speak again.

"Tell me what's wrong."

Her tears seeped through his shirt. It was a few moments before she spoke.

"For once I'm trying to do what's best for everyone. Why won't you let me go?"

"I don't care what's best for everyone. I won't let you go. Not ever again. And if you run away, I'm coming after you. And I promise you, I'll pull down the walls of that priory one stone at a time, if I have to. And that goes for anywhere else you try to hide."

He wiped away the wetness from her silky cheeks and lifted her chin until he could swim in the violet depths of her eyes.

"Diarmad told you," she wept. "Weren't you listening? They're after me. I'll only bring danger to you, wherever you take me. I can't do that to your people."

"And how will you protect yourself by running away? By facing those villainous vermin alone?" He touched her cheek. "Not as long as I live. There's no battle ahead of us that you and I won't fight together."

"Alexander—"

"Hush, lass." He stepped back and sat down on the edge of the bed. He drew her down onto his lap. "But there's something else. Something you promised to tell me before. It's time. Tell me."

She looked into his eyes and nodded. There was no hesitation. She batted away the wetness on her cheeks.

"After you hear what I have to say—after you know the truth—I want you to know it's not too late to send me away."

"Kenna, I don't care what you've done. I don't care if you've bedded the pope or murdered him. I will *never* send you away."

"It isn't something I've done." She took his hand, tracing his fingers with hers. "First, I want you to know that what I'm about to tell you, and show you, is mostly a mystery to me. I have so many unanswered questions. And I don't even know who to go to for answers."

He said nothing and waited for her to continue.

She reached inside the neckline of her shirt and pulled out a leather pouch. Lifting the cord over her head, she placed it in his palm.

"This was given to me by my mother. Well, not exactly given. I found it on the day of our wedding, tucked among other gifts she'd left me. I think this is what Evers is after. This is the reason he's offered a bounty for finding me."

"What is it?"

She opened the pouch and dropped a piece of carved stone into his palm.

It was cold to the touch. The edges were rough, as if it had been broken off of a larger tablet. Alexander lifted it to the light and stared at the unusual markings that had smoothed with age. The markings meant nothing to him, but the fragment seemed to be very old.

"Do you feel it?"

"Feel what?" he asked.

"The warmth. The power that runs through it."

He met her gaze. "I feel nothing. To me, it's just a piece of stone."

"Touch my hand."

He did. Her smooth palm was cool and steady.

Kenna took the stone out of his hand and held it out in her palm for only a moment. Then she dropped it in her lap and touched his forearm. Her hand radiated heat, and Alexander felt a surge of energy race up his arm from the place where her hand lay.

"I feel that, by 'sblood." He took her hand and turned it over in amazement. "How . . . ?"

"It's not my doing. It's the tablet."

He picked up the piece again. It was cool. The feel of it was no different from before.

"It reacts to you, but not to me. You said this was your

mother's? Do you have memories of her using it when you were a child?"

"I never saw the stone before the day of our wedding," she said. "What I remember is that she always wore the pouch around her neck. She never parted with it. And she was a gifted healer. I thought it just a lucky charm, the same as many folk wear. When I ran away to the priory, I wore it because it belonged to my mother. It was no precious jewel, so it also matched my new life of simplicity and poverty. I never thought it held any power."

"When did you realize there was something different about it?"

"Sometimes, when I was tending to people who were in pain, I would feel it through the pouch. It became warm against my skin. It still meant nothing. I saw no connection between the feeling and the people I was tending to." She looked into his eyes. "Until you."

"Aye. You saved me, Kenna, when you cared for my wounds."

"It was this tablet," she said softly. "Those wounds, all the blood you'd lost. There was nothing I could have done to close that gash. I was frightened. Desperate. I thought you were going to die."

"What did you do?"

"I hoped, I wished, I prayed that this piece of stone was something more than just a lucky trinket that my mother carried around out of habit. I took it out. I held it in my hand."

"And then what happened? How did you know what to do?"

"I didn't know. But as soon as my fingers wrapped around it, something went through me. Heat. Lights. And there were faces and voices, directing me. Telling me what to do."

She touched his side where the wound had been. He felt the soothing warmth in her fingers even now.

"It was a miracle. I didn't understand it, but I thought I had mastered it. I thought I knew all there was to know about the power it held. But I was wrong."

"The pain was even worse the next day."

She nodded. "I knew what I had to try again. I hoped for the same miracle," she said. "So at the standing stones where Jock led us, I tried again, grasping for faith—and magic, if that was at the heart of it—and it worked. This time it worked even better. You became whole. You had your strength back."

"You saved my life twice."

"Not I. The power lies in this." She looked steadily into his eyes. "And I am more certain than anything I've ever known that the power doesn't come from witchcraft or from the devil. This power of healing comes from somewhere good and holy. I know it."

Kenna lay the stone in his palm and held his hand in hers. Alexander felt a rush of heat where their skin touched. The power traveled up his arm, into his body. The sensation was soothing. It settled into his joints. It moved outward into his limbs.

"But you bring it to life. Only you," he reminded her. "And it appears your mother had the same ability before you."

She nodded and slid the tablet into the pouch. "And the way it responds to me has changed since the first time I used it on you."

"How?"

"It's becoming a part of me. I don't need to take the stone out and hold it. Back at that camp by the loch, I never once reached for it, but I still felt it in my hands. The power of the stone was now mine to command." She put the pouch beside them on the bed. "I'm learning how to use it, and in return it's . . . it's accepting me."

Alexander was enveloped in a state of serenity. To his thinking, there was nothing improbable about a healing stone. He'd grown up in the Highlands, a magical and mysterious land. The facts were simple and clear. Kenna had a gift, and it was his responsibility to protect her.

"Have you noticed any feeling of, I don't know, threat coming from the stone and directed toward yourself?" he asked. "Any sense of danger when you hold the relic?"

"Not from this." She touched the pouch. "Not at all. But I had strange feelings when we were at Hermit's Rock. The underground chamber. Those walls. The door."

"The markings on them."

She shivered. "When I reached out to touch them, I had a sensation of burning. Whatever spiritual power, whatever magic exists in that chamber, it didn't want me in there."

Alexander wished he'd paid closer attention to the old stories about the hermit who lived in that chamber. There were people he could ask at Benmore Castle. His father might remember it, too. He gathered her closer to his chest. She was much calmer now.

"Are we done with this foolishness of running away?"

She looked into his eyes. "Somehow Sir Ralph Evers knows about the tablet. That's the only explanation of why he would want me."

"I don't give a damn what he wants. He'll have no chance against us once we reach Benmore Castle."

"But how could I lead him to your door? I am still the woman who ran away from our marriage, though contracts were signed and vows exchanged. Your people would never forgive me. Hell could freeze over before they accept me."

He drew her mouth to his and kissed her deeply. By

the time he ended it, she had her arms around his neck, kissing him back with equal fervor.

"The Macphersons will accept you and vow their allegiance to you and fight for you," he whispered against her lips. "You're my wife. You're their mistress. And you've saved my life. Not once, but twice. That alone places you up there with Saint Fillan, at the very least."

"But I'm no saint."

He smiled, feeling her breast through her clothing. "And that's the best bit of news for me, but they don't have to know that."

~

The river ran strong with the recent rains, and Sir Ralph looked from the water rushing beneath the nine stone arches of the bridge to the letter in his hand.

The message from the duke of Hertford was crystal clear. On no account was Evers to take his troops north of this river. All military engagement was to focus on the Borders. All treasure recovered was to be sent south to the duke and thence to the king's coffers.

Julius Caesar faced this moment, Evers thought. Do not cross the Rubicon, the Roman Senate warned. Do not advance any closer to Rome with your armies. Caesar knew his moment of destiny was at hand. Cross the river and defy the

Senate, or remain and follow orders. Take command of his own fate . . . or disappear into the oblivion of history.

Most men would have greatness, but fear to do what they must to achieve it. And then there are the few who see the tide rising and use it to carry them to the heights.

Caesar crossed the Rubicon with his army, burned the bridges behind him, marched into Rome, and became emperor.

This river is my own Rubicon, Evers thought. Cross the bridge, and there is no turning back. This bridge will take me to greatness . . . or ruin.

North of the river, three more pieces of the stone tablet awaited him. Great power awaited him. Thrones and immortality awaited him.

I'll not deny my destiny, he told himself. I will be king.

Signaling to his commanders, he spurred his horse across the bridge.

At the horizon to the north, beneath the cloud-covered peaks of distant mountains, lay the heart of Scotland.

Chapter 19

And when I liv'd I was your other wife;
And when you lov'd, you were my other
husband.

Kenna leaned her back against the door and glared in the dim light at the trunk. Who was he to be ordering her to wear one of these dresses? Nobody ordered her what to do, what to wear, how to behave. When these men were done in the commander's cabin, she was tempted to stuff her husband into one of these dresses and parade him on deck.

Kenna kept her temper under control. She knew what Alexander was trying to do now. He was making arrangements as if it were their wedding night. A clean cabin and a sumptuous dinner.

Even as she thought of it, she felt herself softening . . . again. The romantic beast.

Still, these dresses! Standing naked in the small closet,

she stared at the wooden chest filled with women's clothing. Her old dress and shift were gone, probably thrown
overboard by her husband.

"Oh!" she fumed, stomping on the shirt and rough
wool jacket she'd just discarded. "Miserable, sweet,
Macpherson worm."

Six months. Six months ago, she'd disappeared into
the night. And that was the right thing!

She couldn't do this. Six months ago, he'd turned up in
that French whore's bed. And now he was asking her to
wear a dress that had to belong to one of his mistresses.
He expected her to wear a dress that he'd probably peeled
off the willing body of another woman.

"By the Virgin, Kenna," she murmured in torment.
"What are you doing?"

Kenna would have walked right out into the cabin and
given him a piece of her mind if it weren't that she could
hear the voices of men coming. She decided they might
notice that she was wearing nothing.

"Almost ready, wife?"

"Wife? Wife? I'll give you a wife, you fickle, wench-
chasing sea slug," she grumbled under her breath, trying
to push the chest open. It wouldn't budge.

"What did you say?"

"The blasted thing doesn't open. It's sealed shut."

Kenna jumped as the door swung open, and Alexander stepped in, closing it behind him.

"I thought I latched that," she told him.

His back was to her, and he filled the closet with his height, his shoulders nearly stretching from wall to wall. This close to him, she felt herself melting. All she wanted right now was to touch him, to feel his powerful body against hers.

That's what making love in that cave had done to her.

She had a vague recollection of being angry with him, but she couldn't remember what she'd been upset about. This man did something to her brain when she was this close to him; rational thought evaporated like a morning mist in the sun. Nothing was left in her head but thoughts of his lips on her breasts and his arousal against her.

"Seriously?" he asked, opening the trunk as if it weighed no more than a feather. "You couldn't open this?"

There wasn't enough room for Kenna to reach for the clothing at her feet without bumping in to him.

"You're weaker than I thought, lass. A solid meal tonight should help."

"Aye, no doubt. Now get out, you lump."

He turned and, as his eyes drifted over her body, a devilish gleam came into his eyes.

"I see I've been summoned here on false pretenses."

Kenna tried to step back, but she had nowhere to go.

The way his eyes raked over her breasts and down the length of her body made her shiver in spite of herself. She tried to cover her breasts, but he took hold of her wrists.

"Nay, woman. Not after doing this to me."

"Doing what?"

He turned her around and pushed her hands flat against the wall. She tried to lower them, but he pushed them back up and held them with one hand. The tip of a finger moved down along her spine, starting at the nape of her neck and slowly caressing every inch until he reached the cleft of her bottom. Gently, he pushed her feet apart with one boot and released her hands. She gasped when he took hold of her hips and stepped between her legs.

"Doing this."

She felt his teeth scrape over the skin beneath her ear. His kilt pressed to her back. No layer of tartan could hide his arousal. She'd done that to him.

"I . . . I didn't plan it," she whispered, already shaking with need as one hand lifted the weight of her breast and the other caressed her stomach and slid still lower. His fingers found her already damp folds and liquid fire instantly coursed through her. He suckled her earlobe, and she leaned her head back against him.

"You don't need to be shy with me."

He squeezed her breast and the play of his fingers in

and out of her flesh had her body humming to the most tantalizing song.

"I... I..." Too lost in the waves of pleasure, she couldn't imagine what she was about to say. Her eyes closed as the pressures within suddenly carried her upward. At that moment, Kenna gave herself to Alexander to do as he wished, welcoming it, aching for it. She had no control. She wanted none. She was his.

Then, the release came in a rush. She grabbed his wrist but then soared an instant later when he didn't ease his touch.

In that moment, she didn't know if she was standing or floating. She couldn't even recall the floor beneath her feet. It didn't matter. His voice came to her from a distant cloud.

"This is exactly how I dreamed you would be. You are the woman I imagined."

She leaned to one side and dug her fingers in his hair, kissing him deeply.

The force of his passion was dizzying. He turned her in his arms and pressed her back against the wall.

"Put your legs around me."

She did as he lifted her. He slid into her, and she sighed with pleasure.

Kenna wrapped her arms around his neck. She moved her hips, drawing him in, feeling the length and size of him inside. Her body ached for him to move.

"I'm sorry that I can't go through that door right now and take my time making love to you."

She shook her head in agreement. "I think we might alarm your sailors."

He lifted her buttocks and then slid hard into her once. His voice was husky with feeling. "Only you and I will be here for dinner."

She arched her back and rocked, wanting more.

"And after?" she asked. "Will you make love to me after?"

Six months ago, no one sang the praises of this aspect of marriage. No one thought to mention the miracle of how bodies fit together. No one even hinted at the pleasures to be found in mating.

He lifted her, slid into her almost to the end of his cock and then drove into her again. She gasped at the exquisite pleasure of him.

"Aye, after dinner," he growled, "and for as many times as you'll have me. So long as you don't kill me."

"Really? I can kill you with lovemaking?"

"Aye, love. And I hope you remember to try."

~

Putting his shoulder to the door that separated them,

James shoved as hard as he could, but his legs couldn't budge it. The door was thick and solid, and the latch and hinges were on Emily's side.

They'd brought her in, awake. He had a dozen questions she might be able to answer. Where they were, where they'd captured her, how many men were guarding them, possible routes of escape. Anything that she had seen that might shed some light on their situation. But all of that would have to wait. He guessed the dawn would bring greater troubles.

"So much has happened since I saw you last. I was so hoping I'd get a chance to speak to you," Emily whispered.

He was trying to keep their talk and any noise to a minimum. He didn't want to attract the attention of their jailors.

"Try the latch ... the hinges. Are you sure there's no way to open it?"

He heard the noise of rusty metal protesting. She was trying the bolt again. There was a grunt, knocking.

"The bolt won't budge. It looks to be rusted in place."

He could tell she was kneeling by the door.

"It looks like we're stuck here," she said. "Can I tell you about a talk I had with my father when I got back to Craignock Castle?"

"Not now. There's no time. We have to hurry," he said.

"There's a high window here in this cell. There must be one in yours, too. If I can get this one open, I'll climb out through and fetch you from outside of your window."

There was a momentary pause. "Oh, please James, don't. Don't leave me with these animals."

"Listen. I won't leave you. I'll be—"

"Wait," she interrupted. "The top hinge. It looks rusted and cracked."

James looked around his cell and tried to imagine if hers looked any different. "Can you see anything you can use to break it? Something heavy to hit the hinge with? Or something to pry it free."

"Wait. I'll look."

James moved to the corridor door, peering through the holes, listening for any steps that might be coming their way. A loud reverberating bang came from Emily's cell. He rushed to the connecting door. "What are you doing?"

"I found a large rock under some sacks of grain in one corner. It's heavy, but I'm trying to knock off the hinge."

"Take aim and do it quickly. Hit it with all your strength, but just once."

There was another loud bang. James looked from one door to the other, waiting for their guards to come charging down the hall.

Another bang and there was the sound of wood splintering.

"I did it! The top hinge is gone."

"Step back."

"Can you push the door open now?"

He backed up until he reached the opposite wall. Steeling himself, he dropped his shoulder and rushed the door. The thick oak portal flew open with a crack and he found himself sprawled on the packed dirt floor of the adjoining cell.

As he rolled over to stand, Emily rushed into his arms, clutching him around the neck.

"Thank you. Thank you, James. You've saved my life."

"Not yet I haven't." Prying himself free, he pushed her back so he could see her. "What did they do to you, lass?"

Even in the darkness, he saw that her clothes were in disarray and her dress and hair were covered with dust and straw. In spite of it all, she looked beautiful to him. Her misty eyes looked up into his with adoration. Her breasts rose and fell with each breath.

"I can't tell you how happy I am," she said, "that you're here, too."

"You wanted me to be captured?"

"Nay, of course not. I mean . . ." she faltered. "But I have so much to tell you."

"Not now—there's not enough time." James knew he had to act quickly. He had no idea how long it would be before dawn. Still, coming face to face with her, he realized that he'd missed her more than he could ever admit. Whether it was Emily who moved into his arms again or James who pulled her in, it didn't matter. She was there, every warm curve pressed against him. And he held on to her for longer than he had any right to. Finally, he pushed her away.

"About my talk with my father," she started.

"Not now." He searched the dark corners of the cell for anything that might be of use to them. The stone was large enough to crush a man's skull. And there were more sacks of grain here than he'd found in his cell.

James peered up at the window. It was barred and latched as his was, but one of the bars was missing. He started stacking sacks of grain on top of each other.

"How did they get you?"

"I went out with three of Kester's men to check on the bairn Kenna delivered. They overpowered us."

"How far away were you from Craignock?"

"Just a few hours north."

"Why would you ride that far away?" he asked, suddenly angry. "You've seen how ruthless these bastards are. But what castle is this?"

"Stop lecturing me." She dragged a sack of oats to him.

James promised himself that he'd give her a serious lecture as soon as they were out of here. "Did you see where they were taking you?"

"They bound me and tied a bag over my head and tossed me in the back of a hay wain."

"How long were you in the cart?"

She shook her head. "I don't know. I was too upset to pay attention."

James climbed up the sacks. Balancing himself, he jumped and his fingers caught hold of the sill. He pulled himself up.

"Where are you going?" She was up on the sacks and tugging at his kilt. James cursed under his breath. She had no idea what a distraction she was. He lowered himself back down.

"I need to see what we're dealing with."

"You said you wouldn't leave me here."

"I'm not leaving you."

James pulled himself up again. As with the window in his cell, this opening was for delivering grain to the cellars. The bars were meant to keep thieves out. But with one of the bars missing, the opening was large enough for a child, or possibly a woman.

He looked out at an alleyway. On the ground across the way, the missing bar lay in the dirt against a wall. He looked in both directions as far as he could.

"What do you see?"

"A dark alleyway. No one is in sight. At the end of the building, there's a hay wain."

"Perhaps the one they brought me in."

He let go and landed on the sacks. She was standing just below him.

"I have an idea," he said. "I don't like it, but if you can squeeze through that window, the other bar is in the alley. You give it to me so that I can pry the window open. Then I follow you out."

"Let's wait here until daylight, when there are more people about. We could blend in and escape then."

James shook his head. "It's not safe to stay here. They could come back for us."

"Not in the middle of the night."

"We have to get out now," he ordered. James reached down to help Emily climb up next to him. But the sacks shifted, and she lost her balance. Clutching at his hips, she pulled him with her, and the two of them tumbled to the ground. She landed with a soft "Oomph!" on top of him.

He tried to cushion her fall, and his hand inadvertently found a breast. He yanked his hand away but somehow ended up holding on to her buttocks as they rolled. Now, with her beneath him and his cock nestled intimately between her legs, James found himself staring into large round eyes.

He couldn't believe it. He was becoming aroused even as danger threatened their very lives.

"Well, lass, this is a first," he said under his breath.

She never pushed him away, but bent her knees, which only made matters worse.

"A first what?"

"I don't think this is a discussion we should be having."

Even in the dim light, he saw the look change in her eyes, and the fire surged in his loins.

He jumped up before his brain ceased to function. Moving away from her, he piled the stacks up again and climbed to the top.

"You're in such a hurry to get out of here. Fine, help me up."

She started scaling the side of his body, using him like a ladder before he was ready to lift her.

He lifted her up. And a sharp knee bone dug into his shoulder. Skirts draped around his head. Another push, and somewhere under those layers of cloth, he touched the silkiest skin he'd ever encountered. And then she was out through the window.

Her blond head appeared. "Stay there, until I come for you."

"Do you see the bar? Hand it to me."

"Wait. I have to hide. Someone's coming."

Chapter 20

Man is a giddy thing, and this is my
conclusion.

The dinner Alexander arranged for his wife was not as grand as something from the kitchens of Benmore or Castle Varrich, but it was the best his cook could prepare, considering the short notice and limited supplies.

Sitting across from Kenna and watching her eye the platters with little interest, Alexander decided the limited selection was not the source of her discontent. She'd had the same expression on her face since coming out of the smaller cabin wearing a green dress that she'd covered with a large blanket. With the bloody thing draped over her shoulder, she'd hidden every bit of herself, from neck to knee.

He knew better to ask what was going on with her. Whatever problem was banging about in that beautiful head of hers, it would surface soon enough, and she'd let him have it.

And when he'd weathered that storm, whatever it was, he'd lure her to bed.

Alexander started eating. He was going to need all of his strength, if there was any justice in the universe.

One savory piece of mutton and a half cup of wine later, and she couldn't hold it in any longer.

"Well, aren't you going to ask me?"

He looked up innocently into the flashing eyes and immediately became hard at the recollection of what they'd been doing in that tiny cabin such a short time ago.

Down, wanton, he told himself. Too soon. Too fast. Focus on something else, man.

She'd braided her hair into a single rope that draped over one shoulder. And if Kenna thought that he wouldn't find that appealing, he'd show her a few ways to use that braid to his advantage when they made love. And that would be soon, very soon. He smiled.

"Ask me," she ordered, stabbing some mutton with her knife and depositing it on her trencher.

"Ask you what?" He should have removed all sharp objects from her reach.

"Ask me why I am wearing this blanket."

"Because you're cold?"

"Nay, I'm not cold."

"Because you were cold?"

"I wasn't cold."

"Because you plan to be cold?"

"Stop with the cold. It's July!" she snapped. The meat was on her plate, but the knife was waving about dangerously. "The cold has nothing to do with why I'm wearing this."

"Very well. Let me see. You were embarrassed."

"About what?"

"Isn't it obvious?' He cocked his head toward the other cabin. "I open that door and find you standing there naked as a sea nymph, intent on luring me in, attacking me, and making what some might call brazen sexual demands. Now you're a wee bit embarrassed, so you're overreacting with this horse blanket."

The colors in her face would have put a bonfire to shame. She opened her mouth a couple of times before the words spilled out. "You ... are ... a ... I never ... I didn't—"

"Didn't enjoy it, wife?" he asked, reaching under the table, touching her knee. She immediately moved out of his reach.

"Don't distract me."

"Did you or didn't you?"

"You're changing the subject entirely."

He sat back in the chair, goblet in hand. "If you're annoyed because our lovemaking was too short ..."

"It wasn't too short."

"But I didn't please you."

"You . . . you . . ." Still holding the knife, she shoved to her feet with such force that the chair tumbled back and the blanket fell from her shoulder.

Alexander's gaze was immediately drawn to the neckline of the dress. The bodice was tight, and her breasts were nearly spilling. Ah, yes. Thank you, Lord. There is justice.

The pouch Kenna wore around her neck was now hanging from a ribbon at her waist. He put the cup of wine on the table. He wanted his hands free.

She came around the table and he pushed back his chair, watching her with a great deal of interest. If today was any indication of what their future life would be, Alexander knew he may have found heaven on earth.

"I'm angry with you and you're smiling."

"I can't help it. You entertain me." He took hold of the hand with the knife as she reached him. "Let go of this, love."

"Why? I have designs on using it."

"Nay, you don't. We both know how you feel about me. So as soon as you'd stab me, then you'd have to heal me. And since we're starting the next stage in our journey in the morning, I think we can find far better use for the night hours."

She paused for a moment, her eyes spitting fire.

Pulling her hand out of his grasp, she tossed the knife onto the table.

"Now, words, Kenna. Not temper. Words."

Hands on her hips, she exploded. "A trunk full of women's clothes, you artless measle. You, a married man and yet you have enough clothes in there to dress ten mistresses. And don't try to tell me that they belong to Diarmad."

"I really don't think they'd look as good on him as this one does on you."

"And then," she sailed on, ignoring him, "you're tickle-brained enough to expect me to wear one of them. How in the devil's name could a beast sink so low—"

"My mother's," he said calmly. "And Tess's."

"What?" She stopped.

"Aye, lass. I'm not the only Macpherson that uses this ship. Colin spends more time in command of this vessel than I do. And more often than not, Tess is with him. And my parents still travel, you know. That dress belongs to Fiona or Tess, though I'll be damned if I know which one."

"Oh."

Alexander held her gaze. "And as for mistresses, when I said I haven't been with another woman since we exchanged our marriage vows, I meant it."

Her blush ran to an even deeper hue than before, and

it spread nicely down the neckline of her creamy skin. He wanted to follow it with his mouth, and he felt the stirrings of sex.

"Speechless for the second time in a matter of minutes." He smiled, taking hold of her hips and drawing her between his legs.

"You should have told me."

"You should have asked me."

"I thought . . . I assumed the worst." She was staring at his shoulder, avoiding his eyes.

He ran his hands up her sides, using his thumbs to trace the curves beneath her breasts, admiring the fullness. He felt the intake of breath, the expansion of her ribs.

"You, my wee, knife-wielding warrior. What am I going to do with you?"

"Keep me, perhaps?" She leaned into him. "And somehow put up with my bursts of temper?"

Alexander raised her chin until their gazes locked. "I will, but maybe you don't need to be pointing a dagger at me anytime you don't have the answer to a question."

"I can't stop being who I am. I was raised by men, and I have a mind of my own. I'll be a complete embarrassment to you."

"I very much doubt that." He brought her closer and brushed his lips across the skin beneath her ear, on her neck, placing soft kisses on top of each breast. "And I cherish this wild side of you. You're a Highland lass, born and bred, and I wouldn't have you any other way."

"I'll remind you of that the next time you're chewing my head off because of something I've done."

"No fear, Kenna. I never lose my temper."

"Alexander?" she drawled. "We're speaking honestly now."

"Just so." He pulled her closer, unable to stop himself. "But you see, I've decided never to be angry with you. You're all passion and fire. This is who you are."

"I'm going to have you say that before witnesses."

"I'll sign it in blood, if you like."

She looked into his eyes. "I see. Now I know why you're talking so sweetly to me."

"Do you, now. And why is that?"

"You're determined that I be carrying your child before we reach Benmore."

Alexander's throat tightened at the thought of their children romping through the halls at Benmore Castle. He wondered if she said it because she wanted it, too.

"Well, wife, making love to you is a noble pursuit." He kissed her smiling lips, but gently, knowing that if he pressed her too much right now, she'd fight him.

Instead, she leaned into his touch as he fondled her breast, and her breath caught as he stroked the nipple.

"But right now, I'd like to take my time."

She edged closer into the angle of his legs, pushing against the cloth of his kilt until his hardening cock pressed against her thigh.

"Impossible," she whispered. "Every time we make love, it's faster and more powerful than the time before. We're like a spark to dry wood. The flame bursts upward, consuming us instantly. How much time can we possibly have?"

"Are you doubting me?"

"I'm questioning myself. You touch me . . . and I come apart." She pressed her lips into his hair as he pulled at the laces that held her gown together.

"Well, that's a high praise, but tonight I intend to feast repeatedly on your body. Unlike our first time, no one will interrupt us."

"And if they do?"

"They will have short shrift before going overboard. And I made that clear."

"So, of the two of us, you're the only one feasting tonight?"

She took a sharp breath as Alexander's fingers pulled open the dress. She sank against him as his lips found the curves above the neckline of the silk shift.

"Aye," he growled. "I'm the *only* one."

Slowly, ever so slowly, he peeled the dress down her shoulders, worked it over her hips, and let it pool at her feet. He pushed it away with a boot.

The thin linen cloth molded to her body. Her breasts strained to break free of the tight confines.

"Everything I tried was too small. I'm larger than your mother and Tess."

She tried to cover herself but Alexander took hold of her hands and pulled them away. He gazed in rapt admiration at the creation before him.

"You're perfect, a goddess," he whispered, his voice husky with desire.

Alexander's thumbs crossed her ribs, and he felt her shiver as he gently caressed the subtle curves of her belly.

"I look forward to our bairn growing inside you." He stopped, cursing himself. He'd forbidden himself from mentioning it, but his mouth ran ahead of his resolution.

He felt her grow tense in his grasp.

"It's difficult to think of such things with so much danger haunting me. We must think about Evers and Maxwell."

He reached up and pressed a finger to her lips. "They'll be taken care of. I promise you that. They'll not be haunting you for long."

She kissed his finger and nodded. "If the time ever comes that we have a bairn, both our clans will be celebrating for days."

"And what about you?" He searched her face. "Will you be happy, too?"

She bit her lip. The blush was back again, blooming in her cheeks. Alexander didn't realize he'd been holding his breath until he saw her nod.

"I believe I will. But I want a child only after we've put an end to the evil dogging our steps."

"I swear that I will keep you and our bairn safe and out of harm's reach."

"And I swear I'll cherish motherhood when I have tamed you enough that you submit to all of my fantasies, to every one of my hidden wishes."

Fantasies? Hidden wishes? It was becoming increasingly difficult to focus on words when she stood before him, a seductress. She would win any battle with him negotiating in such state of undress.

"Tell me about these . . . these hidden wishes."

One of the shoulder straps fell on her arm, revealing the milky-white flesh of her breast.

"You will obey all of my commands."

"You know we'll have summer flowers in winter before such day comes." Alexander pulled both of the straps down her arms and drew her onto his lap, holding her captive.

"Barbarian."

"But before you pull your dirk on me again, know that

failing to obey commands has always been a quality I take pride in. I follow my own path."

She punched him in the chest. "Even the most beef-witted of men can do that."

"But I will respect you, my wife." He placed a kiss on her exposed shoulders, tasting her soft flesh. Kenna didn't try to resist. "Now tell me about these fantasies of yours."

"The list is long."

"We have all night. Tell me."

"In a moment. But first, before we reach Benmore Castle, I want you to tell me everything there is to know about your family. Your parents, your brothers, their likes and dislikes. I want the absolute truth and no tomfoolery. I want to make a good impression on them. I've put myself at a disadvantage already."

"To hell with all of them. You've married me. Not them."

"Alexander?" She pulled open the front of his shirt and paused with her lips hovering over his skin. "I thought you were going to be agreeable."

"Very well. I'll tell you everything you need to know."

She kissed him and then laid her head on his shoulder. He traced the edge of her gown where the tops of her breasts rose and fell alluringly.

"And I want to go home to Castle Varrich for a time."

"Nay, lass. That's impossible."

"I need to make peace with my father."

"He'll be coming to Benmore. I've already sent a message to him."

"It's been too long since I've seen my brothers."

"I'll make arrangements for them to come to you, too."

She looked into his eyes. "You're being disagreeable."

He pulled the chemise down below her breasts. He ached with desire for her. "I want to hear about the fantasies, whatever that means."

She pulled the silky fabric back up. "I've been sharing my wishes with you."

"So far, they've all been orders."

"They're *my* wishes."

"Then perhaps you should throw in a fantasy here and there to keep my attention."

Her fingers stroked the soft wool of Alexander's kilt, moving from his knee toward his groin.

"Will you be agreeable to going north to Castle Varrich if I go along with this game of yours?"

"Nay, lass. I'll listen to your arguments, but that's the end of it."

"Not enough," she snorted. "You need to learn to compromise."

Alexander looked into her flushed face, working hard to ignore the heavenly pleasure of her hand on his thigh.

She wasn't giving up. Finally, he nodded.

"We'll both compromise." He kissed her lips. "Now, it's time for a fantasy."

She stared at his bare chest.

"I want you to show me how to please you."

This is what she calls fantasy? he thought. This *is* heaven.

"Please me? Lass, you *do* please me. I am ... beyond gratified."

Kenna stood and turned in his arms until she faced him. Their gazes never wavered when she leaned down, placing a kiss on his lips. "Tell me or show me or I have to venture into this on my own."

Alexander's eyes dropped to her breasts, the nipples barely holding on to the silk. The heat was pulsing into his loins. He was in trouble. All he could think about was having her straddle him where he sat and burying himself in her.

She grabbed a fistful of his hair and pulled back until his gaze lifted from her breasts to her face. "Tell me what I should do or I go back to wishes."

Alexander gripped her thighs. Then, slowly—very slowly—he began to gather the shift below her knees. "Just use your imagination, Kenna. Do whatever you want to me."

She shivered when his hands slid under the raised

hem, moving his palms across her naked buttocks. Taking his advice to heart, she tugged his shirt up over his head. Dropping the linen garment beside her, she let her hands travel, exploring his back, his shoulders, his chest, tracing the scars and muscle.

Alexander groaned when she followed her fingers' trail with her mouth. She watched him—waiting for his reaction to the effect of her mouth on his skin. He tried to touch her, return the pleasure, but she pushed his hands away. She was in command of her curiosity, his body, his mind.

Slowly, she lowered herself in front of him, and as her mouth traced a path down his stomach, he took a deep breath and held it for so long that he finally gasped for breath.

Alexander's hands reached for Kenna's braid and pulled it back. Their eyes locked. "What are you doing to me?"

"Using my imagination."

"You're making me lose my mind."

She smiled. "You have my permission."

She placed her hands on his thighs and slid them slowly upward, pushing the kilt away. As her fingers found his manhood, encircling it, he closed his eyes and tilted his head back. She moved closer and reached down and, hesitantly, rubbed the warm crown against her cheek, her ear, her throat. Alexander groaned.

The moment she slid her lips over him, taking him deep in her mouth, he lost control.

Within him, passion surged, filling his chest with a tightness that constricted all breathing. With her lips and tongue, she was driving him to the edge of release. When he knew he could take no more, he again grabbed her hair and pulled her head back until her face looked up into his. Their eyes met, and he saw her own matching desire. Desire that permeated the space between them. Desire that hung like a glistening jewel in their locked gazes.

His mouth descended upon her still-parted lips. His tongue thrust deeply into her warmth. He tasted all she had in her. Alexander's hands cradled Kenna's face, then moved to draw the silk shift up. He lifted it over her head. Taking her hands, he gazed on the vision looking up at him. She slowly, wordlessly, stood up.

Kenna shone as if lit from within. Like a goddess of some pagan rite, she stood motionless and hid nothing from him as his eyes did homage to her resplendent beauty. His gaze traveled from her face, down along the braided hair draped over one breast, past the curves of her belly to the triangle of soft hair that graced the junction of her long legs. He looked up into her exquisite face and violet eyes.

"Like flame to tinder. I ignite with your gaze alone."

"It's time I showed you a fire hotter than you've ever

imagined."

Kenna touched his cheek, and Alexander kissed the palm of her hand. Then, placing her arm on his shoulder, he lifted her effortlessly as he stood, moving to the bed and laying her across it.

He looked down at her as he kicked off his boots and unfastened the belt that held his kilt. Unwrapping it, he stood naked beside the bed, and Kenna watched him.

She moved restlessly against the bedding. "I need your weight on me."

"Not yet." Reaching down, Alexander took hold of Kenna's legs, dragging her slowly toward him until her knees dangled at the edge of the bed. She began to raise herself, but he met her halfway, taking her wrists and pushing them back, trapping them with one hand above her head.

"Do you remember the tree in the clearing when we camped on our first night on the road? There were things I wanted to do to you that night."

She smiled. "You tied me to that tree."

He nodded, eying her squirming body and trying to keep his sanity intact.

"Imagine me tied."

Alexander's mouth was rough as he took possession of hers, and Kenna responded, hooking one leg around his thigh.

He tore his mouth from hers and kissed the hollow of her throat. He felt her body arch against him as his mouth descended, suckling a hardened nipple.

She seemed to hold her breath when his lips moved slowly down the softness of her belly. He parted her legs and draped them over his shoulder. Their eyes locked when he reached under her buttocks and lifted her to his mouth.

She gasped and Alexander's tongue thrust into the sweet, moist darkness.

~

Kenna could not take air into her lungs, but she was beyond caring as the blood roared wildly in her head. When she thought she couldn't take another moment of this erotic torture, he still held her down, tasting, probing, and teasing her until she cried out with release.

Moments later, she felt his weight upon her. Alexander took her into his arms and slid into her. Like two clay forms, their bodies molded together with a completeness that Kenna sensed more than thought. As they lay momentarily still, she felt his arms tightly around her, and she felt cherished, valued, loved.

When Alexander began to move, Kenna went with him. Looking up through the haze that clouded her vision, she saw her husband's eyes burning into her with intensity. Her hands moved over his chest to his face, and she clutched at his hair as he once again slid molten heat into the very center of her. A moan escaped her lips, and a new urgency swept into her.

Kenna felt no bedding beneath her, saw no ceiling above. The only things she knew to be real were her husband and the wild sensations that were threatening to lift her out of herself and into another dimension. She clung desperately to him, but still more quickly she rose, ever higher and higher, until her spirit tore through the gauzy curtain of the world as she knew it. With blinding speed, the sky opened above her, and like a bird thrown into flight, Kenna soared upward into an unknown, crystalline sphere.

And Alexander was right there with her, stretching and circling, climbing into the blue-white reaches of another realm.

~

Two voices drifted down through the window. Two men were coming down the alleyway, and James didn't know where Emily was hiding. She was definitely in danger.

The men were almost on top of the window.

"And they already paid?"

"Aye." James heard the clink of coins. "Right here."

"Then where to?"

"Beyond the new kirk and past the glen. Said just to take it to the bridge by the old mill."

"This ain't a godly hour to be doing such a job."

The coins clinked again and the two men laughed.

James shook his head. Scots doing their enemy's bidding like it was nothing. He waited at the wall below the window.

Steps. They were above him.

"When's that bairn o' yers coming?"

"Afore the harvest."

"Gor, lad. That must make a baker's dozen you got running about."

"Aye. Shame the baker won't feed 'em."

They laughed as they moved away. The steps never faltered.

James pulled himself up and looked out through the opening. In the dark, the two appeared to be just farmers, one older and limping. No one else was in sight. No sign of Emily.

The bar was now close to the window. Emily must have had moved it before she disappeared. James reached for it, and a moment later, he'd pried the window open. Squeezing through, he stood and pressed his back against the stone wall. By the time he reached the muddy alley at the end of the passage, the men had harnessed the oxen and were climbing up on the cart.

He had to find Emily. He looked about. Even in the moonlight, he couldn't identify where they were. Castles were constantly changing hands these days, some falling into enemy hands, but there were a few instances of turncoat lairds, too. It would be good to know if this holding belonged to someone they mistakenly counted as an ally.

A whip cracked and the cart began at a crawl. That's when he saw her. She was in the back of the cart, half buried in the stacks of hay, waving at him.

He waved back, his mind racing. If he went back down the alleyway where the two men had come from, perhaps he'd recognize the castle. On the other hand, he couldn't let her out of his sight and risk her safety. But he had no weapon, and if a guard at the gate spotted them, he needed to be ready to fight.

He made a motion that he'd follow, then turned in the opposite direction.

James had not taken two steps before he realized she was out of the cart and running toward him.

He caught her by the waist as she barreled into him.

"Where are you going?" she whispered.

"Get back inside that cart. I'll catch up to you."

"How? Nay, you have to come with me now. That's

our way out." She started pulling him toward the creaking cart.

"I need to know where we are."

"Later; we have to go now."

He couldn't get her hands off of him. Also, she was much stronger than he would have imagined—and much more persistent. "Nay! You go. I told you—"

"I won't go without you," she snapped. "You promised we'd stay together."

"I have a responsibility here. I need to find out where we are, so I can come back here."

"Die here if you wish, James Macpherson, but my blood will be on your hands as well. Go ahead—let us be captured again. You don't care that I'll be back in shackles down there with those brutes doing God knows what to me."

James looked in the direction of the cart. It was almost at the end of the alley. This blond demon was right. Above all, he couldn't jeopardize her safety. "By the devil! Very well, woman. Let's go."

He ran after the cart. She kept up with him and they jumped onto the back. Burrowing in, they pulled the hay over them, covering their bodies. The sky was beginning to brighten with the hint of dawn. He raised himself, hoping to get a glimpse of the buildings or the yard, but Emily rolled over him, pulling more hay over them. From somewhere ahead, voices reached them. The smell of a fire.

They lay perfectly still, face to face. Their lips almost touched. Their breaths mingled with the scent of fresh hay. Emily's soft body lay sprawled on top of his. The cart rolled and bumped. Someone shouted a farewell from above them as they rolled through an enclosed passage. The cart wheels clacked over stone and then wood. They were through the gate. Another bump and they were on a country road.

James's relief was only momentary and immediately replaced by his awareness of this woman stretched out on him. He could feel every curve, and a tendril of her blond hair lay across his lips. Before he could move, he felt himself growing hard.

He turned his attention to other things.

"Move, lass," he breathed. "I need to see where we are."

He tried to push her to the side, but she slipped her arms around his neck. As they rolled, James found himself on top.

And before he could push away, Emily pulled herself up and kissed him.

~

This castle held little for Sir Ralph except food, and women for his men, and a few paltry chests of plate and gold.

Leaving his men to it, he strode to the small chapel a few paces from the tower. As he entered, the dying sun threw his shadow into the long rectangle of light that cut the darkness of the nave. The chapel had already been emptied of anything of value.

But he could smell it. The bitter, ashy taste of the dead was in his mouth.

Descending the few steps into the crypt, he paused as the tablet in the leather pouch beneath his shirt warmed. He smiled. No longer did he need to wait for the spirits of the dead to rise. With every passing day, the power sank its roots deeper within him.

He raised his arms in the darkness.

From the very center of the crypt floor, a shape rose and stood before him.

"Speak and tell me who you are."

"John Comyn, Lord of Badenoch, Lord of Lochaber, and Guardian of Scotland."

"Indeed. The Red Comyn."

The specter nodded.

"Stabbed to death by the Bruce himself in a church in Dumfries."

"Aye," the ghost replied. His voice, deep and gruff. "Carried back here under cover of night. Buried here in secret like an unchristened whore."

"*You would have been king of Scotland, they say.*"

The spirit nodded again.

"*Instead, your descendants were banished from these lands. Exiled to England. They live there still, fighting with us against the Stewart rabble that now rule.*"

The Red Comyn stared, his dead, black eyes seething with hatred that centuries had not diminished.

"*And I raised you from hell. You died in your blood two centuries ago.*"

Sir Ralph felt for the stone tablet.

"*This is true power, Red Comyn. Think of what I will gain from the secrets of the dead. With these hands, I will raise an army of the dead. Their riches will be mine. And no one living will stand before me.*"

Chapter 21

Thou and I are too wise to woo peaceably.

As Alexander and Kenna lay together in each other's arms, the following breeze shifted and the ship heeled slightly, breaking the spell.

Lying there, he couldn't help think of his past experiences with women. They all paled in comparison to this. Not one even came close to the lightning blast of passion, to the ironbound union of souls he shared with Kenna. They were destined to be together. He recognized the truth now with a fierce certainty. The past no longer existed. They had only the present and the future.

Propped up on his elbow, he traced the lines of her beautiful face with his fingers. She turned and gave him a smile that took his breath away.

"I don't believe I have ever seen you look as happy as you do now."

"How could I not be happy? I am married to a beautiful, confident, intelligent, independent, spontaneous, and sensual woman. And for the first time, I'm not worried that she'll run away the first time my back is turned or put a blade to my throat when I close my eyes to rest."

"In spite of your compliments, you're being far too confident." She edged up against him.

"I know how you feel about me."

"And how do you know?"

"Because that was the greatest lovemaking since the Garden of Eden, and the first words out of your mouth confirmed it."

"Did they?"

"Aye. You told me you had no idea what you were running away from six months ago."

"I didn't say that."

"But you meant to."

She ran a finger across his lips. "You and I have made many mistakes. But perhaps those six months apart might be the reason why everything has worked out between us now."

He shook his head in disagreement. She nodded.

Alexander sighed, gathering Kenna even closer in his arms. "I know it's foolish to think that we could agree on even the simplest matters."

"Perhaps we can agree on this. I'll not run away and I'll not stab you, unless you give me a reason."

"This makes me happy." He rolled onto his back, and she propped her chin on his chest. "I intend to give you no reason."

She laughed. "A very wise husband. Then, as a reward, I have a compliment for you."

"Only one?"

She raised herself up, and her gaze traveled down his naked body and back to his face. "Scars and all, you are more handsome than any man has a right to be. And you are brave and honest and strong of heart."

"Handsome? Do you mean it?"

"And is that the only compliment you heard?"

"Were there others?" He ran his fingers up her spine, enjoying the shiver it produced.

She gathered the blankets to her chest and knelt up, smiling. "Before you distract me, there are a few things that we need to discuss."

"I don't have any idea how to distract you." He tried to pull the blanket down from her breasts, but she playfully slapped his hand away.

"Emily."

"There's nothing to discuss about that wedding. You're not going."

"And there, you see? You've just opened the door for another argument."

"Kenna, be reasonable." He put his hands behind his

head. "Going back to Craignock Castle would be descending into the dragon's lair. Even if I turned this ship around and we sailed there, Evers would soon know of it. And how long do you think it would be before his troops were battering down the MacDougall's gate?"

"I agree. I don't wish to go anyway."

"Then why bring it up?"

"It was a test. And you failed."

"How?"

"You ordered me, Alexander," she said flatly. "You have admitted you don't take orders well. Well, I don't, either."

He started to reply but then stopped. He was the commander of the Macpherson fleet. At Benmore Castle, his father encouraged him to make decisions that affected the clan. He was accustomed to issuing orders. And people obeyed.

Perhaps, he thought, this is part of marriage. He and Kenna would fight many battles, until one of them softened.

"Think of this as a teaching moment," she said gently, breaking into his thoughts. "We must teach each other, and we must each learn."

"Go on," he said.

"I know my own temperament. I know I'm impulsive. I often say and do things before thinking them through. So I'm asking you to discuss things reasonably with me, rather than issuing a command. If you can do that, we'll both fare much better."

He settled back against the pillows. He couldn't help but to be amused. And she was right about this. He *was* capable of being reasonable. Many of his men swore to it.

"And you have a cleverness of wit, too," he replied. "Did you bring up Emily's wedding for the purpose of creating this 'teaching' moment?"

"Actually, that was an unexpected bonus. I never mentioned the wedding. I only said 'Emily.'"

She reached down and traced the scar in his side with the tip of her finger. Alexander breathed in deeply, feeling heat seep through his skin. The wound, fresh only days ago, now appeared to be healed. In fact, he no longer even thought about it.

"Very well. What about her?"

"I was thinking she might have some information about the tablet."

"Emily? How?"

"Our mothers were sisters. I could be wrong, but it's at least a possibility that the stone was handed down from my grandmother to Sine. I used to hear stories that my mother had inherited the gift of healing from *her* mother."

"And you think Emily may have heard stories from her mother."

"My mother died when I was twelve, but my aunt died just two summers ago. Perhaps Emily knows something."

Alexander propped himself up on an elbow.

"You and Emily spent some time together growing up."

"Anytime my father thought I was spending too much time with the men, I was sent to Craignock... for months at a time."

"But neither your aunt nor Emily ever mentioned any of this?"

Kenna shook her head. "It never came up. But I never asked. I didn't know the tablet was waiting for me at Castle Varrich." She paused.

"What is it?"

"Now that I think of it, if I had known about this gift when my aunt took sick, I might have helped her. Saved her life even."

"But you were at Castle Varrich when she died?"

"I was."

"Three weeks of hard riding in good weather, if not more. How long was she ill?"

She shook her head and stared at her lap. "Not very long. But now that I know what I'm capable of, what I could have done . . ."

Alexander grabbed her hand. His thumb caressed the warm palm. "You didn't have the stone. And you didn't even know about it. But you also need to remember that you can't save everyone. You can't be everywhere. Sickness and death are part of this world we live in. We're all mortal, Kenna. Your mother was. And those who had the stone before her were, as well. Put that guilt behind you. Think about those you've already saved. About those you will save."

Her eyes were misty jewels when they met his. She brought their joined hands to her lips and kissed his fingers. "When did you become so wise?"

"It's a gift. I've always had it." Alexander smiled and touched her lips. He wiped away a tear that fell onto her cheek.

The power that the stone bestowed on Kenna was no trifling matter. It was truly a matter of life and death, and the ramifications were not lost on him. If word ever got out beyond the rumors Evers and Maxwell were spreading, if the truth of her power were ever made public, she would always be hunted. By everyone. He couldn't let that happen.

"You understand that we must keep your gift secret," he said gently but firmly. He was not ordering her, but he needed her to understand. "And that's from everyone. My family. Your family. Everyone. You said your mother never even spoke of it to you. When you talk to Emily, somehow you mustn't reveal anything to her."

"I know." Kenna sighed. "Revealing this secret cost an old man his life, and because of that, the Englishman knows whatever Cairns knew. That's why he's coming after me."

He nodded.

"Alexander, I need to find the other two women Evers is after . . . before he finds them. They must hold a gift that is somehow connected to mine. And what happens if they have no way of protecting it?"

"Not you . . . *we* will find them. The two of us." He knew it would be only a matter of time before Kenna brought this up.

She squeezed his hand.

"We don't even know their names," he continued. "But once we land, I'll set Diarmad on their trail. This far north, we're in a far better position to find these women than Evers and his armies could ever be."

Kenna appeared more in control of her emotions. The look of confidence was back in her face. "I'd still like to see my cousin. Perhaps not before that mess of a wedding, but soon."

"Sir Quentin Chamberlain will be taking Emily back to the Borders as soon as he can. You can be certain of that."

"Aye," Kenna spat. "But how could a father make such a disastrous match for his only daughter?"

"You didn't think too highly of *your* father's decision, either."

"By comparison, you're a prince. Chamberpot is a festering piece of aged, elf-skinned baggage."

A prince. Alexander smiled. A yet another complement from his wife. He could get used to this.

"But you haven't even met him."

"Nor has Emily, and that makes it worse. This is the sixteenth century we're living in, not the Dark Ages, by the saints!"

"I met the man. At court."

Curiosity lit her face. "And . . . ?"

"Sir Quentin is puny and vain. An ill-bred peacock. But he has wealth and position at court. And for his second wife, he wants a young, beautiful, submissive wife with a good name and breeding potential. And this union with the MacDougalls only adds to his power and influence."

Kenna shuddered and lay down next to her husband. "I still can't believe Emily is going along so willingly."

～

She wanted to be on top. He let her.

Though he knew this would be trouble, James didn't resist when she edged over on top of him beneath the warm hay. She ran her fingers along his rough growth of beard. Her curiosity was guiding her as she tenderly, repeatedly touched his lips with hers.

He lay still, frozen between what he should do and what he wanted to do. He was already aroused by her. Moving would mean taking charge, and his body craved far more than kissing.

Smart, spirited, and eager for him, she was an alluring dream in flesh and blood. In the recesses of his mind, he realized the absurdity of the situation. But in his loins, he felt the same thrill that the hunter feels when coming face to face with the stag. The connection between them was palpable; it was undeniable. Inwardly, he thanked the hand of fate for throwing them together, for giving them this last chance before she was married and gone forever. This was their moment. Perhaps their last moment.

He ran the tip of his tongue along the seam of her lips. She paused and then mimicked what he had done. This time he delved in a bit deeper, rubbing his tongue against hers. He felt her intake of breath. Emily was a diligent student. Her tongue explored his mouth, her body molding itself to his.

If she wanted to drive him beyond reason, it was working. His hands caressed her as they kissed. He kneaded her back, her buttocks, pulling her tight against him. A soft moan escaped her throat.

One last vestige of reason asserted itself.

"We should stop," he whispered under his breath. "Worlds are about to change, perhaps forever."

But even as he said it, he hooked one of her legs with his, keeping her captive.

"I know," she breathed in his ear. "But not yet. I've never done this before, and . . . and it feels so right."

A bump in the road jolted them, and her body ground against his now obvious erection. Her eyes opened wide and then her gaze immediately went to James's mouth. She attacked it with a new vigor, this time an open mouth assault of lips and tongue.

When he could take no more, he turned his face away and pressed her head into the crook of his neck. It was becoming harder and harder to remain passive. He tried to focus on anything and everything instead of the urge to bury himself deep inside of her virginal sheath. He tried not to see her, not to think of her, not to smell her intoxicating scent. He couldn't let his cock make decisions that they would both regret.

He pushed some of the straw away. Sunlight and fresh air and glimpses of leaves on the trees.

"I wonder if kissing Sir Quentin will be anywhere near as good as kissing you."

"Nothing about us will be the same," he murmured, fighting down irrational anger.

In spite of himself, he rolled her beneath him. Pushing her knees apart, he shoved himself between her legs where the cloth of her torn dress was the only barrier. "Do you feel this?"

Her eyes half closed and she nodded. She tilted her hips, nestling him even more tightly against her. She wasn't getting it.

"Is this what you want?" He pulled at the neckline of her dress, harder than he intended, and cloth ripped, exposing one of her breasts. Before he knew it, his mouth descended, latching onto the nipple as she gasped and lifted her knees. She held his head tight against her breast.

"Oh, James," she breathed. "Please, what's happening to me?"

He broke off and took her mouth in a bruising kiss. One hand reached between their bodies. He lifted her skirts and found her wetness. He stroked her with one finger and delved into her tightness. She convulsed in his arms—gasping, pulling his hair, squirming, her heart pounding so hard that he could feel it in his own chest.

Rational thought returned, and he slowly, gently withdrew his hand and rolled to his side, still holding her in his arms. He ached with how much he wanted to take her. And he knew she'd let him. But he wouldn't do it.

Not here. Not like this. He'd already done more than he'd intended.

Her blue eyes looked into his with awe. She caressed his face, her thumb brushing his lips. "How ... ? I never expected ..."

James tensed at the sound of the farmer calling out to his oxen, and the cart creaked to a halt.

"Hush."

The two men were talking, but he couldn't hear the words. He heard the sound of the team being unharnessed from the cart. James edged away from Emily, ready to fight when the men came around to the back.

But they didn't come around. Their voices grew fainter as they led the animals away.

James pushed his way out and dropped off the cart. The two men had crossed an old bridge with the oxen and were about to disappear over a hilltop. A moment later, they were gone.

He looked around him. They'd left the hay wain by an abandoned mill. The yard was overgrown and the thatched cottage was clearly deserted. There was no one else in sight.

Emily climbed from the cart, her hair and clothes covered with hay.

Her dress was torn in front, and her perfect breasts drew his gaze. By the devil, he thought. He'd done that to her. She saw him looking and immediately pulled the material together, covering herself.

"Where are we?" she asked.

Before he could answer, the sound of approaching horses reached them. Whoever they were, the riders were coming from the direction of the castle.

"What do we do?" The note of panic was evident in her voice.

The open meadows around them offered no place to hide. From the sound of the horses, he knew they didn't even have time to get over the hill beyond the bridge.

The mill was a trap. The old dam had given way, and the river below it was shallow but wide. The mill would be the first place they'd search, but it was their only chance. Maybe there was something he could find there to use as a weapon.

He dragged Emily across the yard to the mill and pushed her inside. "Look for anything that we could use to fight them."

A moment later, the riders came into view, and relief poured over him.

"It's all right," he called over his shoulder at Emily. "Kester and six of his men. And the abbot is with them."

He went out and crossed the yard as the group reined in their mounts.

"By Saint Andrew, it's good to find you here," Kester

said, not dismounting. "But we're looking for—"

"I'm here, too," Emily said, coming out of the mill.

All eyes were on her. James cursed himself as she tried to hold the pieces of her dress together. When he turned back to the riders, he saw a look of horror on the abbot's face. Kester's eyes flashed with murder.

"What goes on here?" the warrior growled.

"Give me a blanket or something to cover her," James demanded.

One of the men tossed him a blanket, and James shook it and draped it around her shoulders. She looked up at him with a grateful expression.

He turned to Kester, who was dismounting.

"Someone kidnapped us. I was drugged and taken at Oban. They were holding us at a castle not far from here. It must be Evers or someone working with him. Where are we? What castle is near here?"

Before Kester could answer, Emily broke in. "What are you doing here, Abbott? Why are you with Kester?"

"Your father, lass. He was worried about you. And with your wedding . . ." The clergyman paused, carefully studying Emily's torn dress and disheveled condition. "Did they . . . ? Were you attacked?"

Emily stared at him, then looked from Kester to James.

The abbot's questioning was clear. James saw it plainly. The man had been sent to bear witness later that Sir

Quentin wasn't being cheated of a virgin bride. It was all business as usual.

In spite of her abduction and the possibility of her being hurt, right now Emily was no more than a bargaining chip in the MacDougall's eyes. She might be his only daughter, but her safety and well-being were secondary to clan business. That might be well and good for some, but in James's eyes Emily had more value than that.

He crossed to her, glaring at the abbot and Kester. "You'll give us a moment."

Taking Emily by the hand, he led her across the yard and into the building. The floor was still covered with oat hulls, though the millworks had long ago been removed. Gathering his thoughts, James looked down through a hole in the center of the floor at the water running beneath the building.

Finally, with no ceremony, no warning, no pleasantries of any sort, he turned and blurted out what was on his mind. "You will marry me. Right here. Right now."

Her mouth opened and closed. There seemed to be confusion first and then her expression softened. "What are you saying to me, James?"

"The abbot knows, and so do Kester and the others."

"What do they know?"

He waved a hand at her disheveled condition, at the torn dress.

By the devil, he thought. She was beautiful.

"I'll not allow you be questioned about what happened and when and by whom. The rumors alone will destroy you. We'll put an end to it before it begins. We'll marry."

"Why are you doing this?"

"You know why," he snapped. "I'm doing it to save your honor and reputation. You're a fine woman, Emily. And we had no choice in being captured. But this . . . this last thing . . . what happened in the cart. What we did . . . what I did . . . went beyond innocence. To everyone out there, it's obvious something happened. And I must take full responsibility for it."

"But I kissed you. I practically attacked you."

She was such an innocent. As if her chaste kisses stood in comparison to what he'd done. The way he'd handled her. The way he desired her. The way he wanted her even now.

"I was more than willing to be kissed by you. But I took it further than—"

"James, wait. I need to talk to you."

"None of that matters. We must marry. Your father's plans have been dashed, and I must make amends. To him. And to you."

"But—"

"Nay. This is the way it must be." He moved toward the

open doorway. "I'll get the abbot. He'll perform the ceremony, or I'll break his scrawny neck."

"James. Stop. I'll not marry you."

Chapter 22

I am gone, though I am here: there is no
love . . .

Emily wrung her hands. His eyes were burning into her.

He'd understand. He had to. She'd concocted an innocent plan. And it had all gone wrong.

"James, this marriage can't take place," she said quietly. "At least, not for those reasons."

"You have no idea what a scandal this will be, here and at court. After what's happened, that pompous Lowlander won't marry you. But he'll make certain that your name and your clan's honor are smeared in every inn and brothel from Dumfries to Stirling," he said. "Nay, lass. I've done you wrong, and I'm determined to set it right. We must marry. It's the only way."

Emily shook her head. This had gone far enough. She couldn't bear to see him so distraught on her behalf when she was the cause. Now, she prayed he'd understand.

"This is all a huge mistake. I never intended it to happen this way. I just wanted time to talk to you, to be with you."

"What are you talking about?"

She took a deep breath.

"The original plan was simple. My people were to put a drug in your drink to make you feel unwell. They were to take you to a cottage in Oban where I was waiting, where I could nurse you back to health. Where we could spend some time and I could tell you about my change of heart."

James stared at her, a puzzled look on his face.

"It was just a draught for sleeping," she continued, trying to stay calm. Perhaps he'd see the humor in it. "Because of your size, we didn't know how much to give you. We just wanted you to feel dizzy. A wee bit ill."

The puzzled look disappeared. His face became expressionless, unreadable.

"That was when the plan fell to pieces. You passed out and everything went wrong. Campbell and Macpherson warriors were everywhere. My men panicked. They couldn't get you to me, so they took you to my aunt's castle, just north of the town. I wasn't there yet, and my aunt knew nothing of the plan. And when she found out, she wanted no part of it. She was afraid of what would happen if you woke up before I arrived. So she put you in the dungeon. For safekeeping."

His silence was beginning to unnerve her. She raced on, trying to explain everything.

"When I got to you, you were already stirring, and I didn't know what to do. I was afraid you'd be angry and leave right away. So I did the only thing I could think of. I pretended we were both kidnapped. I had the guards drag me in to the adjoining cell. I thought we could still have a chance to talk. I kept trying. I wanted to explain, to tell you how I felt about you and me, about Sir Quentin, but you wouldn't listen. You just wanted to get out of there. You were relentless. So I had to go along with you, improvising as I went. When I realized we were actually going to escape, I was afraid someone might get hurt."

She knew she was beginning to babble, but she couldn't stop now.

"Actually, you gave me the idea. In what you did for Alexander and Kenna. I thought if I could arrange the same thing for us . . . a chance to be together. You said that you knew they were made for each other, and they just needed time to realize it. I wanted that for us because . . ." She faltered and then plowed on. "Because I love you. And I know you care for me, too. I couldn't bear to walk away and marry someone else. Not without knowing . . . without knowing about us. So I had to do something. But I made a mess of everyth—"

"Stop."

His curt order cut through the air. Emily winced at the cold fury she saw in the depth of his gray eyes.

"You poisoned me. You tricked me. You lied to me."

She'd wanted to make James see that everything she'd done had been done out of affection, but his eyes told her that he didn't. Tears welled up and splashed down onto her cheeks.

"You used me for your amusement," he snarled. "You are the lowest woman I've ever known."

"Don't say that. I understand that I went too far, that I ruined everything. But I love you. And I was so desperate to know what you felt for me. There was so much that was left unsaid between us. I couldn't marry Sir Quentin. Not when I'm in love with you. I tried to steal some time for us, the only way I could think of. Only an overnight." Emily stopped. She stretched a hand out to him. "I'm sorry, James. Please forgive me."

"Never," he rasped in a voice of cold steel. "My only hope is that I never lay eyes on you again."

~

She lied. Everyone had lied. She lied.

The sound of her crying followed James out the mill door. He came to a dead stop in the yard, anger washing through him. Tears meant nothing. It was far too late for tears.

Bloody hell. Bloody hell.

The morning sun framed the men and horses standing in the cart path beyond the mill yard, but it was no match for the fires blazing inside him. His face burned. How could he be such a dolt?

The Highlander's fists clenched tight. His eyes fixed on Kester, who stood with the abbot near the others.

"You knew about this?" James demanded, spinning him around.

Kester frowned. "What did she tell you?"

"Who knew about this? Her father?"

"Nay, lad. Not her father nor her aunt nor the abbot here."

"But you knew."

"She meant no harm. Her plan went awry, but the lass just wanted some time to talk to you."

The blow to the jaw sent the MacDougall warrior staggering back across the cart path.

She was a monster. Aye, beautiful on the outside, but with a devious soul that seethed within. She was a poisoned apple. And he hadn't seen it. He was a fool.

And this one was just a minion, doing her bidding.

But when it came right down to it, he had no one to blame but himself.

With one hard look back at the mill, he climbed onto Kester's horse and wheeled the animal toward the hills.

~

Wiping the blood from his face, Evers knew he'd been duped. Going west, following the shore of the long lake, they'd been hemmed in by a ridge of impassable mountains to the north. The way had turned out to be a death trap.

Sir Ralph scanned the hillside around him. Acres of heather and clumps of pine, and the ground covered with blood and bodies. Such a small force of Highlanders, and yet they had come screaming out of the west and fallen on his forces with such wildness. Such ferocity! He'd encountered nothing like this in the Borders.

The feeling was coming back into his left arm where the barbarian had struck him with his hammer. The red-haired giant had breathed his last a moment later with Evers's sword embedded in his heart.

Every Highlander lay dead on the field. Not one escaped. But at what cost?

Sir Ralph moved slowly over the bloody ground. His best officers were dead. Too many of his English fighters were dead or dying. Many of the Lowland Scots were sitting or kneeling, catching their breath.

The price had been too high. He'd lost too many men.

He flexed his left hand. Usable, once again.

The shadows were growing long by the time he reached his forward company. He turned to a grove of trees by the lakeshore where the battle had been wildest. The leader of the enemy lay on his back, his torn and bloody tartan spread out like a great eagle's wing on the rock and grass. Unseeing gray eyes stared vacantly into the Scottish sky.

"Speak to me, Highlander," Evers commanded. "Rise and speak."

The specter lifted out of the body and faced the Englishman.

"How was it that you knew where to attack us?"

"Every clan in the Western Highlands knows you are coming, butcher. You're on Graham land, but we're only the first that you will meet. The MacNabs and the Campbells gather to the west. You will die in your own blood before you reach the sea."

Evers waved his hand, dismissing the ghost. "Away, spirit. To hell with you and all your barbarous kind."

Sir Ralph looked out to the west. He would never get past a larger force of Highlanders, not with the men he had remaining. He had to reverse his course, go east, and meet up with his forces there.

Turning his back on the orange sky, the Englishman worked his way back across the battlefield, ignoring the spirits rising up from every bloody corpse. Around him, his men had begun stripping the bodies of their weapons.

Maxwell was still pursuing the woman. The last message he'd sent said she'd slipped the noose but that the Lowlander had a new plan.

Whatever it was, it had better work, Evers thought, or he would gut Maxwell like a sow and eat his miserable heart.

Chapter 23

Charm ache with air and agony with words.

Kenna leaned down and whispered enticingly in his ear.

"Slow down, you beast. Make this last."

But there was no slowing him. He was heading for home.

"If you'll at least throw a shoe, I'll see that you get extra oats for your supper."

Her horse shook his head with a neigh, and Kenna had her answer.

The animal couldn't walk slow enough to suit her. Kenna would travel on foot the rest of the way if she thought she could get away with it.

They crossed into the river valley that marked the beginning of Macpherson land yesterday. They were getting close to their destination. With the long summer days, they'd started out very early this morning. After two days of riding, they'd arrive at Benmore Castle today. Much of the valley's meadowland was covered with heather, but Kenna barely noticed the blanket of purple spreading out around her.

Side by side at the head of the Macpherson warriors, Kenna and Alexander crested another ridge. The Grampian Mountains, covered with snow even now, rose up majestically to the south.

Kenna sighed. She wished her husband would take his men and ride ahead and let her alone with her misery on this last day of their journey. But he stayed with her.

Unconsciously tightening the reins of her mount, she cringed at the thought of how different her entry into the Macpherson stronghold would be compared to six months ago. Last winter, the plans had included ample ceremony and grandeur. A large company of MacKay warriors would escort her with pipes and drum, and two young women would ride on either side, serving as her lady's maids. Carts had been loaded with trunks filled with dresses and fine cloth and an abundance of gifts that her people had spent weeks preparing for practically everyone at Benmore. She, Kenna MacKay, daughter of Magnus MacKay, laird of the North, was to represent the best of her people in this union. She was to make her clan proud.

How different from today, Kenna thought with growing anguish. She was to arrive wearing a borrowed dress and cloak, carrying no gifts, bringing with her nothing from her people, escorted by none of her clan. She was a runaway bride who had dishonored the MacKays and Macphersons on her wedding day and was now being dragged back like some captured renegade. She had no more value than a sprig of trampled heather.

Kenna's mind raced with uncomfortable and hostile situations she would surely face. She fought imaginary arguments, resisted penalties she'd be forced to pay. The folly of Alexander's blunder on their wedding night no longer mattered. Everyone seemed to know that Kenna's plans had been made days before the wedding. Fault lay with her. Bumping along on this trail, she broke out in a cold sweat thinking how she'd be received by the laird and by Lady Fiona. Considering everything, how could they be expected to treat her?

She knew her own temperament. Would she be able to keep a cool head? What were her options? What was she to do?

"If you ride any slower, we might not reach Benmore before winter."

"I would like that. So much more time together. Just the two of us. I imagine we'll not have a chance like this again for quite some time."

He wasn't fooled.

"Plainly, something is bothering you." Alexander pushed

his horse so near that their knees rubbed. "Talk to me, Kenna."

She hesitated, but for only a moment.

"Your family hates me. They have every right to. I've given them reason enough."

She was relieved to throw off the weight she'd been dragging for days. Running away was no longer a possibility. She wouldn't leave him. She wouldn't break her promise. But that didn't make any of this easier.

"How do I apologize?" she continued. "Do I get on my knees and kiss your father's ring? Your mother's feet? Should I do penance working in the kitchens? I need an answer. I need to know what I can do to make the past go away."

"Difficult problem."

Alexander was taking her seriously. His frown told her so. She followed his eyes as he turned his gaze out across the wild, green Highland hills, across the patchwork of hawthorn and pine groves, across purple flowering fields toward the white-peaked mountains to the south.

"Kenna, if it's penance you think you deserve, there is one thing you can do." His face was grim as he reached over for her hand.

She looked up into his face, feeling his support.

"The next time we're in bed, I'll show you."

Kenna tried to pull her hand away, but he wouldn't

let go. She slapped his arm with her reins, but he just laughed heartily.

"This is no time for humor, vile beast. I'm genuinely upset at the situation I'm riding into."

He brought both of their horses to a stop and waved his men by.

"Kenna, I've told you before: there's no basis for you being upset. What happened after the wedding was between the two of us. We've reconciled. Better than reconciled. From now on, all will be well. I'm telling you."

"It can't be," she told him. Why couldn't he understand? "Even if the immediate aftermath of our wedding were unblemished—which it's not—look at me. Look at the wild woman you're taking home to present to the daughter of King Jamie."

"This is just my mother you're talking about," he reminded her.

"You're no help." She let out a frustrated sigh. "Look at me. See me for who I am. For the qualities I lack. I'm not fit to be the wife of the laird of a clan like the Macphersons. Your family will see this, if they haven't already. I knew this in my heart when I ran away before."

"Kenna."

"But don't worry—I'll not run away again," she assured him. "I just have to learn to accept my lot in life. I need to grow accustomed to a life of misery."

"You'll not be miserable. I promise you that. This will all work out to the satisfaction of everyone. Let me explain it the way I see it. The way my family and the rest of the Macpherson clan will see it."

"You've told me already," she reminded him. "You jest about doing penance in your bed, but there's truth in that. Your people will be satisfied so long as I produce a child every year for all my child-bearing years, which will make you the pride of the Highlands and me an old woman before my time. If I survive. And we both know how that worked out for my own mother."

He leaned forward and took her chin. His blue eyes bore into hers. There was no hint of humor in them now.

"I don't want a single bairn, if the price is your life. You, alone, are all I want."

Kenna shook her head. "I'm sorry I said that about my mother. I didn't mean it. I'm just overwrought with everything."

"Let me tell you why the Macphersons will *love* you." He caressed her cheek. "Six months ago, I was to marry a bonny lass in an arranged marriage that was sound business for both of our clans. I didn't know her any better than she knew me. I was doing my duty. My people respected me for it. Still, she was a stranger to all of us. But today, I'm bringing back a beautiful and courageous young woman that I'm deeply in love with. A woman I now know as well as I know myself. She's a lioness without fear. She's a woman fit to be a queen."

Kenna's troubles evaporated like morning mist in the Highland sun.

"What did you say?"

"I said you're beautiful."

"Nay, after that."

"That you're fit to be a queen."

"Before that."

He brushed her lips with his. "That I'm deeply in love with you. And my people are no fools. They'll know that you're the first woman to claim my heart."

She wasn't a crier. She never had been. She despised women who couldn't control their emotions. But here she was, weeping like a child.

"My love."

Suddenly, one of the warriors shouted back at them. "Riders coming."

She batted her tears away and looked where he was pointing. Three mounted warriors had emerged from a grove of oaks and were racing down into the valley. The hard-charging riders were coming directly at them, and Kenna looked questioningly at Alexander.

"Macphersons," he said to her.

The thundering hooves grew louder as the riders approached. It seemed that in only an instant they'd covered the ground between them. The air was suddenly filled with the sound of shouts of welcome and friendly banter. The smell of leather and sweating horseflesh and men. The ruddy faces, the plaids, and the flash of metal in the morning sun.

The confidence that had been eluding her seeped back into her bones. This was the world she'd grown up in. This was the world she knew best.

Kenna recognized the dark blond warrior. Alexander's youngest brother, Colin. Kenna sat up in her saddle. The Macphersons looked with interest at her, and she heard murmurs of approval as they streamed around them.

Colin rode directly to Alexander. The two brothers embraced one another from the backs of their horses. He then turned his young and smiling face to her.

"Kenna." He bowed.

She bowed back. "Colin."

"My wife told me, in no uncertain terms, that I'm not allowed back at Benmore until I apologize to you with all the eloquence I can summon, and convince you to forgive me."

Colin had the same sincere blue eyes as her husband, but his expression bespoke mischief.

"Eloquence? You?" Alexander said. "Plan to be sleeping with the horses, then, laddie."

"Again," one of the others added, to laughter around him.

Colin ignored them all. "Accept my sincere apology. The night of your wedding, I played a misbegotten prank, but please believe me when I tell you I had no idea that this doddering old barnacle would fall fast sleep the moment he fell into the wrong bed."

"Oh, you hoped he would remain awake. And what would that have led to, I wonder?"

"Led to?" Colin's demeanor lost some of its mischief. "Uh, nothing. Nowhere. What I meant to say was that he would have recognized he was with the wrong wench . . . uh, woman, and left her immediately."

"To end up with the next 'wench' you had waiting for him?"

"There was no other wench. I mean 'woman.'"

"Unrivaled eloquence, brother," Alexander commented with a smirk.

"And you expect me to believe that?" Kenna asked Colin.

"Aye. You should. You must. You see, I was only returning the favor to my oldest brother for a dozen pranks he's played on me. This has always been the way between the three of us. There was no harm intended—"

"But with that prank, an insult was directed at me."

The roguish look was gone. In its place, Kenna saw remorse.

"I apologize. Truly. It was a foolish, untimely prank.

And what troubles me most about it is that I caused you pain. It was never my intention." He reached out for her hand. "Could you forgive me?"

"If you don't," someone said, "Tess may decide the stables are too good for him."

"Then it's off to the sty with him," another added.

She took Colin's hand tentatively. "Your wife has never shown me anything but kindness and friendship. But are you really here because of Tess's threats, or did you wish to make peace with me yourself?"

Colin lifted her hand to his lips. "It was my wish. Well, mostly mine. I've been looking forward to your homecoming for months, just for the opportunity to tell you this."

She smiled. "Then we shall travel to Benmore as brother and sister, and I'll make certain to tell Tess that I have accepted your apology without reservation. No doubt due to your eloquence."

A cheer went up from the men around them. She withdrew her hand and placed it in the folds of her cloak as she turned to her husband.

"Ah, those teaching moments," he murmured. His eyes shone with what she now knew to be love for her.

Colin maneuvered his charger between the two, breaking their moment.

"Out of the way, gargoyle," he said over his shoulder

at Alexander. "M'lady, now that I've been forgiven, may I escort you the rest of the way to Benmore Castle?"

Before she could answer, their attention was drawn across the valley to a dozen more riders.

"Are you expecting more Macphersons to escort us?" she asked, looking from Colin to Alexander.

"Look again, lass. Is that not the MacKay banner?"

"MacKay?" Her people. The surging and ebbing of emotion she'd been feeling today was swept away in an instant. Her heart swelled. Her clan had come. In spite of all she'd done, she hadn't been deserted by them.

Kenna watched the Macpherson warriors part as two men rode through the throng.

Robert. Allister. The best of the MacKay warriors and stalwart defenders of the clan. These were fighters she'd doted on, followed about like a puppy as a child. These two men had been generous with their time and kind to a lost girl with a mother dead and a father withdrawn.

"My two friends," she began in greeting. She stopped.

Another man rode in behind them. A man she thought would never come.

Her father.

The immediate joy she'd felt at seeing the MacKays evaporated into thin air. The smile disappeared from her face.

The two eyed each other silently. His hair was grayer.

Deep lines that were absent six months ago etched patterns around his eyes. He'd aged in ways that were easy to see. But he was still fit. He had no paunch about the middle like many men of his years. He sat astride his stallion with the confidence of a commander ready for battle. His eyes were clear and sharp.

"Daughter." He nodded his head.

It was one word, but it was said with that same tone she knew so well. She took it like a slap, that chilly air of formality she'd faced for eight years. But she'd never become accustomed to it.

Magnus MacKay had forgotten how to be a father to her after Sine's death. Keeping her at arm's length, he'd showed no interest in what she did or where she went or who she spent her time with. Kenna simply didn't exist, until it was time to marry her off. Only then did she have some value in his eyes.

The words came back. The insults he'd heaped on her before the wedding. The reminder that he thought so little of her. That she was so unworthy of the mantle she was to assume . . . and of the man who was to be her husband. She'd known for a long time how he felt. Their argument that night had only sealed Kenna's decision.

Magnus MacKay was the reason she'd run away on her wedding day. To succeed in discrediting him, to dash his elaborate plans and alliances, was to be her revenge.

Magnus glanced only once at Alexander, nodding his greeting before fixing his gaze again on her.

"Father, it wasn't necessary for you to come."

She knew a message had been sent to the MacKays about her pending arrival at Benmore. But she'd never thought he would come. When he wasn't feuding with the Sutherland lairds, he loved to hunt at this time of year at a lodge in Altnaharra, at the southernmost edge of MacKay territory. He was here not to support her, but to remind the Macphersons of the terms of the marriage.

"And how are my brothers?"

"Giles and Ninian are fine strapping lads, growing an inch a day, it seems. You'll not recognize them."

"I think I will."

"Perhaps. This is their first summer at Altnaharra, you know. Why, the pair of them even managed to kill a boar that was twice their weight together. The beast charged out of a thicket at them. The lads drove their lances clean through that tough old hide and right into the heart."

Kenna saw the way light shone in his eyes at the mention of his sons. She'd killed her first boar with a lance at the age of thirteen after being thrown by her horse. It had been a near thing. Kill or be killed. Allister had been proud of her. All the men had been proud. But she'd begged them not to tell her father. She'd been foolish enough to think that he'd care enough to punish her for riding steeds far bigger than she could handle, never mind trailing after MacKay hunters.

"They wanted to come," her father added. "They've missed you."

And she'd missed them, too. Kenna loved the twins, and Giles and Ninian adored her. From the time they could crawl on their pudgy hands and knees, she'd been the target of their affection. The eight-year-olds' bedchamber was her last and most difficult stop before fleeing Castle Varrich on her wedding day.

She and Alexander would make arrangements. She'd see her brothers. Right now, there was nothing else that she wanted to say to her father. A heavy silence fell over the company. Kenna wanted to order him to leave. To tell him that he wasn't wanted. But for the sake of her husband, she wouldn't make a scene.

"I've sent for your trunks to be brought down from Castle Varrich," the MacKay said, breaking the stalemate. "They should arrive soon enough. But Lady Fiona has assured me you'll not be wanting for anything before your things arrive."

"That wasn't necessary, either."

He ignored her. "Now we need to proceed to Benmore Castle. There, I'll present you to the laird. The Macphersons will ride ahead. You will ride beside me—"

"Nay," she interrupted. "I'll ride with my husband."

Kenna didn't have to look for Alexander. He was beside her, taking her hand.

"A fine idea, Kenna," he said breezily. "In fact, how about if you and I ride ahead and beat the rest of this company to Benmore. You're one of the best riders in the Highlands. So how about it? Shall we leave them in our dust?"

She looked into his laughing eyes and wished she'd told him already how much she loved him. He praised her in the face of denigration. He stood with her when she was alone. He buoyed her when she foundered. And he was here for her, protecting her from her father, and from herself.

"This is her first visit to Benmore Castle, Alexander," Magnus MacKay said, the words chopped and icy. "As her father and as laird of—"

"Hold a moment, Magnus, if you would," Colin broke in.

Another rider, this time coming after them from the west. In a moment, Kenna recognized the man.

It was James Macpherson, riding like the devil was on his tail.

Chapter 24

*With anger, with sickness, or with hunger, my
lord,
not with love.*

He looked like James. He acted like James. He spoke to
Kenna's father like the politician the family always knew
him to be.

But I'll be damned if it *is* James, Alexander thought.

Something was definitely not right.

Alexander grasped his brother's forearm once everyone was past the excitement of his sudden arrival.
"What's wrong?"

"Nothing." He wouldn't look Alexander in the face.
"Let's get along to Benmore."

Colin joined them. The look the youngest brother exchanged with Alexander said that he too had noticed
something was amiss.

"By the devil, James, they normally mistake you for

a Highland steer, but right now you look like some whipped ginger cur."

"One more word and I'll show you whipped," James retorted.

"Where are our men?" Alexander asked.

"At Oban. I wanted to catch up to you before you reached Benmore. Hell, I arranged your reunion with your bride—I should be part of the celebration."

"A fine mount," Alexander said, glancing down at the steed. "Borrowed from the MacDougalls?"

"And he came all this way with no sword and no dirk," Colin added. "Naked as an infant."

James's hands tightened around the reins. The horse pawed the ground.

"Did you hear that Evers turned east?" James asked, trying to steer the topic. "The Grahams stopped him, but at the cost of good men and too much blood. Still, the lads turned him."

"Aye," Alexander replied gravely. "Heard it when we first came ashore."

"Any more news of Maxwell?"

"Nay. Maybe he's slunk back to the Lowlands with his tail between his legs." Alexander stared at his brother. "But about you—"

"Not now." James dug his heels into the side of his horse and moved off.

"Let's go," Colin said. "The horses are rested and watered. We can beat the truth out of him when we get back to Benmore."

Alexander looked past the MacKay men at Kenna and caught her eye. She was sitting stiff and silent beside her father. He rode over to them and spoke directly to the MacKay.

"Colin says you've already been to Benmore and visited with my parents."

"Aye, we rode in yesterday."

"Then we're finished with formalities, Magnus. My wife will be at my side as she sees the land and her people for the first time. She rides with me."

He stretched out his hand, and Kenna took it.

The matter was settled.

~

She rides with me.

A husband's command. That was all it took to remove her father's hands from her throat.

The day was clear and beautiful as they emerged from a woody glen, and a great valley stretched out before them. Round-topped gray mountains Alexander called Monadhliath formed one border to the north, and rising forestland of fragrant, red-limbed pines rolled upward to the south. The great River Spey wound like a sparkling jeweled serpent along the wide floor of the valley, and Kenna's breath caught in her chest at the beauty of the scene. The pasturelands of the valley were green and the farm fields midharvest. As she and Alexander led the Macpherson and MacKay warriors, the men and women gathering the grain raised their hats and shouted welcome to them.

James had long before disappeared ahead of them, and Colin stayed to the back of the line, riding with Magnus MacKay.

"I'll bring you back another day when you can meet and speak to some of the crofters."

"I'd very much like that," Kenna told him, thinking of how her gift could be of use to this community.

Shortly after the sun passed overhead, they rounded another bend in the river and Alexander pointed to the great castle sitting atop a mound overlooking the waterway. Groves of tall pines flanked the north side of the edifice, and drawbridges crossed the series of ditches and moats that protectively encircled the high stone walls. To the right, a stone bridge spanned the river on seven arches and led into a friendly looking village of wood and stone buildings that clung to the south side of the Spey.

"I'll race you to the gates," he challenged.

"You're on."

A few moments later they reined in their panting steeds and rode under the arched entry into Benmore Castle. As they passed through the shadows, another wave of uncertainty clouded Kenna's mind. Hopes. Expectations. Disappointment. What lay ahead?

"Are you coming?"

She blinked and saw Alexander beside her. She looked down at his outstretched hand. She took it.

"You're home, Kenna." His thumb softly caressed the back of her hand. "Look around you. This place. These people. Give them a chance to love you, as I do."

She took a deep breath and let his words of reassurance flow over her. She trusted him as she had never trusted anyone.

"Nudge me, trip me, do something if you see me wallowing in self-pity."

"I can think of something better to do if I notice any frown darkening that beautiful face of yours."

She looked at him. "Can you?"

"Aye. I'll steal you away to a quiet corner and have my way with you. A closet. A hallway in the upper floors. In one of the tower rooms. Actually, there are quite a few private spaces in Benmore that I plan to drag you into."

Kenna blushed at the suggestive gleam in his blue eyes. This was another thing to get used to. Receiving his affection in public. Not to be embarrassed before family and clan. So different from her own family.

The courtyard was ringed with buildings that huddled beneath the curtain walls. As they rode in, Kenna greeted men and women on both sides who stopped their work and approached. All around her people cheered their arrival.

Kenna's gaze traveled upward. On the wall of a great building across the close, a large stone medallion displayed the Macpherson family crest. Her eyes were drawn to the lion at the top of the shield. This was the same design on the brooch that Alexander wore on his tartan. The same design adorning the flags on Macpherson ships.

She stole a glance at Alexander beside her and couldn't help but say her thoughts aloud. "Blond, blue eyes, majestic, untamed, fierce, and protecting."

"Aye, lass. Your own lion!" His low growl made her smile.

Kenna surveyed the interior of the castle courtyard. With its three towers, Benmore Castle was far more impressive than Castle Varrich or Craignock Castle or anywhere else she'd ever been.

Alexander was reading her thoughts. "From the outside, it has the look of a fortress. But inside—you'll see for yourself—Benmore has many comforts."

Kenna heard the pride in Alexander's voice. Sitting astride her horse, here in the heart of the Highlands,

Kenna promised herself that she would face whatever challenges lay in her path. Somehow, she would find a way to belong.

A group of people had gathered on the stone stairwell leading up to a large doorway. She saw James had already arrived. Next to him stood a friend, an ally, a person that Kenna already knew she could rely on to teach her whatever expectations they might have of her. Colin's beautiful wife, Tess.

A step below them, the striking redheaded woman stood with the tall, distinguished-looking man with graying hair. Alec and Fiona Macpherson. Her in-laws, she thought, feeling the blood drain from her body.

Alexander was standing beside her horse, ready to help her down. He squeezed her hand.

"Be prepared," he murmured. "You're their daughter now. It does not matter how old or tall or accomplished we become, those two have no reserve when it comes to showing their affection. So be ready."

Kenna looked down into his smiling face. She was glad that her father had not yet arrived.

Alexander helped her from her horse, and the two walked side by side. In spite of her resolutions, in spite of his support, Kenna felt a weight dragging down her every step. Six months of fretting. Six months of doubt and fears. It all came down to this moment. She wanted so badly to make a good impression.

She tried not to think that she was in the presence of Lady Fiona Macpherson, half-sister to the late king himself. In her entire life, Kenna had never met anyone with nobler blood flowing in her veins. She tried to push away the memories of what she'd done at her wedding. Of how their introduction had gone before. Of how lacking she still was in sophistication and charm. She could only imagine how horrible she must look right now.

In spite of all of it, she had to wipe the slate clean. She had to make a fresh beginning. This was her only chance.

By the time they reached the group on the stairs, Kenna's insides were as taut as knotted rawhide. Fiona was standing quietly beside her husband, her long red hair loosely braided and cascading down her back in glorious waves. Kenna realized this was the first time that she was really looking her in-laws in the face.

Fiona's gray eyes had the same shade as James's. The Macpherson laird was an older and more distinguished version of Alexander, and even taller than James. The love they had for their son shone brightly in their eyes as they looked at Alexander first before turning their attention to her.

"Welcome to Benmore Castle, Kenna."

The laird's voice was deep and resonant. She extracted her arm from Alexander's and curtsied politely.

"Thank you, m'lord . . . m'lady," she whispered, her head bowed. She had to do it now. The apology that was long overdue. "I'm dreadfully sorry to inconvenience you for all these months. I—"

Lady Fiona reached out and took hold of Kenna's chin, putting an end to her stammering. She gently raised her face, and Kenna looked into eyes that conveyed nothing but kindness and affection.

"Welcome home, daughter," she said softly. "We were eager for you to come, and we are now overjoyed that you're here."

~

After the disaster at the mill, Kester took Emily back to Dunstaffnage Castle to give her time to mend the hole in her heart. But the gentle care at the hands of her aunt made no difference. Days later, Emily was still a raging, pacing picture of anguish.

The ocean winds were sharp and gray skies threatened rain when Emily ordered the warrior to meet her in the empty chapel.

His disbelief and then alarm became evident as she told him her news.

"Your father will put my head on a pike when he hears this."

"He won't. He relies on you."

"Emily, you must return to Craignock Castle. You've got a wedding to attend to. Sir Quentin has certainly arrived by now."

"Nay, I'll not go," she said emphatically. "And I'll not marry Sir Quentin, either. When you go, you can tell my father exactly that. He must call off the wedding. Cancel any agreement he's made. Do whatever needs to be done."

"If it's a matter of you spending time alone with the Highlander, the abbot will not say a word. Your reputation is intact. And you told me the man was honorable."

"He was," she said fiercely. "James Macpherson is the most honorable man alive."

Kester gentled his voice. "You're angry now. Upset. In another day or two, perhaps another week here with your aunt, you'll feel differently about all of it."

"I will not. And I'm not staying here."

"What do you mean, you're not staying here? You're with family. You're safe. Where do you think you're going?"

"To Glosters Priory."

"By Saint Andrew!" Kester threw his hands up. "And now you're pulling the same tricks as your cousin Kenna."

Emily might be a slow learner, but she now understood very clearly what Kenna had lectured her about. What she had before was not a life. What she was walking into with that arranged marriage was no better than imprisonment. She'd tasted passion with James, no matter how brief. True, she was in love with a man who would never look upon her again without hatred and suspicion, but she could not undo the harm she'd done. She had her memories, and those would have to be enough.

"What Kenna did was no trick. And besides, I have no plan to work with the nuns like my cousin. I've already sent word to the prioress there. I'll become cloistered, a bride to the Lord."

"Have you talked to your aunt about any of this?"

"Aye, of course."

"What did she say?"

"She says I should do as I wish," Emily retorted.

Kester ran a tired hand down his battered face. "Listen to me, Emily. I have gone along with your plans and schemes for too long. You're a smart and caring young woman. Think about your responsibility to your father. To your clan. You have—"

"Would it be better if I jumped into the sea?" She asked. "Or perhaps took poison or stabbed myself in the heart? Would my father or my clan prefer that I be dead, rather than giving myself over to God's work?"

"Now, see here—"

"I'll not marry Sir Quentin Chamberlain, Kester. So what should my choice be? Life or death?"

"Very well." The warrior shook his head in resignation. "Though your life will certainly mean my death at the hands of the MacDougall."

It wouldn't. She was certain of it. Her father trusted Kester with his life, with all of their lives.

What it would mean, she guessed, was that a marriage would soon take place. But it would be her father who was marrying. And another heir would follow. And all would be well for her clan. Perhaps not today, but in due time.

"Thank you," Emily said without joy.

"But on one condition. If you insist on going to Glosters Priory, then I must see you safely there."

~

Lying in the gorse at the top of the ridge, Maxwell saw the storm sweeping down the valley. The rain would be on them soon, but it didn't matter.

He'd found them.

Below, a black, foam-pocked river flowed along the narrow valley before disappearing into a pine forest that stretched as far to the south as the eye could see. To the north, the valley's hillsides rose steeply to peaks shrouded in mist.

Beside the river, smoke rose from two fires in the fenced-in yard of a hunting lodge. And in the yard, two dozen men and boys gathered in a large circle, raucously enjoying the combat between two lads no more than eight years old and identical in size and ability. The boys were fighting with short swords and sticks, and the battle was pitched. With every blow, the lads' cries reached them.

"If that ain't them, I'll fock one o' them shaggy red cows yonder," the man next to him said, nodding to the cattle grazing untended across the valley.

"Is or ain't, you'll fock the poor beast anyhow," another man sniggered, drawing low laughter from the line of men lying along the ridge.

"Quiet, fool," Maxwell ordered. "Or I'll cut your throat here and now."

Silence descended immediately.

Maxwell turned toward the lad standing with the horses and gestured for him to approach. The boy came quickly. His lip was still swollen from a blow he'd gotten the last time he was slow to answer a summons.

The Lowlander grabbed him by the collar and dragged him to the ground beside him.

"Look down there, Jock," he demanded. "Think you could beat either of them lads?"

The boy peered at the two battling in the farmyard. He shrugged sullenly.

"Didn't think so," Maxwell sneered. "Just a fishing lad, and no fighter, I'm thinking."

He scanned the number of adversaries and looked at Jock again. "What do you think? Should we attack? Can we take 'em?"

"Aye," he answered. "They've only a few more men than you. You should attack straightaway."

Maxwell shook his head, looking in grim amusement at Jock. "You'd like that, wouldn't you? Seeing us caught in a fight we might not win?"

The boy said nothing.

"Nay, we'll not bleed here in these godforsaken Highlands for a pair of miserable whelps. We'll take the MacKay lads, but at a time and place of our own choosing. Back to the horses."

Jock scrambled away.

Below, the line of rain reached the lodge, and the boys were soon slipping and falling and covered with mud. The laughter and shouts of encouragement only increased, and the two fought on.

"With their spirit, those lads will be out hunting again in the morning," Maxwell said. "And when they go, we'll find our chance to separate them from the others."

"Judging from the sound of them, them young curs'll put up a yowl that'll bring their keepers down on us quick."

Maxwell drew his dagger and held it up in front of the man's face. "Well, if they do, then we'll just cut out their tongues and see if they can muster even a whimper."

Chapter 25

None, but to desire your good company.

Looking into Lady Fiona's face, Kenna saw the warmth in those gray eyes and knew that all would be well between them. Her eyes misted. The older woman drew Kenna into her arms and that was her undoing. A mother's embrace that told her she was at home now. Kenna returned the hug even as she tried to tame the raw emotions bubbling to the surface.

"How about me?" the laird protested.

"You shall wait your turn," Fiona whispered, holding on to Kenna.

More horses were arriving in the courtyard. Kenna heard the laird shout out a welcome to the MacKay laird. Tension crept up from the base of her spine.

"See to our guest, my love," Fiona told the laird. "My daughters are coming with me."

Wrapping an arm around Kenna, she started up the

wide steps with Tess at her other side.

Alexander was beside them as they reached the door. "And no welcome for your son, mother?"

"Oh, I suppose you deserve one," Fiona laughed, embracing him.

Alexander lifted his mother off the ground and whirled her around, causing her to shriek. Kenna worried that he might hurt her. She needn't have feared.

"No sooner they cross the threshold of Benmore," Tess whispered, kissing Kenna on each cheek, "and the ruffian comes out in all three of them."

"So I see," Kenna replied with a smile.

"And they get it from their father." Tess nodded toward the laird. "So be prepared to get tricked and tripped and occasionally knocked off your feet. It is just their way of showing their affection. And it doesn't matter that you married the one; you are now sister to the other two, and that makes you a fair target."

"Which makes me a sister to you, too."

"I know." Tess's dark eyes reflected the brilliance of her smile as she hugged Kenna. "I was an only child and spent most of my years without the company of anyone my own age. I think I've been more impatient for this day to come than anyone else."

"Outside ... with the rest of them." Fiona's order to Alexander drew the two women's attention. "Your father needs you. The MacKays need to be seen to. And I believe your brothers need to see you down by the stables."

"The stables?" Kenna asked quietly.

Tess nodded. "It doesn't matter how old they are, the three always need to fight about politics, harvests, horses, religion, tides, and anything else that occurs to them," she whispered. "And I think before you and I were in the family, every other argument was about some woman or other."

Kenna didn't think she could ever think about Alexander and another woman—no matter how far back—without wanting to scratch out someone's eyes. He belonged to her now.

"Wait, but why the stables?"

"She sends them to the stables to protect the furniture in the Great Hall."

Fiona was pushing him across the landing. "And the three of us need some woman time."

As he let his mother move him, Alexander's gaze found Kenna's. She nodded and motioned to him to go. She felt perfectly at ease with Fiona and Tess.

Fiona patted Kenna's hand as they made their way through a throng of people toward the Great Hall. "I'm giving him less than an hour before he comes searching for you."

"He has the look," Tess agreed.

"What look is that?"

"A man in love." Fiona smiled. "You've done it, child. You've captured his heart."

Kenna blushed. A mother could see.

"And he has captured mine," she whispered.

Fiona squeezed Kenna's hand. "I know. Regardless of what your father likes to think, with your free spirit, you wouldn't be here unless you loved him."

She had no chance to say more as Lady Fiona introduced her to an aging steward named Robert inside the wide doors of the Great Hall.

"No trunks. No baggage. Just like the day you arrived, Lady Fiona," Robert observed. "The same with you, Lady Tess. Women with no possessions. Nothing to haul to the upper floors. I'm delighted to meet you, m'lady."

"Don't take to heart anything he says," Fiona said. "He means no insult. He has been here with us for so long that we can no longer even discipline him, though my husband occasionally threatens it. Robert is family."

"Aye. Family. So it is." The man's thin face creased in a smile. "I've served my lady for many years. Before coming to Benmore even. Aye, she was the Angel of Skye then."

"Angel of Skye?" Kenna asked her mother-in-law.

"Aye," Robert continued, ignoring the warning look from Fiona. "As Lord Alec still says, my lady here wasn't only a king's daughter. She was the fairy princess who rescued those in danger. She was a wood nymph who guarded the lepers. She was a kelpie who swam the lochs. She was a beloved rebel who broke every rule. Aye, this lady before you here is the Angel of Skye."

Kenna hadn't thought she could be more impressed, but here she was, awestruck.

"Will you tell me about it?" she asked Fiona.

"Someday, perhaps." She patted Kenna's hand. "We have far more important things to do first. I want to show you around. Then we need to get you ready for the banquet tonight."

"You'll be formally presented to the Macpherson clan," Tess told her.

Fiona turned to the steward. "And I believe you have work to do?"

"Aye. And why is it that you felt the need to move the newlyweds to the Roundtower Room?" he complained. "Those are perfectly good chambers Alexander occupies."

"Robert!" Fiona's sharp tone sent the steward scurrying off, grumbling under his breath.

"A tradition that began when I first arrived at Benmore," Fiona told her. "That was my room. Then Tess stayed there before she and Colin married and took charge of Ravenie Castle. I thought you could use that room while you decide which chambers in the castle suit you and Alexander. This is your home now. The decision will be yours."

The rush of emotions came quick. Kenna somehow managed to murmur her thanks. But no words were enough to describe how welcome Fiona had already made her feel.

"And the builders and construction." The older woman waved at the crew of men working on ladders and scaffolds in the Great Hall. "It's Benmore Castle's destiny always to be undergoing renovations. My mother-in-law was determined to improve the place. I've done my share over the years. And now you're next. Decide what needs change, and you'll have an army of helpers to do it for you."

Growing up, there had been no expectation of Kenna getting involved in doing anything at Castle Varrich. There had been no changes since her mother's death. The household ran just as her mother arranged it. No one offered to teach her or involve her. Everyone always knew that one day she'd marry and go.

Kenna had much to learn from these two women.

"The Great Hall is magnificent." She let her eyes travel the length of the chamber. Each of the plastered walls was covered with colorful tapestries and hangings of embroidered velvet, silk, and damask. The floors were covered, as well, with ornate rugs fine enough for hanging on the walls. From behind them, the chatter of people starting to file into the hall filled the air with laughter and good cheer.

Lady Fiona led Kenna toward an arch and into the quiet of a long corridor.

As they made their way along, Kenna asked the other women about the history of the castle and the improvements that had been made.

Fiona was delighted at the show of interest and made a point of taking her through every room they passed. Her mother-in-law's pride in Benmore had no bounds. Kenna saw glazed windows and the new fireplaces in living quarters. She was led through new kitchens and the brew house, and then up one floor to some smaller guest chambers directly above. By the time they had worked their way around to the other end of the castle, Kenna was amazed at the effort and expense that had gone into the castle's renovation.

Kenna took Tess's hand. "Alexander told me before that you and Colin spend a great deal of time at Ravenie Castle. Why don't you live here?"

"I ask them the same thing."

Tess smiled. "Ravenie Castle burned and lay in ruins for years. Colin and I are rebuilding it. For all that time my clan was abandoned. It's our responsibility to be there, to help rebuild and strengthen the clan. But, as you'll find out, we enjoy spending time here with the family."

Moments later, Fiona led them up a winding stairwell. Kenna held her breath as she entered the Roundtower Room.

"This is absolutely exquisite."

"I remember thinking the same thing," Tess whispered, standing beside her in the doorway.

The room was large and airy, with leaded glass windows to keep out the cold Highland wind but still provide a sweeping view of the hills outside. The base of each window was corbelled, with a bow-shaped oak sill wide enough to sit on. A large canopy bed with richly embroidered curtains sat against an inner wall. The floors were made of oak, and a handmade rug covered only part of the burnished wood.

"I've kept everything here the same." Fiona motioned them to the middle of the room.

"I can see why."

"It's delightful how much the three of us have in common."

"Me?" Kenna replied, surprised, looking at the other two.

Fiona nodded, helping Kenna out of her cloak and drawing her down beside her onto a bench. Tess moved to the window, looking out at the view.

"I was torn from my family as a child. Drummond Castle, where my mother and I lived, came under attack the same night I was to meet my father for the first time. I left there that night, knowing that I would never see my parents again." Her voice wavered. "I was raised simply, without the comforts and finery that life in a good family offers."

"But you were a king's daughter."

"To those wonderful nuns who raised me, I was a castoff." She looked at Tess.

"I was taken away from a burning castle as a child, too," Tess said. "There was so much that I didn't remember. I washed ashore on the Isle of May and was raised by a kindly old couple who lived alone on the island."

"The reason why we bring this up is to let you know that we understand," Fiona explained. "Although you grew up at Castle Varrich and among your clan, we know the hardship you went through after your mother's death."

Kenna shrugged. "My clan folk are good people. Many showed me kindness when I needed it."

"But your father didn't," Fiona corrected. "I know."

"How . . . do you . . . ?"

"I was in the room when he was trying to order my husband about and telling James to use whatever means possible to bring you back to Benmore. It was clear to me that he wasn't concerned about his daughter. He was discussing property of his that needed to be delivered."

Anger flowed through her veins like a river of ice. "When was this?"

"It was just before James made the arrangement with the MacDougalls to hide one of our ships and fool Alexander into going to Craignock. Of course, you know the rest."

Kenna did and she didn't. So she and Alexander had been tricked. She harbored no resentment toward James for what he'd done. He'd been doing the best he could with the task he'd been given. But what she was feeling about her father was another story.

"Where is Magnus MacKay staying while he's here at Benmore?" she asked.

Fiona and Tess exchanged a quick look of alarm.

"He's in the guest chambers in the wing beyond the next tower."

"Would you forgive me if I leave you for a few moments, m'lady?" Kenna asked, standing and heading for the door.

"Where are you going?" Tess asked. "You can get lost. Can I come with you?"

"I'll find my way," Kenna said, pretending calmness while her heart pounded with fury. "I had no opportunity to greet my father properly when I met him on the road."

Without another word, she disappeared through the door.

Chapter 26

O God, that I were a man! I would eat his heart
in the market-place.

"I'm looking for my father. Have you seen him?"

The steward was coming into the corridor from the stairwell. Tess had been correct. The castle was a maze of wings and twisting passageways. Finding Robert was a blessing.

"Nay. That I haven't. I've just come up from the Great Hall. I can tell you he wasn't down there with the laird and your husband."

"Do you have any suggestions where I might find him?" she asked, trying to remain patient.

The steward looked at her closely. "I should think the MacKay went off to his chamber to rest and prepare for tonight's events. Would you like me to take you there?"

"If you please."

"Aye, then. This way." Robert pointed back the way she'd come.

It had all come to this moment, after a lifetime of being silent. Well, not exactly silent, she conceded inwardly. But in any event, it was time to face him. She would speak her peace or she would explode. Six months ago, he'd inflicted the deepest of wounds and she'd run away. No more. It was time she faced him and spoke her peace. She wouldn't start her life at Benmore dragging the past behind her.

"Shouldn't you be doing the same?" Robert asked, casting a side-glance at her as they moved down a few steps into a different part of the castle. "Shouldn't you be resting? You've been on the road for quite some time, I hear."

"Thank you, but I'm fine."

They walked along in silence for a while.

Any show of daughterly decorum be damned, she fumed. She would no longer do this. She would not build a marriage with Alexander while Magnus MacKay went around taking credit for it. She would not allow him to belittle her before her new family. And she would not tolerate his dark cloud over every joyful event of her life.

They climbed a few stairs into yet another part of the castle.

Robert paused by an alcove. A torch sputtered above them. "I was not always a steward, you know. In fact, that wasn't my intention, at all, when I was a lad."

Kenna stood waiting. When Lady Fiona had taken her through the castle, the place had seemed large, but it was clearly even more extensive than she'd thought. Still, she'd said the MacKay's chambers were just in the wing beyond the next tower.

"I was squire to Lord Alec when he was sent to Dunvegan Castle on the Isle of Skye. Did you know my lord and lady met on that island?"

Kenna motioned with her head that she was listening.

"Aye, that was a wild place. But Lord Alec soon set it aright. With my help, of course. Nothing like the peaceful haven we handed over to Malcolm MacLeod a few years ago."

"Of course," she said shortly. "If we could continue—"

"Certainly. Certainly."

Robert started along the corridor again.

"You know Malcolm is step-brother to your husband. Raised by Lord Alec and Lady Fiona, he was. Like he was one of their own. Have you met Malcolm's wife, Jaime? She is another Macpherson." The steward never waited for acknowledgment, but continued talking. "Daughter to Ambrose and Elizabeth. Jaime is a spirited lass, to be sure. Used to chase after Malcolm and call him 'husband' from the time she was just a wee sprite of a thing. Always saw herself as the 'intended' and never settled until he married her. A great adventurous tale, if it were to be told.

Would you like to hear it?"

"Perhaps another time." Kenna looked around her. This passageway looked familiar. "Robert, didn't we just come through this hallway a few moments ago?"

"I don't know that we did, mistress. Benmore is a braw, great place. And the way Lady Fiona had it rebuilt, everything looks the same, but finer." Robert waved in the air and motioned her to follow. "As I was saying, when I was much younger, my one wish was to become a fighter, a warrior. I wanted nothing more than to go out and train with the men instead of looking after the low tasks that squires need to see to."

"And did you train?" Kenna asked.

"Aye. In fact, Lord Alec encouraged me."

"And?"

"A woeful tale, it is. I found out soon enough that I'd become afraid of heights. Not just afraid. Petrified. I'd look over the edge of some cliff or wall, and I couldn't move. Felt like I was about to fall, or worse, leap off. It sounds mad, I know, but there it is."

"That must have been difficult for you."

"Aye. Devastating. Now, I know wielding a sword at the edge of some cliff is not necessary for a warrior, but it still made me question what exactly it was I wanted."

"And what did you decide you wanted?"

"To belong. To be part of a family. To be with people

who care about me. Folk I can care for. To be useful. That's what mattered."

As they entered another corridor, Kenna looked at the set of doorways. About halfway down, she spied an alcove with a sputtering torch.

"Stop right there," she told him. "I recognize this. You are taking me down the same hallways."

"Am I, mistress?"

"Why?" she asked, facing him. "Why are you doing this?"

The steward looked down at her. "Are you armed, Lady Kenna?"

"What?"

"Are you carrying a knife or a weapon of any kind?"

"Perhaps I am. Why?"

"May I see it?"

Kenna glared at him for a moment. She didn't know what this was about, but she decided to go along. She cautiously drew her dirk.

"May I, if you please?"

He stretched out his hand, palm up. She placed the knife in it, and he inspected its blade and tested its weight and balance.

"A fine thing, this. I'll hold onto it for the moment, if you don't mind."

She bristled. "What's this all about, Robert?"

He motioned to the door they were standing in front of. "These are your father's chambers. I'll be standing guard with your dagger until you come out."

The merry chase he'd set her on became clear. Robert had been trying to give her a chance to cool her temper.

"You're a strange man."

"Thank you, mistress," he returned with a smile. "I've been called far worse."

"And you talk too much."

"A unanimous position, I believe."

"But I hope you don't think I'd stab a guest—never mind my father—inside the walls of Benmore."

"I could never think such a thing, mistress."

"Very well." She held out her hand. "Then you'll give me my knife back."

"Nay. I won't." He took a step back and hid the weapon behind him. "I'll tell you the honest truth, Lady Kenna. I saw the look in your face. And your reputation precedes you. I'll just be holding it for you here."

She considered wrestling him for it but decided there was no point in that. She wasn't planning to use it, anyway. And he'd succeeded in diffusing her rage.

"We're not finished with this, you and I."

"As you wish, mistress."

"You will not eavesdrop on our conversation."

"I swear." He nodded and crossed himself. "The wood is too thick, in any event. I've tried before."

Kenna turned to the door, her mind clearer on what she wanted from this meeting with her father. She knocked once.

~

The library instead of the stables. Conversation in lieu of physical combat.

Alexander had known the traditional homecoming of two brothers teaming up against one would not be a wise move today.

James was upset, and while that didn't generally stop them from showing their fraternal "affection," he had a feeling that today someone might get seriously hurt.

And after forcing their brother to tell them what had transpired—the kidnapping from the tavern in Oban, the dungeons at Dunstaffnage, the involvement of Kester—Colin and Alexander exchanged a look, knowing they'd done the right thing.

"And you never suspected a thing?" Colin asked.

"Nay, the bloody chit is a wily thing. You wouldn't know it to look at her."

"Aye, she's a right bonny lass," Alexander put in, drawing a sharp look from James.

"But why?" Colin continued. "Why go through such a scheme?"

"I don't know," he spat. "But I guess she wanted to teach me a lesson. We hadn't included her in the plan for Alexander and Kenna."

"You never told her it was staged?" Colin said.

"Not until later."

"So she turned the tables on you."

James scowled and stalked to the fireplace.

"That is one smart woman," Colin said admiringly. "Though it seems strange that she'd jeopardize her future, with her wedding so close."

"Aye, she's daft, for all I can tell," James snapped.

"And you proposed marriage to her?" Alexander asked to make certain.

"Aye, to save her reputation."

"And she didn't accept."

"Of course not," James raged. "That was when she admitted it was all a lark."

"A lark?" Alexander repeated.

"Aye," he nearly shouted. "She was playing me for the fool."

"And what did you do?" Colin asked.

"I bloody well lost my temper. What do you think?"

"You didn't kill anyone?" Alexander asked cautiously.

"Nay. But Emily and her lackey Kester and all the rest of

those bloody MacDougalls are lucky I'm not a violent man."

"And no one was hurt?" Alexander had to make certain.

"Kester needed a lesson. But I left him with only a bleeding lip."

"The bastard deserved a beating," Colin agreed. "But it's probably a good thing you didn't seriously hurt or kill him. That would certainly have added a complication between our clans—"

"He's fine," James spat, sounding like he wished it were not so.

"And then you ran for home," Colin suggested. "I mean, you stole the man's horse to teach him a lesson."

The murderous glare James sent their younger brother didn't go unnoticed by Alexander. He guessed they weren't being told the whole truth. The dark cloud hanging over the redheaded beast said James had been more than just a victim of a reprisal prank. He'd met Emily. She was a sensible young woman. And there'd certainly been something developing between her and James on the road. He'd seen that from the moment James pulled the hood from her head at the abbey.

"Where is Emily now?" Alexander asked. "Did she go back to Craignock for her wedding?"

"I have no idea where she is," James hissed, moving to the window and staring out. "But she can burn in hell, for all I care."

Alexander and Colin exchanged a look as their brother whirled to face them.

"And I don't want to hear her bloody name ever again!"

~

Robert's interference didn't work.

The moment Magnus MacKay opened his door and she spied his sour visage, the fires of her anger ignited again. She remembered their last private meeting. The night before her wedding. A scared young woman reaching out to her father, hoping for help, guidance, assurance, some thread of hope to make her feel adequate in what she was embarking on. It had been a disaster.

That was not even a year ago, but that woman was long gone.

"I need a moment of your time," she demanded, moving past him into the room.

She didn't see walls or furnishings or the view from the windows. The surroundings floated about her in a reddish haze.

She whirled on her father. "Your behavior is reprehensible, and I've grown sick and tired of it."

"My behavior?" he growled. "You show great nerve coming in here and accusing me of anything."

"Lady Fiona told me of your latest underhanded interference in my life. I think you would have done just about
anything to deliver me to Benmore."

"It needed to be done." His hard stare hid whatever emotion brewed inside, if any. "It was time to put an end to your
nonsense. The Macpherson laird agreed. And James was
invaluable in taking charge of the arrangements. Alexander Macpherson could have requested an annulment. That
would have put an end to everything I planned."

"*You* planned," she repeated, tasting the bitterness in
her mouth. "Aye, you told me, in no uncertain terms.
Right before the wedding. For the good of the clan, you
said. For the safety of your sons. Everything planned to
make a better life for those *you* care about. And it didn't
matter that your plans included trading away a 'woefully
inadequate' daughter before the buyer had a chance to
discover the fraud she was."

"I recall that night. I was angry with you. Tired of your at-
titude. I said those things to motivate you, to wake you up
to the real world." He shrugged and turned away, moving to
the window and looking out. "I am clan chief of the MacK-
ays. I do as I see fit. It was not for you to be questioning my
decisions. You wanted me to stop the wedding."

She'd been frightened. She'd gone to him, hoping
against hope that her father had her well-being in mind,
too.

Kenna thought of Alexander and how much she loved him now. She thought of the warmth and welcome of the Macphersons. Staring at her father's back, she thought of how loveless and indifferent he was. This man had shut her out, treated her more coldly than he would treat a stranger. And that wasn't for a day, or a month, or a year. That had been for all the years after her mother's death.

Well, this was her home now. How different, how much better her life would be now. She had far more worthwhile things to do than waste even a moment trying to change his mind about her, or trying to win so much as an ounce of his affection.

"Very well. You did it. I'm exactly where you intended me to be. And I am staying. Benmore Castle is my new home. The Macphersons are my new clan, my new family. And the surprising thing is, they want me here. When have I ever felt that before?"

He half turned but did not look at her.

"You've delivered on your part of the bargain. The articles of agreement on the contract have been met. The Macphersons will honor their part."

His gaze drifted to her, but his face showed no expression.

"And I want you to go," she said, trying desperately to hide the hurt and anger in her voice. She wouldn't cry in front of him. "Now. Immediately. Before the clan gathering tonight. Before I am presented to my new people."

Her father said nothing.

"Do you hear me? Let me make this clear. I no longer want you in my life. I want no visits from you. Go and leave me to live in peace."

His guarded expression revealed nothing. His voice was low when he spoke.

"As you wish. I'll be gone this afternoon."

The gaze returned to the window.

She nodded and turned on her heel as her tears broke free. The door was only a few short steps away. She closed the distance. Her hand shook as she reached for the latch. She hesitated.

This would be the last time she'd ever speak to him, Kenna promised herself.

"One last thing before I go, before you're out of my life forever. Tell me, at least, why you treat me like this. What have I done that you should harbor such resentment?"

"There's no resentment."

"Don't lie to me," she cried, turning around. "At least have the decency to tell the truth this once. I'm your only daughter!"

He was watching her from the window. "Let it go. Best not wake the sleeping hound."

"Wake him! I need an answer. There once was a time in my life when I was loved by a mother *and* a father. I recall a time when I was the jewel of your eyes, the center of your attention, the child you doted on. I want to know what I did to turn your affection into loathing."

"What *you* want? Must it always be what you want?" He shook his head. "I have nothing more to say, Kenna. Enough."

"It's not enough," she cried. "Don't you see? You buried your love for me the day you buried my mother. But why? Why? Someday, God willing, I will bring a child of my own into this world. For the sake of that child, tell me what a little girl can possibly do to destroy the love of a father."

Through the blur of tears, Kenna couldn't see his eyes. All she could see was an aging Highlander who threw up a shield between them whenever she was near.

"Please, Father."

He had no answer, offered no explanation.

She turned once more to the door, but her fingers froze at the sound of his voice.

"I hold you responsible for your mother's death."

~

The tinker's eyes opened wide as Maxwell and his men strode out of the darkness into his camp. In the firelight, the Lowlander saw the look of fear the man immediately tried to hide.

"Welcome, friends," the man said, rising slowly and struggling to straighten his old back. "I've naught but some bannock cake, but yer welcome to share it 'round."

Maxwell waved him off and gestured to one of his men. "Bring our new friend some of that beef we had for our supper."

The tinker raised an eyebrow as he received a slab of roasted meat. "Why, thank ye. The laird of these parts, a mean fellow to his very bones, ain't usually so generous with his cattle."

"So right you are," Maxwell replied, sitting by the man's fire. "But since the man wasn't about, we didn't think he'd mind us helping ourselves."

Maxwell's men lurked on the edges of the darkness rimming the camp. The tinker had seen them in the distance earlier in the day. He'd pretended not to notice them and turned his ox-drawn cart to the west, but Maxwell wasn't fooled.

"Well, a fine job ye did with this meat, I'm thinking."

Maxwell drew his dagger and pressed the point into the soft ground in front of him. "But you'll not be telling tales on us, I hope."

"Devil take me, if I do. I'm just an 'umble journeyman. And I don't mind telling ye that the MacKays north of here are not the most welcoming of strangers like you and me."

"So you're not a MacKay?"

"Damn me and my pap's kilted arse if I am. I'm a Sutherland, through and through."

"A Sutherland, traveling in MacKay land."

"Och, this was all Sutherland land up to a dozen years ago or so. For now, the MacKays hold it, but not for long, they say."

They sat for a few moments, the silence broken only by the sound of the crackling fire and the tinker chewing.

"So," the craftsman said. "Would ye be in need of some polishing of yer swords? Ye wouldn't want to be seen at a disadvantage by the lassies at the festival."

Maxwell drew his dagger from the ground and looked at it. The polished metal gleamed in the firelight. He looked up at his men. Their faces glowed red in the darkness.

"You hear that, lads? A festival . . . and lasses." A murmur of approval came from the men. "And what festival is that?"

"Why, in these parts, it's the grandest festival of all. I'm going there now. Five days of feasting and revelry. At the Abbey of the Oak. Just beyond the glen away to the west of here."

"And folk travel from all about here to go to the festival?"

"Aye, everyone. And from far off, across the sea, even. Pilgrims. The abbey ain't much to speak of, anymore. Only two or three monks left. But they have the third finger of Saint Brigid's right hand!"

This could be the chance they were waiting for, Maxwell thought. During the hunting each morning, the two MacKay boys were being watched over like a pair of matched pearls, *and he was starting to think they might need to take them by force. But if they went to the festival—and they very likely would go—then he could either snatch them there or surprise them on the road somewhere.*

"And do you think strangers like us would be welcome?"

"Aye, I'm certain of it, if—begging yer pardon—ye have money in yer purse. Why, last year they had pilgrims from as far as Inverness and Belfast even. Quite the festival, it is."

Maxwell considered his options and decided. Some of his men would go as pilgrims. They could use some salvation, and Saint Brigid's finger was sure to do the trick. He turned and slapped the man on the shoulder.

"You've convinced me. We're going. And as for polishing weapons . . ." he began and then paused.

His dagger flashed in the light and the blade disappeared into the chest of the tinker. The man stared down at Maxwell's fist on the hilt, tried to turn his head, and slumped over.

"That's all the polishing my weapons need."

Chapter 27

Yea, and I will weep a while longer.

How? she thought. *How could I possibly be responsible?*

Kenna's mind raced, and then as if stepping out of a fog, years peeled away. She was in the room with her mother, clutching her hand, refusing to be taken away, as Sine's voice faltered. She moaned in pain. The twins were born the night before. Kenna only saw them in passing.

"Teach her. Tell her what to do."

Her father's voice rang in the room. Kenna didn't know what he meant and who needed to be taught. Women crowded around the bed, fussing, seeing after the patient. Kenna gazed into her mother's eyes while fighting the tears. She kissed the weak fingers, desperate to show her love, as words would not claw out of her throat.

"Please, Sine. Do it now."

Her mother's lips moved. She squeezed Kenna's hand

and mouthed the words. "Go . . . you go now. See your brothers."

Kenna shook her head. She wasn't leaving her mother's bed.

Sine's gaze drifted over Kenna's shoulders where Magnus MacKay stood. "Take her."

Her father paused before taking hold of her arms. Kenna sobbed. She wouldn't let go. She didn't want to leave the room. Her cries for her mother rang in the bedchamber when he finally was able to carry her out.

In the shadows of the solemn Great Hall, he put her down.

"Listen to me, Kenna. Go see your brothers but then come back," he told her. "I want you to tell your mother that you are ready. That she has to let you try. It is your right. Your duty."

It is your right. She has to let you try. You are ready. The words continued to repeat in her head.

The next time Kenna saw her mother, it was too late.

She now understood. She had the power to cure any injury, to save a life from the very edge of the abyss. She had been there, holding her mother's hand, as Sine lay on her deathbed.

He'd been trying to tell her what to do back then.

She looked up at her father and a dark curtain was torn asunder. He knew. Her mother had entrusted him with the knowledge of her gift.

"You're talking about the stone," she said. "The tablet. The fragment that belonged to my mother."

"Aye, the healing stone," he replied, letting out a weary breath. "So you know what it is and what it can do."

"I only just discovered the power of it. When Alexander was badly injured, when we were on the road, I was certain he'd die. There was nothing humanly possible I could have done to save him. And then I reached for the stone."

He nodded, leaning against the wall, as if he'd delivered a weight and now he was allowed to rest. "How did you know what to do?"

"I didn't know. The stone showed me. I remembered seeing it on Mother. It was with my wedding dress and other things she left for me. I held it . . . and it worked. It came alive in my hand and guided me. I was able to heal him."

He sank onto a bench by the window. His elbows rested on his knees, his head hanging.

"This is exactly as she said it would be." His voice sounded as if it were coming up from a deep well. "She told me it needed to happen this way."

The memory was back. She remembered his face that day. The tearful eyes when he told her to come back. He was hurting and she didn't know what to do—how to make him better.

"I remember your words. I recall what you told me to do. But I didn't know what they meant. I had no idea of what I could do or I would have never left my mother's side."

Large hands covered his face. She knew he was reliving the same moments.

"You hold me responsible. But I didn't even have the stone until six months ago," she said softly. "Why? Why would you punish me? What did I do wrong?"

Silence hung in the room.

"She didn't want me to see her die. She had you take me away because she loved me." Kenna couldn't hide the tremor in her voice. She was way past holding back her emotions. "You loved her. But how could you blame me . . . the daughter she loved . . . your daughter . . ."

"I was desperate for someone to blame."

He ran a hand down his face and she saw the tears he batted away. "I've never moved past the grief I still have at losing her."

"And the same goes for me," she reminded him. "She was my light, my air, the sunshine, my happiness. Losing her was the end of my childhood."

His eyes welled with tears when he met hers. "Kenna, it's not you. It's *she,* your mother, that I've never forgiven."

Kenna could no longer be a distant observer. She moved to his side, sat on the bench beside him. This close, his pain became hers—her sorrow gripped by him.

"It was a terrible thing, a difficult birth. After the boys finally came, there was nothing the midwife could do to stop the bleeding. I asked Sine . . . I begged her to give you the stone. If she had done it, you could have saved her life."

"And why didn't she?" Kenna asked, having no control over the tears that blanketed her face.

"She said you were just a child. She said the stone brought great responsibility and immense danger. The relic was both a gift and a curse. She told me you were not ready."

"So you blamed me because I wasn't older? And you think I wouldn't have taken it that day?"

"I know. But I needed someone to blame. I told myself that if you'd only come back in, told her that you were ready, convinced her somehow, that maybe . . ."

"But I didn't have any idea!"

"I know. I . . . I've been a fool, Kenna. A blind, angry fool."

She reached over and took his hand. His other hand, rough and calloused, covered hers.

"I loved her. More than a man should, perhaps. I couldn't accept that she chose death over me. Over us." He took a deep breath to steady himself. "She worried about your safety. But I told her I would protect you as I protected her. But she wouldn't have it. She wouldn't listen to anything I said. She'd made up her mind, and I had no say in the decision. She just wouldn't listen to reason. I was frustrated. Angry. That's why I tried to tell you . . . make you ask for it . . . make you talk her into giving it to you. But then she was gone."

Kenna tried to imagine how Alexander would suffer watching her die when there was a way to keep her alive. Kenna tried to understand her mother's decision. A gift and a curse. Would she pass such a responsibility on to a child of hers to save her own life? Would she rob her own offspring of a childhood? Moreover, was there more to the curse that Kenna still didn't know?

She wiped the tears from her face. She felt at peace, sitting here with her father. Still, there was a great deal that they hadn't talked about yet.

"Do you know how she came to have the stone?"

"From her mother. She inherited it on her wedding day, too," he told her. "And like you, she had no one to show her what to do. Her mother had been dead for years. And yet she knew how to use it. When she needed it, the stone came alive for her."

Kenna looked up into his face. For years, she'd suffered from his coldness, his lack of affection. Now she wanted answers.

"You can say what you will about blame," she said.

"But it was your heart that spoke loudest. You took out your anger on me. Why?"

"Because you have been a constant reminder of her," he said. "The way you look, your manners, your independence, your reckless courage. From that day to this, every time I've seen you, I could not help but think of Sine. And I couldn't get past the belief that she should have still been a part of our lives."

Many told her that she was a mirror image of her mother.

"And you could have handled the stone. You had the strength, even then. You had a spirit in you that was so much older than your years. But then it was too late."

She was surprised when he brushed the fresh tears off her face. Such a simple act, and yet how many years since he'd last shown her any affection? He stood up and walked across the room.

"And in time, my anger and frustration turned to bitterness. I see that. I suppose I thought by holding back my affection from you, I could punish her. As if she would look down and understand how much pain I still felt." He began to pace. "Your mother loved you. She loved you more than me. She loved you more than those newborn twins, I think. She loved you more than life itself."

Kenna dabbed at the tears that wouldn't stop.

"All the instructions on her deathbed were about you. All her worries were about what would become of you."

Kenna hugged her middle. Her grief over the loss of her mother was as fresh a wound today as the day it happened.

"To her last breaths," he said, turning to her, "she was consumed by what I needed to know, what I needed to do for you. I must choose a worthy husband for you. One with enough power and position to protect you and the responsibility you would be burdened with. She made me promise that the stone would be kept for you until you married. But even then, I was not to speak a word of it unless you asked. She told me, 'The stone will show her the way. It will teach her what she needs to know.' She said, 'It would become one with her, in body and soul.'"

And it had, Kenna thought. Her mother knew. And she also foresaw the dangers. Today, she had Evers and Maxwell chasing her. Tomorrow, it would be someone else.

Kenna closed her eyes and wiped her face again. When she opened them, she found her father on one knee before her.

"I never thought I would say this," he said, taking her hand. "But it breaks my heart to see you and know I've failed in my promise to her. So lost in my own grief, I see now—though I suppose I've known it for a long time—that I've failed you as a father."

She couldn't find her voice.

"I do love you, daughter. And when you ask me, tell me, that you no longer want me in your life . . . this is death for me. Once again, I know I'm losing a piece of my heart."

She looked into his tearstained face. Her heart nearly broke to see him like this.

"Tell me, Kenna. Tell me where we go from here."

~

One more minute and Alexander would have taken down the door.

But when Kenna appeared, he took one look at her tearstained face and started past her to shove open the door again.

"I'll kill the bastard."

"Nay. Don't. All is well." She held his arm and turned him around. "All is *very* well. We talked, Alexander. We've settled our differences."

He drew her to him, holding her so tight that there wasn't a breath of space between them. A year ago, six months ago, he didn't think such a thing was possible. But he knew it now. His love for her ran deeper than the waters of Loch Ness, deeper than the western ocean itself. Just seeing her troubled made him want to tear something down. Only the smile on her lips calmed him, made him want to rebuild it again.

"But what are you doing here?" she asked, pulling back far enough until she could look up into his face. "What happened to Robert?"

"He came after me as soon as you went inside. He was terrified that he'd put you at a disadvantage somehow. He kept jabbering on about hotheadedness and knives and reputation."

She smiled. "He thought my father might stab me?"

"He must think you inherit your temper from somewhere." He kissed her brow, her damp cheeks, her lips. "Enough about Robert. What happened in there, and when is he leaving?"

They started down the hallway.

"He's not leaving. Not right away. I told him I wanted him to go, and he agreed that he would. But then, after we talked, I asked him to stay."

"You want him here? Truly?"

"Let's go back to our chamber where we can talk privately."

He nodded.

"Wait, you're not going to lead me on a merry chase around the castle like Robert, are you?"

"No chance." He smiled. "But going back to the

Roundtower Room is out of the question. My mother has an army of dressmakers and servants waiting for you there."

He ducked under a low archway and took her up a narrow, airless stairwell. He didn't want them to see or be seen by anyone.

"Is this one of those private spaces you warned me about?"

"It could be."

"Seriously, where are we going?"

"To the chamber I slept in before my mother made other plans for us."

"Why?"

Alexander knew his father wanted to meet and welcome Kenna personally before the festivities tonight. His mother had threatened him to not detain her; the dressmakers were waiting. Tess was insisting on helping Kenna prepare so she could tell her what to expect. Colin was probably already off somewhere planning some mischief. And James . . . well, James wasn't a problem. He just looked miserable and wanted to be left alone.

Alexander knew he was being greedy with her time, and he felt no guilt whatsoever.

"I want you all to myself."

With her hand in his, they ran up the curving stone stairs. Coming out into the hallway near the rooms, they nearly barreled into Robert, who looked tremendously relieved at the sight of them.

"She's alive, praise the Lord," the steward exclaimed. "And I knew this would be where you'd bring her."

"Did you do as I told you?"

"Aye. When have you known me to fail you? Why, I—"

"Listen to me, you old rattle," Alexander threatened. "You didn't see us. You didn't speak with us. You have no idea where we are. Is that clear?"

The lanky steward considered his order.

"I telling you, if you let on to anyone Kenna is here with me, I'll nail your carcass to the stable door."

Robert turned to Kenna. "He always talks to me this way, mistress. I'm sorry you have to hear such nonsense. He's actually quite—"

"Robert," Alexander drawled threateningly.

"Very well. I never saw you. You'll not be disturbed." He began to turn away.

"Wait." Kenna put out her hand, palm up to the steward. The two eyed each other for a lengthy moment.

"He'll be safe with me," she told Robert.

With an amused shake of his head, the steward handed over the weapon. "I do believe you two deserve each other."

Once the door was closed behind them, Alexander could wait no longer. Pushing her up against the door, he kissed her hard. He explored ravenously, and her enthusiasm matched his own.

As he'd expected, the moment she tore free to catch her breath, she spotted the huge tub filled with steaming water. She smiled up into his face.

"You're taking a bath."

"*We* are taking a bath. Robert had it delivered here for the two of us."

"But your mother expects me to return to my room."

"Of course, she does. But we do what we want," he said, bolting the door.

A soft blush immediately spread across her flawless cheeks. "But we can't. It's daylight. Everyone in the castle would know what we're doing. And I have no clean clothes to put on after." She shook her head. "If anyone were to see me, it would be a scandal."

Alexander wanted to laugh out loud at her innocence, but he wouldn't hurt her feelings for the world. Where did she think they'd be sleeping after the banquet tonight?

"As you wish. You wanted a place where we can talk. Here we are. Just the two of us. I'll sit in the bath while we speak. I have enough road dirt on me to fill the moat. Tell me about the conversation with your father."

She moved into the spacious room, talking as she looked at everything.

"My father knows about the stone. My mother told

him. He says she inherited it from her mother. He knows nothing of its origins or how my grandmother came to have it."

He watched her as her fingers trailed along the bed-clothes, as she looked out the window, tested the chairs, all the while telling him everything that was discussed with her father. She told him that Magnus wanted Sine to give up the stone so her life could be saved.

"If it were the two of us, I would have forced you," he asserted. "I would have pulled down the sky and torn the earth asunder to save you."

She paused. "You say this now because we have no children. Imagine the responsibility we would be putting on a child. Perhaps it would be too much for her to bear."

He didn't want to think of it. He wouldn't want to be in that position. He wanted Kenna with him forever. That's all he knew.

"You matter above all things," he said quietly. "My love for you will rule any decision that I make, from now till the end of time. I'm telling you now that I will fight for you—and I will not fight fair."

She came across the room and embraced him, press-ing her face against his chest. "I love you, Alexander. And today, right now, I will not fight you over choices that I hope we never have to make."

He pulled her hair back until her face turned up to his.

This woman was the very air in his lungs. "You love me."

"I love you."

And his lips met hers.

"I have other things to tell you," he said, unfastening his brooch and yanking his shirt over his head.

She stared at his chest.

He sat on the edge of the tub and pulled off his boots. "I've learned that all of that business in the west—the ship, the kidnapping, leaving us in the wilderness—it was all arranged. The whole thing was just to get you and me back together."

"I heard the same thing earlier today."

"To be honest, I've known it since we boarded my ship at the Hermit's Rock. Diarmad told me."

"And you made no mention of it."

He stood and pulled his hair free of the thong holding it back.

"Nay, I didn't. I think I was too grateful at the moment to James for being so cunning ... and happy that our clans wanted it so badly." He smiled. "Also, my thoughts were too intent on ravishing you in my cabin. I didn't want you to be distracted."

"I also learned today that you never requested an annulment."

He gazed at her for a long moment.

"Aye, lass. That's true."

He unfastened his belt, and the dark wool of his kilt pooled at his feet.

"Why?"

Her eyes drifted over his chest, stomach, and lower.

Alexander turned away. He was starting to enjoy this.

She aroused him with a mere look. He stepped into the tub, sitting down.

"By the devil!" he cursed, lifting up and then slowly settling back into the water. "That bastard Robert just scalded my scallops!"

She laughed and then grew serious again. "Why didn't you go to the bishop for the annulment?"

"Because I knew this would be the way between us. And if James hadn't acted as he did, in another month I would have kidnapped you myself from those nuns at Loch Eil."

"You wouldn't have," she said. "I know you now. You would never have forced yourself or the marriage on me."

"Perhaps." He leaned back. "But I might have spirited you away and kept you locked in a tower somewhere and forced you to watch me bathe."

"And you think that would have won me over, I suppose."

"No doubt. How is it working now?"

She reached up and slowly pulled at the laces that secured the front of her dress.

"You're not the only one who can be tempting by sitting naked in that tub. Two can play that game."

His eyes followed the movement of her hands. "You have on far too many clothes. I'm not tempted at all."

She pulled at the neckline of the dress and started pushing the garment over one shoulder, holding on to the strap of her shift. "How about now?"

Alexander fought the urge to jump out and drag her back in the tub with him. "Not even close, woman."

Kenna pushed the dress over her other shoulder and down over her hips. The garment fell to the floor.

"And now?"

His gaze traveled down her body. Although he had a thorough knowledge of what lay beneath her thin shift, that knowledge did nothing to diminish the desire he felt now.

"I'll be honest. You're getting close." He smiled faintly and nodded. "But you're still wearing more than what I have on. Not the same level of temptation, I shouldn't think."

She approached the tub. "Well, that's all you'll be tempted with today. As I said, I don't plan on getting wet. The only reason why I removed the dress was to wash your back."

He shifted in the tub and her eyes widened at the sight of his wet and fully aroused manhood.

"As you can see, I may not have been completely honest. You are a wee bit of a tease, Kenna."

"Am I?" she replied coyly.

He studied the rich brown hue of her long gleaming hair, the violet-blue eyes that he fell asleep thinking of, the dark nipples pushing through the shift, the long legs extending from beneath the thin fabric.

"Tease or no, you can't touch me," she ordered. "I'm only washing your back."

He held up a wet cloth.

"My gratitude knows no bounds, to be sure. Here you are, lass," he said. But as she reached for it, his other hand darted out, and she was on his lap in the water before she could even cry out.

"Ah! Now this is so much better," he growled. "I love it when I get my way. I think I'll wash you first, my sweet."

With her feet still dangling on the outside of the tub, and her arm around his shoulder, she looked up and met his gaze.

"Why do you have to be such a temptation? I can't believe I just walked into your trap."

"It's a gift. The water's not too hot for you?"

She shook her head slowly.

Alexander poured bowls of warm water over her breasts, soaking the thin garment until it was transparent.

"But how am I going to face everyone when I leave here? They'll all know what we did."

"Aye. It's safe to assume they all know." He pressed his lips to the bare skin of her neck. "Robert had his folk deliver the tub and this water to this room. And drying cloths enough for two."

Kenna went limp for a moment in his arms. Then, turning and placing both hands on his shoulders, she looked into his face. "And he won't hold his tongue?"

"I could threaten him with torture at the hands of Torquemada himself—the man couldn't hold his tongue."

"So who knows we're here together?"

"The entire household. My parents," he lied. "They're probably all gathered in the hallway outside at this very moment, waiting to celebrate your moans and cries of marital fulfillment."

She laughed. "You are the devil, Alexander Macpherson."

He pulled her against him, and she shivered as his hand caressed her breast. He placed soft kisses on her face.

"I'm glad we've settled that. Now, let's work on those moans and cries."

His hand dropped into the water, and his fingers slid up along the skin of her thigh. Kenna held her breath and curled into him.

"If you insist."

Chapter 28

Use it for my love some other way than swear-
ing by it.

Kenna looked at herself in the mirror.

This was as fine a gown as the one she had worn on her wedding day. The dress of pale yellow laced with threads of gold clung to her body and then flared to a long, full skirt below her hips. The tight sleeves hugged her arms, and velvet cuffs extended over her fingers.

This had been one of Fiona's dresses. And the seamstress had worked her magic in letting out just enough material to make the gown fit her body like a second skin. Kenna eyed the neckline. It was far too revealing.

For six months now, she'd been wearing the pouch with the healing stone around her neck. Now, she was wearing the stone at her belt. Understanding the power of the relic, she was constantly alert as to where it was. She would not lose it.

Looking in the mirror again, Kenna gathered her long brown hair and pulled it over one shoulder, trying to hide some of the exposed skin. She didn't want another exhibition. This afternoon, after they'd made love, Alexander had brought her back up here using secret hallways and hidden stairwells. Still, quick exchanges of looks and the averted eyes of the maids and dressmakers waiting for her left no doubt that they knew what the two had been doing.

Before leaving, Alexander had kissed her soundly on the lips and reminded her that this bedchamber belonged to both of them.

Kenna needed to get used to this. She was married. And it was absolutely acceptable for her husband to parade his affection in public. And deep down, she was thrilled each time by the feeling it gave her.

The rest of the afternoon had been a mad dash of preparations. Another scrubbing, but without the luxury of the tub. Women measuring arms and legs and waist and hips and bosom before trying out different colors and textures of cloth against her skin and hair.

Twice, Tess had poked her head in, making certain that everything was under control and that Kenna wasn't being overwhelmed by the cadre of workers buzzing about her.

In the span of a few short hours, Kenna was amazed at the array of dresses, gowns, and accessories that were delivered to her room.

In an odd moment alone, she picked up a fine silk nightgown left on her pillow. She marveled at the soft suppleness of the material and the finely stitched handiwork. Running it over her hand, she noticed the delicate feel of the fabric and how it molded to her outstretched fingers beneath. She trembled with excitement imagining Alexander's reaction to it when she would put it on.

This afternoon in his chamber, he'd torn the shift from her body. The two of them made love in the tub and then again on the bed while they were still wet with the bath water. It seemed that he could not get enough of her, and she felt exactly the same way. He played her body like an instrument. She sang, she soared, and she came back again and again for more.

A knock on the bedchamber door broke into her reverie. She opened it to find the man she'd been thinking about on the threshold.

"May I come in?"

Kenna took his hand and pulled him in, closing the door behind him. He looked around, surprised to find her alone. Rising to her toes, she took hold of his neck and kissed him on the mouth, before pulling back quickly and sliding out of his grasp.

"I can see you've missed me as much as I've missed you."

She smiled and nodded. He was no longer the roguish Highlander who terrorized the western shores and the captains of Spanish treasure ships. At this moment, he was impeccably dressed in exquisitely fitted clothes. His face was clean-shaven and his dark blond hair tied back. Looking at him now, she felt the heat descend into her belly.

"My parents forced a promise from me that I would escort you directly downstairs." His eyes took in the swells of flesh that beckoned from the neckline of the dress. "I can see now that was a mistake."

Alexander lifted her in his arms and his mouth settled on hers, crushing her lips in a kiss.

"They were afraid I'll do what I did this afternoon," he whispered in her ear, his mouth grazing the skin of her earlobe, her neck. He kissed the hollow of her neck.

"What was that?" Her hands moved over his chest. She could feel his heart beating hard and fast.

"I may have mentioned to a few people that you and I made love four or five times. Or six."

"Alexander!"

"But that was only because Robert complained that we splashed so much water out of the tub that the hallways and the chambers below were flooded."

"Now I know you're lying."

His hand gently caressed her breast as he placed a kiss on the exposed skin.

"Nay, lass. There was water everywhere."

"Really? And was there a great deal of damage?" she whispered vaguely, watching as he slowly tugged at the neckline of her dress. Slowly, ever so slowly, he was exposing more of her skin.

"Aye. Nearly a disaster. They may need to renovate this entire wing again." His fingers grazed over the line where silk met skin.

"Is that . . . is that so?"

"But my father says it's all for a good cause."

"I'm glad."

"But my mother insists that we wait to wreak that kind of destruction again until after the banquet tonight." He tasted her freshly bared skin.

"Of course, your mother is right."

"I am more inclined to side with my father on this." He pulled the material even lower until one breast popped free.

She took a sharp breath and ran her fingers into his hair as he slid his hand beneath her breast, lifting it. She gasped as his mouth took possession of the nipple.

"We can't make love whenever we wish it," she said hoarsely, the sweet torment overtaking her senses. Her fingers raked his shoulders and moved again through his hair. "We should stop. I need to make a good impression before your family."

"Aye, that's true, my love." He pulled back, smiling. "But it might be too late. From what I understand, everyone in the Great Hall heard your cries this afternoon."

"Don't tease me like that. I'm nervous enough as it is," she growled, pushing at his chest. She pulled her dress back up, covering herself. "Time to go."

"Nay, I'll not have those lusty fellows in my clan down there eyeing you in this condition. Your skin carries a mark of every place I kissed you."

She freed herself of him and looked in horror at the mirror. He was right. Red marks stood out on her fair skin.

Grinning, Alexander went off searching among the pile of garments brought in this afternoon and returned a moment later with a shawl of Macpherson colors. She watched as he arranged the cloth around her shoulders.

He stood back in open admiration. "Aye, that should do it."

A few moments later, Kenna smiled brightly as they slipped into the festive hall. A huge fire at the end of the hall lit the festivities, and the smell of roasting meat and breads filled the air. Pipers played and children danced. On every side, laughter and merriment enveloped them, so that amidst the revelry, almost no one noticed their entrance.

Kenna spotted her father sitting beside Alec Macpherson and for the second time today, her heart warmed knowing he would be part of her life. Now she understood him. His silence. His pain and grief. There was still much more they needed to talk about. They both had emotional wounds that still bled. But they now had a chance to heal. At that moment, Magnus MacKay spotted her, and he immediately came to his feet.

An immediate hush fell over the entire hall. The musicians ceased playing, and all eyes turned to her. Alexander took her arm and stopped her from taking a step back.

The laird and Lady Fiona got to their feet. One by one, others followed.

"What's happening?" she asked in a whisper.

"They're your family, my love," he answered reassuringly. "They've been waiting for you, and none too patiently, for six months now."

"Why are they so quiet?" she murmured back to him. "I told you this would happen."

"Nay. You've rendered them spellbound, from the looks of things. But how can you blame them?" Alexander said. "You're a vision. You're far more stunning than they ever expected." He brought their joined hands to his lip and kissed hers. "I am proud to stand beside you."

Magnus MacKay crossed the floor and bowed to them. Her head high, her back straight, her eyes met her father's for a moment. The words they'd spoken this afternoon were her salvation. The confidence she felt now came from the realization that she'd never lost her father. She curtsied.

"Daughter," he whispered, taking her into his arms.

Kenna felt his affection run through her limbs and reach her heart.

"I pray and I hope I've done well by you here," he whispered in her ear.

She was misty-eyed pulling away. "You have, Father." Magnus took Alexander into his arms.

Alec Macpherson was not going to be denied this time. With a booming welcome, he crossed the floor with Fiona at his side.

"At last!" he thundered. "At last I get to welcome my daughter to Benmore Castle."

The final vestige of Kenna's nervousness vanished, and a smile spread across her face.

"At last," she responded with a low curtsy. "I'm honored to be here—a daughter, a wife, and a member of this generous and dignified clan."

The room suddenly erupted with cheers, and the old laird beamed with delight.

Alec Macpherson opened his arms, and Kenna placed a kiss on the chieftain's cheek, only to find herself crushed in a bear hug as his powerful arms wrapped around her.

"And now it's my turn, Alec," Fiona put in, warmly welcoming her with a hearty embrace.

The pipers began to play again, and Kenna found herself surrounded by crowding faces of well-wishers.

Tess was right there; so was Colin.

"You do know that with this declaration tonight, you are now fair game. I can play any trick I wish, and you can no longer run away."

"I won't need to run, brother," she replied. "Because you might not be able to crawl."

They laughed as Alexander moved beside her. "Colin, you pathetic whelp. I nearly succeeded in drowning you once but Tess saved you. Next time, little brother, I'll make sure the water is colder, the distance to shore farther, and there is no one around for miles to save you."

Colin wasn't deterred. "You do anything to me, and you'll have to answer to my wife." He wedged himself between Alexander and Kenna again. "Has this brute told you anything of the lunacy in our family?"

"Move along, lad," Alexander growled. "The only lunacy in our family, my love, is in the third son."

Kenna and Tess exchanged a look. This was exactly what she'd warned her about before. She expected a brawl to break out at any moment.

"As I was saying—" Colin continued, holding on to her hand.

"Tess, would you be kind enough to control your husband?" Alexander asked, pulling Kenna away.

"Aye, that I can do." Tess brushed a kiss on her husband's cheek, and suddenly Colin's attention was only on his wife.

Kenna glanced about her. She hadn't seen James.

The warmth she was feeling—the welcome, the cheerful banter, the loving feel of Alexander's hand on hers—all had been made possible because James had accepted the challenge of bringing them back together.

She saw him across the room. Their gazes locked. He slowly pushed his way through the crowd, and when he reached her, he kissed her gently on both cheeks.

"Welcome to the family."

Something was wrong with him. She saw that instantly. The troubled look that Fiona sent her confirmed that she guessed the same thing.

"Thank you, James," she told him. "Thank you for stealing a ship, for kidnapping me, for stranding us. Thank you for any other trickery you played on us that I don't even know about."

He nodded, but a mask hid his emotions. "My brother is a good man. You two will do well." With a curt bow, he turned and walked away.

"You see," Colin put in. "Lunacy has taken hold of that one's brain."

She looked up at Alexander. "What's wrong?"

"A matter of the heart." He shook his head and looked off in the direction of his departing brother. "He's left a piece of it elsewhere, I'm thinking."

~

Sir Ralph Evers sat on his charger, ignoring the cold rain running down his face.

A dozen villagers dangled from nooses in the oak tree behind him.

His soldier half dragged the woman through the mud, yanking her by the hair. She was dressed only in a filthy wet shift, her white flesh visible through the tears. The man forced her to her knees and pulled her head up for Evers to see. She was bruised and bloody, her bottom lip gray and swollen to the size of a fat mouse.

She was almost past caring what happened to her now, Evers thought, but perhaps not quite.

"They say you're a witch, woman."

She mumbled something, shaking her head from side to side.

The soldier slapped her hard. "Speak up when his lordship asks, bitch."

"Nay," she whispered.

"You don't understand. I'm looking for a witch, one with great power. They told me you come from a long line of them."

She stared up at him, confusion evident in her face. Then her eyes narrowed with suspicion.

"I'm not trying to trick you. This is why I came here to this godforsaken hole. They say that you can read a man's past by touching his hand or his face. Is that true, woman?"

She said nothing for a moment and then cowered as the soldier raised a fist to strike her.

"Aye," she murmured, glancing furtively from her tormentor to the mounted leader. "A man's skin, m'lord. It speaks to me."

"Approach," Evers commanded. "Touch my hand and tell me my past."

As the woman struggled to her feet, Evers tugged off his gauntlet. She moved toward the warhorse, keeping an eye on the soldier. Reaching out hesitantly, she placed her fingers on the back of Evers's hand.

She closed her eyes and a moment later began to sway back and forth.

"Did she have a stone?" Evers asked his man.

"Nay, m'lord. A bag with acorns and seeds and dried flowers and a shell from the sea was all."

The woman's eyelids began to flutter and her breathing came in short bursts.

Evers pulled his hand away, and she slumped to her knees in the mud.

"What did you see, woman?"

She steadied herself and then looked into his face. "You're a warrior much feared. I see you in many battles. You have seen faraway—"

"Enough," he said, cutting her off.

Evers pulled the pouch from around his neck. He held it out in front of her.

"Tell me how I came to have this stone."

The woman rose to her feet, eying the pouch. Reaching up, her fingers came within inches of it. Suddenly, she snatched her hand back as if burned, and backed away.

"Tell me about this stone."

She stared at him, and he saw her face change. "A lying heart. A devil's eyes. Always false and full of lies."

"Hold your tongue, vixen."

"A stone. A stone. You die alone." She backed farther away and covered her face. "Nay, Englishman. I can tell you nothing. Nothing. Nothing."

"We shall see," Evers said, tucking the pouch inside his shirt.

Her black eyes flashed with hatred as he pointed to the tree behind him.

"Hang her. I'll wait."

Chapter 29

Everyone can master a grief but he that has
it . . .

At the sound of sharp knocking, Kenna sat bolt upright, looking about in momentary confusion.

The Roundtower Room. Sunshine pouring in through the open windows. The damasked bed curtains were pulled back and pleasant summer smells of cut hay and flowers wafted through the chamber.

More knocking, accompanied by a muffled voice.

Her nightgown lay across a pillow, and she pulled it on. Alexander was still sleeping, sprawled naked across the bed, his head partially buried beneath another pillow.

After days of celebrations, there had been yet another banquet last evening, with introductions and toasts, a singer and dancing. This time, the guests had included neighboring clans and allies of the Macphersons. This morning, many of the men—including the laird and

Kenna's father—were to go hunting. Alexander told them all in no uncertain terms, to great laughter all around, that he had no interest in rising early to traipse through Benmore's woodlands.

The knocking continued.

"Bloody hell," her husband cursed, lifting his head and staring menacingly at the door. Kenna pulled on her robe and hurried to the door.

A lad whom Kenna recognized as Robert's helper stood in the hallway.

"Begging yer pardon, mistress. But I was told to—"

The panicked face instantly registered the boy's relief when he glanced past Kenna. Alexander appeared beside her, dressed in his shirt and donning his kilt.

"M'lord, Robert said to fetch ye. It's urgent, he told me to say. The laird is out riding, and Lady Fiona fell."

"Fell?" Alexander barked. "What do you mean, fell?"

"She's awake and struggling to speak. But she can't move anything. Not her hands or feet. She can't raise her head. Robert is sitting with her, but he didn't know what he should do. He told me to come fetch you."

That's all Kenna needed to know. She rushed back into the room to get the pouch.

"Where is she now?"

"On the stairwell by her chambers. We found her a few moments ago."

Kenna looped the pouch around her neck and rushed after her husband. Her mind raced with all that could be wrong. Broken bones. A broken back. She'd seen men at the priory brought in who'd taken too hard a blow to the head and couldn't remember a thing. She'd set bones. But this.

She'd only been at Benmore for a few days, but Kenna already loved Fiona Macpherson. Her kindness and her compassion extended to everyone, but she had been consciously giving her new daughter-in-law room to adjust, while still making her feel included. Fiona was the mother figure that she had lost eight years ago.

Cold fear gripped her heart. There was so much about the stone that she still didn't know. Could she draw on the talisman's power every time she needed it? Could she do the right thing for Fiona? As they hurried through the castle, she felt the stone, already warm against her chest.

Alexander looked over his shoulder at her as they reached the stairwell. He didn't have to say anything. His look showed his fears, too, as well as how much he relied on her.

The boy stood back, allowing them to push past.

The stairwell was dark and steep. She hadn't been in this one, though she and Alexander had been using others like it to get around the castle.

A whisper floated up the steps as they descended to the landing.

"By the saints, Robert, say something," Fiona ordered softly. "Your silence is a wee bit frightening."

"I can't, m'lady. My throat is choked shut."

"Robert."

"I hate these stairs."

Kenna forced herself past her husband as they reached the landing.

Robert was sitting on the steps below, holding Fiona's head on his lap. The woman's body was sprawled awkwardly on the stones. How far she'd fallen, Kenna had no idea.

"Look what you've done now." Fiona admonished the steward weakly. "No need to look so worried, my loves."

"Mother." Alexander's voice was choked as he crouched beside her.

"What should I do," Robert asked, tears welling in his eyes. "Get the surgeon? Get the priest? Send someone after the laird?"

Kenna sat down on the steps in Robert's place. Her fingers grazed over Fiona's brow, her head, her ears. With feathery touches, she moved her hand over her neck, down her arms.

"Aye, get them all," Alexander ordered. He turned to the boy standing above them on the stairs. "Get Master James and Colin . . . and Tess, too."

"Should we move her first from this stairwell?" Robert asked.

"Nay. Go, both of you."

Kenna could feel no broken bones in her arms and legs. But when she touched Fiona's shoulders and then her neck, Kenna's hands warmed instantly. Alexander looked at her, and she motioned to him to speak to his mother.

"Tell me what hurts, Mother."

"I have to feel something for it to hurt," she replied. "Right now, I feel as if someone cut off my head and laid it on my chest. I feel no pain. I feel nothing. But I am beginning to feel light-headed."

Kenna reached into her robe and took hold of the stone. She waited for voices to direct her. But there was nothing.

Unlike Alexander's wound, Fiona's injury had no blood or gash from a sword's entry to direct exactly where to touch, where to focus her attention. Blackness surrounded Kenna. Fear raised its ugly head. She pushed it back, positioning herself lower on the steps, her fingers touching Fiona's neck again. Heat emanating from the spine flared.

"Help me roll her to the side."

Alexander helped her, though it was difficult in the confined space.

Kenna ran her hand down Fiona's spine. The heat drew her hand to the spot.

"Listen to me," Fiona whispered. "The two of you. Kenna, you are to be the mistress of this house. And Alexander, your father will step aside now. You will be laird. Life is about change. Even the final moment is simply another change. But I will not accept a change that makes me a burden to you. Not like this."

"Mother, perhaps you're worrying about things you shouldn't dwell on."

"Nay, Alexander. I know what has happened to me. I saw it once on Skye. A warrior fell from a horse and landed on his neck. It was terrible, and there was nothing we could do. But he lived, unable to move at all, growing more bitter and querulous for months and months. By the time he died, he hated the world and everything in it. I want no part of that."

"Mother—"

"Listen to me. I've done irreparable damage. I'll never move again," Fiona said. "I refuse to be dependent on others for everything for the rest of my days. I will not live to hate anyone. So I ask you . . . to help me . . . go in dignity."

"What are you asking of me?" Alexander asked angrily. "Are you asking me to end the life of the woman who brought me into this world?"

There was silence.

"You're asking your son to do something that—if it

were I lying there—something that you yourself would never do." He shook his head. "If I had fallen, you would nurse and cheer me on until your own final breath. You would stay near me and protect me like a lioness from anyone that meant me harm. You would help me find a purpose for living, no matter how little of my old self were left."

Perhaps it was Alexander's words of love, or perhaps it was the stone itself. But as he spoke to his mother, Kenna's hands came alive with the heat of the tablet. Suddenly, as they moved over Fiona's upper spine and neck, she knew exactly where to touch. She closed her eyes, focusing on the injury she could now see in her mind's eye, transferring the power running through her into Fiona's back. Her hand moved of its own will as her mind followed some ancient intuition.

Kenna no longer heard the words being spoken. She faded from the present. No time existed. She was vaguely aware that she no longer occupied any physical space. She hovered suspended in the infinite power of healing.

The next words she was conscious of were her husband's.

"You've done it, my love. Look—she is moving her hands, her legs."

Kenna opened her eyes. Fiona struggled, but after a moment she raised her hand. She motioned that she wished to be helped to sit up.

Voices could be heard. Running steps. Colin's and Tess's voices called from above. James came up the stairs three at a time.

"I'm fine," Fiona said calmly. "I slipped, but I'm fine now. I'll see you all in the Great Hall in a moment. Let me just gather myself."

Alexander stood up and nodded to his brothers. Fiona caught Kenna's hand before she could push up to her feet, too, pulling her face close to hers.

"Your gift. It's no rumor, after all."

Kenna smiled.

Fiona kissed her on the cheek. "Thank you, daughter."

~

Fifty years ago, Maxwell thought, this town must have been alive with trade lasting beyond these few days.

Standing in the shadow cast by the market cross, he scanned the bustling square from the abbey walls to the livery stables at the end of the "high" road. After hanging about for three days, he'd gotten word from his men that the boys and their keepers seemed to be preparing for a trip to the festival.

He wasn't going to miss his chance to grab them here. Snatching them on the road would be a bloodier affair.

"So where in bloody hell are you?" he muttered.

If I were one of those lads, he thought with disgust, I would have been here every day, and nothing would have kept me from it.

The town had the look of a Calais whore. Brilliant flags and banners—both Sutherland and MacKay—flew from every gaudily painted shop and house and inn. Colorful tents filled the market square, with vendors hawking everything from fruit and baked goods and ale to wool and household goods and fine woven cloth. Indeed, the face of the town looked fine and alluring in the summer sunlight, but Maxwell had a feeling the place would look a wee bit old and tired when the crowds were gone and the winter darkness descended.

At one end of the square, beyond a herd of sheep being driven into the packed town, two drunken pipers where competing for the worst renditions of the "Plough Song," and the equally drunken revelers around them were adding unintelligible lyrics to the performance. In a cattle pen at the other end of the square—where livestock auctions had been taking place every day—a boisterous assembly was rooting on two fighters, who were staggering about with flailing fists and spraying blood everywhere. And throughout it all, festivalgoers went in and out of market tents, and young lads wrestled for attention in front of giggling lasses by the stone wall around the kirk yard.

A shouting match behind him drew his gaze. Two finely

dressed women were jostling for a place going in to the abbey. The two pilgrims had paid for admission to the shrine of Saint Brigid's finger, but the line to salvation was apparently not moving quickly enough for one of them.

The only thing missing, Maxwell thought, was a fire to break out and burn down half the town.

Then, just as it looked as if a pitched battle were about to break out, a whistle from one of his men alerted him of the boys' arrival.

Five MacKay warriors, looking relaxed and off their guard, strolled in a loose formation around the lads. All was in readiness.

A company of acrobats drew the attention of the boys. As they started over toward the performers, Maxwell signaled a waiting band of Gypsies. Immediately, black-haired women with flashing eyes and tambourines floated around the warriors, distracting them with silk veils, murmured promises, and flashes of milky skin.

And by the time the MacKay men tore their eyes from the women, the boys were gone.

Chapter 30

O that I were a man for his sake!
or that I had any friend would be a man for my
sake!

Just as Robert had said, Alexander found Kenna alone and crying in the garden.

He moved quickly along the path toward her, his heart aching at the sight of her on the old stone bench. The steward told him Tess was there with Kenna, comforting her, but there was no sign of his brother's wife.

"What's going on? Why the tears?" He crouched down, trying to see into her tearstained face, gently covering her hands with his own.

She never lifted her head or looked at him.

"Bad news? Robert told me that Kester came and went already this morning. The man didn't even stop to speak to your father, or mine." He paused, hoping she would pick up the conversation, but Kenna just sobbed softly, her hands taking hold of his. "What did he say? Come, my love. Tell me what's wrong."

She only shook her head. There seemed to be no end to her misery. He stroked her hair. It wasn't like her to surrender to trouble. She always attacked it head-on.

"Speak to me, my love. When did tears ever solve a problem?"

She leaned forward and buried her face against his chest.

"You'd best tell me or I'll ride after that worm and drag the truth out of him."

"It's Emily," she murmured finally.

"I guessed that. But what about her?"

"She's gone to the priory at Loch Eil. Kester escorted her there before he came here." She wiped at her face. "She's decided to become a nun. A *cloistered* nun!"

Alexander's thoughts turned immediately to James. Robert also said he'd seen his brother walking near the garden.

"A nun? I don't imagine that will suit Sir Quentin too well."

She sat straight and wiped away the tears on her face. "She won't marry him."

"I assumed as much. A good decision, anyway."

"Decision? Her reputation is ruined. But even if the Lowlander agreed to marry her, I doubt they'd be able to force *her* to go through with it. She's in love."

Fresh tears streamed down.

"Emily is in love?" he asked, already knowing the answer, but asking anyway. Out of the corner of his eye, he saw a shadow move behind the trellis near the gate. A red-haired shadow. James. "In love with whom?"

"With James," she replied. "With the most undeserving lout in the Highlands."

"But before we get to my lout of a brother," he said, pulling her against him, "what else did Kester say?"

"He told me everything. He said Emily made a mistake, but it was because she acted according to her heart. She allowed her emotions to rule her reason."

"What do you mean?"

"After they left us, she fell in love. And by the time she got back to Craignock Castle, she'd made up her mind she wasn't going to allow her father to sell her off to that Lowland chamber pot. So she came up with a simple plan to snatch James away for a few hours. Just so they could spend some time together. But as the bad luck would have it, everything went wrong. The MacDougalls ended up taking him to a dungeon at Dunstaffnage Castle."

"And the scoundrel took exception to that?"

"Aye." Kenna continued, telling him details he'd already heard, and some that he hadn't.

"But then, after he proposed to her—"

"He proposed marriage to Emily?" He already knew this, too, but he also knew that James was listening to every word. "He proposed marriage to a woman already contracted to marry someone else? So she thought she could trap him into marrying her?"

She shook her head. "Nay. Her love wasn't supposed to be a trap. She only wished to buy some time to test the depth of their affection. But she only did it because she thought he cared for her, too."

"She kidnapped him," he reminded her.

"A bad plan, as it turned out. But she did it out of love. You'd kidnap me for love, wouldn't you?"

He would indeed, though she'd probably cut off his balls in a fit of temper. But Alexander decided this was not the time to have that discussion.

"And was there more that Kester told you?"

"When James proposed, of course she confessed it all. It would have been dishonorable to accept him ... trap him, as you say. But when she told him that she'd done it all because she loved him, he threw it back in her face and stormed off. And then he came here, the coward, while her life is ruined."

Fresh tears ran down her face. He caressed her back, placed kisses on her hair. This was indeed a mess, but he was glad James was still by the trellis.

"So she declared her love to him?"

"Kester said she did, over and over. But James had made up his mind. Nothing she said was enough for him."

"He *was* drugged and kidnapped," he reminded her.

She pulled away and stood up, facing him with her hands on her hips. "I said nothing about him being drugged. I never said anything about how he was kidnapped."

"James told us some of this when he first arrived. But I couldn't make any sense of it, to tell the truth. He never said Emily declared her love. I had the impression the whole thing was done as revenge for secrets he'd kept from her when they left us on the road to Oban. Truthfully, he portrayed her as heartless and conniving."

She walked away from him and plucked a leaf from a pear tree. He wanted to get up and go to her, but he waited.

"You saw how he looked, Kenna. I've heard you wonder out loud why he's been so miserable since we've arrived at Benmore. This explains it all."

"You might have told me."

"Told you what? That my brother was miserable because of the underhanded actions of your cousin?" he reasoned. "That would hardly have been fair to you. You've had enough to think about since arriving at Benmore. And then there was the accident with my mother."

She turned slowly to face him. "Don't worry. I'm not upset with you for not telling me."

"But these tears are for Emily."

She nodded. "In many ways, these are tears of frustration, as well as sadness for her pain. What choices did she have? What choices does any woman have? Weeks before a wedding arranged by men, she's abducted by men and used as a pawn in a ploy to put us together to consummate another marriage arranged by men. She was powerless."

Alexander considered arguing the point, but he didn't know where to begin. This was all true.

"And then," Kenna continued, "when she turns the tables and tries to use the same ploy with James that he had used, she's—what did you say?—heartless and conniving. So he rejects her, spurns her. And in the end, her life is ruined because she listened to her heart and to her head and acted independently, perhaps for the first time in her life."

Something deep inside of Alexander was telling him that, as a man, he should put a stop to this kind of talk, this kind of reasoning. But something else, something stronger, was telling him that, as a man, he needed to own up to the truth of what this woman—who only by chance was the woman he loved—was saying.

She stood before him now, her hands at her sides, the summer sun illuminating her face. "For a long time, Alexander, I never thought it could be possible, but I love nothing in the world as much as you. And even this makes me understand Emily better. What she did. Why she did it. And why she suffers for it now."

"And I love nothing in the world more than you. I told you before that I would pull down the sky for you, and I will."

Still, Emily's whole plan had been dangerous. Knowing his brother, it was a miracle no one was dead or severely injured.

Alexander glanced upward, pretending to watch a hawk that was wheeling far above them. James had not moved.

"You say you will do anything for me?" she asked.

"I will. To make you smile again, I swear. Anything."

"Something to right a wrong?" she asked, stabbing at the tears.

"Aye." He would. And he hoped she knew it, too. She mattered so much to him. "Name it."

"Justice calls for action."

"Aye, perhaps there's something in what you say. I need to talk to him."

"To start with, if he would just consider what she told him now that the heat of the moment has passed. Of course, if she was wrong, if he cares nothing for her . . . if he thinks it's right that she lock herself away for life, then so be it. I won't forgive him, and I'll never speak to him again, but I'll not harm him, either. But try to make him think this through with a clear head."

"I'll try. I will," he said, raising both hands in peace. "And for your sake, I'll even beat it into him, if I must. But I can't make his decision for him. I can't force him to take the next step."

She gave a curt nod.

"But I'll say this," Alexander continued, pulling her into his arms. "He's certainly acting like a man in love . . . and stung by it."

The shadow moved, and Alexander watched James slip away in the direction of the stables.

"Did he finally go?" she whispered.

"Aye, love. In a few moments, if we look to the west, I'm certain we'll see a cloud of dust from his horse's heels."

Kenna smiled and kissed him on the cheek.

"You knew he was there, listening?" he asked.

"Not at first. But your eyes gave him away." She took his hand as they started walking back from the garden to the house. "I am glad it turned out this way. That he saw reason on his own."

"James cares too much for her. Anyone could see that.

It was only a matter of time before he came to his senses. But that was clever of me, wasn't it?"

"Wickedly clever." She smiled back, slipping her arms around his neck. "I love you."

He kissed her on the lips. "So, tell me. Which of my wicked qualities did you fall in love with first?"

"With all of them. Together, they create such an entirely attractive person." She kissed him. "But tell me. Which of my angelic qualities made you first fall in love with me?"

"Angelic! That's it. You're truly an angel. What other creature but an angel could make me love her even against my will? I loved you when you ran away from our wedding, and I've never stopped loving you."

"And I loved you even as I ran, hoping that you'd come for me and woo me."

"But you and I were too wise to woo peacefully," he told her.

"Here we are," she said contentedly. "For the moment, at least, at peace."

"But how long can that last?" he laughed, leading her through a door and down a hallway toward the Great Hall.

When she said nothing, he decided it was best to change the subject.

"I saw my mother earlier, walking about the castle.

Here it's only a week since her fall, and she's doing all the things she was doing before."

"Aye, just as you were doing, not even a week after nearly dying from a sword wound."

"But I was completely healed."

"She is, too," Kenna told him. "Forcing her to stay in bed for a few days worked well. Your father and the rest of the household needed to see that her recovery was gradual. But in truth, she regained her strength in just a few hours."

Robert came into the far end of the hallway and ran to them. His face was flushed.

"You need to go to the library immediately," he told them. "They need you. They need you both."

"What's wrong?" Alexander asked.

"A messenger just arrived, mistress. Your brothers, Giles and Ninian . . . they've been kidnapped."

Chapter 31

Do not you love me?

Emily had no talent for healing like Kenna. Working with the sick was out of the question. In fact, she found she grew squeamish at the sight of blood.

But the good sisters of the priory had quickly reminded her that the jobs in the chapter house had to be earned. They were not given out freely, no matter how highborn an entering postulant might be. The prioress decided the safe place for her to start was in the kitchens.

After only a few days, the stocky, red-faced nun running the kitchen was begging her superiors to find Emily something else to do. Anything. Indeed, the prioress was now searching frantically, before she burned down the entire priory or poisoned the staff.

Emily's hands were beginning to look like skinned meat from the scalding and the cuts from sharp knives.

And the burns up and down her arms were dreadful. She had two egg-sized lumps on her forehead from slipping on a wet floor and from banging her head on an iron cooking pot. She seemed vulnerable to any accident.

She knew she was paying the price of a lifetime of being pampered. What bothered her was that she was being taught some very basic lessons about real life and she was a disaster.

But she wasn't giving up. There was no going back to Craignock. She'd written a letter to her father and sent it off from Dunstaffnage. He would be angry, she knew. But she'd decided it was best if she told him in her own words, rather than putting it all on Kester.

Taking responsibility for her actions. That was what she was going to do.

And she'd told Kester that contacting Kenna was out of the question. Not right now. Not when her cousin was still new to her own circumstances. Also, she knew that any communication with Benmore Castle would come across to James as another effort to deceive him. She'd done him enough harm.

"Do you see how stiff the dough is, Emily? Add a little more water. Pour it right over my hand."

Emily focused on the old nun she was helping today with the baking. The wrinkled hands were wrist deep in the dough she was kneading. She added the water.

"Nay," the nun directed sharply. "Too much. Add more flour."

"We've finished this flour. I'll be right back with more."

As Emily headed to the special pantry where they stored the flour, she thought she heard the wizened old nun cursing under her breath. There was a problem when she tried to help any of them. These gentle women gave her orders, assuming Emily knew how much to pour or how to mix or how to take the loaves of bread out of an open oven. She didn't. But she would learn. She had to. This was her new life. True, the obstacles were humbling, but they made her realize how much she lacked. Correcting her mistakes also made her work harder and gave her less time to cry over James.

Emily grabbed a large wooden bowl off a shelf and shoveled flour into it. She tried to guess how much the nun would want. It was better to bring out more than less.

She stepped out of the pantry and her heart stopped dead. A giant was standing in the doorway to the kitchen. The sun was behind him, so she couldn't see his face. But there was no mistaking the long red hair, the tartan, the way he filled the opening with his height, the width of his shoulders, his presence.

Don't show any weakness, Emily told herself. Be strong. Be fearless. You are a baker now. You don't need him or anyone.

Clutching the bowl to her body, she started forward. One step and she went into a puddle she hadn't seen before. One moment she was striding confidently, the next she was lying on her back with a coating of flour on her and a cloud of white hanging above.

~

He'd overheard what Kenna and Alexander said about her being distraught, but James never imagined she might try to choke herself with flour.

He strolled inside. Several of the nuns were already leaning over, trying to help her. She was covered with white powder. It was in her eyes, her nose, her mouth, and in both dimples. She looked like a fish out of water, gulping for air, as she struggled to wipe the flour away.

Looking at her now, only a step away, he realized that for the first time in more than a week, his head didn't hurt. His heart wasn't aching. His mood wasn't foul. He was actually smiling.

She was sitting, struggling to get to her feet. The nuns saw him, nodded in acknowledgment. He motioned for them to say nothing and pointed at the door. An old nun smiled.

"My heavens, child, but we can't clean you up here," she chided. "Come with me. I'll take you outside."

James slipped through the kitchen door. Outside, the morning sun was shining through the smattering of clouds. He waited near the door. It took only a minute, but it felt like a year before the kindly nun led Emily out. He offered his hand, and the old woman put Emily's hand in his.

She immediately tensed, but James held on and drew her out into the sunshine. The nun disappeared back onto the kitchen.

"I thought it was you," she sputtered, trying to wipe the flour from her eyes. They were finally open, and blue orbs peered out at him from the chalky white features.

"Is that why you took such a graceful tumble? Trying to run away?"

"You're the one who runs. Not I." She looked down at the ruined dress, at her hands. She touched her face and grimaced. "I don't know why you're here, but I'm certain that it can have nothing to do with me. The prioress's office is just that way." She waved in the direction of the buildings. "Now, if you'll pardon me, I need to clean up and get back to work."

She started around the building. He followed. Her dress was plain homespun wool of a dull, indefinable color. Somewhere between gray and brown. The white veil she'd been wearing when he first saw her had disappeared in the fall she took. James stared at the blond curls escaping the thick braid bundled in a knot at the back of her neck. He wanted to touch them, feel their softness against his lips.

She spun around on her heels. "What are you doing?"

"I've already finished my business with the prioress. What I have left to do involves you."

"I have nothing to say to you."

Her face was still covered with flour, and the blue eyes glaring from beneath thick, powdery lashes were fierce.

"I have a great deal to say to you."

"If it is more of an apology from me that you're after, then you can just march out of here. I have no more to give. And there is no point in it, anyway. You don't hear. You don't understand. You don't forgive. You have no heart."

She walked away before he could say anything in his own defense. He followed. This time, she stopped by the well, dragging out a bucket of water and grabbing a drying towel from the rough-hewn table sitting nearby.

"Will you please go? I don't wish to be harassed."

"Am I harassing you?" he asked softly, reaching over and wiping the flour from the tip of her nose.

She leaped back as if she'd been burned. He had to reach out and grab her arm as she nearly toppled backward into the well.

"A wee bit susceptible to accidents, I see."

"Nay, not in the slightest!"

"So none of this is accidental. The damage you're doing is intentional."

"What damage?"

He took the towel out of her hand and dipped it in the water. "These bumps and bruises. The accidents. The prioress told me that you have good intentions. You are committed to become part of their community. You work hard. But you're a disaster as a nun."

"Who are you to talk to the prioress about me?"

"I had to make sure of your plans. I wanted to be certain this was not another trick."

She tried to step away; he gave her no room. She was trapped between him and the well.

"What I'm doing, where I am, how I live my life today, tomorrow, or forever has nothing to do with you. So be on your way. Get away from me. I never wish to see you again."

"Liar." He smiled. "Making that arrangement to kidnap me. Then telling me the truth when you could have had what you wanted. Then throwing away your future with Chamberlain. Even walking away from your family and settling on this. Everything you've done has to do with me. What kind of nun fabricates lies such as these?"

James used the towel to swab lightly at her brow

and nose, and then her cheeks. Her eyes stayed open, watching him. He dipped the towel in the water again and ran it across her full lips, causing her to take a sharp breath.

"Now, tell me again that you don't want me here."

Color bloomed in her newly washed cheeks.

"Why are you doing this, James?"

"Because I want to hear your words again. What you told me that day in the mill."

She shook her head. "Nay, never again. I no longer care for you."

He leaned toward her. "Don't you?"

His lips were inches away from hers. James realized that her breathing had become ragged, unsteady. The blush was spreading down her neck. She didn't turn her face away.

"Very well," she said, frustrated. She pushed at his chest. He didn't budge. "Perhaps a little."

"Well, I care about you, too. And far more than a little."

She shook her head, forcing herself to think clearly. "This doesn't explain why you're here. How did you know where I was?"

"Your man Kester told Kenna. I overheard Kenna and Alexander talking, and here I am."

This time she slipped around him and walked off.

"Where are you going?" he asked, keeping up with her.

"I will not allow you to be manipulated because of a sense of guilt."

"Guilt?" He took her arm and turned her around.

"Aye, guilt," she retorted. "You come here and see my meager lifestyle that I have *chosen,* and right away decide to do the honorable thing. But I will not have it. I will not tolerate it. Go away. I don't want you here. You're interfering . . . with my life."

She walked away.

Riding from Benmore, a dozen possible conversations ran through his head, but this was not one of them. In the best-imagined discussion, James had pictured arriving and finding that she was delighted to see him. Immediately, Emily would again declare her love, and he would admit how much he loved her, too. And then, they'd set their wedding date.

She wasn't making this easy.

But all the people moving about the open area and gawking at them were not helping, either.

He caught sight of Emily disappearing through a doorway and ran after her.

The building was ancient but smelled surprisingly of mint and lavender. The hallway was narrow and dark. He heard footsteps going up the stairs and he followed. She was closing a door behind her, but James put his boot in the jamb and then shoved the door open. He stepped in behind her.

"What do you think you're doing?" she cried.

He closed the door behind him. The room was small and cramped, with only a narrow bed along one wall for furniture.

"Let's begin again."

"You're not listening, as usual. I'm a nun now. Get out."

"You're not a nun. You're far, far from even becoming a nun. And frankly, the prioress wishes you'd stop trying to be one."

"That is between her and me. But this is still my cell, and I'm ordering you to get out."

He raised both hands. "Why won't you give me a chance to start again?"

"Why? So you can come up with more reasons why poor Emily should be saved, and why you're the man to do it?"

"How about if I list a dozen reasons why it's James who needs to be saved, and Emily is the only woman capable of doing it?"

Her eyes met his. She stepped back until she bumped up against the wall. "Please, James. Don't play games with me."

"No games." He moved closer to her. "I've been miserable since the day I walked away from you. And you can ask anyone if that is true or not."

He wanted to reach for her, enfold her in his arms, but he was afraid she'd run. And he wanted to finish what he had to say.

"True, at first I was angry that you'd bested me at my own game. Before I even reached Benmore, I was stupid with misery because I realized that I still loved you. My gloom only increased as I thought back on your words, on the way you tried to make me understand your reasons and how everything had gone wrong. And how I had rejected you. Then, I lay awake at night searching for a reason to go after you, to stop your wedding to Chamberlain, devising plots to break into Craignock Castle and steal you away."

He closed the distance between them, cradled her face. Her eyes were misty when they met his.

"I can't tell you how happy I was, hearing that you were at this priory. That you'd rejected the marriage to the Lowlander. I knew then that you truly loved me. I rode here on the wing of an eagle to say this . . . I love you, Emily."

Her fingers moved up his chest. "I love you, James."

"Then you'll marry me."

As she kissed him, the priory on Loch Eil lost yet another nun.

Chapter 32

They swore that you were well-nigh dead . . .

In exchange for the safe return of Giles and Ninian, the healing stone had to be delivered by Kenna and her father the next day.

Maxwell's demands were clear. The exchange was to take place at midday at the market cross of a small village a half-day's ride to the southeast of Benmore. No armed company of Macpherson warriors inside the village. If more than three accompanied Kenna, the twins would be killed.

The messenger carrying the letter was a poor farmer who had no idea of the severity of what was at stake.

Alexander exploded on hearing the demands. He wasn't about to endanger Kenna's life by letting her go anywhere near Maxwell. The man was a snake, as ruthless as he was deadly.

Kenna had other ideas. She was going. There was no

question of it. And she worked hard to make him see that he would do the same thing if his brothers' lives were in jeopardy.

A score of Macpherson and MacKay warriors accompanied them from Benmore to a field at the outskirts of the village, and that was where they set up camp. They would wait there while the exchange took place. Alexander wanted Maxwell to know that, while they were not breaking the terms of the exchange, the Macphersons were not to be trifled with.

She and Alexander, Magnus MacKay, and Colin rode in alone. The place was a muddy market village, consisting of three or four dozen cottages of stone and wattle and thatch, clustered around a low kirk at the bend of a wide, slow-moving river. The market square was filled with farmers and craftsmen, buying and selling. Smoke from cooking fires hung in the air beneath a lowering sky. Sheep and cattle grazed on the fields by the river, and the rugged Cairngorms stretched away to the south.

The village was like a hundred others that Kenna had seen in her life. Around the square, craftsmen and women plied their trades beneath overhangs of thatch in front of cottages. Children and dogs ran wild, and every stranger was greeted with a crowd of wee folk and barking hounds and curious looks from the villagers.

Though the village was at its farthest border, this was

still Macpherson land, and the village elder ushered the laird's son into his cottage and then left them. Time was growing short, but when Magnus declared that he and Colin would go to the market square to make the exchange, an argument ensued. They were his sons, the MacKay asserted. He would make the exchange. Kenna and Alexander would wait there together.

She wasn't happy about it, and neither was Alexander, but it was midday. She shook her head and shrugged in resignation.

"We've spoken about this, and we're at peace with it," Kenna told her father, holding out the pouch and the stone. "I would give far more for the lives of Giles and Ninian."

The MacKay laird held up a hand. "Nay. There's no need. I had this made."

He placed a piece of stone into her hand. It looked similar in size and color to what she had. Lines and figures had been etched into it to make it look genuine.

"Aye," her father said. "It's a fake, but how will this bastard Maxwell know the difference? I'll give him this, and we'll have the boys."

Kenna glanced at Alexander. He looked as doubtful as she was feeling. "Perhaps he's seen whatever it is that Evers has. Father, we can't take a chance of him realizing the deception and hurting the boys."

"I won't let him. I don't give a damn about what he realizes. As soon as we see the boys, I'll cut the villain down."

"It might not work out as you think. You should still take the one I have, just in case."

Magnus took the fake tablet out of her hand and put it in a pouch similar to hers. "Nay, daughter. I made a promise to your mother that I would protect the stone. And my sons were kidnapped when they should have been with me. I will get them back, and I'll not renege on my promise to Sine."

"Father."

He turned to Alexander and put a hand on his shoulder. "Keep her safe here. We'll bring the lads back."

Even as Kenna watched her father go, the claws of fear raked at her heart. She'd lost her mother when the stone could have saved her life. Now her father was walking into what had to be a trap. Her brothers had been taken for the same relic. She hugged her middle, unable to fight down the panic that was taking hold of her. What she had was no gift, but a curse.

"What my father is trying to do won't work. If something happens to my brothers, I'll never forgive myself."

"Last night, we had a half dozen men slip into the village, my love. I don't know how many people he has, but when he shows his face, we'll spring the trap. And Colin will be there. I trust him."

She looped the pouch around her neck and paced the empty cottage. Alexander stayed near the door, his hand on his sword. She knew there were others nearby, watching the cottage. Time dragged on. The young faces of Giles and Ninian were constantly in her mind. Kenna wished she'd insisted on Alexander sending for them as soon as she arrived at Benmore. Her heart broke at the thought of how frightened the two of them must be.

When a distant cry of a woman rang in the air, Kenna rushed toward the door. Something had gone wrong. Cries of "Fire!" followed.

"Stay inside," Alexander ordered, pulling open the door.

People were running on the muddy road in front of the cottage. She followed him outside.

"The cur is burning the village," he said.

She looked along the row of cottages. Every thatched roof was on fire, it seemed, and black smoke was billowing thickly all over the village. As they stood there, the cottage they were in burst into flames.

"I am getting you out of here." Alexander took her hand.

He motioned to two men who ran to them. Macpherson warriors, she realized with relief. The sound of the fire had grown to a crackling roar. People were shouting over it.

"Take her out of the village to the camp." He turned to her. "I'm going after your father and Colin and the boys."

Kenna wanted to go with Alexander, but he was already running in the direction of the market. One hut after the next was now engulfed in flames.

"Come on, mistress."

The two men shielded Kenna on either side and urged her up the road. As they passed a cottage, a young girl ran out, shrieking in panic. Her dress was on fire.

Kenna broke free of the men and rushed to her, throwing her cloak over the child, pushing her down into the mud and crouching beside her. She slapped at the cloak, smothering the flames while the girl cried hysterically.

The air was so thick with smoke that it was burning Kenna's eyes and lungs.

The girl's eyes suddenly focused. "My sister! She's still inside! She's just a bairn!"

Kenna motioned to the men to go in. Without hesitating, they dove through the open doorway.

Just then, as if in a dream, two boys with hoods on their heads, their hands bound at their waist, appeared. They were just a few short steps from her. A man stood behind them, holding a knife. She didn't need to wonder if he was Maxwell.

"The stone," he demanded, his Lowland accent harsh. "Toss it to me and you can have the boys. If you hesitate for even a moment, they die."

She pushed slowly to her feet. "First, I need to see their faces."

The man raised his knife to one boy's throat and pulled off the hood of the other. Giles cried out her name when he saw her, but Maxwell cuffed him hard.

"Now, woman, or they both die."

Kenna took the pouch from around her neck. She held it up. "Send them to me."

"Throw it to me."

They both moved at the same time. The pouch with the stone flew through the air just as the two boys sprawled at Kenna's feet.

When she looked up, Maxwell had disappeared into the smoke. Holding Giles close to her, Kenna pulled the hood off his twin brother.

But it was not Ninian.

She stared as the shock of recognition struck her hard.

It was Jock.

~

Alexander was not about to lose Maxwell.

There was no time to gather his men, and Colin and Magnus could fend for themselves.

The two Macpherson men had come out of the cottage as the roof collapsed, one carrying a baby under his arm, and both hacking from the smoke. Turning Kenna and the boys over to them, he leaped onto his horse.

Breaking out of the smoke and chaos of the village, he galloped east along the river road. He hadn't gone far when he realized Kenna was right behind him.

"What are you doing?" he shouted. "Go back!"

"Nay. Save your breath. There they go."

Alexander looked ahead and saw two riders on a rise. The boy was draped across the neck of one of the steeds. They were following the river road, which made a great sweeping arc around a woody glen just ahead.

He didn't have time to fight with her. He knew he wouldn't win, in any event.

"This could be a trap, Kenna. Stay behind me and go back for help if you see more men join them."

If she heard anything that he said, she didn't acknowledge it.

Maxwell had enough of a head start that their only chance was cutting them off. Spurring his horse off the road and into the glen, Alexander rode hard through the woods. Branches tore at him. He heard Kenna's horse crashing along behind him. Her safety was the most important thing in the world to him. But he knew regardless of what he did, she wouldn't stop chasing these blackguards.

It wasn't about the stone. She had decided already to

part with it. It was Ninian. She would never give up until she had him back.

His steed vaulted over a fallen tree, and he heard her horse land safely. She was as good a rider as anyone, and she was fearless in the face of danger. He'd seen that already.

And that did nothing to ease his worries. She would take any risk.

Moments later, they broke out of the glen and into open meadow. Not an arrow shot away, Maxwell and his man turned in their saddles and saw them.

Encumbered by the boy, they were quickly losing ground.

Seeing the Highlander hot on their heels, Maxwell motioned to his man to move away from the river and up toward higher ground, where craggy boulders jutted up from brush and patches of scrub pine. He could see a long ridge ahead. If they were going to shake their pursuers, they stood the best chance of doing it there.

Snatching that fishing lad from the hills by the western sea had worked out better than he'd expected. Maxwell had planned to use him in place of one of the twins from the first moment he laid eyes on them at the hunting lodge.

The MacKay heir would serve many a purpose once they joined Sir Ralph Evers—who should be waiting not a league from here. Those Highland fools would surely pay handsomely for the lad, but getting clear looked to be the challenge now. He glanced back at the Highlander and the woman. They were steadily gaining on them.

Returning with the stone was his mission. To hell with the boy.

"If they catch us," Maxwell shouted to his man, "you cut the brat and drop him near the ledge. That should give us time."

Standing there with the boys in the village, he'd seen the look on the MacKay woman's face. Never mind the stone—she'd have given her life to get them back.

Cresting a rise, Maxwell was stunned to see Alexander Macpherson riding up the sheer face of the ridge. Drawing his sword, he quickly rode behind a large boulder where the Highlander would reach the top.

As Macpherson galloped past, Maxwell swung the sword, but the Highlander was too quick. In a flash, he had his own sword up, catching the full weight of the blow.

The Highlander's sword was shattered, and the man was thrown from his horse. But it took Maxwell a length of the heartbeat before he felt the searing pain. He looked down. The point of Macpherson's blade was lodged in his chest.

Bellowing in fury, he rode to where his man waited with the lad.

Macpherson was getting back on his horse when his wife appeared.

"Cut him. Leave him."

Maxwell's man didn't hesitate for an instant, driving a dagger deep into the boy's back and dumping him at the edge of the cliff.

Spurring their steeds, the two galloped off.

A forest lay beyond the next hill. Beyond it, Evers waited. Bending over his mount's neck, Maxwell pressed his hand to the wound. The blood flowed freely from around the jagged steel. He couldn't stop the bleeding, and he could taste his own blood. His breaths were coming harder, and his vision was becoming distorted as he struggled to stay on his horse.

"We've lost them," his man said.

Reining in, Maxwell slid off his horse and hit the ground. He blinked, looking up at the patches of the sky above.

The hooves of a horse circled around him. The rider dismounted. Maxwell looked up at the blurred face of his man.

"In the pouch ... at my belt ... the healing stone. Take it. It's magic. Use it on me."

The man reached down and took the pouch. Maxwell

closed his eyes. A miracle. Magic. The object of his quest would make him whole again.

The feel of the blade slicing across his throat caused the Lowlander to open his eyes, but the light was now blinding. And as he drowned in his own blood, Maxwell's last thought was that no miracle would be coming.

~

Alexander reached the boy before Kenna did. They'd stabbed Ninian for nothing.

Blood already soaked the boy's clothes. He pulled off the lad's hood, and blue eyes so much like Kenna's stared back at him.

She was beside them in an instant.

"You came for me," he said weakly. "I told Giles not to worry. I told him you'd find me."

"Of course, my love." She gathered her brother against her. She looked at the wound. How much blood the lad had already lost!

"It hurts, Kenna," Ninian whispered. "Can you make it better?"

She glanced up at Alexander in despair, her eyes burning with tears.

~

Sir Ralph Evers stared at the renegade soldier. So Maxwell was dead. But this man had been able to keep the tablet and deliver it.

"When a commander loses a trusted fighter," he said, "it is important to have a good man to replace him."

"Aye," Maxwell's man said. "That's what I figured. And I'll do whatever the job calls for."

Evers nodded and emptied the pouch the man had delivered into his palm. He gazed at the stone: the color, the markings, the edges. Right away, Evers knew it was genuine.

He walked away from the line of men standing and waiting for his reaction. He took out his own portion of the tablet. He held one in each palm. He brought them together.

They fit perfectly. Like a puzzle. He had two links of the chain. A rush of pleasure washed through him. He was halfway to his goal. He would have it all.

He walked back to those waiting.

"No Highlander would be tricking us, Sir Ralph." Maxwell's man was all swagger now. "Brought the genuine article, didn't I?"

Oh, it was genuine. He had no doubt.

"Let's test it, shall we?" Evers asked.

Taking out his dagger, he stabbed Maxwell's man in the belly. The Lowlander's eyes rounded in shock. He stumbled backward.

"Hold him up," Evers ordered.

Men moved on either side and took hold of the Lowlander's arms, keeping him upright.

Stone in hand, Evers reached out and touched the bleeding wound. Moments went by, but there was no sensation within him, as there was with the other stone. No heat. He felt no change at all. Blood continued to run from the wound.

And then it came to him.

Cairns. The stone sat for some time on the shelf in that dungeon. Many could have touched it, picked it up, studied it. Redcap Sly had done so. But the power had passed on to no one but himself, Evers thought. No one had been able to possess it.

Not until Cairns was dead.

Sir Ralph stared at the healing stone in his palm, anger building within him. He had the stone that could provide the gift, but Kenna Macpherson would have to die for him to possess its power.

And die she would.

∼

Kenna had nothing to save him. She felt helpless, terrified, but she wasn't about to let her little brother know the depth of her despair. His time was growing short.

Alexander continued to talk to Ninian, showering him with praise for his bravery while Kenna looked on. Somewhere in the back of her mind, a faint glimmer of hope was teasing her. But what could she do?

After giving birth to the boys, her mother had known that she was about to die. But Sine had done nothing to save her own life. Why hadn't she given the stone to her husband? Why not give it to the midwife, or to someone else she trusted in the household? To anyone? There had to be so many people who could have handled the tablet and then returned it when Sine recovered. Her own father could have done it. But she didn't give it to him. Why?

Kenna's hand hovered over the wound. Without even touching it, she felt the heat emanating from it.

She closed her eyes, allowing her fingers to move where they willed. In her mind, she focused on the place where the dagger had pierced the flesh.

Suddenly, inside of her, a storm gathered. From the sky above and from the earth below, she felt the surging column of light colliding, swirling, filling her with energy like never before.

Harnessing the power, she directed it, pushed it, willing the healing to flow out of her arms, through her hands and fingers, and into the thin, cold body of her brother. The ancient instinct was still there, rooted in her mind, in her heart, spreading through the tips of her fingers.

As always, she didn't know how long it lasted, but the sound of Ninian's voice as he spoke to Alexander made Kenna become aware of them.

"I like Jock. He's very brave, you know. They treated him very badly, too. Do you think he could stay with us?"

Kenna stared at the wound. The bleeding had stopped. Ninian's face was regaining some of its color. He was acting as if he wanted to sit up.

"It's you." Alexander was smiling at her. "It's not the stone. *You* are the gift."

Kenna leaned her head on her husband's shoulder. She now knew the truth as her mother had known it before her. The power of the stone stayed with you.

It was a gift for life.

Epilogue

> In brief, since I do propose to marry,
> I will think nothing to any purpose that the
> world can say against it;
> and therefore never flout at me for what I have
> said against it . . .

The wedding was to take place in the village kirk, across the river from Benmore Castle.

For a sennight, the clan folk had all been in high glee, with flowers and banners decking the windows of every cottage and shop. Pipers, dancing, and feasting were the order of the day.

No one loved celebrating more than the Macpherson clan, and weddings provided the most joyful reason of all.

For his part, Graeme MacDougall was gratified beyond measure at the prospect of gaining as a son-in-law the second son of the powerful Macpherson laird. James, he felt, was a man with a great future at court, and losing a Lowlander was no great loss. The Macphersons were strong allies to have for a clan perched on the western sea, as the MacDougalls were. Indeed, he would have agreed to have the wedding anywhere, so long as vows were exchanged and he had someone to whom he could hand over responsibility for his beloved Emily and her newly discovered willfulness, impetuosity, and independence. She, he was beginning to think, would be a handful.

Many guests had arrived for the wedding. Family from far and near. Friends and allies from across the sea. And Alexander's protectiveness had grown proportionally with the number of guests. Kenna saw it and felt it every time she turned around.

Descending the steps into the courtyard of the castle, she glowered over her shoulder at the four warriors in gleaming armor who flanked her and Alexander. They were becoming too familiar a sight.

"Husband, this will not do," she said.

Alexander followed her gaze. "It will have to for now, my love. We need to take care since Evers put that bounty on your pretty head."

"And what about the even greater reward you've offered to anyone who foils an attempt on my life? What has that accomplished? We have a line of blackguards at our door every day with their hands out for the reward, just for *saying* they've stopped some attack."

"It's worth it. You're worth it." He kissed her hand. "And stop planning ways of escaping your guards."

"How do you know what I'm planning?"

He kissed her lips, paying no attention to all the heads he turned, showing such affection for his wife. "It's a gift. You have yours and I have mine."

It had taken a little time, but Kenna was now used to Alexander's ways. It was more than that. She cherished his love, his affection, and his passion—whether it was in public or in private.

Alexander's eyes scanned the gathered family as he continued. "But I want you to know that there may be an end in sight to Evers and his bloody bounty. I have some news about the other two who hold pieces of the tablet."

"What news?"

"Their names are Innes Munro and Muirne MacDonnell. They're the ones he's searching for now."

"Do you know where they are?"

"We are looking for them. We'll find them before Evers does."

"And then?"

"Then we set a snare for Evers. We'll get him, my love. He's cut himself free of his king, it seems, and I swear to you that he'll never see England again."

Kenna had to be satisfied with that. For now, at least. She'd lost the tablet that her mother had entrusted to her, though the gift remained within her. Still, she needed to get the stone back. She knew that she couldn't live the rest of her life looking over her shoulder at Macpherson guards. She couldn't live with her family forever troubled by every new face, never sure if it was a friend or foe.

Finding the two women also gave Kenna hope that perhaps she might learn more about the power behind the gift. Her father knew nothing more than what she herself had discovered. Perhaps Innes and Muirne knew more.

They made their way through the courtyard to Colin and Tess. Kenna's father was with them, and he hugged her warmly in greeting. Behind them, Giles and Ninian and Jock stood jostling one another. She smiled at them. The twins had become triplets.

Standing with Tess, Kenna realized the lads weren't the only ones growing restless. Across the courtyard the entire party looked ready to go. By the castle gates, grooms were struggling to hold prancing steeds in check.

A hint of anxiety edged into her. Emily and her father had not yet appeared. And neither had the bridegroom.

"Where's James?" she asked.

"He hasn't come out yet," Tess replied.

The two women looked at Alexander and Colin, who were both gazing innocently at the crowd.

"Colin?" Tess asked.

Colin turned to one of the boys who had tumbled against him.

A stir in the crowd drew all eyes to the great doors of the castle. Emily and the MacDougall came out onto the landing and descended the steps. The expression of concern on her face and the frown on her father's did nothing to diminish Kenna's fears.

She turned to her husband. "Do you know what's going on?"

Before he could answer, the whispers reached them.

No one could find James. He was to meet the bride at the doors of the Great Hall.

Kenna knew something was wrong. James, ever the organizer, had planned the day from hour to hour. He'd orchestrated each step with the precision of a military campaign. Every event was arranged, scheduled, and rehearsed.

"Look!" Tess pointed at the south tower.

Every eye turned.

James was clambering out of the uppermost window and slowly descending from a makeshift rope.

"Who is he shaking his fist at?" Tess asked. "And why is he dressed in a nightshirt?"

Kenna turned to her husband, who was gazing up at his brother with a look of badly feigned surprise.

"I can't imagine."

Author's Note

To begin, we'd like to thank William Shakespeare for deciding to become a writer rather than pursuing a lucrative career in glove making. We're certain his father went to his grave happy that Will had something to fall back on. We'd also like to thank him for writing one of our favorite plays.

As most of you have probably guessed, Kenna and Alexander's story is the first in our Scottish Relic Trilogy. In *Taming the Highlander* and *Tempest in the Highlands,* you will meet more strong women and courageous heroes, as well as Kenna and Alexander again, as they battle Sir Ralph Evers in protecting these ancient artifacts and the power they hold.

Also, as many of our readers know, we can never let our characters go. We hope you enjoyed this romp with our old friends in the Macpherson clan.

Finally, we need a favor. If you enjoyed *Much Ado About Highlanders,* please leave us a review ... and recommend it to your friends. You the reader have the power to make or break this book. We greatly appreciate your support!

All the best!
You can contact us at:
www.MayMcGoldrick.com

Read on for a sneak preview of the second installment of the Highland Relic Trilogy!

———————

Taming the Highlander

———————

Available August 2016

Prologue

NORTH HEAD, SCOTLAND

Death one step in front of her. Death behind.

Innes Munro stood at the edge of the world, and a cold, watery grave lay ready to take her.

The grey fog swept up the jagged cliffs, swirling about her. She'd run as far as she could, but another step meant certain death. Her lungs burned, and Innes stared down through moving breaks in the mist at the waves crashing against the rocks far below.

Trapped.

The brambles clinging to the edge of the precipice caught at her skirts as she turned to face her pursuers.

A dozen men, their mail shirts gleaming dully beneath filthy, dark-stained tunics, spread out like hunters at the end of the chase. They'd run their prey into the ever-tightening enclosure on the cliffs. All that remained was the kill.

They eyed her and awaited their master's signal.

The commander sat astride his black steed behind the

line of men. He rode no courser, but a warhorse. A leather cloak, tied at the neck, was thrown back over one shoulder, revealing a heavily marked chest plate, a long sword, a pair of daggers. His eyes never left her.

Trapped.

Innes knew what they wanted. Merchants traveling from Aberdeen this week had brought the news to the castle. A band of Lowlanders and English soldiers were roaming free in the hills, looking for a certain woman from clan Munro. By the time Innes heard the tale, fact and rumor had woven together into a thick noose. The Munro woman was a witch. She possessed a mysterious relic given by Satan himself. She could turn a person into stone if he looked into her eyes. Most important, gold would be paid to any man, woman, or child who pointed them in her direction.

Someone would talk. Her secret would be exposed. She'd feared this moment for so long. For years.

For Innes, the past held no mystery. She knew so well the power of the stone that passed on to her from her mother. Only one piece of the whole tablet. Three other fragments. Each carried across Scotland fifty years ago by men who'd survived a shipwreck not far from this northern shore. Innes knew the powers that the other stones held. And she knew the disaster that would rain down on their heads if the wrong person brought all the pieces together.

The commander spoke to her. "Give it to me."

Innes said nothing. His eyes were fixed on the pouch she wore at her waist.

She cursed inwardly. Why had she left the safety of the castle? She knew why. Because she'd *trusted*.

All her life, Innes valued trust above all other things. She knew, better than anyone, that mere knowledge was a curse. Trust was the only true gift, the pearl of great price. But love had made her blind. She'd followed when she should have hesitated. She'd stayed silent when she should have questioned. She'd refused to use her power, assuming it was betrayal of that trust. What a fool!

The sea breeze whipped her tangle of midnight black hair with its blaze of white. Behind her, seabirds floated on the wind, their cries breaking the silence.

"Give me the stone and I'll not harm you or anyone around here."

He was lying. He was an Englishman, risking his life here in the Highlands. He had to know. For all its ancient power, the stone was a useless bauble to anyone until the moment that its bearer died. But perhaps he didn't. She had to touch his skin to see into his past, to learn whatever it was that he knew, to find out which of the stones he already possessed. But she wouldn't go near him to find out. What if her fragment was the last that he needed?

"Go and take it from her."

The men advanced a step, and Innes backed to the very edge.

"Stop right there or I'll jump into the sea . . . and then you'll never have it."

The men hesitated.

Innes had been a child of seven when she sat at her mother's sickbed and was told the secret of the stone. The history, the power of sight that was soon to be hers, the knowledge that no one she touched could hide anything from her. At that moment, none of it made any sense. She'd only wanted her mother to stop talking, save her strength, and get better.

Later, standing at the funeral, she'd learned exactly what it all meant. Holding her father's hand, Innes felt his past flow like a gushing stream into her brain. Hector Munro had been so keenly disappointed with her mother, the woman who'd given him two daughters and no sons, that he'd already chosen his next wife and negotiated for her hand. All of this came to Innes without speaking a word. It was at that moment, as the hot pain that came with *knowing* cut through her, that she realized what she'd been left was no gift, but a curse. The next morning, she awakened to see the white blaze in her long black hair.

"She won't jump. Get her."

Innes turned toward the cliffs.

She welcomed death. It would put an end to all of it. She was ready to part with the heavy weight she'd been forced to carry for much of her life. But she paused at the brink, thinking of him. The man she loved.

Innes winced as someone grabbed her hair, yanking her back from the ledge. She twisted and fought the men who latched on to her arms. She'd been too slow.

One of them cut the string of the pouch and ran with it to his commander.

Held captive, she watched their leader take the stone out of the pouch and hold it up. Inside her, hope fought a losing battle. Perhaps he knew nothing of the power of the relic he held. Maybe they had come because of the rumors, and he now realized that the quest had been for nothing.

Those desperate hopes sank when she saw him produce two other pieces of the tablet and fit them together. He knew what he had.

The Englishman's gaze shifted to her. He'd done this before. He knew how to take from her the power of the stone.

Innes saw a movement at the top of the rise behind the raiders. A great gray wolf appeared.

The Englishman nodded to his men.

"Kill her."

About the Author(s)

Authors Nikoo and Jim McGoldrick (writing as May McGoldrick) weave emotionally satisfying tales of love and danger. Publishing under the names of May McGoldrick and Jan Coffey, these authors have written over thirty-five novels. Nikoo, an engineer, also conducts frequent workshops on writing and publishing and serves as a Resident Author. Jim holds a PhD in medieval and Renaissance literature and teaches English in northwestern Connecticut.